LINGUA GALACTICA

S. J. Schwaidelson

ISBN: 978-0-692-98684-4

Also by S.J. Schwaidelson
DREAM DANCER

In loving memory of two of the bravest women I have ever known
Sarah Savitsky Schwaidelson
and
Jane Savitsky Skolnick

Jane and Sarah

They crossed an ocean with £10 between them.
The rest is our history.

ACKNOWLEDGEMENTS

Lingua Galactica started as a dare: *If you're so smart, why don't you write a sci-fi novel?*

So I did.

Lingua developed a life of its own, including an underground following that I could never quite understand. After ***Dream Dancer*** was published, I was urged to whip this one into shape to get it out the door.

So I did.

Funny thing about beating on a manuscript, my initial ambivalence toward the characters turned into passion. The more I re-wrote them, the more I liked them. They have, in so many ways, become very real…at least to me. And while I want to see them all in print, it means letting them go; I will miss this crew taking up space in my head.

All that banging away could've been done in a vacuum, but it was not. First, I have to acknowledge my late husband, Steve, for the dare and the first round of technical edits. He saw potential where I saw a gag. He was the first one to say, "I really like these people; I would want to know them in real life."

Thanks go to Sean Murphy and Eric Pasternack for talking me into taking on ***Lingua*** for real. Without their prodding, I would've left it to the underground. Joan Naidish joined the fray, and her editing skills were invaluable and when coupled with her opinions, talking things through with her was core to my process. Morgan MacBain became the content/continuity coach; her insight into my characters was incredibly helpful. Sally Lorberbaum's willingness to line edit was also a tremendous help. Joan, Morgan, and Sally were my extra sets of eyes when I could not see the forest through the trees.

The cover art was contributed by Misha Siegfried, a fine graphic artist when he isn't playing blues and jazz in clubs. It's the product of a lotta late night IM conversations and a whole lotta patience on his side. I am grateful he took on this project despite his initial misgivings.

I am grateful for all the support and encouragement from family and friends. Without it, I would not have had the courage to finish this book on my own.

CHAPTER 1

The U.S.S. *Washington, D.C.* docked at Kennedy Space Center just long enough to take on cargo and new personnel. The side trip home was just that, a side trip and it would be only eighteen hours before they shoved off again. Three officers were going stateside and two passengers were being deposited at Kennedy. In addition, there was a routine crew rotation for thirty-six, including one couple married that morning by the captain.

Lieutenant Krieg stood on the observation deck, relishing the fresh air as she watched the ship maneuvered into docking position. Any landing of a major vessel was a sight to behold, but a command ship was the biggest and most complex type of craft in the fleet. Almost magically it set down on the pad, precisely aligned on enormous concrete pylons. The ship seemed to nestle into its dock, letting out a loud sigh when the procedure was completed. The officer watched as the landing zone came to life with trucks, ground crew, and supply trams positioned themselves while they waited for the all clear. The intricate dance of departments happening on the tarmac was riveting and the officer watched with a sense of awe and anticipation.

Hoisting a duffle, the lieutenant headed back inside and briskly walked navigated maze that led to the outer gate closest to the waiting ship.

A young woman, her curly mop of red hair trying desperately to escape from her cap, hurried down the gangway. She looked around until she saw a crisp set of khakis striding purposefully in her direction. "Lieutenant Krieg?" she called, adding a tentative smile, and a salute.

"That's me. " The salute was returned.

"Oh, good," she breathed, relieved. "I'm Annabelle Winter and you're assigned to me, or rather, I'm assigned to you. I'm your yeomate." She shook the newcomer's proffered hand vigorously. "May I take your bag?

"Thanks, but I can manage." She preferred to do things for herself and this was the time to make that known. "Do I have time to stop at my quarters before meeting the captain?"

"Sure. Anyway, you just missed him; he left the as soon as they lowered the plank."

~

The *Washington* still gleamed with that first coat of paint shine. Divided into five operational sectors, the ship carried over two hundred crewmates when on routine patrol but could easily handle another three hundred. The engine, reaction chambers, and engineering sections were centrally located above the ventral hull. Flight decks for shuttlecraft and in-space supply transports were on both port and starboard sides, linked together cargo and storage bays. Above that was the rec deck: recreational facilities, sickbay, mess halls, a chapel, and an auditorium. The main crew quarters were on the port side, rising above the rec deck while the officer and guest quarters were starboard. Linking the two sides together were three working decks and the uppermost deck with the bridge, wardroom, and an observatory that doubled as a sort of living room when guests were aboard. The whole thing was linked together by miles of passageways, corridors and an internal transportation system, referred to as the cage.

Winter matched her officer's strides pointing out various attributes as they passed through an endless corridor. The lieutenant did not have the heart to tell her guide that she already knew the *Washington* backward and forward; it would have been impolite. When they reached the cage, Winter stopped to catch her breath. "Captain Morgan will be back before for dinner and said you should plan on joining him at seventeen hundred in his ready room. You'll dine with him and the other officers at 1800 in the wardroom." The cage arrived and the crewmate stepped aside to allow the lieutenant to enter first. "E-deck-2."

When the door slid open, the crewmate followed the same procedure before taking the lead once more. "Your quarters are here, on E-deck section two, with the other department heads, Lieutenant. The captain's at the end of section 4, dead ahead and to the right. You've got a station on the bridge, of course, but you also have a good-sized office on B-deck-2. Did you send a trunk through cargo?"

"Yes. When can I expect to see it?"

"Probably within the hour. We're pretty efficient on the *Washington*," she said proudly. "Captain Morgan runs one tight ship."

"So I've heard." Lieutenant Krieg stopped when the yeomate stopped in front of a blue door. The plate, *Lt. S.J.R. Krieg*, was already in place to the right. The lieutenant allowed a small smile at the sight.

Yeomate Winter slipped a card key into the slot to the left of the handle, withdrew it, and handed it to the officer. "Don't lose your key if you can help it; Mr. Butts, our key master, can be a real pain about those things."

"I'll try to hang on to it," chuckled the lieutenant.

The door opened onto a spacious sitting room, furnished comfortably with a small sofa and easy chair at one end, and a table and two chairs at the other. The Floridian sun poured in through a porthole to the outside, a real luxury on a space ship. One wall held built-in shelves and a desk. A terminal sat in the middle, combined with a full communication console.

The door on the right opened into the bedroom. The lieutenant dropped the duffle on the bunk. There was a long dresser and a closet with a sliding door. A private bath was one more luxury a command ship provided, and this one had everything she could want: a shower, a commode and a sink set into a real cabinet, over which hung a mirror. It looked more like a stateroom on a cruise ship in the Caribbean than a working vessel.

Winter was unzipping the duffle when the lieutenant turned around. "Any special requests, ma'am?" she asked as she started putting things into the dresser drawers. As the lieutenant's yeomate, she automatically helped out.

Lieutenant Krieg thought about stopping her but realized the woman was only performing a routine function. "You do the clothes, I'll do the personal items," she answered with a grin. "Tell me about the *Washington*."

"It's a great assignment, Lieutenant. We get all sorts of weird stuff on this ship and most of it's pretty exciting. Lots of diplomatic missions and we see more of the galaxy than almost anyone else. We've been in a few skirmishes, but the *Washington* is so imposing no one wants to mess with us once we arrive. Captain Morgan is a good C.O., even if he's a stickler on rules and regs," explained Winter. "He's very fair and he doesn't make us crazy...usually. He can be a bit of a micro-manager, but he really tries to keep it in check. When it's just us, things can be pretty informal, very relaxed, but once we have passengers, watch out; he's big on protocol. If you work hard and do your job, he's great. If you screw up, he's a bear to be around. Morgan expects everyone to be in top shape and he notices if you even think about putting on any weight." She stood up and patted a very flat stomach. "We're expected to exercise regularly and he periodically checks the gym log. He thinks we don't know, but we do. By the way, we have a full-size gym, so there's intramural basketball and volleyball. There's a mirrored studio for exercise classes and yoga. We are also the only ship in the fleet with a full sized swimming pool. With a diving board, thanks to the captain and our chief engineer. There's a really nice base-exchange on G-five and an all-night coffee on G-seven."

The lieutenant knew about the swimming pool and she already heard about Morgan's penchant for physical culture, but it was not an area where changes in her own life would have to be made; exercise was part of her personal regimen. When Winter paused, she jumped in. "And what exactly do you do, Winter?" she asked, wondering how a bubbly woman like this found her way into the service.

"Data analysis and simultaneous translation. I'm almost as multi-lingual as you, Lieutenant," she quipped with a grin. "I read your list when I was filing the new personnel log. You've got twenty-one languages, I've got fifteen."

Lieutenant Krieg was impressed. Usually people like that ended up in officer candidate school and she said so.

"Next year, Lieutenant. I've got to finish one more rotation on the *Washington* and then I'll have enough credits to go to OCS. I'm finishing my bachelor's in linguistics while I'm on board." Her pride in her accomplishment was evident. "Actually, Captain Morgan already put in my application and it was provisionally accepted; they said I had to finish my degree first. The captain manages my tutorial." She blushed just a little, telling the officer that the Captain was more than just a superior officer to the crewmate. What, exactly, the lieutenant wasn't sure.

"How did you end up in the service?" she asked changing the subject at the same time hoping to make the pretty yeomate relax and slow down.

Belle laughed, but her cheeks turned bright pink anyway. "An accident, I guess you'd call it." She paused, wanting to check whether or not the lieutenant really wanted to hear the story. "I was very depressed, you see. I was a senior in college and I was all set to go on to grad school. I got accepted at Stanford and Duke, but I didn't get a decent grant so I couldn't afford it. When the last hope for money fell through, I went on a very juvenile bender with one of my roommates. There was this Stellar Two Language Conference and the night before I was supposed to deliver part of a paper on Venusian poetical grammar, we went out drinking. I was bent on getting plastered and did exactly that. We were sitting in a bar near campus and there was this guy. Anyway, he was older, like my father's age, and we started talking. He told me if I enlisted, I could build up an educational account and then use it for grad school. To make a long story short, the old guy turned out to be someone you know... Lester McCormick."

"Les McCormick tried to pick you up in a bar?" blurted the lieutenant, completely astonished by the thought. McCormick was a major player in language analysis and not the biggest fan of the Fleet. Jane had spent two years under his watchful eye while she was at Yale; she could not imagine him in a campus bar, let alone picking up a student.

"He wasn't trying to pick me up," protested Belle, "at least I don't think so. He was very sympathetic. I don't remember much about that night, but I do remember the next day and the monumental hangover that went with it." She sighed dramatically. "I was so embarrassed the next morning when I met him at the conference. He was so nice, so solicitous, asking me how I felt when it was obvious from the color of my face I was sick as a dog."

"So how did you end up here?" Jane prodded.

"He convinced me it was the best means to a desired end. After the conference was over, I went to the recruiting office in Minneapolis and signed up. It turned out there was an opening for a polyglot here on the *Washington*. This nice lady called and asked if I would be willing to come on board when the ship docked. I thought I'd have six or eight months; I had five weeks. So I quit school and signed on for crash basic. Best decision I ever made."

Jane could tell Winter wasn't lying; it was obvious from the sparkle in her eye that she loved what she was doing. "What about your parents?"

Belle shrugged. "My parents thought I was crazy enough when I decided to be a linguistics major. You have to understand, I grew up in a small town in Iowa. My folks are dairy farmers; they figured I'd study agriculture at Iowa State, maybe go on to veterinary school or marry a farmer...something like that. They didn't object, but they didn't dance for joy either. I'd never even flown on a sub-orbiter before I went to Florida for basic training!"

A sharp rap on the door startled them both. "Hey, Winter," called a male voice, "is the looie on board yet?"

"Yes, I am," answered Lieutenant Krieg, suppressing a smile.

"Sorry, ma'am." A burly crewmate poked his head in the door. "Your trunk is here. Where would you like it?"

"In the sleeping quarters, please."

He lifted the trunk as though it was made of cotton fluff and carried it into the bedroom. He wiped his hand on his pant leg and saluted smartly. "Crewmate Dresher at your service, Lieutenant. Welcome aboard."

She returned the salute. "Thanks, Dresher."

"If there's anything else you need moved, just holler." He grinned sheepishly, relieved she hadn't taken offence.

"Thank you, again." She waited for the crewmate to leave. "Nice guy. I hear that everyone on the *Washington* is pretty nice."

"I think so, ma'am. I'll be sorry to leave when I go off to OCS, but with any luck, I'll come back here as an ensign." She waited while Lieutenant Krieg opened the trunk. "I guess you'll want your books at the desk."

The officer nodded. "Just help me carry the big stuff out to the sitting room, and then you can finish unpacking the clothes." She hoisted a row of hard copy texts from the trunk.

For the next hour, Lieutenant Krieg sorted through her personal belongings while the yeomate took care of the rest. When everything was unpacked, Winter used the intercom to summon Dresher back for the empty trunk.

"There's another couple of boxes for you, ma'am," announced the crewmate when he arrived. "They're labeled office, so that's where we put 'em."

"That's great; I'll stow those later. There's another small container that should be arriving separately. Please bring that here."

"Sure thing, ma'am," replied the burly Dresher before he saluted and disappeared into the passageway.

A soft, but very masculine voice emanated from the console. "Is the lovely Lef'tenant Krieg to home?" it asked.

A broad smile lit up the officer's face. "Tapper!" she cried, pushing a button. His face appeared on the screen. "How are you?"

"Just fine, S.J. Welcome aboard the floating palace. Are your quarters to your liking?"

"After eight months on the venerable tub *San Diego*, they're deluxe accommodations. I heard you finally made commander as a tech chief. Is true fact?"

"Is true fact, S.J.. And speaking of true facts, I damn near fell over when I heard you're gonna be our lingo looie."

"Are you pleased?"

"What do you think? You know I like having you around." He blew her a kiss. "That's the last one of those you're gonna get from the likes of me, madam officer. But enough of the social call, I've got a vidcom for you. Wanna take it now or should I tell her to call back later?"

"Her?"

"Herself, her. Who else?"

"Tell herself to hang on." Lieutenant Krieg turned to Yeomate Winter. "You can take off for now, Winter, but please come back for me in about an hour. I really appreciate your helping out."

It was a pleasant dismissal, but a dismissal all the same. Winter wondered who could be calling the lieutenant this soon after her arrival. Personal calls were rarely put directly through to a cabin. Winter would have preferred to stick around and find out who was calling. "See you later, then." Winter saluted and left, closing the door softly behind her.

Jane turned back to the screen. "Go ahead, Tapper, put her on."

"Will do, S.J. Wander down to engineering if you have time, okay?"

"Sure thing." She pulled up a chair and sat down. In a few seconds, Elizabeth Rothko, wearing the dark blue dress uniform of an Air Force Brigadier General, appeared on the screen. "Hi, Mom. Are you in the office...and why the get-up?"

"Yes, but only for a few more minutes. Your father is coming to get me for a dinner...hence the sparkle duds." She smiled at her daughter. "How's the new posting?"

"I've only been here an hour, how can I tell?"

"Sorry, Sarah Jane," laughed the general. "I'm only being a mother."

"I wouldn't have you any other way. How's Dad taking all this?"

"Fine, but his punching finger is itchy. He wants to call you but won't. Said it's behavior unbefitting an officer."

"He's right, y'know. But he'll be checking up on me all the same if I know him." She leaned back and sighed, "I guess I am a little nervous. I figured I get the *New Orleans* or one of the smaller cruisers, so I was really surprised to get the *Washington*. I went over the assignment with Malcolm Dodge before I left the San Diego, and he said this is the perfect job. Did Dad have anything to do with it?"

General Rothko shook her head. "Actually, he stayed out of it completely. He even passed up candidates' review; claimed he had a speech to prep, but I didn't buy that at all. Your brother said it was because he wouldn't be able to keep his mouth shut."

"Dad could keep his mouth shut anywhere he wanted. But I'm glad he didn't go. I just hope no one associates me with him."

"I don't blame you, sweetheart," smirked the general. "I don't always like being associated with him myself."

"Mother!"

"Sarah Jane, I love your father dearly, but he can be a serious pain when he goes all military on us. I shouldn't have to remind you."

"No, I guess not."

There was a soft buzz in the background. "Uh oh, he's here. Take care of yourself, darling, and do send a vidcom every once in a while. Tapper will send it classified and then no one will know where it's going."

For a moment, the lieutenant was little misty. It would be a long time before she saw or even spoke to her mother directly again. General or not, once they were en route, there would be no more calls. "I'll try, Mom. And you take care of yourself, too. Give kisses to Becca and Isaac for me, and if you see Jonathan, shoot him a salute."

"I will, dear." The general put her hand up, but it was not for a salute. "Remember, we love you."

"And I love you. Bye, Mom."

"Gei gezunt und kum gezunt, Lieutenant S.J.R.Krieg."

By the time Winter returned, everything was as though the lieutenant had been living there forever. "Ready to see your home away from home?" she asked brightly.

"I am. Let's do it."

In the office, the lieutenant and the yeomate set to work creating order from new-arrival chaos. Winter went through the files left by the last linguist, prioritizing as she went. Manuals and assorted documentation lined up on the credenza behind the desk in need-to-know order. Down to the personal stuff, Winter asked if she could go tend to a few personal things for herself.

Winter paused at the door. "Dinner tonight is informal, so you can either change or stay in the khakis. The only time officers dress for dinner is when we've got guests on board. Some people will be in khakis because we're home, but anyone who's been back aboard for a while will probably wear reds." She frowned a little before she went on. "Oh, one last thing: the reds I hung up are kinda not our reds."

"Oh?"

"Yeah, yours are *really* red. Engineering wears that color. Staff officer reds are more maroon. Medical wears like an eggplant color. Senior staff wears dark blue."

"Wow," Jane whistled. "On my last three postings, everyone had regulation reds. Do I have time to see the quartermaster?"

"Already called in. Three new reds will be delivered to your quarters within the hour. There's a guy who does finish tailoring at the ship stores, and he'll get you fixed up once we're in flight. He works pretty fast. You should be fine. Everyone knows you're new."

"Thanks for thinking ahead," said Lieutenant Krieg looking down at her rumpled uniform. "They're much more comfortable."

"Good choice," Winter agreed. "Everyone wears them around here. Even Captain Morgan. He says khakis are for landlubbers. Can you find your way back?"

"No problem, and you really don't need to escort me to the bridge. I'm sure you have other things you'd rather being doing. Like shopping..."

"There are a few things I'd like to pick up. Do you need anything from town?"

She thought for a minute before digging into her pocket for some cash. "If it's not too much trouble, bring me back a couple of big jars of chunky peanut butter. I forgot to get them this morning." She handed a folded bill to Winter who took it with a knowing nod.

"No jelly?"

"Jelly I've got. It's the peanut butter I missed. I could've sworn I packed some." She watched the crewmate go; sure she had done the right thing. She had some in her kit, but extra peanut butter could go a long way on a voyage.

There was plenty of hot water, unlike on the *San Diego* where water was rationed like fresh milk; Lieutenant Krieg used it to her best advantage. She washed her long hair thoroughly, and then just stood under the stream until guilt from waste took over. The new reds had been delivered as promised. The fit was not perfect, but it was close enough to pass an inspection. There would be plenty of time to get them altered once they were underway. Instead of regulation boots, she opted for the white leather sneakers she always wore on the *San Diego*, having noticed other crewmates were wearing them, too. With a fresh towel, she dried her hair as well as she could before twining it into a braid to be clipped into a knot at the back of her neck. It took a minute of rummaging before she found the correct insignia for her new position, and she fastened it to her suit. She removed the rest of the necessary regalia from the discarded khaki uniform before tossing it into the standard issue laundry sack hanging on the closet door. There wasn't much to pin on, but the few pieces she had were important. She checked herself in the mirror, and satisfied that everything was in place and straight, she parked herself on the sofa and began reading the dossiers left for her by the last language specialist.

It was 1650 before she checked her watch. Tossing the reports aside, she grabbed her posting packet and headed to the Captain's office on the bridge.

"Come in," called a voice as she approached the open doorway, "and sit down." He did not look up from the screen. "Put your packet on the desk and sit down."

She did as she was told and the door slid shut behind her. "Lieutenant Krieg reporting for duty, sir." She saluted and watched a hand return the salute without the face looking up. She sat down.

The captain's office was a study in simplicity. Other than a scale rendering of the *Washington*, there was no decoration on the walls. Behind the wide, precisely arranged desk, three large portholes allowed him to see whatever lay ahead of his ship. "Welcome aboard the *Washington*, Lieutenant," said Captain Morgan, clicking off the terminal. "I trust you found your quarters satisfactory." It was a statement, not a question.

"Yes, sir."

"And I take it you are surprised to find yourself assigned to the *Washington*." Another statement.

"Yes, sir."

"Yeomate Winter said you've already been to your office. Was everything in order?" This was a question.

"Yes, sir."

"And you were just at your bridge station."

"Yes, sir."

Captain Morgan shot a piercing glance at the lieutenant. "Do you say anything besides 'yes, sir?'"

"Yes, sir."

"Well, there's a start." He opened her packet and withdrew the papers from the envelope. He quickly glanced through the documents. "Graduated number two in your class, *summa cum laude* from Dartmouth. Masters in Semantics and Applied Linguistics from Yale. A year in Officer Candidate School, two years in Super School, six months on the *Saratoga,* six on the *Monitor*, a year on the San Diego. Lots of initials, S.J.R. Krieg. What do they call you at home?"

The moment had come. She hesitated for a briefest second. "Jane, sir."

"Jane?" He raised an eyebrow; if he knew differently, he said nothing.

"Yes, sir; Jane."

"You come highly recommended, Lieutenant Jane Krieg. Let's hope you can live up to your reputation." There was a distinct note of sarcasm in his voice she did not like.

"Permission to speak candidly, sir."

"Ah, she talks." He looked across the desk into a determined pair of grey eyes. "Certainly, Krieg, what's on your mind?"

"No offense intended, sir, but I earned my reputation through hard work, not through any connections you may or may not think I have. My record stands on merit, Captain, and I hope that I shall exceed the expectations of your command."

"Let's all hope so, Lieutenant." His words were as crisp as his intent. "I expect my officers to perform at peak efficiency whether we are alone or playing host to a member of the diplomatic corps. What seems like an easy float to some is, in actuality, a difficult and complex assignment. We are expected to coddle our passengers and we are expected to observe local custom when we are called in to perform duties of presence. Your function on this vessel is to ensure that we understand those we come in contact with and that we, in turn, are understood. In addition, you will be expected to maintain and upgrade our computer language banks."

"I understand my role and the posting, sir; I am fully qualified for the position."

"Good. Then we understand each other, Lieutenant." He pushed back in his chair and regarded her silently for a moment. "Dinner will be served at 1800 in the wardroom. No need to dress for the occasion; we will be dining *en famille* this evening. We sail at 0800, but you need to be on the bridge by 0700."

"Yes, sir."

"Dismissed, lieutenant." He gave her a more precise salute than his earlier one.

Lieutenant Krieg returned the salute and left. Captain Morgan was nothing less than she expected. He was, as she had been warned, outrageously good looking, with a dark beard and darker blue eyes. His hair was longer than regulation, but it would look ridiculous cropped too short. There was no doubt that he was from Boston; his accent gave him away. His voice did have a cynical edge, but she couldn't decide if it was because he knew the truth or because he was always that way. Only time would tell. That he knew who she was was unquestionable; her personnel dossier would have that information. Whether or not he used it against her remained to be seen.

Alone in his office, Asher Morgan leaned back against his chair and closed his eyes. S.J.R. Krieg was not at all what he expected. Looking at her was like looking at a female version of Speed and why that surprised him, he did not know. Willowy, not very tall, she looked almost ethereal in her reds. Her hair, he suspected, was quite long, judging from the size of knot at the back of that long neck. Her face was fresh scrubbed and glowing, but it was the eyes that threw him. They were the same murky grey that on her brother threw women into a veritable frenzy; they were undeniably sexy on her. She was a potential, very dangerous, distraction.

Morgan thought back to candidates' review. None of the dossiers had names, only numbers, to prevent any untoward discrimination. As captain of the *Washington*, he had first choice of all candidates from the five academies. Each of the four service branches sent their top students to first round candidate review, plus the ones who had survived super-school, the academy that instructed only those with advanced degrees in specific areas. He was a super-school survivor, as were most of the captains in the fleet. Like this new crop, he had been selected blind by his first commanding officer, a situation which proved to be disaster. Every time he sat at the review, he remembered that, and looked for hidden signals hinting whether or not a candidate would fit in. He was not interested in grades; he was looking for something else. Candidate 871-135-7112K had that something. On paper. Once he had flagged the folders that piqued his interest, hardball began.

The review had, on more than one occasion, been compared to the NFL draft. Commanding officers traded in-coming officers like star players: *I'll give you that one, if you give me this one*. But Morgan needed a multi-lingual data specialist with engineering capabilities and he wanted 871-135-7112K. It never occurred to him that the K stood for Krieg. He heard Admiral Rothko had a daughter in the draft, but assumed that, like Speed, she would use the Rothko name. Once he discovered who she was, he fought tooth and nail with his superiors to rid himself of the double-service brat. Now he had her and he was stuck with her. Speed would think it was just desserts.

Putting thoughts of the lieutenant aside, Morgan hit the intercom and waited for Tapper to come online.

"Yes, boss?"

"Give me an outside link, will you? And scramble it."

"Calling home, are we?" He knew his captain well.

"What's it to you, fella?"

"Say hello to the kid for me."

"Sure, Tapper." He waited for the line to open and punched the number. It took a little while, but soon his father's face appeared on the screen. "Hello, Papa," said Morgan, forcing a smile.

"You're healthy?" asked the bearded man who looked more like eighty than sixty-five.

"Yes, Papa, I'm healthy. How are you?"

"Just fine, Asher. Are you observing mitzvot?"

"As best I can, Papa." It was the same routine every time he called. The old man never said *Hi, son, how are you?* The conversation was always strained, never friendly.

"Are you eating strange foods?"

"No, Papa. You know I don't."

"Are you coming home?"

"I wish I were, Papa, but I can't right now. How's Mama?"

"As well as can be expected. The boy keeps her young." He paused and stroked his beard. "I'll get her; she'll want to talk to you."

Morgan watched as his father left the viewing area. He could see the kitchen, looking as wonderful as it always did. His mother's great pot sat on the stove and he could almost smell the brisket he knew must be simmering inside. No matter how old he got, he felt like a child when he saw his mother's ultimate domain. Soon she was scurrying across the room, wiping her hands on her apron.

"Asher! Where are you?" she asked, her face flushed, her hands tugging at the head scarf to make sure it was in place.

"In Florida, Mom. We had a personnel rotation, so we're here for eighteen hours. If it was longer, I would have come home."

"I know you would have, my darling. Are you in good health? You look tired."

"Yes and yes. It's been a long couple of days, but once we're underway, I'll get some rest. How are you feeling? Are you taking the medication?"

"Of course, *mein kind!* I have a family to look after so I can't afford not to do what the doctor tells me." She called to her husband. "Aaron, go get Reuben, he's playing in the yard. But don't tell him who's on the screen." She beamed at her son. "It's always better to surprise him."

"Is he giving you a hard time, Mom?"

"No harder than you and your brothers. Oy, he's a joy. He works hard in school, that boy, and his grades show it. Better than yours, Asher. But he misses his papa."

Morgan smiled sheepishly. "And I miss him. With any luck, I'll get home sometime in the summer." They heard a commotion and a tall, gangly ten-year-old bounded into the kitchen.

"Hey, Dad!" cried the boy as soon as he saw the face on the screen. "Are you coming home?"

"Sorry, champ, I'm in Florida for a few hours. We had a quick stop here." It seemed the boy had grown a foot since he'd seen him in May, six months ago. "Tell me about school."

"School's okay. I'm doing really well in math and science, but Mishnah class is tough. Grandpa Stein is helping me, but boy, am I spending a lot of time at my desk."

Morgan laughed; Mishnah had been tough for him, too and said so. "Ask Zayde to find my yellow notebooks. They're in the basement in a box labeled 'Talmud stuff.' Maybe they'll help you."

"Thanks, Dad. I can use all the help I can get. Will you be coming home soon? I'd rather have you help me in person."

"Maybe in the summer, like I told your Bubbe." He watched his son push up his Red Sox cap and wipe his forehead with the back of his arm, a mannerism which had driven his mother crazy when he was a boy. "Do me a favor, Reuben, give my mom a big kiss for me."

"Sure." He threw his arms around his grandmother and gave her a noisy kiss. "That good enough, Dad?"

"Yep, that oughta do it." They talked for a few more minutes, and when Morgan finally said good-bye, it was with a wave of guilt; he should be there for his son, not cruising around space. When his wife passed away two years earlier, it had been her wish that he not give up his military career. Tovah had been so proud of her officer husband, never complaining about the months of separation, always ready with encouragement when he needed it most. She had stood by him during the years when his father had fought his decision to give up the rabbinate and become a full-fledged officer rather than just a chaplain. Tovah had worked hard while he was at super-school, supporting them while the money was scarce. When Reuben was born, she opted to stay in Boston, near their families, rather than become a camp follower. He had agreed with her decision and in the end, it was the right one. Both her parents and his were there when the cancer was discovered and together they cared for her and the boy until he could get home. He had taken a posting at Super-School for a year while he watched her slowly fade away. But he was there when she died, and the last four months of his assignment were spent living alone with Reuben in the house Tovah had found for them. The decision to return to active duty had been a hard one, but one made together with Reuben who was not unhappy to be living with his grandparents. After all, he had pointed out to his father, at least Bubbe can cook, a skill Morgan had never managed to perfect. This was the best way and he knew it, but it did not make him feel any less guilty.

The officers of the *Washington* gathered at precisely 1800 hours in the spacious wardroom. Tapper was there, but after a quick hello, he left Jane to her own devices. Introductions were made and Lieutenant Krieg found herself sitting between First Officer Joseph Newhouse and Ensign Robert Davies, both graduates of the Fleet Academy. During the first course, they plied her with questions about super-school and Jane felt as though she were under a microscope. Rescue came when Lieutenant Commander Barbara Lucas, chief protocol officer, addressed her from across the table.

"Ignore the men on this vessel, Jane," she instructed with a laugh. "They are positively in awe of anyone who comes out of Super School with head intact."

"And you would know, wouldn't you Barb?" countered Joe Newhouse with a wicked grin. "Since you are a victim yourself."

She pointed a knife directly at him. "Your fangs are showing, Joey, dear. And you are green with envy." She turned to Jane and studied her for a brief moment. "Have we met somewhere?"

Thinking for a minute, Jane shook her head, "I don't think so."

"Hmm. You look a little familiar." Barbara shook her head. "After a while, all the kiddies look alike." Her smile did not extend to her eyes, which seemed to be flipping through a mental flip file.

The banter was lively and the newcomers enjoyed the slice of casual life they glimpsed in the wardroom. There was a strong sense of camaraderie, not the competition which could make even the most amazing ship a hell hole. At the head of the table, Morgan presided with good humor and fine manner. His staff was relaxed but respectful; it was that respect which impressed Jane the most. Obviously they thought highly of their commanding officer.

At seating, an attending steward asked each officer for a menu choice. "Unlike most of the other ships in the fleet, we have a most able chef who respects our peculiar eating habits," explained the captain as he sampled the wine poured into his glass by the steward. "Make a point of visiting him in the galley and he will be your friend for life."

When the crewmate approached Jane, she selected fresh yellow snapper for her entree. Fish of any sort would be a rarity once they left port, so the choice was a natural one. Morgan ordered the same, as did several others. A platter of stone crab claws was passed around the table, but Jane declined.

"Are the claws not to your liking, Lieutenant Krieg?" asked the captain. "They are a specialty of the area."

"Thank you, but no, sir," replied Jane, handing the platter to Newhouse. "I'm not one for shellfish." The excuse seemed lame under the circumstances, but she was not forthcoming with an additional explanation. She did, however, notice the captain did not take them either.

The conversation returned to the ship; the old timers regaled the newcomers with adventuresome stories about their last year in space. Captain Morgan said little, but seemed to enjoy the tales as they unfolded. Jane was fascinated by the intensity of the experiences, and eager to be underway. Life aboard the *Washington* was unlikely to be dull.

When dessert was served, a wonderful chocolate confection was presented by the chef himself. As much as she would have liked to have eaten the entire thing herself, Jane resisted the impulse and allowed a small amount to be set before her. Between the food and the wine, she was stuffed, but mousse topped with strawberries was irresistible. Strong Jamaican coffee was served but it took all her strength not to fall asleep at the table. It had been a long, exciting day and she was ready to call it quits for the night.

But the captain had other ideas. Leading the way, he took his staff to the window-walled observatory where more coffee and brandy awaited. Everyone found comfortable seats and waited for Captain Morgan to begin the traditional pre-sail briefing. He spoke about the need for constant teamwork on his ship and reiterated his own set of rules of decorum. His rules varied somewhat from the norm, but they had been carefully devised because of the sensitive nature of most of their missions. "The bottom line, ladies and gentlemen, is that we must never give a passenger or a host the impression that we are not the best of friends on this ship. I will not tolerate divisive behavior aboard ship. If you have a problem, either solve it yourself or find someone who will. If you can't manage that, come to me or you will find yourself waiting for the next shuttle back. Respect your shipmates, kiddies, and they will respect you."

His use of the word "kiddies" was not demeaning; it was clarifying. As captain he served as mother and father to his crew and he took the responsibility seriously. Yet, there was no indication that he would coddle a recalcitrant crewmate. Satisfied that he had made his point, Captain Morgan leaned back in his chair and sipped his brandy. "Now, I'd like to go around the room and give everyone a chance to introduce themselves. State your name, rank, academy, and anything else of interest."

The old timers looked at each other, puzzled by the request. He never played parlor games in the past and they wondered why he was starting now. Still, it wasn't a particularly bad idea. The captain began with himself.

"If you don't know already, I'm Ash Morgan, from Boston, Massachusetts. I come out of Super School, like some of you others, but I also have degrees from Columbia University and MIT. This is the second ship I've commanded, and I am a survivor of the Great Training Mishap." There was a titter from his audience. Everyone knew about the G.T.M.; survivors were folk heroes.

Which means he knows Jonathan, Jane realized Her brother was there, one of the wounded. She wondered why she had not thought of that before.

Captain Morgan caught the slight furrowing of Lieutenant Krieg's brow when he mentioned the G.T.M.; it amused him to watch her put two and two together. Turning to the officer closest to him, he said, "You're up, Tapper."

The chief tech cleared his throat dramatically. "I, too, am a survivor of the G.T.M. My name is Joshua Bear and I got the name Tapper because of a little bit of Morse code I once tapped out." There was more laughter from the assembly. It was his ability to rig a radio from found material that had finally brought rescue squads to their location. "I'm out of MIT and Super School, but it doesn't mean me and the Captain come as a matched set, even though some people like to think so. I've been on this tub since before it left port and I'll probably stay here the rest of my career. Such is the plight of a designing technocrat." He, too, glanced at Jane, but said nothing more. He had practically lived in the Rothko house while the *Washington* was being designed, working day and night with her father. But because she was using Krieg, her mother's maiden name, he stopped himself from mentioning he had known the new officer since she was a noisy, skinny teenager.

Jane listened attentively while the others took their turns. When it came to her, she was ready. "My name is Jane Krieg. I also come out of Super School, but my other degrees are from Dartmouth and Yale. It's true I handle twenty-one languages, but only eighteen are spoken. The others are computer communication. I come from Maryland, originally, but I've also lived in New York, London, and off-planet. This is my fourth ship, having just come off the San Diego." She smiled when everyone groaned. The San Diego was known to be the oldest and least comfortable ship in the fleet. "So I guess the *Washington* is a reward for time served on a tub." She flashed a smile and relaxed, waiting for the next officer to perform.

When it was over, the officers milled about, socializing as Captain Morgan made the rounds, spending a few minutes with each small group. Jane and Tapper were sitting in a corner, heads together, when the captain approached them. "I take it you know each other," he said, perching on the arm of Tapper's chair.

"More or less," replied the chief tech, unusually guarded in his answer. Morgan knew his history; he knew the commander had been close with the Rothko clan for years. But Jane had made it clear to him that she was not to be associated with her family in any public way. If Morgan missed the connection, it was not Tapper's place to point it out.

"Are you boring the lieutenant with tales of the G.T.M.?" asked the captain.

"Nah, she already knows 'em all. We were just catching up on news of the world." As close as they were, he was not letting his friend in on the conversation. "Well," said the captain, standing up, "don't keep her up too late. The lieutenant has first watch." With a last glance in her direction, Morgan left them alone.

As soon as he was out of earshot, she whispered, "How well does he know Jonathan?"

Tapper shrugged. "He's the one who pulled Speed from the wreckage. I'm surprised you don't know him; he and Jonathan were really tight; they still are."

Jane's brows knitted into a V above her eyes. "Why don't I remember a guy named Morgan?"

"Because, dummy," chuckled Tapper from deep within his throat, "his name is Morgenstern. Asher Morgenstern. Does that ring a few bells?"

"The chaplain?"

"The rabbi. Ash was the chaplain on the Montpelier when it crashed. After that, he more or less left the rabbinate and went back to Super School. He's got *smicha* from Yeshiva University, though he never mentions it, a bachelors and masters in math from Columbia, and did double doc in math and engineering at MIT. He was a veritable whiz kid who just couldn't decide what he wanted to do with his life...until, that is, he found himself in the service."

"I had no idea that's who he was. Is. I just never connected the two. How come the name change?"

"You're asking that question? You know a lot of Jews in the service who go anywhere besides your family?" He took her hand in his. "Even I opted for tech chief rather than buck the system. Your dad disagreed, but General Liz said I would be a helluva lot happier doing what I do best rather than trying to be a regular bridge officer. I've got the rank, but I don't get the bullshit that goes with it. Give me a crack engineering department and I'm a happy camper."

"My father wasn't too pleased with my decision either, Tapper. He said that a twenty-four-year-old girl had no business opting for the military no matter what her qualifications and that I was too old for any academy. When I got into Super School without his help," she said with a wicked grin, "he threw a fit. So now I'm a twenty-nine year old looie with no marital prospects in sight. In spite of my mother, he does not believe a woman's place is in the military. Or rather, his daughter's place..." Her voice trailed off.

"But he's proud of you all the same. That's more than Morgan can say for his father. His dad has never reconciled himself to a son in the service of anything less than that of God."

Jane said nothing; it was a lot of information to digest. She looked about the room and saw the captain, drink in hand, talking animatedly with Lt. Commander Lucas. Her elegant hand reached up and patted her C.O. on his bearded cheek, and he threw his head back, laughing heartily. He seemed so relaxed around her, not at all like he was in his office. Turning back to Tapper, she asked, "What's he like to work for?"

"He's the best there is, S.J. As a C.O., he goes out of his way to be fair. We have our disputes on this ship, but he works hard to keep them to a minimum. Ash is approachable, definitely not an aloof sorta guy. He's not afraid to get his hands dirty and he knows this ship from stem to stern. Including the mechanical. Pretty unusual these days, from what I hear from other tech chiefs...like Dodge on the San Diego... Dodge is a great administrator, but he doesn't know squat about how a power source functions. He makes sure his staff is competent, because he has to rely on them for knowledge he lacks. Morgan, on the other hand, has made it his business to learn what he doesn't know and he isn't too stuck up to ask questions when he doesn't understand. The crew thinks he has eyes in the back of his head because he knows everything that goes down on this vessel."

She was about to ask another question when Barb Lucas joined them. "Anyone for a dip in the ocean?" she asked with a twinkle in her eye. "A few of us are going to sneak down to the beach for a last touch of *terra familiar* before we shove off."

Tapper readily agreed to go. "I could use a swim. Wanna come, S.J.?"

"Thanks, I'll pass. I was out there this morning so I think I'd better stay here and finish up a little reading."

"Don't whine you're homesick later," laughed Tapper. "Oh, S.J.," he said before he left her. "I've got something for you." He pulled a small disc from his pocket and tossed it to her. "See you later, Squirt."

Jane watched them go, Tapper's arm draped casually about Lucas's shoulders. She wondered how much fraternization actually took place on the *Washington*.

The observatory was emptying slowly. Jane took the opportunity to chat with a few of the other officers before slipping out into the passageway. She was almost to the elevator when someone asked her to stop. She turned and saw Captain Morgan coming toward her.

"Aren't you going with the beach bums?" he asked pleasantly.

"No, sir, I have some reading to do."

"Take time to play now, Lieutenant Krieg; there will be precious little of it later." He eyed her carefully.

Jane straightened her shoulders under his stare. He was much taller than she had thought; she came barely to his shoulder. Whenever you're unsure, her father instructed once upon a time, look your fear in the face. She tilted her chin and looked directly into the Captain's blue eyes.

"I understand that, sir, but if I am to take my post on the bridge for lift off, I had better be prepared." She had the sense that he was expecting her to make mistakes and she immediately decided that there would be none under any circumstances. She was fairly certain he did not want Fleet Admiral Rothko's daughter on his ship and she would be damned if she was going to give him the opportunity to say "I told you so." He was standing close enough for her to smell the faint scent of brandy on his breath. It was, she knew, a position meant to intimidate but she did not move. Instead, she used the tension of silence to state her own, fearless position.

"Have it your way, Lieutenant," shrugged the captain.

"Goodnight, Captain Morgan." Jane saluted and marched toward the cage, annoyed at his attitude.

Ash Morgan watched her disappear into the cage. "Dangerous woman," he muttered under his breath. "Definitely her father's daughter."

In her quarters, Jane exchanged her reds for a flannel nightgown. She was about to curl up on the couch with her manuals when she remembered the disc Tapper had given her, still in the pocket of her flight suit. She retrieved it and shoved it into the vidcom. Her brother's face materialized on the screen. He saluted smartly and broke into a smile.

"I guess if you're watching this, you must be aboard ship. How does it feel, squirt, to be a big leaguer? It isn't every girl who gets herself posted on a command vessel, you know.

"I'm sorry I'm not calling you in person, but this is the best I can do. Ran into Tapper last week at the lunar station and he suggested I do this before I ship out to the Middle East, assignment classified. Poor Dad, Mom won't tell him exactly where I've been sent. Anyway, it's good for him not to know, it'll give him something else to worry about...beside you.

"I just wanted to wish you lots of luck on this assignment; I know it's an important one and I think you'll do a great job for Morgan. I saw him, too. I didn't mention you're my kid sister, but he probably knows by now, so don't get in a lather about it. Just do your job and keep your smart-ass opinions to yourself. And stay outta trouble; I won't be there to bail you out like I used to do on the playground. If for any reason, you need to get a hold of me, tell Tapper. He's got enough contacts to get a message anywhere I might be. Remember, he's more than a good friend, so don't hesitate to ask him for advice. Trust Tapper; he knows us all and it's never gotten in the way. The best advice *I* can give you is to keep your connections to yourself. The fewer people who know who you are, the better. Trust me on this one, I know from experience. I shoulda done what you did, using Mom's name, but I never thought of it.

"Make us proud, squirt, and use every chance you get to send a vid home. And don't forget to send special ones for Becca and Isaac. They're your biggest fans, you know.

"Have a great voyage and remember, I love you, Sarah Jane." He saluted again and the screen went to black.

Jane popped the disc and put it in her desk drawer. She was touched by his message and pleased that Tapper had thought to arrange for her to get it. Of her three siblings, Jonathan was closest to her and was the one she would miss the most. They were almost six years apart, but that had never gotten in the way. Jonathan was the one who encouraged her to apply to super-school and was there when she told her parents she'd been accepted. He had gone to war with their father on her behalf and it was Jonathan who had finally smoothed the way. He was the best brother a girl could ever want.

Back on the sofa, the manuals waited. She picked one up and soon was lost in its complex text. When she next looked up, it was after one in the morning. Reluctantly, she put the books away and crawled into bed. As excited as she was, sleep came quickly.

CHAPTER 2

When the lieutenant opened her eyes, the first rays of late autumn sun were drifting through the porthole and the digits on her beside clock glowed 0555. Stretching slowly, she relished the sensation of impending adventure. Too excited to stay in bed, she headed for the shower.

Dressed in the requisite flight suit and white sneakers, she collected the things she wanted at her station on the bridge and left her quarters. The passage was empty and still dimly lit for night. Jane had the cage to herself as it lifted her to her first day's work on the *Washington*.

The bridge was deserted save for a lone ensign finishing the night log. He yawned as he looked up, his eyes already heavy with oncoming sleep. "S'long as you're here, I can go," mumbled Cartier, struggling to his feet. "I should never have gone swimming with them last night. Should've taken a nap." He ambled toward the cage. "If you're hungry, call down to the all-night coffee and they'll send up some breakfast," he called before the door slid shut.

Taking Cartier's place at the center console, Jane logged her ID number and established herself as bridge watch. It wouldn't be long before the others arrived; lift off was set for 0800. Looking over the log, she noted that the pre-flight had been completed at 0530 and all that was left to do was clear the cargo bay doors. The screen told her provisions were still being loaded; the amber symbol would not go to green until the cargo bay doors were secure. As with any watch, she walked from station to station, verifying that nothing else was going on. Fairly certain that her review was complete, she still checked herself against the list in the front of the log book.

Back at her own station, Jane switched on her screen and waited for the password request to appear. It was customary to set one's own tertiary password when logging on officially for the first time. It was the spot check, the one thing that would always be hers. Without hesitation, she typed JONATHAN; she knew her brother's tertiary was SARAHJANE and this seemed to have become a tradition between them. *Password entered. Please verify* appeared on the screen and she retyped the word for verification.

Settling in, she began reviewing entries for the past month. Lieutenant Commander Emilio Trieste had been a most thorough fellow, she decided as she watched his notes go by on the screen. His careful notations gave her a decent idea of how Captain Morgan wanted reports: terse, yet thorough.

Jane pulled up the flight plan. First glance told her this was a show-and-tell cruise for the new flag ship. The first leg would be out to Titan, Saturn's moon, where Captain Morgan and First Officer Newhouse would be representing the fleet at IGCC, the annual conference of deep-space commanders and diplomats. Other specialists would be meeting their counterparts. The prospect of an interplanetary conference was an exciting and propitious way to begin her posting. A couple of ambassadors from Jeylos were then expected to hitch a ride home, two star systems away. The next stop, beautiful Amitides, was one of Jane's all-time favorite places; she was hoping there might be a little shore leave to visit friends, a fun loving bunch known for their all-female galas. From Amitides to Taapusor, from Taapusor to Lomos, from Lomos to Kotuchar, from Kotuchar to Bagnamba. Some of them Jane visited with her parents, others would be new. At Bagnamba, a new flight plan would be filed. It wasn't a long voyage by most standards; still, every minute was planned by the Admiralty to make the most of a command ship in flight.

"Can you handle the languages?" asked Captain Morgan from behind.

Her reaction was to startle at the sudden intrusion, but she checked herself. "Nothing out of the ordinary, sir," she answered calmly.

"Good." He tossed several files on her desk. "Sift through these before we get to Titan. You'll have a better shot at participating intelligently if you know what they're talking about."

If she didn't like his tone, she didn't mention it. "Thank you, Captain. Any assistance is appreciated." She looked up at him, towering over her. *He uses his height to his own best advantage,* she thought once more. Her eyes met his and did not waiver.

The captain backed off. "There's coffee over there, if you want some," he said, pointing to a dispenser near his office.

"Thank you, Captain."

When she didn't move, he asked "Would you like me to pour?"

It was a tempting offer, even if offered with an eyebrow raised and a mocking voice. The sane part of her told her to say no thank you, but the Rothko part took over. "If you don't mind?" she replied with a too sweet smile.

I deserved that, thought the captain; "My pleasure." He went over to the dispenser and carefully aligned a cup beneath the spout, feeling her eyes on his back. "Cream? Sugar?" he called, drippingly polite.

"Black, thank you."

He brought two cups and sat down at the console beside her. "Let's get something straight right now, Lieutenant," he said, handing her the cup. "We both know from whence you've come, and as you so assiduously pointed out, you've accomplished what you've accomplished on your own. But don't expect that there will be any expectations different from those I already subject my senior staff to."

Swiveling her seat to face him full front, Jane held her temper in check. Her lips formed a tight line as she considered her reply. "What I expect, Captain Morgan," she began slowly, "is to be treated like any other officer aboard the *Washington*. I would also expect you to respect my privacy; specifically the obvious desire that my full name not be used by you or anyone else. That information is classified. To my knowledge, the only other person who knows is Tapper and *he* will not slip."

"Implying that I would?" There was ice in his voice.

"Take it as you will, Captain."

"I believe, Lieutenant, you have made your position perfectly clear."

Jane eyed him carefully. His eyes were even darker than before and in them she could read distrust. An adversarial relationship with the captain was the least desirable of all possible scenarios. In an attempt to diffuse him, she spoke quietly. "I am not a spy for my father. I was raised, as was my brother, in a two-service household, where privacy and respect are top priorities. What takes place on this ship is our business except where it concerns the Admiralty and then, Captain, it is up to *you* to decide what to report and how to report it. *My* first loyalty is to my ship and her captain, *not* my father nor the admiralty. I'm well aware of how rules are bent to meet the need, and I am in no way expected to report them. All I ask is that I be given the same opportunities given to other officers of my rank. If I screw up, tell me. If I screw up royally, get me off your ship. But don't discard me simply because my surname is Rothko."

Captain Morgan had anticipated something hostile; instead got a lesson in decorum. He was duly chastised, but loath to admit it; Jonathan would have just punched him in the nose. He grudgingly admired the way she sliced right through his misplaced anger; this wisp of a girl, with the proper training, would be a crack negotiator yet he caught himself thinking that he would not have expected anything less from the daughter of Admiral and General Rothko. "Just do your job, Lieutenant," said Morgan with reduced hostility, "and I'll stay off your case." Without another word, he went into his office and closed the door.

Lift off was almost anti-climactic after her confrontation with the captain. The bridge crew arrived and began the pre-flight routine. She was nervously excited and her eyes kept darting to the count-down clock where the seconds crept by with painful slowness. When Lt. Commander Lucas called off the last 10 seconds to departure, Jane was counting with her. The ship rose smoothly from its moorings, the movement almost imperceptible until they had cleared the tower. Captain Morgan, sitting in his chair at the center of it all, gave each command to Helmsman Ryan in a casual voice, as though he was doing nothing more than backing a hovercar from a garage.

"Twenty kilometers," announced the navigator from his station.

"Maneuver 180," answered the captain, looking at the large screen which displayed their location.

"Maneuver complete," said the helmsman. After a moment, he announced "Thirty kilometers."

"Maneuver 25," Morgan instructed, still watching the screen where Kennedy Space Center was not even merely a speck on the coast line. The ship tilted upward twenty-five degrees.

"Maneuver complete," Ryan announced.

A voice from the control tower came over the speakers. "You're clear to go, *Washington*. Have a nice trip."

The captain pushed a button on the arm of his command chair. "Thanks much, Pete. See ya' round." He glanced in the direction of the helmsman. "You ready to go, Mr. Ryan?"

"Yes, sir."

"Then let's do it."

"Increasing power, sir. Hang on, folks, we're heading into outer space."

There was a slight vibration as the *Washington* picked up speed. Jane checked her harness, clutched the arm of her chair, closed her eyes, and said a quick, silent prayer in honor of her first voyage on the *Washington.* In a matter of seconds they were through the upper level of the earth's atmosphere and speeding in the direction of Saturn. When the departure lights went out and the crew relaxed, Captain Morgan stood up. "Very nice, ladies and gentlemen. Thank you very much. Staff meeting for linguists, systems, and protocol in fifteen minutes in the observatory." He left the bridge.

Barb Lucas came over to Jane and plopped down in the empty chair beside her. "Well, how do you feel?" she asked although she could guess.

"Exhilarated. I can't believe I'm really on the *Washington.*"

"Believe it, Jane, 'cause you're gonna be here for a while. Take your time and get used to the way we do things. If you ever have any questions, just ask. We try to behave like a team around here and it's important that the old timers help you new recruits as much as we can."

"Thanks, I'll remember that."

"A piece of advice, if you'll have it." offered the Lieutenant Commander.

"Sure."

"Schedule your first staff meeting for immediately after the lunch hour. That's the best time to grab everyone before they disappear for the day." Barb patted her hand. "Don't worry, kid, you'll do just fine."

Jane arrived at the observatory in time to get a comfortable seat near the back. Several of the other specialists had already come in and they spent the few minutes before the captain arrived reintroducing themselves to Jane. Although she had met them the night before, this was a better chance to associate names with faces and specialties. Winter was there, along with other non-officers with special assignments.

"I've got your Skippy in my cabin," whispered Yeomate Winter. "I'll drop it off at your quarters later." She took the chair next to Lieutenant Krieg.

Captain Morgan showed up a few minutes late. He graciously apologized for the delay and then launched into the business at hand. His eyes roved constantly as he spoke, making sure everyone got what he was saying. When a face looked puzzled, he paused and asked for questions. Jane was impressed with the way he read his senior staff; he seemed more like a professor than a commanding officer in his delivery and response. With a change of thirty-six crewmates at Kennedy, Captain Morgan reviewed the personnel roster according to assignment. When he came to linguistics, he handed Jane a docupad.

"Lieutenant Krieg, you've got six staffers of your own. Their names and qualifications are listed there. Considering that you'll be involved in the conference on Titan, you need to finesse your duty roster as soon as possible. Stop by my office later and I will give you an agenda for the conference." He turned his attention to one of the other newcomers.

Jane studied the pad carefully. Annabelle Winter's name was at the top of the list as aide-de-camp/factotum. The other names were unfamiliar to her, but their credentials as listed seemed to cover all bases. As soon as the meeting was concluded, Jane sought out the other woman. "Let's call everyone in at 1300. I'd like to meet them and get started on the duty roster."

"No problem, Lieutenant," answered Winter with a smile. "They're kinda anxious to meet you, too. I'll see if I can grab the conference room on B-Three."

"Great. Would you bring the lingo-log with you and I'll take care of getting the rest of the documentation we'll need."

"Aye, aye, ma'am." She liked the way the newcomer operated. There was an ease about her which the others would like, too. Their last area chief had been a nice enough guy, but not very sure of himself. He would drive the captain crazy by constantly deferring to his wishes even when he knew a better way. There was a certain electricity between Captain Morgan and Lieutenant Krieg that almost crackled when in close proximity; Winter could not yet tell if this was good or bad. Either way, it to be promised an exciting voyage.

Jane went back to her station and ordered extra discs of the language structures they would be working as a team. According to the roster, Winter was fluent in both Jeylosian, and Lomosean, two important communicator languages. Cadet Thomas Peters, on board as an intern from the Fleet Academy, had lived on Taapusor and spoke the three languages used there. Kotuchar, however, had a special place in her heart. For several years, while the Rothko children were growing up, their father had been stationed on the planet. Although they spent the school year on Earth, summers were for living within the palace walls in Petuchar City, where the children of the Hokhma Baga were her friends. Jane spoke Petuch almost as well as she spoke English. Winter also spoke Petuch, which was a valuable asset for anyone who wanted a career in linguistics in the Fleet. But the yeomate's best work seemed to be in Stellar-5 language theory. This was an area where Jane had some experience, but had not yet mastered the nuances of the language group. Cadet Peters had intro classes in the language, and crewmate Ho Ngyuen also had had some exposure, but his specialty was in Stellar-4 languages; his talent would come into play when they reached Bagnamba in that system. That left two on her staff, Chakrabati and Olukotun, both had exposure to Amitidean, but also to languages that would not come into play at this time. She would find other things for them to do.

Annabelle Winter found the lieutenant eating lunch alone at a small table in the commissary. It was not unusual for officers to dine there, but rarely alone. Her first impulse was to ask her why she wasn't eating in the wardroom, but she quashed it. "Mind if I join you, Lieutenant?" she asked instead.

"Sure," smiled the officer, clearing a space for Winter. "The officer's mess was very crowded and I didn't feel like waiting for an opening. Besides, I wanted to read through this stuff again before the meeting."

"The guys are ready for anything you can dish out. Trieste had a tendency to do everything himself and give us only the slop work. A lot of the time, we were bored stiff."

Jane swallowed a sip of tea and laughed. "I promise you won't be bored. One of the things I want to do is have you who are fluent in useful languages offer classes to other crewmates who might want to pick up another lingo. On the San Diego we tried it and it was a very popular way to spend an evening. Plus, the Admiralty wants us to add six new dictionaries to the bank, and that has to be done manually. I've also brought a bunch of discs to learn Stellar-6 languages and anyone who wants to join me, can."

"Sign me up, Lieutenant. Stellar-6 is the up and coming thing to know."

"Oh, and that's another thing, Winter, on the bridge, lieutenant is fine, but my name is Jane so you might as well use it. I prefer to be on a first-name basis with my staff; it makes it a little less stuffy."

The yeomate grinned in approval. Most officers were on first name basis with their immediate staff, but Trieste would have gone into a snit if anyone called him Emilio, even the captain. "Most everyone around here calls me Belle."

They began discussing what would be needed from each specialist for the duration of the cruise. Jane listened carefully to what Belle had to say;

the woman had a keen insight into the people she'd been working with over the last eighteen months. It was a competent group, with a strong sense of teamwork that had not been nurtured under Trieste. She understood why he had opted to go stateside after only a year on the *Washington*; as qualified a linguist as he was, he must not have fitted well into Morgan's game plan.

By 1300 hours, Jane was better prepared to face her staff. Armed with the new, informal information Belle provided, she was able to set the tone without having to gauge their reactions as closely as she might have, had not Belle filled her in. She addressed everyone by first name and watched them all relax visibly. Next came her personal standards and philosophy. Sitting at the oblong conference table, she slid a stack of papers in the middle and asked everyone to take a copy. With her crew present, she formulated and finalized the duty roster.

"You have 'em right where you want 'em," Belle told her as they walked back to her office. "Those guys will follow you anywhere, especially the plebe. I think he's in love."

Jane blushed in spite of herself. "Now comes the hard part: toeing the line between casual but commanding respect and utter disregard for rank."

"Then just don't drink with us," shrugged Belle, adding a wicked grin.

They reached the office in time to see Captain Morgan coming around the corner. "Good afternoon, ladies," he said with a pleasant smile.

"We're just coming back from our staff meeting; we finished the duty roster," offered Belle enthusiastically.

He stopped at the door and waited for Jane to go in. "Mind if I take a look? I like to keep close tabs on my new people at the start of their hitch."

Jane handed him the docupad. She busied herself at the desk while he took the visitor's chair and read. His presence annoyed her, but there was no way to ask him to leave. Belle stood at his shoulder, making a few comments about the choices.

"Looks good, lieutenant," said the captain, tossing the pad on the desk. He made no move to leave.

"Anything else, sir? Jane asked, carefully modulating her tone to disguise her discomfort.

"Not for you." He turned toward the yeomate. "Tutorial in half an hour, Winter."

"Where, sir?"

"In the library."

"Then I'd better be going; I've got to get my act together. See you later, lieutenant." She gave them a snappy salute and left the office.

For a moment, Morgan watched Jane at her desk. His eyes bore through her back until she spun around to face him, although she said nothing. He stared at her until she inclined her head in his direction, waiting for him to speak. In truth, he had nothing to say, but the moment demanded some sort of statement from him. "Treat Winter well," he announced gravely, "she has the makings of a top-notch officer and I won't have her spirit dampened."

Jane gritted her teeth. *Of all the nerve*, she thought angrily, *she is not a horse about to be broken!* She returned his unwavering stare.

Feeling somewhat foolish and knowing why, Captain Morgan rose stiffly and left. Once outside, he waited for the door to slide closed behind him before he allowed himself a guffaw. From within, Jane heard him and was angrier than before.

They took their time getting to Titan. With several new crewmates in the reactor room, Tapper wanted to give them a chance to play with the power before letting them loose. Each department was busy getting resources together while Captain Morgan spent the bulk of his time overseeing orientation for the new crewmates. Jane and the other new officers were left pretty much to their own devices, the captain's attitude being that they were officers and should be able to find a niche without a babysitter.

By the end of the week, Jane was settled comfortably into a routine. Her people were working on various projects, including the loading of new dictionaries into the computer banks. She got to know her team: where they hailed from, how they ended up in the fleet. Because she was a member of the bridge crew and in the chain of command, albeit a low position, she was expected to know everything about the operation of the *Washington*, and made it a to point spend time at each of the work stations. Tapper was invaluable walking her through the technical end of the spectrum. They were often seen together, eating in the wardroom or at the all-night coffee. On her first overnight watch, Tapper stayed up with her, going over blueprints of the *Washington* and coaching her on tech operations.

"If you're going to be a first rate officer," he explained that night, "you'd better know this stuff cold. I won't have you asking dumb questions and looking like a moron. Your mother would never forgive me, S.J."

She appreciated the time spent with her as much as she loved his company. There were rumors, however, that a relationship was building between them. It was unfortunate, thought Jane, but understood how it happened. Where she thought there was a little hanky-panky going on was between the captain and Winter.

When she asked Tapper about it, he laughed and slapped his thigh. "She would like some hanky-panky, but Ash wouldn't. The man is steel when it comes to women."

"That's not what I heard," countered Jane, glad to be taking a break from ionic fusion theory.

Tapper looked at her askance. "And just what have you heard, Lef'tenant Lovely?" When she blushed just a little, Tapper caught a fleeting glimpse of teenage Sarah Jane.

"Just that he's a heartbreakin' ladies' man who loves 'em and leaves 'em in every port."

"That's quite an accusation for someone you just met."

"Maybe, but is it true?"

"Partially true. He does break hearts, but usually because he doesn't love 'em. Women fall all over Asher but he doesn't pay much attention. He was married, you know."

"Was?"

"Widower. Cancer, if you can believe it. And he's got a kid."

"Really?" Jane was surprised. She could not imagine Captain Morgan as a father.

"A real nice kid. Reuben lives with his folks in Boston, but Ash is very close to him. He vidcoms the kid at least twice a week and I treat vidcoms from Boston as top priority. The kid goes to the same yeshiva he went to and, if you can get him to talk about Reuben, which he doesn't, he would tell you the kid is a *chachem*, a real Talmud whiz, even at 10. He's one proud papa although you'd never guess Reuben exists. Ash keeps his private life very, very private."

"So why are you telling me?" asked Jane.

"Because I think you need to know about him." Tapper got up, stretched, "Coffee?" Jane nodded. "The captain," he said, as he refilled their cups, "is a difficult man to know, but a fiercely loyal one. Speed could tell you that. He knows Asher as well as anyone could. I'm just surprised you didn't know it."

"There are things my brother and I never got around to discussing. I knew about his friendship with 'the reb,' but he didn't come up much in conversation. The stuff I do know is mostly about your adventures...or maybe misadventures is a better word. I mean, Tap, I know some things, the funny things, but he never discussed anyone's personal life with me. We're usually too busy blabbing about family stuff. We just don't see each other face to face much these days."

"I wonder why?" retorted the chief tech with an understanding grin.

"Speaking of Jonathan, do you know where he is?"

"Somewhere in the Middle East. Maybe Tel-Aviv, maybe Amman. He's fluent, so God only knows where they sent him. But he's probably flying fighters in any case, so I'd guess he's happy."

Jane nodded; her brother was happiest when soaring above the clouds. It was a high risk occupation, one her father disapproved of, but could never dissuade him from. "He's stopped seeing Chava, you know."

"Yep, he told me. Fool. He should marry her and get it over with."

"Mom thinks so, too, but you know Jonathan, he's avoided marriage this long, so he'll probably avoid it a little longer. Besides, I think she wanted him to settle down and quit trying to kill himself."

Tapper laughed. "That'll never happen."

"What'll never happen?" Captain Morgan was standing at the portal; he was wearing a black woolen *djallabah* and looked only slightly sinister in the robe.

"Speed getting married, that's what," frowned Tapper.

"Nope, it'll never happen. Too bad, though; Chava's a nice lady."

The captain went to pour himself some coffee.

Jane watched him surreptitiously. Her new-found knowledge caused her to think about him a little differently. In the djallabah he looked exotic and very handsome. He went into his office and came out with several docupads under his arm. Instead of leaving the bridge, he came over to where they were sitting and parked himself in a chair. Automatically, Jane straightened up and picked up her pen.

He noticed the slight movement. "Relax, Krieg, I'm not checking up on you. I merely came to get some reading material."

"At this hour?" Tapper looked at him sideways.

The captain shrugged. "Couldn't sleep. And since when do I answer to you?" The question was not accusatory.

"Since the day I pulled your sorry butt off the *Alabama*." He glanced at Jane who was still ramrod stiff in her chair. "That was after he pulled Speed out. He went back in and…well…let's just say I pulled him out. What do you want to do next, S.J.?"

"Alloy reaction."

Aware that he had altered the mood, the captain considered leaving, but decided against it. It was too much fun to watch them both squirm. He wondered, glancing at Tapper, whether or not the chief tech was actually developing a "thing" for the pretty lieutenant. She was, after all, a nice Jewish girl and Tapper only liked nice Jewish girls. Besides, Morgan knew Joshua Bear was de facto a member of the Rothko clan; he must have watching the lieutenant grow up. "Carry on with whatever you were doing," he said amiably.

"We were indulging in a little gossip, but we had been doing scientific analysis," said Tapper defensively.

"Then gossip. Don't let me stop you." Morgan leaned back in the chair and extended his legs before opening the docupad.

Tapper raised an eyebrow and clucked disapprovingly at the captain. "Let's do this instead," he said as he unrolled a blueprint. "Here's the high tech difference between us and the rest of the world, S.J.," he said, picking up a pencil. "Alloy fusion done this way is new and we're the only ship outfitted with a reactor like this one."

With her eyes on the diagram, Jane found it difficult to concentrate on the lesson with the captain so close. She could feel his presence as acutely as she could smell the soap he must have just used in the shower. Every sense was heightened and it was oppressive. She was conscious of her every movement, feeling as though she was beneath a microscope; it was the same feeling she used to have when she sat at one end of the kitchen table doing her homework while her father sat at the other reading the newspaper. She didn't like it then, and she didn't like it now, but as then, there was no escape. She could see the captain through the corner of her eye, absently stroking his thick beard as he scanned his files. She wished he would go away.

As if reading her mind, Tapper suddenly stood up. "As long as you're here, Captain, mind if I steal the lieutenant for a few minutes and walk her through the lab?"

Morgan realized he didn't want her to leave, but shook his head "no" anyway. "Be my guest, but don't keep her too long."

He even sounds like my father, Jane frowned silently as she followed Tapper into the cage and waited until it moved before saying anything. "He makes me so nervous," she complained.

"He's supposed to, sweetie; he's the captain. If he didn't make you nervous, he wouldn't be doing his job. But give him a chance, S.J., you've only been here a few days; you'll get over it."

When they returned an hour later, Captain Morgan was sitting at his command post speaking softly into the vidcom recorder. Tapper extended his arm and kept Jane back, whispering "He's talking to Reuben." He waited for a moment and then rapped on the bulkhead, letting the captain know they had returned. Morgan acknowledged them, but did not immediately stop and they waited for him to finish. The disc popped out of the machine and Morgan brought it to Tapper, flashing him a warning look as he handed it over. Silently, Tapper took the disc and slipped it in his pocket. Jane kept her eyes as steady as she could. Her heart ached for a man who could not be with his son, but as a service brat, she ached more for the child.

"Carry on, troops," said the captain as he went past them into the cage.

The door slid shut and they both visibly relaxed. "Don't let on," instructed Tapper needlessly because he was sure she wouldn't.

The Washington slid into orbit around Titan right on schedule. Those crewmates scheduled to participate in the conference shuttled down with enough gear to last two days. Jane was excited, anxious to see who was there, who she knew, and who she needed to know.

The first session was long but informative. Stellar-6 languages were the hot topic and any new information was devoured. By dinner time, the two women were exhausted, but exhilarated. They sat with other linguists at the dinner and even managed to stay awake long enough to attend the department reception, but planned to cut out early and retire for the evening.

Fleet members in fantastic uniforms from a dozen different systems milled about the enormous reception chamber. Jane and Belle, drinks in hand, tried not to stare at some of the more decorative outfits. Although Jane had encountered many of them at one time or another, she was hard pressed to remember which was which. Captain Morgan, tall and elegant in his dress blues, stood near the center of the room, talking to three exotically attired officers from Taapusor. "The really short one with the spiky hair is captain of their flagship," Belle told her lieutenant. "He toured the *Washington* when we were at Vega Base last month."

"Who's the woman in the lavender gown with him?" asked Jane, trying not to point. Captain Morgan was moving away with the woman on his arm.

Belle peered in their direction. "I'm pretty sure that's Field Marshall Hacha. She's head of their diplomatic corps since the old man died." Everyone knew the "old man" was General Taamsori, one of the most famous military negotiators in their system. His treaties were required reading for all cadets no matter which academy they came from. "Somebody, maybe Tapper, told me she always wears purple as a sign of perpetual mourning for her husband. He died ages ago in some battle, but Taapusor ladies never really come out of mourning." Another officer approached the captain and the lady.

"What about the one who just walked up with Commander Bear… in the green flight suit? Any ideas?"

"I'm not sure, but I think that's the new commander from Zedni in Beta Omega-6. Newhouse said they were making their first appearance here."

"Oh," said Jane, trying to think of his name. Her CO on the San Diego had mentioned meeting him on his last exploratory. The planetary governments of the Stellar-6 system had only recently joined the League of Planets and no one from any of their fleets had been seen outside the negotiations. "What do you think about getting out of here, Belle?" asked Jane, tired enough to pack it in.

"Okay with me." She put her empty glass on the nearest tray. "The stuff they serve at these things always gives me a headache in the morning." They started to move toward the door when Belle stopped and pulled on Jane's sleeve. "Look, over there," she pointed. "Look who's joined them!"

Jane maneuvered herself into a position from which she could see Captain Morgan and the field marshal. Her eyes widened and her mouth would have fallen open had she not clamped it shut. A tall, silver haired man in the dress blues of the U.S. Fleet stood with Morgan, Tapper and the lavender lady, but even from the back, she knew who it was. "Oh, shit," she swore softly.

"Come on, let's go over. Maybe the captain will introduce us," begged Belle eagerly.

"You go, I'm going back to my room."

"Oh, no you're not. This is the opportunity of a lifetime, Lieutenant Krieg and you're going to take it. This is one place where rank doesn't matter and now's our chance." She grabbed Jane's arm and dragged her in the direction of the captain.

Tapper saw them first and suppressed a smile, but Captain Morgan almost growled. The silver haired man looked up and smiled politely. There was a split second of awkward silence before Tapper leapt in for the rescue.

"Admiral Rothko, Field Marshall Hacha, allow me to introduce two of our linguists," he began gravely, "Lieutenant Jane Krieg and Yeomate Annabelle Winter."

The admiral opted to shake hands rather than salute. When he took his daughter's, he shook it firmly, but added a tight squeeze. He then turned his attention to Annabelle Winter. "I am delighted to meet you, Ms. Winter. Tapper and Captain Morgan were just telling me about the work you've been doing on Stellar-5 language. I hear you are going to present a paper tomorrow. Congratulations; that's quite an honor."

Winter blushed and smiled charmingly. "Thank you, sir. It's just one piece of the linked languages theory; it's not much, actually." On the contrary, it was a very big deal and one that had caused the name *Winter* to be noticed in several circles.

In a friendly manner, he went on. "And I also hear you would like to transfer to OCS when you complete your degree tutorial. Have you set your sights on a particular academy?"

"I think Fleet Academy, sir, although I haven't really decided." She was now deeply flushed.

"What about super-school? Have you given that any consideration?"

Her eyes flashed with disbelief; his words were an uncouched invitation to apply. "But, Admiral Rothko, I won't have an advanced degree when I finish; I won't meet the pre-reqs."

The admiral laughed at her widened eyes. He was well aware of what he had said and he meant it. "Then write your thesis on Stellar-5 theory; if it's original, breakthrough work, I'm sure someone would grant you a master's. It's been done before."

She looked from the Admiral to her captain, who nodded with a tight lipped smile and a raised eyebrow, sure signs of approval. "Thank you for the advice, sir," she stammered, "I'll see what I can come up with." She backed slightly away, still in shock, not listening to anything else around her.

"And you, Lieutenant...Krieg, is it? How are you enjoying the *Washington*?"

"She's just fine, sir." Her face remained an immobile mask. She shot a look at Tapper, who shrugged his shoulders.

The Admiral kept going, not letting her off the hook. "It must be a far cry from any other ship you've been on, Lieutenant. And certainly you must consider yourself lucky to have gotten such a plum assignment." Silently, his eyes added *With no help from me, kiddo.*

"Yes, sir, I am lucky." There was a fine note of sarcasm in her voice which did not go unnoticed by the others. Even Winter heard it.

Tapper, ever resourceful, grabbed Winter's arm. "Let's go get a refill for the Admiral, shall we, Academician Winter?"

"Thank you, that would be nice," agreed Admiral Rothko, still smiling politely. He waited until they had walked away. He wanted to hug his daughter who looked so marvelous in her dress blues, but he resisted the impulse, choosing instead to maintain his distance. Morgan had not offered any information about Sarah Jane, nor did he ask although he was certain the captain knew. "I'm glad to see you looking so well," he said quietly.

"Thank you, sir. I'm feeling quite well."

His eyebrows knit beneath his forehead the same way hers did when distressed. Captain Morgan stepped back slightly, giving them a little more space. It was an awkward position in which to be in the middle, yet there was no real way to make a graceful exit. Field Marshall Hacha was watching with a bemused expression on her elegant face.

"I was hoping this would be a pleasant surprise, Lieutenant," said her father.

"It certainly is a surprise, sir." She was not about to loosen up in front of the captain and the field marshal.

Tapper and Winter returned with a round of drinks. "To your health and smooth sailing," pronounced Admiral Rothko, looking directly at Jane.

"To smooth sailing," they echoed.

They stood together for a few moments. Finally, unable to stand it any longer, Jane spoke up. "If you would excuse me, sir, I am quite tired and would like to retire for the evening."

"Please, don't stay on our accounts," interjected Captain Morgan, speaking for the first time since the women arrived.

"Pleased to have met you, sir, ma'am," said Lieutenant Krieg, forcing a smile. She saluted sharply and caught Winter doing the same thing from the corner of her eye. As soon as she could, she made her escape.

In the corridor, Belle, angry and confused, turned to face Jane. "How could you, an officer, walk out on an opportunity to stand around with the highest ranking admiral in the whole damn fleet?"

"You don't understand, Belle, it was very awkward for me in there. You didn't have to leave; you can go back if you want. I just couldn't stay there."

"Why the hell not?"

"Let it go as I just couldn't. Besides, I'm too tired to stand up any longer. I'm going to the room." She walked away from Winter.

Inside the reception room, Field Marshall Hacha eyed the admiral carefully. She waited until Captain Morgan and Commander Bear had gone before she mentioned the encounter with the young women. Taking his arm, she leaned toward him and asked in delicately accented English, "Tell me, Edward, which one of those lovely young things would you have?"

The admiral blushed in spite of himself and let out a hearty guffaw. "The redhead, should I be so inclined, for with the brunette, it would be incest!"

"Ah," sighed Yellina Hacha knowingly, "so that *was* Sarah Jane. She goes by Krieg? What name is that?"

"Elizabeth's maiden name, Yellina dear."

"This is no surprise, Edward; the girl looks just like you."

"Yes, I know. Isn't she lovely?" he added with a satisfied grin.

"Quite beautiful despite the obvious resemblance. She and Captain Morgan shall make a striking couple."

"Hah! That'll be the day." He suddenly stopped and stared into the field marshal's face. "Is that the seer in you or merely speculation?"

"Neither. It's intuition. Surely, you are not blind?"

"When it comes to Sarah Jane? Indubitably."

"Just as a father should be. But my, how he looks at her! Why, he doesn't even know it himself." Field Marshall Hacha patted his arm. "How Elizabeth ever lets you out of her sight is a wonder, Admiral Papa."

Winter didn't hold a grudge for long and by the time they reached the lift, she was chatting away about the admiral. "Isn't he a piece of work, Jane? I never thought an older man could be that handsome."

"He's very married, you know. His wife's a Brigadier General and not too bad looking herself." Jane found the conversation borderline amusing, so long as it stayed away from the serious.

Belle would not be dissuaded. "He's a very sexy man, but do you think he's any good in bed? I mean, he is kinda old. Wouldn't that be a coup...to be the Fleet Admiral's lover?" she asked wickedly.

"Annabelle Winter, what an awful thought."

"Yeah, but," she giggled, "it never hurts to imagine."

"Go to your room!" Jane was still laughing silently when she slid the key card into the lock. This, for sure, she would repeat to her brother.

CHAPTER 3

Jonathan Rothko stood in the blazing sun of the Negev, his hand shielding his eyes from the intense glare shimmering off the runway. Two F-class fighters were on final approach and he waited impatiently for them to land. He was not happy with the performance he had witnessed, not happy at all. The pilots maneuvered their crafts sloppily, without the precision he demanded. Granted, this was new equipment, but they should have been paying closer attention to what they were doing up there. They had come perilously close to colliding.

The first craft touched down lightly on the tarmac and screeched to a halt, followed quickly by the second jet. The ground crew ran out to secure the twin fighters while the pilots finished shutting them down. By the time they reached Major Rothko, he was fuming. "What the hell kind of flying do you call that?" he demanded in Hebrew as soon as they were in earshot.

"Come on, Major, give us a break, we're new at this," groaned Yaniv Evron, pulling off his helmet.

"You'll be dead at this if you don't get it right, Evron. There are no good excuses at those heights."

"Maybe you'd like to show us again, Major," the other pilot, Eli Zahavi, drawled.

"Maybe you'd like to go to hell," spat Jonathan, walking away. As much as he loved working in Israel, he found the casualness of their air force difficult to take at times. He went toward the Quonset hut where he had established a make-shift office. He sensed the two pilots were not far behind. Once inside, he tossed his cap across the desk and sat down. Evron and Zahavi strolled in and draped themselves over the ladder back chairs. They seemed not to be bothered by the close call they had just had.

“Everyone makes mistakes, Yoni, even you,” Zahavi said, his mouth in a tight line. “You are supposed to be teaching us, not expecting us to know what we haven’t learned.”

Evron pushed his sunglasses over his thick hair. “We can only do so much, Yoni. F-511s are much different from what we’ve been flying. We need to log many more practice hours.”

“I’ll say you do.” All things considered, they hadn’t done too badly. He merely expected perfection. “Come on, guys, let’s go have a beer.”

For two weeks, Jonathan drilled and grilled the two pilots. They would, once certified, be the ones to teach the others. The presence of F-511 fighters in Israel was considered top secret. Until now, only the United States was using them; it was through a crazed set of circumstances that the Israelis gotten not one, but two of the aerodynamic marvels. Not only were they the fastest, quietest, and most agile fighters ever built, they had a unique hull surface which rendered them virtually invisible to both the naked eye and laser tracking when lit from beneath the metal skin. Israeli engineers had tripped across and improved the Pitanese paint formula that made it all possible.

Jonathan loved the jets. They were sleek and lovely to behold, engineering works of art. Each time he took one up, he was an eagle soaring deftly between clouds, free from all human restraint. More than speed enchanted him; it was the total experience of being alone in the heavens, invisible to all below at his whim. Now, with tension running high, the jets could mean all the difference to the Israelis. Their political situation was volatile and their very survival depended on having better technology than their Arab brothers. After almost two hundred years of relative peace in the region, a new, fanatical imam in Syria was preaching jihad, and a new intifada had begun in earnest. As a Jew, Jonathan felt a responsibility to aid the Israelis. As a military man, he felt a responsibility to prevent war. The only way to do that was to give Israel the technological edge she needed to stay ahead of the other guys.

In the canteen, a few of the men stationed at Machaneh Ein Geshem were sitting about, trying to keep cool. The name, Ein Geshem, was a double *entendre*, meaning either spring of rainwater or no rain, depending on how it was spelled at any given moment. Lately, though, it was spelled with an aleph instead of an ayin, for there had been no significant rain in the Negev for over a year; not unusual for the relentless desert, but the men were always hopeful. The temperature was well over 100 degrees Fahrenheit at 0800, and no one had the nerve to check at noon. The primitive conditions did not allow for air conditioning; the only cold air was to be found in the canteen freezer. Jonathan took three beers from the case and tossed a few coins to cover them in the jar beside it. Eli and Yaniv took the table in the far corner, away from the others.

"Let's go up to Jerusalem for the weekend," suggested Yaniv, holding the cold bottle against his forehead.

Jonathan took a slug of beer and nodded. "I think we all can use a break." Any place but Haifa, he said to himself. Chava was in Haifa and the last thing Jonathan wanted to do was run into her. "If we leave tomorrow at 0600, we can be there for dinner. Steak at the King David?"

"Sounds good, Yoni. We can sign a hovercar out of the pool." Whether or not one was actually available, Eli would be sure to commandeer one. "Can we stay at your place, Yaniv?"

"Sure, why not? My sister's been living there but she's in England for a couple of weeks. I don't think she'd mind, so long as we don't leave a big mess."

The other two laughed; Yaniv was a notorious neatnik, always taking his bunkmates to task for their less than pristine ways.

"Good," said Jonathan, finishing the last of his beer. "It's all set. Let's take another look at those stat reports one last time before we call it quits for the day."

They got to Jerusalem just as the city was shutting down for the Sabbath. Last minute shoppers scurried home with bundles tucked beneath their arms. A few Hassids, their black hats pushed back on their foreheads in deference to the late autumn heat, were already walking toward the Western Wall, the *Kotel,* the last remnant of King Solomon's Temple. Near Yaniv's flat, they found a grocer not quite ready to close and stocked up on the items they would need for the duration of Shabbat, when all stores were dark. In good humor, they bounded up the stairs to the flat, anxious to change and make it over to the King David Hotel where they could get a good piece of meat, yet pay for it before the Sabbath when no money changed hands. While Jonathan was in the shower, Yaniv called the hotel to make sure they could be seated, not that they would ever turn soldiers away.

Lingering over dinner, the three comrades-in-arms talked about things not military. Jonathan had known Eli and Yaniv from previous missions in Israel, but this was the first time he was serving as their commanding officer. Although he found teaching them to be a strain, he still enjoyed their company off the base; their ease of conversation was a far cry from the way he was treated by other trainees back in the States. At home, he would never have gone off with a couple of the guys unless they were fellow officers. Israel was different, but as a Jew and one who was more than fluent in the language, he felt right at home with them.

After dinner, Yaniv decided to walk over to visit a relative; Eli was more interested in going back to the flat to sleep. But Jonathan was not tired. He wanted to walk about the city he found a constantly changing mystery. The men parted ways outside the hotel.

Alone and out of uniform, Jonathan joined the other Sabbath strollers. Total strangers wished him "*Shabbat Shalom* " as he passed. Feeling a little undressed, he dug into his pocket and pulled out his *kippah*, the little skull-cap he always kept with him. He paused before a shop window and clipped in place. It felt good to have it on, like it naturally belonged there although he did not wear it every day. He walked with no set direction until he realized he was in the Old City.

Crowds were still gathered there when he arrived at the *Kotel*; the men on one side of a barrier, the women on the other. Children of both sexes raced back and forth between parents, their exuberance undampened by the sanctity of the Sabbath. Jonathan eased his way through the throng of dark coated Hassids mixed with short-sleeved Israelis until he stood at the Wailing Wall. The enormity of the stone blocks was undeniably awesome no matter how many times he stood there. All Jewish history was made real by their very existence, unscathed by time nor war nor politics. He touched his lips to a golden block before he accepted a prayer book from one of the Hassids standing close to him. As he recited the familiar ancient words welcoming the Sabbath Queen, he could feel tears form in his eyes. At no other time or place did Jonathan weep, but at the *Kotel*, emotions surged through him at breakneck speed. Prayers were a link to his past and his future. His parents, despite their military ways, had taught him well to love his God and his people, something others had shucked as trappings of superstition. His voice joined hundreds of others as praises to God rang out in the warm autumn air. He was a part of it as much as it was a part of him.

When he was ready to leave, Jonathan was happy to be carried along with the crowd. He reveled in his anonymity; there were no soldiers to salute or ask him questions he was in no mood to answer. He was merely a part of the crowd making his way home. It would have been nice to be going home to someone, he thought a little wistfully, but his own family was far away and he would have to satisfy himself by conjuring their faces in his mind. Hands in pockets, he saw them, one by one, and would have never looked up had someone not bumped him, bringing him 'round to the present.

Chava was standing a few feet away from him, in a stone archway, talking to another woman. Jonathan stopped dead in his tracks; the walkers flowed around him, a stone in a stream. When she glanced up and saw him, she blinked, then smiled a small, tentative smile, unsure of what to expect in return. He crossed the short distance to her and kissed her on the cheek.

"Shabbat Shalom, Yoni," she murmured shyly.

"Shabbat Shalom, Chava," answered Jonathan. "How are you?" It sounded lame as it came out of his mouth.

"I'm fine." She quickly introduced him to her friend who then made her excuses and left. "What are you doing in Jerusalem?" she asked.

"I could ask you the same question," countered Jonathan.

"I asked you first."

"I came up for the weekend with Yaniv and Eli. We needed to get out of the desert."

"I hear there's been no rain whatsoever."

"None." The conversation stalled; he was at a loss for words.

"How's the training going?" Chava was no better off.

"Difficult, but it's going. Are you visiting your sister?"

"Yes, she had a little boy Tuesday morning, so I came up to help get ready for the *bris*. Will you still be here for it?"

Jonathan shook his head. "We have to get back on Sunday. Wish her and your parents *mazel tov* for me."

"Thank you, I will." She reached out and squeezed his hand. "It's nice to see you, Yoni."

"It's nice to see you, too."

"Take care of yourself." And then she added, "Be careful."

"I will, Chava." This time, he kissed her on the mouth, lingering there but for a second. "Shabbat Shalom."

"Shabbat Shalom." She released his hand and melted into the crowd.

With a gnawing, empty feeling in his stomach, Jonathan watched until her black curls disappeared. That he loved Chava was not a question; that he could not bring himself to settle down with her, was. He never knew a woman like Chava Gutman before. She was beautiful and intelligent. No, more than that; she was quick witted and sharp, very sharp. Nothing escaped those proud, brown eyes. Her gentle laugh was as musical as her voice, easy to listen to for a lifetime, if he so chose. When she wasn't standing before a classroom filled with would-be pilots, she was on her knees digging for history, her devotion to technology matched by her passion for antiquity. Everything about Chava was, believed Jonathan, perfection, yet he was afraid to commit to her. Even his parents, who normally took his romances with a shrug and a sigh, were in favor of this match. *Match*. It was a good word for Chava and Jonathan together.

The crowd was thinning. Jonathan came back to the present and started up the stone paved street toward the New City. It was time to go home, he thought, and then, idly wondered where home really was these days.

CHAPTER 4

The conference hummed with activity as participants raced from one session to the next. Yeomate Winter delivered her paper, *Syntax and Transformational Grammar Delineation in Basic Stellar-5 Language Groups*, at the second session and was relieved to see Captain Morgan slip into the back row just in time to hear her speech. Her paper was well received and she handled the requisite Q and A with aplomb. When an invitation to join Commander Naftjan and his linguistic team for lunch arrived, Belle almost broke down.

"What will I say to these people?" she cried to Jane. "These are Stellar-5 officers and I'm standing around talking about their languages! I'm going to look like an idiot!"

"No, you won't," said Jane, putting her arm around Belle. "They would not have invited you if they weren't impressed. I've met Naftjan; he is a terrific guy. If anything, he'll probably ask you a lot of questions about how you reached your conclusions and then request a copy of the paper. It's a good paper, Belle; don't be ashamed of it." She knew exactly how the other woman felt; it was always tense when a native wanted to talk to an outlander about his own language.

"What will you do for lunch? Can you come with me?"

"No, Belle, I wasn't invited." She wished she had been. "I'll find Tapper or Newhouse or someone. Don't worry about me."

A Titani page approached them and handed Jane a folded note. She opened it and smiled. "I've just been invited to lunch with Tapper and some of his cronies."

Jane went in search of the suite specified on the invitation. After some difficulty, she found it. Her father was standing at the window looking out over the lunar landscape.

"Now can I get a hug and a kiss?" he asked when she came in.

"Sure, Dad." Jane put her arms around her father and snuggled against his broad chest, not minding that his insignia scratched her face just as it had done all her life.

"You look great, Sarah Jane. You like the *Washington*?"

"How could anyone not like that floating palace." She pulled away from him and looked up into his face. "So tell me, Dad, what are you doing here? You weren't slated to come, or at least Mom didn't mention it."

He poured himself a glass of wine and then one for her. "Last minute decision. Naftjan and Hacha are having difficulties negotiating for karonite with the folks down below. Yellina called me and asked if I would come out, ostensibly to attend the conference, but in reality to sit in on their meetings. The fact that the *Washington* was coming in was, of course, an added attraction. I hitched a ride with the Russians."

"The Russians? I didn't know they were here?" The Russians usually didn't send delegates to conferences unless they were slated for presentations.

"They're not. They had a personnel crisis on the surface, so Admiral Yevchenko decided to take a ride. We flew one of those new speed shuttles and left after you, but arrived before."

"Yeah, well, we took our time. New crew in the reactor room."

A waiter wheeled in the luncheon cart set for two. "Tapper opted not to join us for lunch, but he'll be here for dessert. I promised him cheesecake," explained the admiral, pulling out a chair for his daughter.

She was glad her father had come; time spent alone with him was always a precious commodity and this was bonus time. They spent little of it talking about military matters; mostly they discussed the family. Tapper showed up for his cheesecake, joining in the lively chatter as though he were a blood member of the clan. Tapper's own father died when he was still a cadet and the Rothkos had taken him in. Jane knew her father was more than pleased that Tapper was on the *Washington*; he knew how lonely life could be when you couldn't discuss certain things with your crewmates. At least Jane had a close family friend on board, one who could serve as mentor to a young officer. Captain Morgan, however competent, could not serve that purpose. When lunch was over, Jane and her father said their good-byes behind the closed doors of his suite; it would serve no purpose to be seen kissing the Fleet Admiral in public.

In the afternoon, Tapper, Jane and Belle went to hear Morgan deliver his address on crisis intervention. The hall was packed with delegates from all the League systems. The *Washington* delegation sat together in the center of the room, anxious to hear what their commanding officer had to say. As a flagship, they were often called in on delicate situations when the involved parties had reached a stalemate. His proposal for a mandatory cooling-off period of three standard days was currently under consideration by the League. In addition, he was in favor of League mediations conducted by designated and properly trained vessel commanders who could be called in on demand, instead of having to wait for a League delegate who might not be in the vicinity. The speech was well received, but it would be a while before the League would act on the proposals.

Once the last session was over, the *Washington* delegation shuttled back to their ship. Barb Lucas was waiting for them. "To your cabins, kiddies, and freshen up," she ordered as soon as their feet hit the smooth surface of the bay. "There's been a change of plan. Captain Morgan is coming up with VIPs within the hour. Ms. Krieg, he has asked specifically that you be present at their arrival."

"Dress blues, then, I take it?" asked Jane, unsure of the procedure on this particular ship.

"Dress blues for everyone." She walked along with the newcomer as they headed for the cage. "Morgan insists on blues for the on-deck welcoming committee. And, unless told otherwise, for all officers for the duration of the entire visit. If you think you need an extra set or two, give the quartermaster a call tonight, after dinner. You can always find him in the shop between 1800 and 2000 hours."

"Thanks," said Jane, "I think I will." She stepped in the cage and hesitated, trying to decide if she should go to her cabin or her office. The thought of a quick shower sent her to her quarters.

She was back at the shuttle bay in forty-five minutes along with everyone else who was available. The crew stood in welcome formation with officers lined up beside them. They could hear the outer doors open and then slide shut before the inner seals opened to allow the shuttle craft to glide in on the docking rails. All chatter ceased as the inner seal opened. As soon as the hatch was lifted, Lucas called "Attention," and everyone snapped a salute. The captain emerged first, followed by four Jeylosians, not two as had been expected. They reviewed the waiting assemblage slowly, Captain Morgan taking time to introduce various members of his staff. When they arrived at the officers, he paused in front of Lieutenant Krieg.

"The lieutenant will be your host for the voyage," announced the captain with a wry smile. "She speaks Jeylosian very well."

"It's always a pleasure to meet someone who has taken the time to learn our complex language," the ambassador commented in his native tongue.

"Your graciousness humbles me," answered Jane correctly in the same language.

The Jeylosians were a formal lot, proud of their ancient heritage, and expected that all outworlders would treat them in the manner to which they were accustomed. Tall and usually very thin, they looked almost human once you got used to their seven-digit hands and blue cast skin. They were dressed in stiff fitting unitogs with knee length surcotes, except for the woman who also wore a floor length skirt wrapped about her waist. When she moved, however, the skirt split in the front, revealing wide trousers. Unlike the others, she did not have the standard violet eyes; hers were bright emerald green and Jane immediately wondered where they had come from.

"Lieutenant Krieg, would you be so kind as to escort our guests to their quarters?" asked Captain Morgan. His eyes met hers steadily.

"I would be honored," said Jane, trying to cover a sense of panic. She had no idea where they would be housed. As though reading her mind, Lucas accompanied them to the cage, and when the door slide open, she waited until the guests were stepping in before she whispered "E-2, 10 through 12. Names are on the doors." Jane acknowledged her with a broad smile of relief.

The guests were deposited in the appropriate cabins and Jane hurried back to the bridge. She found Lucas there and pulled her into the small conference room. "Quick, what do I need to know?"

Lucas laughed as she pulled out a chair. "Ambassador and Lady Xinthi-Ang are the big two you have to worry about. She's nice; he's a head-breaker. The one with the orange sash, that's Lalo-Fa, he used to be the chief tech advisor at their science exchange on Amitides, but now he's a technical consul at large. Smart guy, though; roams around the galaxy picking up scientific odds and ends they might find useful. Watch out for him, he's got a penchant for Terran girls. The one in the green sash is Kora Pana-Di, the third son of the Emperor, late of Oxford University and a randy sort of chap; doesn't really have a job but what he does have is a reputation for getting into trouble. I'm not surprised you don't recognize them; they don't photograph well."

"They don't photograph at all!" cried Jane. "How could he do this to me?"

"Easy. It's a diplomatic baptism of fire. Besides, I'm really tied up with getting ready for Taapusor and I need some time to finish. You speak the lingo and even though you're not in my department, we'll overlap more than you probably realize. May as well get used to it." Lucas leaned back and closed her eyes. "Your predecessor was totally useless to me. Trieste had his head buried so far into his damn dictionaries that he couldn't help at all. When we heard we were getting rid of him, at long last, I might add, I practically begged Morgan for a linguist out of protocol division. But when he showed me your dossier, I stopped harping so loud. On paper, you look terrific. In person, frankly, you show promise; even though you're a bit young to be heading up a department of this magnitude, you'll do just fine, Jane. Stick with me, kiddo, and I'll see you don't screw up from my end."

Jane slumped into a chair. "Thank you. I was beginning to think I was out there on my own. You're making me feel much better." She meant it.

"You've got Winter and she's great. The others, well, they're okay but they need a human, not a lexi-jockey, for a leader." She paused and looked at the lieutenant. "Not to change horses mid-stream, but how did you like the conference?"

"It was great; learned a lot. How come you weren't there?" Jane asked, thinking it would have been a natural place for the protocol chief.

"Too much to do up here. There's been a government change on Amitides and we've got two new protocol systems to master, to boot. I've got input coming from all over the galaxy and we're short staffed in protocol for a change." She paused, thinking for a moment. "I wish you could've known this before the conference. You could have said something to Rothko."

"Huh?" said Jane, sitting upright.

"Huh, nothing. I heard you had a private meeting with the Silver Fox down there."

"Who told you that?"

"Neeley from engineering. He shuttled down to deliver some papers to Newhouse and said he saw you going into the admiral's suite. What's the story?" Lucas sounded casual, but she wanted an answer. When one was not forthcoming, she continued. "I've been around a long time, Jane, and I've even been around the admiral before. If memory serves me correctly, and it usually does because that's what I get paid so highly for, there's a picture of you on Rothko's desk. In the right hand corner, I believe, facing him."

"You must be mistaken," countered Jane, a little too defensively.

"Okay, so it's in the left hand corner."

Jane sat in silence for a minute. There was no point in lying about it. Barbara had already figured it out. "Wrong again," she sighed, "It's on the credenza."

"Older daughter?"

"Yep, number one of two."

"Sarah?"

"Yep."

"Does anyone else know?"

"Tapper and the captain, but I think that's all. Am I missing anyone?"

"Nope, I don't think so. And they won't hear it from me." She leaned forward and whispered conspiratorially. "And you know why?"

"Why?"

"Because my maiden name is Makeba. And yes, my grandfather is William. And my father is Jeffers."

Being a Makeba was just as big a deal as being a Rothko. General William Makeba, long considered to be the greatest negotiator the Fleet had ever had, had been chairman of the Joint Chiefs of Staff some twenty years ago when Jane was a little girl and her mother was attached to his personal staff. Jeffers Makeba, a prize-winning economist, had been chairman of the Federal Reserve for two terms, and her mother, Aliyah Jefferson Makeba was dean of Georgetown Law. Her older brother was director of cardio-vascular research at Johns Hopkins. "*You're* Barbie Makeba? Oh, God, I don't believe it," groaned Jane.

"Yep, the family underachiever. By the way, the only one who still calls me that is my mother." She shuddered. "I heard rumors you were in the service. Good move on the name. I wouldn't have guessed until it clicked when I heard the admiral was on the surface. My first training CO found out and could not let it go and I damn near quit before the end of my initial space trial. My sympathies, kid; it's hell when they know the truth."

"Does the captain know?"

"I was married before I signed on. I was working for the State Department back then and I had the great good fortune to meet your father at a diplomatic reception. We got into this conversation about the lack of protocol training in the fleet. It was a little fractious, but I found a sympathetic ear. The next thing I knew, he called my office and offered me a job; the only hitch was that I needed a hitch. It seemed like a good idea at the time, so I came into the Fleet as a lieutenant."

"But your family? Didn't they mind?"

"I was a newlywed and my husband thought it was cool. I stayed assigned to State, but as an officer, and began developing a new protocol standard for on and off world. Oh, I traveled a bit, but mostly within our solar system. This is actually my first real ship…after training, that is," grinned Barb. "Before this, I managed to shuttle out and back on locals. Morgan was the one who talked me into taking a three year tour on the *Washington* so I could finally beat the standard into shape in real time."

"And your husband didn't get bent out of shape?" asked Jane.

"Not at all. Kip thought it was a great idea. He was heading out to Lomos, so I would've been a single parent on Earth. The boys wanted to go to Lomos anyway, and they thought it was cool that I was offered a job on the palace. So, after a lot of discussion and a string of sleepless nights, I took it. To answer your original question, all my records are under Lucas, and I've never seen fit to tell Morgan otherwise, so he may or may not know. Kip thinks it's funny. He kids me about it mercilessly, especially whenever we make it home for family functions, which is rare these days. You'll meet him when we get to Lomos. He's a helluva nice guy; you'll like him."

"Oh, good, someone who doesn't care!" Relief poured out of Jane like a flood. They were laughing so hard that they did not notice when Captain Morgan opened the door and stood there shaking his head.

"Care to share the joke, ladies?" he asked.

This dissolved them into further gales of laughter. "We were merely sharing a least common denominator," said Lucas, trying to catch her breath.

The captain looked them over with a puzzled glance. *Women*, he thought, *a complete and total mystery.* He left as quietly as he came, leaving them to their laughter, hoping it was not on his account.

"I won't tell if you won't tell," gasped Barbara.

"Not this girl!" Jane sputtered, wiping a tear from her eye.

Barbara tried to right herself in the chair and smoothed her trousers. "We'd better pull ourselves together before we go out there, Jane. Otherwise, we might be suspect and there is nothing this crew likes better than suspicion."

In the Rothko family, the kids had always stayed with mom when the parents were split. Jane knew more people in the Air Force end of the military hierarchy than she had in the Fleet end. Dad had been careful to protect them from too much exposure. Because of the dual-service problem, Admiral and General Rothko had a pact to leave their work at the office and to keep their social life just that, social. The Makebas, on the other hand, were Georgetown folk and Jane wondered how Barbara had managed to keep anything a secret. Later, when there was more time, she would have to get some pointers.

They did the best they could to recompose, and walked out of the small conference room with great dignity. Lucas went to her station and Jane to hers. Two crewmates had been assigned to help the dips get settled, so for the moment, Jane could check her mail and get ready for the next encounter. A yellow vidcom disc sat in her box. The color told her it was personal mail, but there was no time to look at it now, so she slipped it into her pocket. The rest of the messages were logged in the computer. Reading through them quickly, she assigned a staff member to handle each item according to the roster. Satisfied that she was current, she logged off and headed down to her office.

Jane did not look up when someone knocked on her door. "Come," she called.

A tiny earpiece and wire landed in the center of her folder. "My PT-5 is malfunctioning," announced Captain Morgan as he took the seat opposite her. "I tried to fix it myself, but..."

Jane glared at him, then looked at the personal translator. From her top drawer, she took out a pair of oversized magnifier glasses and a well-worn leather case. Adjusting the glasses to a precise spot on the bridge of her nose, she examined the offending instrument before taking a thin probe from the case. "Hasn't anyone ever told you not to monkey with a PT if you don't know what you're doing?" she asked in exasperation, pulling a broken wire from the earpiece.

"No," responded Morgan, refusing to be chastised. He reached across the desk and turned the tool kit toward him. "EMR?" he asked, looking at the worn gold initials in the corner.

"My father's," murmured the lieutenant, intent on her work. With agile fingers, she stripped the hair-thin wire from the receiver.

Morgan watched her, impressed with the way she maneuvered the minuscule connections, despite the fact she looked like a bug with those glasses. Instead of making her appear awkward, they gave her an aura of competence, professorial in a classic way. Periodically, the glasses would slip and a slender finger would push them back into place, at the same time brushing back a stray lock of hair. Morgan caught himself wanting to see just how long her braids actually were. *Dangerous woman,* he thought for the hundredth time since he met her. Tapping his fingers against the arm of the chair, he tried to distract himself.

"Please stop that; it's annoying," said the lieutenant, still involved in the operation.

"Sorry." It came out a little more sarcastic than he would have wished. He got out of the chair and walked around the back of the desk, leaning over her as she worked.

"If you don't mind, Captain."

"Sorry," he repeated. He picked up one of the pewter frames and studied the photo. It was a family picture, taken at enough of a distance so that the faces would be unrecognizable to anyone who did not know the subjects, but he easily picked out Jonathan, the admiral and the general. The other children, and they were children, must be Jane, her younger sister and younger brother. They were all smiling as they sat at a picnic table beneath a large tree, a lake in the background. He wondered where it was, but did not dare ask. He replaced the photo exactly where it had been and picked up the other one. This same photograph traveled with Jonathan everywhere he went and Morgan knew it was a picture of their four grandparents taken at Jonathan's *bar mitzvah*, the last time all four were together before death claimed them. The two old men still reminded him of his father and father-in-law as they were now, gray and grizzled, but beaming with pride at the accomplishments of a grandson. He replaced this one, too.

"There," said Jane, putting a probe back in the leather case, "it's done. Now don't monkey with it again. If it doesn't work, bring it to me."

"Yes, ma'am." He pushed the translator into his ear and adjusted it.

"*V'k'sh'ani la'atzmi, mah ani,*"said Jane in Hebrew.

The captain looked at her, his eyebrow raised. "If I am only for myself, what am I?" he said, pretending to check the translator which obviously worked.

As if you don't know without that thing, Jane thought silently, lips pursed. "That's correct. It appears to have been a damaged connector."

"Thank you, Lieutenant." Captain Morgan went to the door and waited for it to slide open. "I promise not to monkey with it anymore." He stepped out and the door slid shut behind him.

Jane went back to her folder, wondering why he hadn't fixed it himself. She knew damn well he could.

Dinner was set for 1800 hours in the wardroom. Jane called for the Jeylosians at 1740 and found them gathered in the Kora Pana-Di's cabin having a pre-dinner libation. Lady Xinthi-Ang was wearing an exquisitely embroidered gown of raw silk, certainly something she had picked up on her travels. The taupe shot through with threads of gold enhanced the exotic blue cast of her complexion and her startling green eyes. The gentlemen were attired in their dress uniforms, an interesting adaptation of the British Admiralty but in vivid shades of purple.

Lady Xinthi-Ang greeted the lieutenant warmly in her native tongue. "It is so kind of you to come to our quarters, Lieutenant." She indicated that Jane should sit with them. "Would you care for some viliham?"

Viliham, a sweet, fragrant liqueur made from native Jeylosian fruit, was an acquired taste Jane had never acquired. Still, to refuse would have been considered exceptionally rude. "Thank you, ma'am," answered Jane. She accepted the glass from Lady Xinthi-Ang and took a tiny sip.

Lalo-Fa had been speaking when Jane came in and as soon as she was settled, he continued. "We would do well to allow a representative from Lomos to visit our hydroponics site, my lord," said the scientist. "They have made great strides in arid land cultivation since we last visited. Would this be acceptable?" The proposition was a formality; arrangements had already been made.

"With His Imperial Majesty's permission," answered the ambassador with a wave of his hand. "Kora Pana-Di, will you relay the request?"

The Emperor's third son nodded, but his eyes were on Jane. For a Terran, she was especially attractive. She exuded *kore'eta,* the sense of mastery of power, which he usually found so lacking in their species. Kore'eta was a learned skill, but some were, after all, born with a propensity for it just the same. She obviously grew up around power; he sensed she knew how to use it.

Lalo-Fa was thinking along similar lines and when he glanced in the kora's direction, he knew so was his prince. If the woman was amenable, it might be an interesting voyage.

In her chair, Jane could feel their eyes. She willed herself not to squirm, feeling uncomfortably on display. Glancing surreptitiously at her watch, she tried to find a break-in point where she might suggest they join the others in the wardroom.

The exchange of glances between Lalo-Fa and the kora was not lost on Lady Xinthi-Ang. She smiled, amused by the undercurrent, and decided to let it go, at least for the moment. But the young lady needed to be drawn into the conversation if it were to become interesting. "Have you visited Jeylos?" she asked Jane.

"Yes, madam, as a child. My family visited your home for a brief time when I was quite young."

"And did you like it?" asked the kora, moving to stand beside her chair.

Jane avoided looking at the kora, for it might be interpreted as interest in him. She kept her focus on Lady Xinthi-Ang. "Jeylos is a lovely planet, rich with many beautiful flowers. That is what I remember most. We stayed in the eastern capital city of Xarath-Tai and I remember walking a great distance to see His Imperial Majesty open the Jeylos Games."

"Ah," sighed the kora, "then you have seen the best of Jeylos. My father is the greatest Emperor we have had since Agna-Di! And the games are always so charming a spectacle." He rested his hand on her shoulder and there was no escape for the moment. The kora watched twin red spots grow on the lieutenant's face and merely acknowledged it with a bemused smile.

Ambassador Xinthi-Ang paid just enough attention to see Jane's discomfort. Standing sharply, he said, "It would be rude to keep others waiting for their evening meal. Let us go." He strode through the door as it opened on his command. In the passageway, he waited for the others to file out, Jane last. He held her back and waited until the others were almost to the cage. "Let them not embarrass you," he said quietly in precise British English. "They are young puppies with bad manners."

Jane smiled up at the ambassador. "Thank you, sir; I appreciate your kind thoughts of me." It was the correct response in a delicate situation.

"Then allow me," he smiled back, offering her his arm.

Jane took it gratefully and allowed him to take her into dinner.

❧

The appearance of Lieutenant Krieg on the arm of the Jeylosian ambassador caused a stir in the wardroom. Jeylosians usually kept their distance and the gesture was extraordinary. Judging by the looks darting back and forth between the kora and Lalo-Fa, Morgan wondered what had happened in the minutes before they arrived. That Jane was under the ambassador's protection was clear; not that Jane needed much protection. She handled herself with impeccable correctness during the meal, translating an idiom where necessary, gently laughing when laughter was called for. Instinctively he knew it had nothing to do with her father, there was something else about it he couldn't quite place. She had a talent for putting everyone at his ease, except, that is, for him.

After dinner, a holofilm was scheduled for crew recreation. Much to the Captain's surprise, the Jeylosians expressed enthusiasm at the chance to watch a movie. "I'm a great film buff," explained the ambassador to his host. "Lady Xinthi-Ang enjoys them as well."

"Then you must attend the showing," said Jane, glad to be off the hook for keeping them amused. A movie would take up the bulk of the evening and she would sit, as protocol demanded, one row behind the honored guests, therefore keeping her out of reach of either the kora or Lalo-Fa. She led the way to the theatre on the upper recreation deck. As they went, she provided a quick tour of the ship's facilities.

The kora seemed fascinated with the number of different amusements offered to the crew, but he was most impressed by the swimming pool. "Would a swim after the show be possible?" he asked politely, eying the water.

"By all means," replied the captain, "Lieutenant Krieg can make the arrangements." He considered the possibility of joining them, almost as much for seeing Krieg in a swimsuit as for keeping an eye on her and the kora. He did not approve of the way the prince ogled her. Jane's raised eyebrow did not escape him either.

The crew was restrained in its cheering for the good guys due to the presence of the Jeylosians, but it did not prevent them from applauding heartily when the sheriff took out the bank robbers. Westerns were timeless and no matter how many versions of the white hats versus the black hats were produced, they were popular. Popcorn and soda were provided; both Ambassador and Lady Xinthi-Ang consumed prodigious amounts. Sitting beside Lieutenant Krieg, Morgan amused himself by sneaking popcorn from her container once his was empty.

Each time the hand surreptitiously crept into the box, Jane had a mind to slap it away. Anyone who knew her well knew enough to keep away from her popcorn. Still, he was the captain and it would have been too personal a reaction. When he nudged her to ask for a sip of her cherry Coke after his was gone, she briefly considered dumping it in his lap, but passed it to him anyway, hissing "Keep it," only to be laughed at. Whatever game he was playing, it was making her uncomfortable.

When the film ended, she saw the Jeylosians safely back to their cabins before dashing off to change into a swimsuit. Jane chose a sleek, unadorned blue racer that, while it did nothing to conceal her body, at least did not accentuate it. She undid the knot at the nape of her neck and deftly divided the long tresses into two hastily braided sections. Tying them off with covered binders, she struggled to check the part in the back to make sure it was straight. Satisfied with the job, she tossed the braids over her shoulder and slipped into a terry robe.

"I'm afraid I'll be thought of as stodgy," said Lord Xinthi-Ang as he opened the door to Jane, "but I shall pass on the swim. I shall spend my time alone and in peace, reading the proposals your captain has kindly provided." He indicated a pile of docupads on the small table beneath the porthole.

Jane smiled and nodded in understanding. "Your presence shall be missed, my lord."

Lady Xinthi-Ang glided into the sitting room wearing another magnificent embroidered robe, but this one was definitely Jeylosian in design. "The others await us in Kora Pana-Di's cabin. Shall we go?"

At the pool, a large basket of towels had been placed beside a table laden with fresh fruits, Californian wine, and other tempting snacks. The kora took a grape and popped it into his mouth, smacking his lips at the sweet taste. It was customary for the kora to partake first, so the others might enjoy themselves at will.

"Last one in is a smelly egg!" cried the kora as he shed his robe and dashed toward the diving board. Lalo-Fa, not to be outraced even by his prince, followed in hot pursuit.

"I don't think I can tell him," sighed Jane, dropping her own robe over a chair, "running in the pool area is strictly forbidden."

The ambassador's wife laughed delicately. "Then don't. Should one of them slip, you must show no sympathy, only a sharp word for a child who should know better." She patted the seat beside her own and spoke easily in English. "Sit for a minute, Lieutenant Krieg. I would visit with you while the little children cavort." Jane sat and waited for the conversation to begin. "Tell me honestly, Lieutenant, is it difficult being a woman in this service? The few Jeylosian women in our fleet often complain bitterly that our men treat them as servants."

"We're certainly not servants here, my lady, but some men have difficulty in dealing with women in command. We have made great strides in this area, but we have a long way to go. There are not as many women in command of major vessels as one would hope."

"Do your parents approve of your vocation, Lieutenant?" She paused, looking a little sad. "I ask this for a reason."

"Both my parents are in the service," said Jane slowly, "but my father was less supportive of my choice than my mother. He has, however, come around."

"Then you are lucky, Lieutenant. My granddaughter, Helia, has chosen to serve our fleet and neither her father, my son, nor his father, my lord ambassador, has given approval. It has been most trying for us all."

"May I ask whether or not you have supported her decision?" Jane knew she was taking a risk in asking so personal a question, but she felt the conversation warranted it.

"Privately, to my granddaughter and her mother, most assuredly. To my son and his father, frankly, no. But I am most proud of Helia and the way she excels in her studies."

Jane took a moment to compose her answer. How she responded to such a confidence was important both personally and professionally. "Then be proud of your granddaughter and never forget to tell her. Your kind words will mean much in the face of disharmony. Your silence would be taken as disapproval."

The Jeylosian lady smiled at Jane. "You are quite wise for your tender years, Lieutenant Krieg. I am sure you will give great pride and pleasure to your own house."

"May your words reach the skies," correctly responded Jane.

Lady Xinthi-Ang sighed and leaned forward to choose a grape from the cluster. "Go swim, Lieutenant. I believe the men are awaiting you."

"Thank you, my lady." Jane rose, pressed her hands together in the traditional Jeylosian way, and walked quickly to the diving board. She waited until the kora and Lalo-Fa were out of range before she ran the length of the board, bounded upward, then dove smoothly into the water.

From the entrance to the pool, Morgan watched the sleek display before approaching Lady Xinthi-Ang at the table. "Good evening, madam," he said as he reached her.

"Have you come to join the little boys at play? Or do you not trust them with your lieutenant?" There were teasing lights twinkling in her eyes.

"Shouldn't I?" he countered nonchalantly.

The lady stood and shed her robe, revealing a lithe, youthful body encased in a modest white and gold swimsuit. "It depends, Captain," she said, tying her hair back with a gold ribbon, "on whether or not you have prior claim." She left him standing open-mouthed as she went to join the others.

It didn't take long for Morgan to follow. Soon they were staging races between the lap ropes, with the kora giving the captain a run for his money. Lady Xinthi-Ang and Jane tread water at the sides, shouting encouragement, their voices bouncing off the tiled wall, echoing loudly. When Kora Pana-Di prevailed, Jane wasn't entirely sure that his victory had not been permitted by the captain.

"Drinks are on me," shouted the kora, emerging from the water. He went to the table and began pouring wine. The others followed, laughing and dripping. Jane handed out towels until everyone was sufficiently dried. The kora handed her a glass and beckoned her to sit beside him.

"Tell me, sir," said Captain Morgan as he took a filled glass from the table, "where did you learn to swim like that?" He turned to Jane, expecting her to translate, but she did not.

"Oxford, Captain Morgan," he answered in English. "I swam on their team while I was a student. But you have an unfair advantage, sir, having a beautiful pool in which to swim at your leisure. Such a thing is frowned upon at home. Water is a precious commodity and collected for swimming only during our too brief rainy season. At any other time, it would be considered decadent and wasteful."

The conversation drifted informally around a variety of topics from there. The kora's time on Earth had, as it had for Lady Xinthi-Ang, left a less formal outlook on life which could be appreciated only away from the home planet. Captain Morgan even found himself relaxing just a bit, eating and talking with the visitors as though they were friends and not VIPs. Jane spoke well on a number of topics, including music, a subject dear to Jeylosians. She surprised everyone by singing a popular, if a bit ribald, tune which had made the rounds on Jeylos.

"Brava, brava!" cried the kora, clapping his hands. "Where could you possibly have learned that?"

"My father," giggled Jane, a little surprised at herself. "He learned it from an old friend who had business on Jeylos. When I was studying the language, he taught it to me as a way of remembering the declination of verbs." She started to sing again, this time substituting complex conjugations for the original lyric. She was rewarded with more laughter.

The only one who did not laugh was the captain who sat with a smile frozen on his face. Since he did not speak the language, he could not understand the joke. Without a translator tucked discreetly in his ear, he felt left out. He wished they'd go back to talking about things he could understand.

Xinthi-Ang sensed his discomfort. "My dear Captain, perhaps this will be incentive for you to master our most provocative language," she offered in a friendly tone.

Morgan flushed just a little at the remark. "Perhaps you're right, my lady, I shall obtain library discs as soon as possible."

"You could take lessons from the lieutenant," suggested the kora, looking at Jane. "She has mastered both vocabulary and nuance. And," he added with a smile, "her accent is delightful."

"Your graciousness humbles me, sir," said Jane, pleased with an acknowledgement of her fluency. It was always nice to hear it from a native speaker.

The captain was about to say something when a soft chime caught his attention. He pushed a button on his pager. "Captain Morgan, here."

"Captain, sorry to disturb you," said Joe Newhouse, "but we need you on the bridge."

"On my way." He picked up his robe and put it on, wrapping it tightly before he tied the sash. "If you will excuse me, ladies and gentlemen, duty calls." He waited for the kora to speak.

"Of course, Captain Morgan. We have been glad for your company."

Jane wondered what could be happening that they called him away. Since she was not free to leave, nor was she asked to go, Jane sat back in her chair and sipped her wine.

The conversation lasted only a few more minutes when Lady Xinthi-Ang stood. "If you will excuse me, Kora Pana-Di, the hour grows late and my lord will wonder what has become of me."

"As you wish. Perhaps we should all think about returning to our cabins." There was no mistaking this signal to end the evening. Jane and Lalo-Fa stood with the kora. "I shall escort you to your quarters, Lieutenant," he said, shooting a glance at Lalo-Fa.

Shaking her head, Jane replied, "Again, your graciousness humbles me, sir, but it is I who must escort you to yours." She thought she was reading something in his eyes, but dismissed it.

"As you wish," he answered with a wave of his hand. He allowed the lieutenant to lead the way.

At the door to her cabin, Lady Xinthi-Ang bid them good night, leaving Jane, Lalo-Fa and the kora standing in the passageway. Lalo-Fa studied his prince for a moment before saying, "A pleasant rest to you, my kora, and to you, Lieutenant Krieg." He closed the door to his cabin behind him.

"Where are your quarters, Lieutenant Krieg?" asked the kora, making no move toward his own door.

"Not far from here, but I must attend the bridge before I retire, sir," she answered sidling away from him.

"I think not, Lieutenant. I would take it as an honor if you would join me for a nightcap."

"Your graciousness humbles me, sir, but I have duties to attend to."

"In a swim suit?" He stepped closer to her, preventing Jane from fleeing in the direction of the cage.

"Sir, I am afraid I am unworthy of your attentions. I bid you a pleasant rest." She took a step to the side, but he blocked her again. His face was close to hers and she could smell wine on his breath.

"Do I repel you, Lieutenant?"

"Not at all, sir, but regulations forbid personal involvement with guests aboard our ship."

"And if there is mutual attraction?"

"I am sorry, sir," she repeated firmly, "but regulations forbid personal involvement with guests aboard our ship."

He was not to be put off. "Is this like name, rank and serial number, Lieutenant?" he whispered into her ear before touching it lightly with his lips.

Jane recoiled, almost jumping across the corridor. "Sir, you humble me with your graciousness, but this I will not permit!" she hissed softly through clenched teeth.

Crossing the short distance between them, he grabbed her wrist and held it tightly. "I would offer you untold delights." His voice was raspy against her ear.

"And your father would offer you untold hell should you do anything to humiliate a daughter of his ally," her voice was deadly calm, not at all afraid as he had expected. Wondering if she was speaking generally or she was the daughter of someone his father counted as a friend, he released her. "As you wish, daughter of my father's ally." There was something about her tone that made him think the latter.

"Problems, Lieutenant?" asked Captain Morgan, coming down the passageway.

"No, sir; I was just bidding the Kora Pana-Di a pleasant rest." Her steady voice belied her jangled nerves.

"And a pleasant rest to you both," said the kora. He opened his door and disappeared.

Jane leaned against the bulkhead and closed her eyes. A long stream of breath whistled slightly through her lips. "Just when you think the cavalry ain't gonna arrive ..."

"I take it, judging by the way you are holding up the wall, that the little prince was showering you with unwanted attention." Morgan looked amused.

"Yeah," snorted Jane indelicately, "he was. But I think he went off to bed unscathed." She looked up at him. "Good thing I wasn't carrying a sidearm."

Morgan's eyebrow shot up. He wanted to ask what exactly she had done, but he thought better of it; he was probably better off not knowing. He had come in search of Jane for a reason. "Let's go to your office," he said, "I left something there I want you to look at."

"Sure, Captain." Jane straightened and retied her robe. She felt a little strange parading about the ship with the captain in a similar state of undress. *We must look like we're on a cruise*, she thought, but kept it to herself.

On her desk sat several pages of hard copy. Jane sat down and started to read while the captain pulled the other chair directly opposite her. "It looks like a Stellar-4 communiqué, but it isn't. What is it?"

"I don't know. I was hoping you would tell me. Lipson in communications picked it up about half an hour ago. It was broadcast on a general channel, but was repeated several times before reception disintegrated. What do you think it is?" He rested his elbows on the desk and rubbed his eyes, still reddened from swimming.

"Was it repeated exactly as it is recorded here?" she asked.

"Yes."

"Hmmmm. The first part appears to be a hailing signal followed by an identification code. See?" She pointed to a brief word, the indicated pause, followed by a series of short words. "My guess is that these are numbers. If it's theme and variation on Hatma, the numbers are seven, nine, six, four, four, eight. In that sequence, it would indicate a cruiser. Assuming it *is* theme and variation of Hatma, this segment indicates they're in some sort of conflict." She paused, "And I think it's the Wa'atsi using it.

"What makes you think it is Hatma?" asked the captain, trying to follow her train of thought.

"You know Pig Latin, aptain-k?" She saw him nod. "Well, this is kinda like that, only a little more complex. If the words are split and a prescribed set of sibilants interjected, you get the same effect. It's a real simple code, but Wa'atsi are not known for their ability to keep a secret. Besides," she added slowly, "I've seen this once before. I mean, another Stellar-4 done like this. They take another language, in this case, Hatma, and stick in their own vocalization patterns. Unless you know the language they're borrowing, plus the dialect of the borrower, you can't make heads nor tails of it. It's textbook stuff."

Morgan raised his head and looked at her. "And if you're wrong about the Hatma?"

"I still think it's a distress call of some sort." She went back to the paper, then hit a button on the intercom and waited for the bridge to answer. "This is Krieg, Lipson. Could you pipe that transmission down to me? I want to hear how it came over. Thanks." She listened as the garbled voice filled the office. "It's Wa'atsi, all right, and they're using a pretty low grade of Hatma. The accent of the speaker is definitely Wa'atsi."

"And the rest of the message.... can you translate?"

"Sure, give me a minute." She took a docupad from her drawer and began writing swiftly, going back and making changes every once in a while until she was satisfied with the result. "Cruiser *Ana'atam* reporting damage sustained in a skirmish with Amitidean cruiser *Tical*. Nish injured. *Tical* incapacitated. Assistance required."

She handed the docupad to the captain. "Did they get her location based on the transmission?"

"Yes." He leaned over and switched on the intercom. "Captain to bridge. Notify Port Misaleta on Amitides that the *Tical* has been in a skirmish with the Wa'atsi and has sustained damage. We are going to their aid. We can reach them faster than they can. Mr. Parker, set a course for the coordinates you've got, and take it at starmach-6."

"Aye, aye captain," responded the navigator from the bridge. "Battle stations, sir?"

"No, but put the ship on a very quiet yellow alert. No use in alarming the passengers."

"Aye, aye, Captain."

"Captain, out." He flicked off the machine. "Get changed and meet me on the bridge in fifteen minutes, Lieutenant. And bring Winter with you."

"Yes, sir." She watched him leave.

The staff was assembling on the bridge when Jane and Belle arrived. No one seemed to care that the yellow alert light was blinking at various stations, not even Winter, who calmly walked to the printer station and pulled a sheet from the machine. Jane could feel her heart beating faster than normal, adrenalin pumping through her system. Morgan sat in his command chair, talking quietly with Newhouse. He glanced up and saw the two linguists. "Let's adjourn to the conference room, ladies and gentlemen."

Like a scout troop, they followed the leader into the conference room. Jane took a seat with a terminal in front; she would need it to monitor incoming transmissions. She logged on and waited until the screen began putting out chains of symbols. "Captain," she called, "there's been a change in the transmission." Morgan walked around behind her chair and watched the screen. "Here," she said, pointing to a line with her finger. "This is now reporting that Nish is dead. They are awaiting a directive from another ship, yet unnamed."

"Mr. Newhouse, who else is in the area?" asked Morgan.

"The closest Wa'atsi vessel is the *Pu'unoti*, about fourteen hours from here." The *Pu'unoti* was another battle cruiser, but one usually used the same way the *Washington* was, primarily as diplomatic courier. Like the *Washington*, its armament capacity was at maximum. "We've been hailing the *Tical* on a security channel, but so far, there's no response."

"What does Amitides say?"

"Proceed to the *Tical*, Captain. They are sending a medical team to meet us, but we'll beat 'em to the *Tical*."

Captain Morgan looked around for the ship's surgeon. "Dr. Vecchio, are we stocked with compatible supplies?"

She handed the captain a docupad. "We've got some antibiotics close enough to theirs to hold us until their own people arrive. Their physiology is not too different from ours." Leaning over, she punched a button on the nearest terminal and waited for data to appear. "O-neg blood we've got, and we've got a number of possible donors on board as well."

"Better get down to sick bay to put together a kit and a triage team, doctor."

"Aye, aye, Captain."

"It's 0013 hours now. Mr. Ryan, how much longer 'til we reach the *Tical*?"

"Six and a half hours, Captain."

Captain Morgan leaned back in his chair, his hands together, thinking. "Our best bet, ladies and gentlemen, is to take advantage of the time with prep and rest. Please review your scheduled procedures, make the appropriate adjustments, and then go catch a nap. Dress uniforms are hereby cancelled; flight suits, please. Be back here at 0530. Mr. Ryan and Mr. Parker, call your seconds and then you are excused from the bridge until 0500. Ms. Krieg will be notified of any changes or additions to the transmissions. Ms. Lucas, prepare a statement of intent for the Wa'atsi. They're gonna ask what we think we're doing in that sector. Mr. Newhouse, you may have the privilege of first watch." He rose and gathered his notes. "Until later, ladies and gentlemen." He got as far as the cage. "Ms. Krieg, awaken the ambassador before you return and ask him to accompany you to the bridge."

"Aye, aye, Captain."

At 0500, Lieutenant Krieg rapped sharply on the ambassador's door. He opened it, already dressed for the day. "Excuse my intrusion, sir," she explained, "but we have received disturbing news." She went on to tell the ambassador of the night's events. "The captain would request your presence on the bridge, my lord."

"Of course, of course," sighed Ambassador Xinthi-Ang. Reports such as these were always troubling to a man whose life had been spent in the pursuit of peace. "Let us go, Lieutenant."

Silently, they made their way to the bridge. Personnel were already starting to arrive. Jane checked her screen for any changes that may have occurred since she last checked it in her own cabin. There were new, coded transmissions from the Wa'atsi base. Quickly she prepared a translation and showed it to Newhouse. "It looks like the unnamed ship *is* going to be the *Pu'unoti*. First Admiral P'nucha is in command, I think."

"By the code name "Star-champion?" asked Newhouse, studying the docupad.

"Yes. P'nucha likes to think of himself as an intergalactic hero. Very showy and always wears full regalia, which is no laughing matter."

Newhouse laughed. A Wa'atsi in full regalia was usually so covered in metal he can hardly move. "Lovely," he said, shaking his head. "Then we're in for trouble."

"No doubt," said the ambassador in English. "P'nucha likes to wage battle wherever he can."

"And he's good at it," added Newhouse. "Show this to the captain as soon as he arrives."

"I'm here," said the Captain coming onto the bridge. He greeted Ambassador Xinthi-Ang, then turned to his first officer. "What've you got?"

Newhouse handed him the docupad. "Doesn't this please you to no end?"

"I'm thrilled," answered Morgan, handing it back. "Mr. Ryan, do we have the *Tical* in view yet?"

"Yes, sir." He punched a button and a broad view of what lay ahead materialized on the large screen at the front of the bridge. "That small object at two o'clock is the *Tical*. The reddish one at ten o'clock should be the Wa'atsi vessel."

The captain, along with everyone else studied the screen. They were still too far off to be able to tell for sure, but Ryan was rarely wrong about these things. "Ms. Krieg, anything from the Wa'atsi ship?"

"Nothing yet."

"Hail them on a general channel and tell them we've come to help."

He paused, then added "Both of them."

"Yes, sir," responded Jane. She took her place at her station and began the hailing process. "Sir, response from the *Ana'atam*. They are asking our intentions."

"Friendly, Krieg."

She sent the message. "Sir, the acting commander has asked that you identify yourself."

"Code M-5756-871."

"Message received, Captain. The acting commander says thank you, but no help is needed by either vessel."

"Bullshit." The word hung in the air. "Tell the *Ana'atam* we are going in to aid the *Tical*. Then hail the *Tical* and see what response you get."

Jane relayed the first message, then the second, on a secure channel. There was no response from the Amitidean ship. She tried again, but still no response was heard. A message came in from the *Ana'atam*. "Sir, the acting commander of the *Ana'atam* says to do whatever you want."

"Gee, thanks," said Morgan amid titters from the crew. He pushed the intercom button on his control panel. "Tapper, get your butt up here."

"On my way, Captain."

"Captain, I've got something coming in from Amitides. Port control says their rescue ship should rendezvous with us at 0945 hours. They ask if you intend to board the *Tical*." Jane waited for Morgan's response.

"Tell them yes, if they would like us to, and then ask them how."

Jane transmitted the reply and waited for the next response. All eyes were on the screen, watching as pinpricks of space vessels grew slowly larger. "Sir," said Jane as soon as the transmission from Amitides began, "Port control says we can get in through the shuttle bay by using a laser code." She transcribed the code onto a docupad.

"Okay, troops, let's get ready to go in." The captain took the docupad from Jane and studied the code.

Tapper bounded onto the bridge with a hearty "Good morning to you all!" He smiled at the captain's glare, unmoved by the visual rebuke. "Did I miss anything?"

Morgan sat back in his command chair. "We're going aboard the *Tical*. Tapper, how much do you know about the ship?"

"More than enough," he answered, leaning against the navigator's station. "Any word on damage?"

"None," answered Jane. "There's been no communication from the *Tical*."

"The following personnel will suit up and meet me in the shuttle dock in one hour: Tapper, Krieg, Vecchio, Anderson, Dresher, and Davies. Doctor, have a triage team ready to shuttle over if necessary." The captain looked around. "Mr. Newhouse and Ms. Lucas, you will stay here and run the ranch while we're gone. Ambassador, I think it might be wise to ask your technician to come up to the bridge. If we need Lalo-Fa, we can shuttle him over."

"Certainly, Captain," said the ambassador. "Any assistance we could provide will be gladly given."

"Thank you, sir." Morgan turned to Jane. "Tell the Wa'atsi that we intend to board the *Tical*. If they have changed their minds and want assistance from us, now is the time to ask for it."

Jane relayed the message and the reply came quickly. "Again they say no, but ask why you are boarding the pirate ship."

The last words caused everyone's heads to turn in her direction. "The pirate ship, Lieutenant? Is that a quote?"

"Yes, sir, it is. They called the *Tical pirate*."

"Ask them to elaborate, please."

Jane turned back to her console. "They claim that the *Tical* was attempting to hijack them." She waited for more information. "The acting commander says they fired on the *Tical* in self-defense." *And if you believe that,* thought Jane, *you believe in the Tooth Fairy.*

"Highly unlikely," pronounced Ambassador Xinthi-Ang with a snort. "I believe the English word for Wa'atsi is carpetbagger!"

The captain suppressed a laugh. It was, after all, a pretty good description of the Wa'atsi. The reptilian Wa'atsi had a habit of showing up on a planet following some disaster and turning a profit before disappearing into the night sky. "We shall see, Ambassador, we shall see."

"Captain," said Ryan, staring at the screen, "there's the flashing coming off the *Tical*."

"Where, helmsman?"

"Over there, sir." He pointed to what appeared to be the stern of the crippled ship. A light was flashing in the distance.

Jane stood and walked as close to the screen as she could get. "Give me a pad," she said to the nearest crewmate. She began recording the blips as fast as she could. "It's Morse code, captain."

"Are you sure, Lieutenant?"

"Absolutely," was what she said, but the glance she gave him said, *are you kidding me?*

She watched and checked as the pattern began to repeat. "Wash we have you in range. Coming here?" She looked at the docupad again. "That's the message. Tapper, can we flash back at them?"

"Tapper, do what the lady tells you," said the captain.

"Come with me, S.J.," said Tapper, pulling her in the direction of the cage. "We're going up to the cap."

Grabbing an extra pad, Jane followed him into the cage. "Good going," laughed Tapper, ruffling her hair. "Glad you told ol' Boston it's Morse and not me." They rode up into the space directly above the bridge where a gunner could sit during battle. Tapper pulled a halogen beacon from a rack in the bulkhead and sat in the chair, pointing the lens out of the window toward the *Tical.*

"Dictate the message," ordered Tapper, turning on the beacon.

"Baloney, get outta the chair." Her voice brooked no dissention and Tapper vacated the seat immediately. Jane took the beacon and flashed out "On our way. Open shuttle bay. What meds?"

The *Tical* flashed "Hooray" and slowly started listing the emergency supplies they required.

CHAPTER 5

The boarding party assembled on deck as the requisitioned supplies were loaded into the shuttle. It was a tight fit, but everyone would get across in one shot. Tapper took the controls while the Captain gave last minute instructions.

"Do what you're told, and stay away from security areas. We are not unfriendlies, merely friends trying to help." He waited until a crewmate on the exterior gave the all clear. "Take it out, Tapper."

The shuttle glided smoothly on its rails until it sat in the outer bay and the inner doors slid shut. "Shuttle 1 to the bridge. Are we clear to go?"

"Go ahead, Shuttle 1. Have a nice time."

"Thanks, guy." Tapper flipped a lever and the shuttle rotated so that its nose was pointing out. "Open outer bay," he said into his headset. The outer doors split, revealing the empty space between the *Washington* and the *Tical.* The *Ana'atam* was barely visible, hovering off the port side of the *Tical.* Tapper engaged the thrusters and they were on their way.

The outer bay doors of the *Tical* slid open very slowly. As Tapper maneuvered into position, he spotted the two pressure-suited crewmen floating nearby, tethered to prevent an accident as they manually operated the *Tical's* shuttle bay. Tapper aligned the craft and brought it through the narrow opening until two more Amitidean crewmen appeared in front of the shuttle, motioning that they could proceed safely. Shuttle 1 slid through a second set of doors until it sat on the deck of the *Tical.* Quickly, they piled out.

Several Amitidean crewmen were waiting for them. "Welcome aboard, *Washington*!" one shouted happily. "We are most glad to see you!" Immediately they began unloading the supplies. An officer, his shirt singed black, stepped forward to lead them onto the ship. Dr. Vecchio remained behind with the Amitidean doctor who immediately began sifting through the supplies for the things he desperately needed.

"Excited?" whispered Tapper to Jane as they passed through a series of portals into the main body of the ship. The *Tical* may have been much smaller than the *Washington*, but no less complex in its form. The thick smell of ozone permeated the air, as if everything hard wired had blown and burned. The passageway was lit with emergency lighting, the main electrical system having been damaged in the skirmish. The few crewmen they saw showed signs of battle; torn, dirty uniforms and fresh bandages. When Jane glanced down one corridor as they passed, she saw crewmen carrying limp bodies. There was no way to tell whether they were alive or dead.

"Krieg!" called the captain from the front of the file. "Come up here and translate. This man is too tired to think in another language."

Jane wondered what happened to his p.t., but said nothing. She scooted up to the captain's side, walking between them, and began translating as fast as she could. "The Wa'atsi were being pursued by a Pitano vessel. The Pitanese captain requested aide from the nearest League vessel. We went after them and caught them here, asked them to halt, which they did. Our captain told Nish that we were only trying to prevent any difficulty between them and the Pitanese, that according to the Pitanese, they were dealing in stolen goods which need to be returned to Pitan. Nish turned and fired on us, and we took the hit broadside. We got our defense shields up but there was much damage; we were already weakened by the first hit." The officer said something that Jane did not understand and she asked him for clarification. Through the corner of her eye, she could see Morgan's face, grim with anger, waiting for her to continue. "He says that the Pitanese captain claims the Wa'atsi have stolen a ritual object from the Temple of the Mountain Oracle on Pitan. The Hamunah Batan."

"The what?" asked Morgan, recognizing the words, but not knowing what they meant.

"The Hamunah Batan is the great bowl the Oracle uses to make her predictions. It's carved from a solid piece of pitanite, about two by two meters and coated with a phosphorescent layer."

Morgan whistled under his breath in amazement. Pitanite, if you were lucky to get any at all, came about the same size as a lump of charcoal. A piece that size would be incredibly valuable. "Any idea as to why they would want it?"

On the surface, it sounded like a stupid question, but it was not.

Jane asked the officer, who shrugged as he spoke. "They want it because without it, the Pitanese believe their strength is greatly diminished. They would then become vulnerable to outland influence. Their government depends on the Oracle to predict all sorts of things, from the weather to the stock market on Earth. The Wa'atsi want a foothold on Pitan and this was their idea of a good way to get it." Jane told the officer to hold up. "The Pitanese are a highly religious people who believe that the Oracle is the key to understanding the cosmos. Have you ever met a Pitanese?"

"Once, but I never had the chance to talk to him about his home world." He paused to formulate the next question. "Ask him what they were doing in this sector." That an Amitidean military vessel was here was out of the ordinary.

"We are here," translated Jane, "because we were invited to attend a ceremony on Pitan in honor of an agreement to supply them with agricultural supplies. It is not a major treaty, but it was a first between our two planets. An agreement with us signaled their desire to become trading partners in the League, something which would hamper any relationship with the Wa'atsi. We had already left for home when the pirates arrived. According to their report, the Oracle herself was badly injured in the raid, but will recover."

The doors to the bridge were yawning open, blown apart by a direct hit to the area. When the party entered, the captain, seated in his chair, tried feebly to rise. "Nice of you to come, Ash Morgan," he said, forcing what was certainly a painful smile. A bandage encircled his head, and both hands were swathed as well.

"Sorry to see you in such sorry shape, 'Mitri," answered the captain, striding over to his friend. "I had no idea this was your crate."

"A loaner, my friend," said the Amitidean sadly. "And how angry that captain is going to be, I cannot predict." He snorted what seemed to be a laugh. The man attending the captain's wounds stood up.

"Well, well, well, if it isn't Blackjack Cardozo in the flesh!" said Morgan, a wry smile on his face. "I take it that was you with the flashlight?"

"Sure thing, Boston," laughed the tall man, extending his arms to embrace the visiting captain. "What the hell else was Ah gonna do?"

"Very clever... for a Southern boy," he growled, returning the great bear hug. He glanced at Jackson's hand; despite a bandage, there was fresh blood. "What happened to you?"

The other captain shrugged. "Nothin' of any import. Ah was trying to hold onto a cable and got mahself zapped. Ah compounded the problem by getting cut on somethin' nasty."

"Let Vecchio take a look at that, Jack," said Morgan seriously. "It looks pretty bad."

He shook his head. "It won't kill me, Boston, so don't you go a-worryin' about it."

Morgan let the comment pass. "Give me your assessment of the situation."

"Y'all ain't gonna like it, Boston.," replied Cardozo, his drawl seeming to thicken as he spoke, "but Ah think someone's gonna have to get that washtub off that pirate ship and get it back to Pitan before we've got a little war on our hands."

"You think so?" asked the captain, one eyebrow raised.

"Ah know so," drawled the Southerner. He bent over and finished wrapping the captain's leg. "You'd better let someone at the League know because otherwise you might find yourself hogtied when you get back to base."

"Sir," interrupted Jane, "the *Washington* wants to know if they should ask the *Merrimack* to swing by. They're about fourteen hours from here and also picked up the Wa'atsi transmission."

"Tell them by all means to join the party." Morgan shook his head. "Some party, Jackson. How do you always manage to find yourself in the middle of these things?"

"Same way you do, Boston. By bein' in the wrong place at the wrong time." He glanced in Jane's direction. "Who's she?"

For a quick moment, he wondered why Blackjack didn't recognize his lieutenant, and she him. "Allow me to introduce my linguist; this is Lieutenant Krieg. She will be translating where necessary and working on jerry-rigging your communications so we can transmit out. What happened to your power packs?"

"Blown to the heavens, I'm afraid, Ash," said Louakis. "We took a direct hit on the bridge and it flamed the system. My engineer is working on it now. Is that Joshua Bear you have brought with you?"

"Sure is, 'Mitri," said Tapper, picking his way through the crowd on the bridge. "I'll head down to your fusion deck and see what I can do." He looked at the others from the *Washington*. "Anderson, Davies, you come with me. Dresher, see if you can find your way to back to the shuttle deck to ply your lock-picking trade on those bay doors."

When they were gone, Morgan turned to Captain Louakis. "Do you still have a communications officer?"

He shook his head. "He was killed in the first hit." Louakis pointed to a burned out station to his left. "There isn't much that hasn't been fried, Lieutenant Krieg, but I would take it as a personal favor if you can do anything with it."

"I'll do my best, sir." She smiled at the man; his manners were impeccable even in his bloodied state. *Typical captain*, she thought.

The communications station was worse than fried; every wire had been smoked by a power surge. The stench was choking, a combination of burnt plastic coating and flesh. Forcing back bile rising in her throat, Jane crawled under the desk and began to pull cable out from the bulkhead. There wasn't much that could be saved; the damage seemed to go through the entire system. Opening a channel to the *Washington* through her portapak, Jane asked for and got Joe Newhouse. "Do we have a freebase communicator we can spare?"

"Possibly. How fast do you need it?"

"On the next shuttle over. I'll also need two UT-40's and three spools of hot wire. Oh, some P-22 circuit boards and a hot glue gun."

"A hot glue gun?"

"Yes, I should have brought one and I didn't."

A voice from above her said "Ah've got a hot glue gun if you need it."

"Forget the hot glue gun. I've got one. Thanks, Mr. Newhouse. Krieg out." She clicked off her portapak. Jane slid out from under the desk and looked up at the man standing there. "Thank you, Captain Cardozo."

"Y'all very welcome, Lieutenant." He offered her a hand that she refused, getting up on her own. "Anything else you might need that Ah have in my possession is assuredly yours, lovely lady."

Jane felt herself blush. So this was *the* Blackjack Cardozo, famous fighter pilot, friend to Jonathan and man most wanted by irate husbands across three galaxies. He was as tall as Captain Morgan, with sandy brown curly hair, grey eyes, and a smile that didn't quit. Handsome as all the descriptions she had ever heard, Jane felt a little like a schoolgirl meeting a movie star. His eyes on her made her shift uncomfortably. "Do...uh...do you have any number five connector pads?"

"Ah'm sure we can find a few strays." He narrowed his eyes and studied her closely. There was something definitely familiar about those grey eyes and dark lashes. "Why don't y'all take a little promenade with me down to what's left of the supply stores and we can rummage together."

Jane glanced over to Morgan, who nodded imperceptibly. "Okay." She started to follow him but the captain caught her arm and pulled her back,

"Watch yourself," he muttered under his breath.

With a glance that could freeze hot coffee, Jane answered "Yes, sir," and hurried after Cardozo.

His long strides caused Jane to almost run to catch up with him. He led her through a maze of corridors still passable but heavily damaged. They reached the supply shop only to find the door jammed shut. "Anyone in there?" yelled Cardozo in Amitidean and a faint voice answered. "Step away from the hatch, Ah'm gonna pop it." He pulled a laser gun from his belt and waited a few seconds before firing. The stench of melted seals filled the passageway and Jane held her nose. Satisfied that the job was done, Cardozo slipped the gun back in his belt and with sheer, brute force, pushed on the portal until it unwillingly slid open. A crewman covered in dark brown ooze crawled out. "You okay, Niko?"

"Barely, Jack."

"Can y'all get yourself to sick bay or do Ah have to carry you?" He extended a hand to the crewman who took it gratefully.

"Thanks," he said, pulling himself up, "but I think I can get there on my own." Seeing Jane standing there, he straightened up and bowed gravely from the waist. "Welcome aboard, madam," he said in English.

"I am pleased to be of service here, but would have preferred to find you in good health," answered Jane in his language.

"Aahhhh, you speak as gently as one of our own. Many welcomes to you, madam officer." He managed a weak smile before limping down the passageway, one hand supporting himself on the bulkhead.

Cardozo made a sweeping bow, "After you, dear lady."

Jane pursed her lips and looked at him doubtfully. *Are you expecting me to faint from the shock of seeing blood or merely from meeting you?* she thought. She marched into the storage bay and began rummaging through the section marked *tapanakiati* in elegant Amitidean cursive, while Captain Cardozo perched himself on a stool and watched. The longer he watched her, the more he thought he knew her.

"Don't Ah know you from somewhere?" he asked after a while.

Jane stopped rifling through the bins and gave the question some serious thought. *Have I ever actually met him?* she wondered and then shook her head no. Something in the back of her mind told her she had indeed met the pilot, but if he couldn't remember either, she wasn't going to suggest it. "I don't think so," she said smoothly.

"Hmmmm." She looked very familiar, but for the moment, he could not place her…at least, not until she turned to face him, holding a micro-welder. "Whoa, don't shoot, Calamity!" The memory of a very skinny little girl in a bathing suit, an oversized cowboy hat and black cowboy boots standing atop of a sand dune at Cape Cod came roaring back to him. There was no mistaking that determined jaw set tight coupled with the grey eyes and black, black lashes.

Jane almost dropped the micro-welder. "Who told you that?" she blurted out, blaming Tapper for the indiscretion but quickly realizing he could not have told him.

Jackson Cardozo threw his head back and laughed. "Well, Ah'll be damned! Krieg my ass! Little Sarah Jane all grown up! Ah knew Ah've seen y'all before, and Ah don't mean on Jonny's wall neither. You don't remember, do you, little girl?"

"Remember what?" asked Jane even though it was all coming back.

"Remember capturin' me on Cape Cod. Y'all tied me up with your lariat and marched me back to the O.K. Corral claiming Ah was Jesse James and that y'all caught me red handed tryin' to rob a bank."

Jane turned bright red. She couldn't have been more than five that summer on the beach when she played at being Calamity Jane day in and day out, insisting that everyone call her that. And there was a boy she tied up and marched back to the house, claiming he was Jesse James. She couldn't remember his name, but she called him Jesse the rest of the summer. Wracking her brains, she tried to recall whether or not it *had* been Cardozos in the grey house so near to their white one. The house *was* owned by her mother's cousins, but she couldn't remember clearly; it was too long ago. The defenses snapped on. "You must have me mixed up with someone else," she muttered lamely.

"Ah don't think so, Sarah Jane Rothko whose mother just happens to be a Krieg of the Philadelphia Kriegs who happen to have Goldsmith relations in New Orleans one of whom happens to be married to a Cardozo. We were all staying at Tante Celine's house that summer. In fact, that's the place Speed and Ah first encountered each other. Ah can't imagine why Ah didn't immediately pick up on that Krieg business, what knowin' the general as well as Ah do, not to mention your elderly siblin'. Shall Ah continue, Lieutenant or should Ah stop now?"

Jane pulled herself together quickly. "By all means, stop now. You've made your point." Her mother did talk about Cardozo relatives in New Orleans, but Jane had never met them. Or at least she thought she hadn't. But it all sounded very familiar now that he mentioned it. And Great Aunt Celine Goldsmith always had a steady stream of relatives in and out of the big grey house during the summer. Jane chewed her lip for a moment. "You're Ezra and Madeleine's son?"

He swept a gallant bow. "At your service, Cousin Krieg."

Vaguely she remembered the very beautiful Madeleine and the handsome judge who was her husband. It was all coming back to her now. "Then I would consider it as a family obligation if you would keep this to yourself, Captain Cardozo." Her voice was very low.

"Call me Jackson, little cousin, and Ah shall consider it done." He said gravely despite the smile in his eyes. "But tell me, Cousin Krieg, what'cha all hiding from?"

The name, you fool, and people like you, she thought, but resisted repeating it aloud. "I want my career to rise or fall on its own merit," recited Jane blandly, "not on a family name."

"But Speed goes by Rothko."

"Jonathan is a guy. And as much as we like to believe gender discrimination went out of vogue years ago, I think you'll agree that it has not completely disappeared. I prefer to use the lesser known Krieg name and be known for my own accomplishments."

"Or fuck-ups," he countered with a grin.

"Or fuck-ups. Whatever." Jane shrugged with nonchalance she did not feel.

Blackjack Cardozo shook his head and smiled. "What a truly small universe we live in, little girl."

"And don't call me that, either. I am not a little girl and I resent being addressed as a child. Just forget the whole thing and let's get back to work." She tossed him the micro-welder. "Make yourself useful and find a crate for this stuff." Jane turned her attention back to the shelves, refusing to look at him.

"Yes, ma'am." Jackson gave her a snappy salute. He went in search of a box and returned a moment later, placing one on the floor beside her. "Y'all need one of these," he said, taking a handful of circuit boards from a bin above her head. "And some of these widgets, too."

Jane looked at the connectors in his palm and shook her head. "That board is too far gone for those. I'll have to hard wire it."

"Can you?" One eyebrow was raised questioningly.

"Of course," she snapped. "Can't you?"

"Under duress, Ah suppose." He went back to sitting on the counter and watching her work. "How y'all getting along with Cap'n Morgan, Cousin Krieg?"

Jane rolled her eyes, certain he could not see them. "Just fine, Cousin Cardozo."

"Y'all don't find him a mite oppressive?"

"No.

"Hmmmm." He lapsed momentarily into silence. "How's Speed doing these days?"

"Just fine." Her fingers were busy sorting through silicon inserts.

"Ah heard he was in the Middle East. Spendin' time with that sweetheart of a sabra, Ah suppose."

"He and Chava are no longer seeing each other." Did everyone know about Chava?

"Hmmmmm."

That sound was beginning to wear on Jane's nerves. She could feel his eyes on her back and her nose involuntarily wrinkled. Satisfied with the pieces she picked, Jane slipped them into her pocket for safekeeping. She checked the crate beside her and tossed in a few things that looked like they might be useful on the bridge.

"Ready, Cousin Krieg?"

"Drop it, sailor!" she growled, her eyes flashing angrily as she stood erect.

"Yes, lieutenant ma'am!" Blackjack Cardozo followed her out of the supply cabin carrying the crate and grinning from ear to ear.

On the bridge, Captain Morgan and the Amitidean commander were deep in conversation with Lalo-Fa. He glanced up at their return, but otherwise ignored them. Jane slid back under the communication console and began taking it apart. She could still see Cardozo's boots directly in front of her and decided to use him as long as he insisted on standing there.

"Hand me a gamma board, please," she asked, extending her hand. The board was immediately dropped into it. "Welder." And that, too, appeared. She stripped two wires, twisted them together, then applied the welder to the joint. There was a quick flash; Jane wrapped the new connection with heat shield tape before sealing it with the hot glue gun. Piece by piece, she stripped and soldered the damaged wires until the fresh connections were secured and ready to be tied into the universal translator/communicator she ordered over from the *Washington*. When she had done as much as she could for the moment, Jane emerged, her face smudged with soot. Wiping her hands on her flight suit, she said "That's it until the shuttle arrives. I'm going to hardwire a UT-40 into the system and support it with a portapak." Her headset began to crackle in her ear. Newhouse was looking for the captain.

"Sir," said Jane quietly into Morgan's ear. "Mr. Newhouse says the *Ana'atam* is maneuvering ninety degrees." She handed him her earpiece and waited while he adjusted it.

"Morgan, here, Joe. What's up?"

"The *Ana'atam* looks a lot like she's moving into battle position. I've ordered battle stations and a code red. What do you want to do?"

"Wrap the ship, Joe. Where's the second shuttle?"

"It's sliding into your bay now."

"Can you patch me through to the *Ana'atam*?"

"I can try."

"Go ahead." Morgan motioned to Jane to stand by. As soon as he had a response from the Wa'atsi, he handed her the earpiece. "This is Captain Morgan of the *Washington* aboard the *Tical*. We request that you hold your position until we can provide adequate aid for you and your crew."

Jane translated and then repeated the Wa'atsi reply. "We need no help from you, Captain Morgan. What are your intentions in this matter?"

"We want to make sure that you are flight worthy, sir, that is all."

"What information do you have about us?"

"We have heard the allegations that you are carrying goods of questionable origin."

"There are no such goods aboard the *Ana'atam*, Captain Morgan."

Morgan frowned and considered his next move. "Are you awaiting a sister ship to aide you?" he asked although he knew they were.

"Yes, and we expect it to arrive within a solar day."

"May I offer you medical assistance, then? We have ample supplies of mattecillin, which would be an acceptable antibiotic for your people."

The Wa'atsi took his time in replying. "What payment do you wish, Captain?"

"No payment necessary. I shall send a medical officer with the medications, if that is acceptable to you."

There was another pause. "We accept your offer, Captain Morgan, but our own surgeon is in attendance. No medical officer is necessary. We shall open our shuttle bay upon your arrival."

Jane waited until the Wa'atsi commander had signed off before handing the earpiece back to Morgan, who immediately signaled the *Washington*. "Joe, get a pressure suit and take a couple of cases of mattecillin over to the *Ana'atam*. And while you're there, collect an air sample on the sly and bring it back to the *Washington*. I want it spectra-graphed for high levels of pitanite and phosphorous."

"On my way, Captain." Newhouse signed off.

Turning to the waiting officers, Morgan smiled. "If they need mattecillin, they're not going anywhere until the other ship arrives. If Joe gets the sample and it's high, we know the bowl thing is on board. Pitanite leaves one hell of a trail when it's moved."

There was general agreement from the assembly. "But what will we do if it's there?" asked Captain Louakis.

"Get it back, naturally." That the *Ana'atam* had shifted positions to face the *Washington* head on bothered the Captain, but he was reasonably certain they would not fire on the cruiser. The Wa'atsi were brash, not stupid. The *Washington* could blow them out of space with a single laser blast and they knew it. But how to get the bowl out of there intact was another story.

An Amitidean crewman arrived on the bridge with a cart carrying the equipment Jane had requested from the *Washington*. She sorted the pieces and laid them on the floor near the communication console before sliding back beneath it.

"How's it coming, Ms. Krieg?" called Morgan from the other side of the bridge where he was sitting with Captain Louakis.

"It's coming, sir. Give me another fifteen minutes and we should be back on the airwaves," Jane answered. Suddenly, bright lights came up on the bridge. There was a round of applause as crewmen resumed their stations. Jane checked for power coming into the console, but there was none according to her meter. With a sigh, she reached for the spare portapak and dragged it under the station. Deftly, she hotwired the power source into the remains of the system and switched it on. There was a loud pop, followed by a great deal of static. By adjusting the connections to the circuit boards, she was able to clear two channels. "*Washington*, this is the *Tical*," she said into her earpiece, "open channel eight and tell me what you get."

Barbara Lucas's voice boomed across the bridge. "*Tical*, this is the *Washington*; do you copy?"

There was a second, even more enthusiastic round of applause. Captain Louakis limped over to the communication console. "May I Lieutenant?" Jane flicked the switch on the portapak and nodded. The Amitidean captain spoke into the transmitter. "We most happily read you, *Washington.* Can you patch us through to Batan City on Pitan with a scrambler?"

"Certainly, *Tical.* Just stand by."

There was a brief silence before a Pitano voice responded. "What is your status, *Tical*?" asked a clearly feminine voice.

"This is Captain Louakis. We have been engaged in battle by the Wa'atsi vessel *Ana'atam* and have sustained heavy damage. Do you know the location of your vessel *Churmat*?"

"The vessel Churmat is en route to you with the battleship *Hamnah* and the carrier *Murnah.* They are twelve point seven khrams from you."

Jane did a quick calculation. "That's about three hours, Captain," she whispered.

"Have you retrieved the stolen goods, *Tical*?" asked the Pitano voice.

"Not yet, but we are confident that we shall. Please advise the *Churmat* that time is of the essence."

"We shall relay your message, *Tical.* Pitan out."

"*Tical*, out." The captain waited for the channel to clear. "What next, Ash?"

Morgan strode to where Jane was standing with Louakis. "Get me through to the *Merrimack* on the scrambler, Lieutenant."

"Right away, sir." She patched through to the *Washington* who patched through to the *Merrimack.*

"What's up, Ash?" asked Captain Coleridge of the *Merrimack.* "Why do you sound like you're in a tin can?"

"Because we're on the *Tical* with a jury-rigged com system. How far are you, Clay?"

"Oh, about three hours or so. We're on our way home." He could almost hear Morgan's sigh. "You want fighters?"

"Every one you've got." Morgan explained the situation to the *Merrimack.* "Play cavalry, Clay. Surround the *Ana'atam* and hold them tight. We can't afford to blow them up; we want what they've got. We need to move fast; the *Pu'unoti* is on its way and I want to be ready for them when they get here. P'nucha is flying that crate and he's crazed when it comes to fighting."

"Sounds like one helluva party, Ash. See you later. *Merrimack* out."

"Nice job, Lieutenant," grunted Morgan.

Flushed with relief, Jane replied "Thank you, sir."

Turning back to Louakis, Morgan shrugged his shoulders. "Now, there's nothing to do but wait."

When Joe Newhouse finally called the *Tical* two hours later, he confirmed what they already knew. The air sample revealed high levels of pitanite and phosphorous aboard the *Ana'atam*. "There are no happy campers over there, Captain," said Newhouse. "They are not in as bad shape as the *Tical*, but their engines were flamed. My guess is that they are waiting for a tow."

"Were they pleasant or nasty, Joe?"

"As pleasant as lizards can be in an arid environment. Their humidity is down to rock bottom levels and they look real uncomfortable."

Morgan frowned. "Who's running the show over there if Nish is dead?"

"Nish is deader than a door nail, Captain. He's lying in state on their shuttle deck waiting to be shipped out on the *Pu'unoti*. Their first officer, a guy named Yeynum is in charge."

Morgan looked around. "Anybody know Yeynum?" There were no takers on the question. "See what you can find out about him from the League outpost on Pitan. Ask what we're dealing with. Can you see the *Pu'unoti* yet?"

"We sense her, but we can't see her. I hear the *Merrimack* is coming."

"Yeah, they should be here soon. Keep an eye out for them and let me know when you've got them in range. Any word from Amitides?"

"The *Dramaxal* is moving as fast as it can."

"Let us know when, Joe." Morgan signed off. "'Mitri, did you figure, the *Dramaxal* was en route?"

The Amitidean shook his head. "I had no idea anyone at home knew of our predicament, but when you said you notified them, I assumed they would send someone out to us. The *Dramaxal* is a good ship, but it's not of the same quality of, say, the *Washington* or the *Merrimack*."

"But can she tow you into Pitan's orbiter station?"

"Probably."

"I hope so. I've got patient passengers, but they have to get to Jeylos as soon as possible." Morgan smiled. "But I won't leave you drifting around up here, 'Mitri, so not to worry."

Tapper appeared on the bridge, his face grim. "Not much we can do with the thruster engines, Captains. We can get them to fire, but output is pretty slim. No great speed is attainable at this point, but you can maneuver well enough to limp over to Pitan. By the way, the *Merrimack* is coming up on the port side."

"I can give you a visual, Captain Louakis," offered Jane, hitting the buttons. The screen was somewhat snowy, but the surrounding space was visible. The *Ana'atam* could be seen, head to head with the *Washington*. Behind the *Washington*, another moving vessel was detectable.

"Hail the *Merrimack*, Lieutenant."

"Hailing, sir." Jane used the scrambler and managed to reach the *Merrimack* without going through the *Washington*. "Captain Coleridge is awaiting your orders, Captain Morgan."

"Welcome to Battle of the Week, Clay. You ready to play?"

"Sure thing, Ash," laughed the other captain. "I've got twelve fighters on deck and ready to fly. Do we circle the wagons?"

"Nah, just outflank the big bugger. Do a Charlemagne and then hold position."

"My guys will like that. They've been itching for a classical tactic for a while."

"How's it going, Clayboy?" drawled Blackjack Cardozo, standing beside Morgan.

"Hey Blackjack! What the Sam Hill are you doing on the *Tical*?"

"Trying to stay out of trouble, Clay. Wish I was on the *Merrimack*, though."

"You just want a fighter of your own, Jackson. Maybe later."

"You're on."

Morgan grinned at his friend. He knew the man would just love to be in the thick of the fight where he could use his impressive fighting skills, but not this time. There was no way to dispatch Cardozo to the *Merrimack* without losing valuable minutes. "Go get 'em, Clay," he said, "and keep me posted."

"Message from the *Washington*, sir," said Jane.

"Put it through, Lieutenant."

"Captain, we're going to pull back to give the *Merrimack* room," said Newhouse.

"Go ahead, Joe, but keep a sharp eye on the *Ana'atam*. We don't know the condition of her weaponry."

"Aye, aye, Captain. *Washington* out."

For a few tense moments, all eyes were on the screen waiting for the tiny dots of fighters leaving the *Merrimack* to appear. One by one, they shot out, until twelve speeding specks were heading in the direction of Wa'atsi ship.

"Captain Morgan, First Officer Yeynum of the *Ana'atam* is hailing us," announced Jane.

"Go ahead, *Ana'atam*," said Morgan. "What can I do for you?"

"Captain Morgan, the arrival of the *Merrimack* and the dispatch of fighters constitutes a provocation."

Morgan chuckled. "No provocation intended, sir. We are merely ensuring that the goods you borrowed from Pitan are returned safely."

"We carry nothing from Pitan."

"Then you'd better check your cargo hold, Mr. Yeynum. I think you'll find a big bowl stowed there." Morgan leaned back in his chair and waited for a reply.

When it came, it was restrained. "You are in violation of League regulations by allowing the *Merrimack* to dispatch fighters."

There was subdued laughter on the *Tical*, including the two captains. It was obvious the *Ana'atam* was not prepared to engage in full battle and the *Pu'unoti* was not yet in sight. "All we are asking is that you hold you position, Mr. Yeynum. *Tical* out." Morgan switched off the communicator. "Let's see how they'll sit. I want the Pitanese ship in range before we do anything else."

Everyone relaxed for the moment, watching the fighters position themselves around the *Ana'atam*. An Amitidean crewman brought in a food cart and was greeted enthusiastically. Louakis, Morgan and Cardozo retired to a corner where they sat, heads together, evaluating the options. With a plate of *doumis* and *chakan*, Amitidean versions of salad and bread, Jane remained at the communications console, monitoring conversations between the fighter pilots and the mother ship. Finally, the *Washington* called to announce the imminent arrival of the Pitanese vessels. Jane relayed the news and the bridge came back to life.

"Tapper," said Captain Morgan into the now functioning intercom, "do we have any fire power at all?"

"One proton laser and one ion laser, but that's all," answered the engineer. "Will that be sufficient?"

"It'll have to be. Can you move us about thirty degrees portside?"

"Nope. Only forward and I don't think you want to do that. At least we've stopped drifting."

Morgan turned to Louakis. "'Mitri, how about we ask the Churmat to prepare a boarding party for the *Ana'atam*, but bring 'em here first?"

"Sounds reasonable. Lieutenant?"

"Hailing the Churmat now. Here it comes." Jane switched them onto the speakers.

Louakis made his recommendation to the captain of the Churmat. Within minutes, the shuttle deck reported their arrival.

"Hail the *Ana'atam*, Ms. Krieg," ordered Morgan.

"Go ahead, Captain."

"Mr. Yeynum, we would like to board the *Ana'atam* at this time to retrieve the Hamunah Batan."

"We do not carry such a thing," replied the First Officer emphatically.

Morgan allowed an exaggerated sigh escape his lips. "Come now, Mr. Yeynum. Are you in any position to play games with us? I think not. We are coming over NOW."

"You will not be permitted to board, Captain Morgan."

"The prepare yourselves to be blown out of the skies, Mr. Yeynum."

There was, for a long moment, tense silence. "If we allow you to board, will you permit us to depart the sector with our sister ship when it arrives?"

"Certainly, Mr. Yeynum," said Morgan easily. "We are not interested in hauling you back to Pitan for prosecution."

"We shall open the bay for your shuttle." The channel filled with static.

Morgan stretched and smiled. "Gentlemen, shall we go?"

Jane was disappointed that she was not asked to accompany the others to the *Ana'atam*; she held her tongue and said nothing.

CHAPTER 6

If it was possible, the *Ana'atam* smelled worse than the *Tical.* The stench filled the nostrils of the boarding party and it was all Morgan could do to keep from retching when he stepped onto the deck. The air was uncharacteristically dry for a species that thrived in rainforest conditions. A welcoming committee of six Wa'atsi snapped to attention on command, delivering their closed fisted salute for the visiting captains and crew. Despite the condition of the vessel, the Wa'atsi crew was impeccably attired in their dress uniforms: knee length black tabards over startling white shirts and white, thickly wrapped leggings tied with bright red bands. To the right, the late Captain Nish lay on a catafalque, his dress uniform almost entirely covered with regalia. First Officer Yeynum, in the custom of the Wa'atsi, made an obeisance to his late commander before addressing the boarding party.

"Welcome aboard the *Ana'atam*, gentlemen," said Yeynum in Wa'atsi, assuming they wore translators. "Although the object you seek was not stolen from the Pitanese, we are prepared to allow you to have it in return for the moneys paid. We were not aware of its ritual importance."

With an unobtrusive grasp, Morgan restrained the Pitanese representative, Admiral Bok. "From whom did you purchase the Hamunah Batan, Mr. Yeynum?" he asked quietly.

"From Pitano traders on the planet."

Anyone who dealt with the Pitanese on a regular basis knew of the Oracle and her temple. Yeynum's insistence that the object had been purchased opened a new avenue for further investigation. The Pitanese Admiral grew blue with anger. "No one on Pitan would sell such a national treasure! The idea is absurd!"

"Do you accuse me of lying, Admiral?" demanded Yeynum. He took a menacing step in the direction of the visitors.

"Ah think, Mr. Yeynum," drawled Cardozo, "that you have been taken in by an unscrupulous peddler. Ah'm sure our good friends on Pitan would be happy to return to their home with you in order to locate the seller for a refund."

Yeynum eyed Admiral Bok suspiciously. "If indeed we were taken in by a thief, Admiral, it is incumbent upon you to arrest and prosecute such an individual according to your laws. We would be willing to come to Pitan to testify in the event you bring this to trial."

The four officers conferred quietly. "I know you're thinking about reparations, Mitri," whispered Morgan, "but give it up."

Louakis agreed. "Cut our losses, so to speak, and get the hell out."

"Exactly. Bok, how does this sound to you?"

"Do you believe he actually bought the Hamunah Batan?" asked Bok, incredulous.

"Not exactly, but Wa'atsi are not known for their ability to lie; they bend and twist the truth, but it's always the truth." Morgan patted his back in a comforting way. "Be reasonable, Bok, do you think they would return even if you managed to produce a thief?"

"I think not, Morgan."

"This way, he saves face and you get the Hamunah Batan back. Offer him some pitanite for being such a nice guy about it." Morgan relaxed his grip on the admiral.

"Would that not mean success at blackmail?" asked Bok, furrowing his braided brows.

"Ah wouldn't exactly call it blackmail, Bok," Cardozo offered, "Ah'd call it a kindly gesture of gratitude for the return of that thing."

Morgan smiled. "And possibly a way of opening up another trade route for you, as well. That is, if you want to deal with the Wa'atsi."

"Just watch your back," added Louakis grimly.

"Look, you can't afford an interplanetary war right now, Bok, and this is the only way to get out of one gracefully." Morgan's chide hit home. Pitan was in no position to be involved with a confrontation nor did they have the fleet power to support one; that they summoned the *Tical* for assistance was testimony to that fact.

Glancing at the waiting Wa'atsi, Bok nodded his agreement.

❧

The negotiations for a specific quantity of pitanite did not take long. The Hamunah Batan was loaded onto the Pitano shuttle and the boarding party departed, satisfied, if not terribly happy with the end result. Morgan called off the *Merrimack* and wished Coleridge and his crew an easy journey homeward.

About the time everything was finished up aboard the *Tical*, the *Dramaxal* was in sight, prepared to tow the wounded ship back to Pitan for makeshift repair. The *Washington*'s personnel assembled on the shuttle deck to take their leave. Captain Louakis thanked them profusely for their assistance, promising a royal welcome when they arrived on Amitides later in their voyage.

"It is always a pleasure to find a skilled officer who also happens to be a lovely woman," he told Jane in Amitidean.

"Thank you, Captain Louakis. It has been my pleasure to serve on your ship, however brief a period it was." Jane knew she was blushing.

Blackjack Cardozo opted to go with the *Washington*. He hugged the Amitidean captain when he made his farewell. "See y'all at your place, 'Mitri. Just make sure that wife of yours has plenty of nesta waiting for this boy!"

Mitri Louakis threw his head back and laughed. "More nesta that you can down in a week, if I tell Amila that you are to be our guest."

❧

On the *Washington*, Belle Winter was waiting for Jane. "You've got to introduce me to Blackjack Cardozo! I am dying to meet him! My God, he's a veritable legend!"

Laughing, Jane promised to introduce her. As they made their way to the bridge, she told Belle about what had gone down on the *Tical*. "I'm just sorry I didn't go to the *Ana'atam* with the captain."

"Yecch, who wants to board a swampy ship like that? The humidity is enough to make you melt!" Belle huffed.

"Yeah, that's true, but it would have been interesting to go all the same." They reached the bridge and went immediately to the comm station. Jane glanced at the documentation Belle entered it into the log. "I'm going to my cabin to get a shower and change. Call a staff meeting for 1100 hours. If we can't get the conference room, we'll do it in my office."

"Sure thing," Belle gave her a quick salute. "Welcome home, Lieutenant."
"Thanks, Yeomate."

Her staff was assembled when Jane arrived, refreshed and ready to work. Sitting at the head of the table, she commended them on a job well done, and listened as each crewmate reported on the monitoring of the *Tical* incident. Cadet Peters admitted he was scared silly at the thought of live battle, but had managed to conduct himself appropriately as transcription monitor. Ngyuen, on the other hand, had botched a message from another Amitidean vessel that called to see if any more assistance was needed.

"Partially their fault, Lieutenant," explained the crewmate. "They used an unsecured channel and then got ticked off because I wouldn't answer any questions. There was no way I could tell whether or not he was on the level. I finally turned him over to Lucas and let her calm him down."

Jane assured him he had done the right thing. "It was a judgment call, and you used your best judgment, I'd say. I'll talk to Lucas and get her opinion, but I'd bet it'll be the same as mine." Jane smiled when the crewmate flopped back in his chair obviously relieved. "Who's next?"

Prakesh Chakrabati reported on the computer's inability to handle some of the code that came in from the Wa'atsi vessels. "We had to do it by hand, which wasn't too bad, except we weren't as fast as we should have been."

"Which brings me to the real reason we're having this meeting," said Jane. "The code the Wa'atsi used was simple enough if you had a handle on two different languages that are mesh-able. Where training short changes us is in general code-breaking, and the computer cannot always be counted on to mix and match the right combination; too much whim involved. The manuals we have are inadequate for our needs, therefore, we are going to develop our own." She went on to outline how the project would work; who would be responsible for which end. "It will go hand in hand with the dictionary project, but it'll mean we'll all be spending extra time in the library compiling the data. Belle, you'll be lead coordinator."

"Can we expect any help from home?" asked Belle.

"Some, I imagine, but mostly we're breaking new ground. I'll talk to someone at linguistics HQ and see what they can send us." Jane stood, signaling the end of the meeting. "I'll have packets ready in 48 hours. In the meanwhile, hit the library and start reading up on your assigned areas. Anything else? No? Good. Staff dismissed." She looked up and saw Jackson standing the doorway.

"They'll love you for this back home, Lieutenant," he drawled when the others had gone. "Ah just hope you haven't bitten off more than you can chew."

Jane gathered up her docupads "If you will excuse me, Captain Cardozo," she said as she brushed passed him.

The officers gathered for a debriefing before dinner. For the first time since she came aboard the *Washington*, Jane felt truly like a member of the officer corps. She knew she'd done a good job on board the Amitidean ship and she accepted the congratulations of her fellow officers easily. When the official portion of the meeting was concluded, Morgan ordered a round of drinks. The Jeylosian passengers joined them for the libation and Ambassador Xinthi-Ang made a point of taking Jane aside to praise her. Kora Pana-Di and Lalo-Fa vied with each other for a place at the table beside Jane, and she ended up sitting between the kora and Cardozo, with Lalo-Fa sitting opposite. Less than amused yet flattered by their attentions, she noticed a look of amusement on Morgan from his place at the head of the long table. Once, catching his stare, she felt herself redden; she was certain he noticed by the grin he was wearing, but met his eyes straight on. *I'll just bet my father knows by now,* she thought, a little peeved.

Coffee was served in the observatory with the talk strictly about events on the *Tical.* Blackjack was regaling an eager audience with the saga of the actual battle. Having already heard the details, Jane found a comfortable seat near Barbara Lucas, where the two of them could talk privately. So engrossed in the conversation were they, that the arrival of Kora Pana-Di went unnoticed until he cleared his throat in an effort to capture their attention. They immediately stood.

"I was wondering, ladies, if you would like to take a swim this evening?" he asked, looking at Jane intently.

Barbara read the look in his eyes correctly and suppressed a laugh. The invitation, most assuredly, was for Jane, not her. "Thank you, Your Highness, but no thank you," she said easily, "I've a great deal of paperwork to catch up on. If you would both excuse me." She disappeared in the direction of the coffee urn.

"And you, Lieutenant?" he inquired, his eyes intent.

"You humble me with your graciousness, sir," replied Jane in the traditional Jeylosian manner, "but I, too, have work awaiting me."

He was not to be put off. "Then perhaps you will join me for a nightcap later in the evening?"

Jane shook her head. "I think not, sir. It has been an arduous day and I would retire early."

"Then a nightcap would help you to sleep. Shall we say, oh, about 2300 hours?"

Another voice was heard. "I believe the lieutenant declined the honor, Your Highness," said Morgan tightly, his voice almost a growl.

The kora backed off. "As you wish, Lieutenant." Shoulders straightened, he went in search of more amenable company.

As soon as he was gone, Jane plastered a smile on her face, but spoke through clenched teeth. "I appreciate your concern for my well-being, Captain Morgan, but you are neither my father nor my keeper!" Spinning on her heel, she left the observatory.

"That," said Cardozo joining Morgan, "is one hell of a woman."

"Don't you start now," he snarled at his friend. "She's dangerous, Jack."

"To who? You? Me? Or men in general?" Cardozo laughed at Morgan's pinched expression.

"I'll let you know."

In her cabin, Jane stripped off her flight suit in favor of a flannel nightgown, picked up a docupad and plopped herself down on the couch, the deciphering project material sitting on the table before her, beckoning. She had barely begun, when her intercom beeped softly. "Krieg here," she answered.

"Hey, cutie, your call to HQ is going through. How come you're not up in the observatory hobnobbing with the notables?"

"Too much ego up there for this girl, Tap," sighed Jane, pulling up a chair.

"The kora?" he asked with a chuckle.

"And the captain."

"Well, you know what they call the kora in certain British circles?"

"No, Tapper, I'll bite. What do they call the kora in certain British circles?"

"Kora Pana-Di Arse." He waited for the laugh.

"Very funny. Where's my call?" Jane leaned back, very tired and not really in the mood for the call to Earth, even though she was the one who placed it.

"Patching now." There was a flutter of static before another voice was heard.

"Hiya, S.J., what's cooking?" It was Erik Bjorgstrom, Jane's mentor and favorite professor, now attached officially to the Pentagon instead of just the Fleet academy.

"Don't tell me there's someone who hasn't heard about our 'incident?'"

Erik laughed. "Good news travels fast, even from deep space. I hear you did a hell of a job on that busted comm-panel."

"Yeah, well, you do what you have to do. But I didn't get to board the *Ana'atam* with the big boys."

"Give it time, Janie, give it time. You've been in flight less than a month! What were you expecting, anyway? Instant status?"

Jane laughed this time. "Point well taken." She reached for a docupad. "Erik, what can you tell me about class-G deciphering?"

"Lots. What do you want to know?"

Jane outlined her plan and listened to Erik's suggestions for improvement. He agreed emphatically with the need for new work in the area, but questioned her approach. Like any student and teacher, they picked the idea apart, then reconstructed it until both were satisfied with the result. "Can you transmit the old manuals with your notes to the embassy on Jeylos within thirty-six hours? I don't think we can tie up the data line to do it on the ship, but I won't need it until after we leave Jeylos, anyway."

"No problemo. I'll even include Dyke's treatise on classical codes. It's interesting, if not outmoded. Promise me you'll let me look at your product before you ship if off to HQ officially."

"Natch, Erik. I'm sure you'll find a thousand loopholes to close."

"I doubt it, Janie. If you're nothing else, you're thorough."

"Thanks for the kind words, teach."

They chatted for a few precious moments about life on the *Washington*. Erik promised to give regards to old friends and by the time she signed off, Jane was feeling much better. She worked for a little while longer, until her eyes could no longer stay open and then she turned in.

∞ ⊖ ∞

Jane slept fitfully until 0330. Unable to go back to sleep, she flipped and flopped and then paced the cabin. "This is stupid," she said aloud, realizing she needed something physical to do. Digging in a drawer, Jane pulled out a canvas bag stuffed with gear. She quickly brushed her long hair into a pony tail before she tugged on tights, legwarmers, shorts and an old t-shit. With a hoodie over that, she grabbed her bag, and went to her office. There, she took out the last box to have arrived on the *Washington* and found the disc she wanted. The passageways, dimly lit for simulated night, were deserted as she made her way to the recreation deck.

The aerobics studio was pitch black, but the lights blazed on as soon as she stepped through the door. Shielding her eyes momentarily, Jane waited for the little green dots to disappear before she shed her hoodie and donned the beat-up black slippers she pulled from her bag. She slid the disc into the audio system and walked to the long ballet barre. Soon, familiar strains of Chopin filled the room. Beginning with easy stretches, Jane picked up steam until the first section of her workout was complete. She exchanged her soft slippers for box-toed pink satin ones. Centering herself in the middle of the floor before the long row of mirrors, she waited for the music to begin again. This time, Stravinsky took her away from the commonplace and into a world of grace and motion.

She danced no set choreography; her movements dictated by the music. Lost in the melody, she did not notice the perspiration trickling down her back, nor the passage of time.

Captain Morgan couldn't sleep either. He sat in his ready room as long as he could stand it and then took his files to the all-night coffee on the rec deck. A few crewmates on break were sitting about and the captain took the opportunity for informal conversation with them. Eventually, however, he was left alone.

By 0430, he had had enough coffee to float an ocean liner. Wound up but knowing he had to sleep sometime, he started back to his quarters. As he ambled along the passageway toward the cage, he noticed light coming through the window of the aerobics studio. Lights left burning bothered him, and he scowled as he reached the door, but stopped when he heard the faint strains of music. Looking in, he saw a woman, *en pointe*, pirouetting gracefully, powerfully, across the floor. At first, he was unsure of the identity of the dancer but when she paused, he could see the unmistakable glint of dark auburn hair. Enchanted, he remained at the window, watching her flow with the music, her slim body seeming unnaturally elastic, bending in ways which would cripple the unskilled. Her face, shiny from exertion, glowed ethereally beneath the mane of hair which fell despite her attempt to keep it back. The damp t-shirt accentuated every curve; there was no extra flesh on Jane, yet she was not angular. Morgan felt like a *voyeur* invading her privacy yet he could not tear himself away from the window. She represented, he knew, the ultimate danger. Morgan lingered until both the dancer and the music stopped, but before she could discover him, he fled.

At breakfast, Captain Morgan carefully kept his distance from Lieutenant Krieg. She sat alone at the long wardroom table, looking as though she had slept a perfect sleep. He greeted her but filled his plate slowly, hoping someone else would show up before protocol demanded he take the seat beside her. Tapper rescued him, bounding in like an overgrown puppy anxious to take on the new day. Joining Morgan at the opposite end of the table, the two men sat talking animatedly about something in which Jane showed no interest. The docupads on the table obviously had her complete attention, much to Morgan's relief. She finished her meal, cleared her place, and was about to leave when Tapper caught her at the door.

"Crewmate Cohen has *yahrzeit* tonight and tomorrow morning. Can you make a minyan?" The observance of a memorial was important, even in deep space.

"Sure, Tap. What time?"

"1900 hours in the chapel, then 0630 in the morning."

"I'll be there." She smiled at Tapper. It was just like him to make sure something like this was covered.

The day passed quietly and quickly. Kora Pana-Di and Lalo-Fa hung around the bridge, hawks looking for quarry. No matter what she did, she could not seem to lose them. They followed her to lunch and back, and then tried to hang about her office. She finally told them firmly, but politely, to seek their amusement elsewhere. They disappeared for a while, but soon returned bringing with them endless questions. Out of desperation, Jane returned to her station on the bridge. Captain Morgan noticed the little procession, but kept his mouth shut; she had to deal with them herself.

Cardozo was nowhere to be seen. He did not appear at meals nor on the bridge. After a while, Jane began to wonder what had happened to the dashing fighter pilot. Belle was still asking to meet him, and Jane would have been happy to oblige if she could have located him. Anything for a diversion.

At 1600 hours, a crewmate assigned to the ambassador and his wife brought an invitation for tea in their cabin. She tried to refuse, citing bridge duties, but Morgan, overheard the conversation and insisted she go. The kora and Lalo-Fa accompanied her to the ambassador's quarters, but were turned away at the door by Lady Xinthi-Ang. "Ladies only," she announced with a smile as she drew Jane through the door.

A look of relief crossed the lieutenant's face and Lady Xinthi-Ang clapped her hands and laughed. "I thought you might need a break from your two ardent admirers!"

"Thank you, ma'am. It's been a most difficult day, having them hovering about." Jane followed her into the sitting area and took a chair near the table.

Lady Xinthi-Ang poured tea. "A most wonderful custom I learned to savor while we were in England," she said, handing her a cup. "I understand you have spent time in London, too."

A friendly conversation about England was launched. As they sipped their tea and ate delicate sandwiches prepared by the ship's cook, Lady Xinthi-Ang and Jane compared British notes. When the ambassador's wife began to talk about meeting Admiral Rothko and his general wife, Jane had a tough time keeping a straight face. Apparently, her parents had impressed her hostess greatly.

"You know, my dear, you really ought to give up this charade."

"Ma'am?"

"Forgive me for speaking most personally, Jane," said Lady Xinthi-Ang reaching for Jane's hand, "but you must not be ashamed of your parents. They are lovely people and I am sure no one would penalize you for being their daughter."

Involuntarily, Jane frowned. "This must be the worst kept secret in the Fleet," she sighed. Looking up, she asked, "How did you find out?"

"I asked the right person the right question."

"Did the captain tell you?

Ladu Xinthi-Ang shook her head. "I asked one of our people and it was confirmed."

"Does Kora Pana-Di know, too?"

"I would think so. Why do you ask?"

"Well, it would explain certain things," she answered simply.

Lady Xinthi-Ang laughed gently. "Certainly not why he is attracted to you! Pana-Di pays absolutely no attention to women because they are suitable, Jane; he's strictly a collector of beautiful women. And as for Lalo-Fa, he is no better."

"So I've heard," admitted Jane with a wry smile. "But as for it not making a difference, my lady, it does. People would be on constant guard around me if they knew I was Rothko's daughter. It was always like that whenever we lived on a base. I would be invited to play with the other children, but I was never treated quite the same,' she sighed. "Frankly, I hated that part of it. So did my sister and my brothers. Finally, Mom and Dad decided we would all be better off if we lived off base somewhere."

"It must have been as difficult for you as it was for our children when they left home to live at school the first time. But luckily for us, our children chose careers in other fields where neither their father nor I had any influence whatsoever. When I discussed my granddaughter with you at the pool, it was because of this very predicament in which you find yourself. You would be in a position to understand her dilemma."

"It is true," offered Jane, "that I would understand and sympathize with the conflict she must feel, but I would stand by what I said: any encouragement from you personally would help to ease the way." She paused and considered her next remark. "Would it help if I spoke with the ambassador? Or would that be too intrusive?"

"You have already shown my lord that skill outweighs birthright. Your performance on the *Tical* had a profound effect on my husband. Do not be surprised if he should seek you out for conversation on this topic. He is a great admirer of your father and especially your mother. I am sure he will, at some point, speak with them." Lady Xinthi-Ang seemed relieved by the conversation.

A little while later, when Jane left the cabin, she felt as though she had made an ally of her own. Being in the good graces of such a powerful couple could, under the right circumstances, be a great advantage. And she believed it would have happened regardless of her parentage.

On the bridge, Captain Morgan noted the lieutenant's return, but did not question her about her visit with Lady Xinthi-Ang. He could see all had gone well by the cat-like smile on her face. As much as he wanted to ask, he restrained himself.

Belle was waiting for her with a list on messages, most of which were congratulatory. Jane sifted through them, her eye catching one from her father, commending the *Washington* on handling so delicate a situation with great finesse. She found her name listed alphabetically with the other members of the boarding party, but there was no specific mention of her. Still, it was a message from Dad. "Has he seen these?" she asked the yeomate, jerking her head in the direction of the Captain.

"Yup. He read every one and seemed to be pleased. You think there'll be commendations for you guys?"

"For what? Doing our job?" Honestly, Jane did not know. Under normal circumstances, there would be a good chance of getting a ribbon, but with her on board, her father might decide to give one only to the captain, or not at all. He would be hesitant, she was sure, to decorate his daughter her first time out. It didn't matter, though; Fleet command had taken notice and that was enough. Not wanting to dwell on it, Jane changed the subject. "Where are we in filing reports?"

"Getting there. I'll do the log as soon as you've read through this stuff." Belle glanced up in time to see Blackjack Cardozo stroll onto the bridge. "Look, Jane," she whispered, "he's here. Introduce me."

Jackson looked well rested and freshly scrubbed. Obviously, he had paid a call to the sick bay, for his hand sported a clean, white bandaged. He ambled over to Jane's station. "Good afternoon, Lieutenant Krieg." He exaggerated the drawl on her name.

"Good afternoon, Captain Cardozo," she answered sweetly. "How's your hand?"

"Dr. Vecchio says Ah'll never play the violin again."

Jane did not take the bait. She wasn't sure whether or not he actually played the instrument, but she was not up for being taken by a gag, however slight. Belle was standing beside her, waiting for the magic words. "Allow me to introduce Yeomate Annabelle Winter, a member of my linguistics staff."

With great Southern charm, Blackjack Cardozo took her hand, raised it to his lips, and held it there for a brief moment. Belle instantly turned crimson. "Ah think," murmured Jackson, "that your captain has cornered the market on lovely crewmates."

Belle was flustered. She stammered as she replied "I...uh...I....uh.... we...are happy to have you aboard the *Washington*, Captain Cardozo." He was everything she had ever expected, only better in real life.

"The pleasure is all mine, Yeomate Annabelle Winter," he drawled.

"Knock it off, Jackson," called Captain Morgan from his chair.

"You a-feared of some poachin', Boston?" Cardozo countered. The bridge crew tittered.

"I'm a-feared of distraction from duties," replied Morgan, the amused look belying his stern voice.

Cardozo turned his attention back to Belle. "Perhaps y'all join me for dinner this evening, Yeomate Annabelle Winter."

Belle coyly looked away. "Perhaps, Captain."

"About eight, then?" he asked using common time.

"We shall see." Her face still pink, Belle smiled.

He released Belle's hand. "Now, if you ladies will excuse me." He ambled over to the captain. "Are you ready to go?"

"Yeah; what the hell." Rising, Morgan pushed a button on the arm of his chair, signaling his departure from the bridge. "Mr. Newhouse, I'll be in my quarters for the next hour. Come on, Southern Boy. It's high time you earned your keep around here." The two captains strolled toward the cage.

As soon as they disappeared, Belle slumped against the desk. "I think I'm gonna faint."

"Great!" sighed Jane aloud. "A yeomate with the vapors. Just what we needed." She did her best not to laugh.

At 1900 hours, Jane made her way to the small chapel near at the end of the observatory. Unlike the main chapel which could seat over 100, this one was for private reflection and smaller religious services. Installed on the far end was a cabinet which contained two Torah scrolls used by the Jewish crewmates. Ten people were already there, insuring a proper quorum by the time Jane arrived. Tapper was standing to one side with Dan Cohen, the man observing the anniversary of his father's death the year before. Obviously a difficult time for him, Tapper had his arm around the engineer and was speaking softly to him. Jane greeted some of the others, and introduced herself to a couple of new faces. She was not surprised to see Jackson sitting in the third row conversing with one of the other crewmates; she had expected him to show up. Captain Morgan, however, was not there.

Tapper looked up and quickly counted heads. "Let's get started," he announced quietly. Everyone found a seat while prayer books were passed out. "Page 126, please," said Tapper as he took the place behind the rostrum. With a pleasant voice, he began chanting Psalm 145.

There was no denying that the words were comfortingly familiar to Jane. Even in deep space, where time was relative and not tied to the orbit of the earth around the sun, the service's progression of *mincha* to *ma'ariv* was reassuring that some things had not changed in thousands of years; the prayers and their melodies remained the same generation to generation. It was easy to lose oneself in the repetition, to put temporal matters aside in favor of more spiritual ones.

At the beginning of the silent prayer central to all services, Jane glanced up and caught Morgan standing in the shadows, swaying back and forth, arms folded. His prayer book rested against his chest, his lips moved rapidly. His eyes were closed and his face poignantly unguarded as he silently mouthed the ancient words. Jane was touched by the tender sight; he seemed a different person from the man on the bridge. She looked over to where Jackson stood with his eyes intently on the page. Close enough, Jane listened to his low Sephardic chanting, so different from the way she had been taught to pray. Like everyone else in the chapel, he covered his head, but instead of a small, crocheted *kippah*, he wore a brightly embroidered cap in the Bukharin style. With a small sigh, Jane turned her attention to the prayers, adding her own words of thankfulness for a crisis averted.

When *ma'ariv*, the evening service, concluded, Jane stopped to express her condolences to Crewmate Cohen, but not before she noticed Morgan had disappeared. Most captains made a big show of attending religious services, but like so many other Jews in the Fleet, Ash Morgan obviously regarded his religion as a most private matter. She left the chapel with Jackson and walked with him as far as the cage. There, they parted company, Jane to her cabin, Jackson to meet Belle.

CHAPTER 7

"Then what happened?" Jane asked Belle between sips of coffee. They were sitting in Jane's office having an early breakfast.

"He was the perfect gentleman. Not at all what I expected," giggled the crewmate.

"You mean he gave you a handshake instead of a kiss," countered Jane.

"Honestly, Lieutenant!"

"Don't *lieutenant* me, you brazen hussy. You wanted more and he didn't make a move!"

Belle kept giggling, her face growing pinker. "Not another word, Jane. You hear me? Not another word."

With a shrug, Jane leaned back in her chair. "Fine. Keep it to yourself, then." She busied herself with a muffin, knowing Belle was dying to talk about her evening with Blackjack Cardozo.

"Aha! I've got it! You're jealous!"

Jane lowered her head, but raised her eyebrows. "Get serious. I'm not jealous."

"That's because you've got your eye on Morgan," countered Belle, "I'd bet my last nickel on that one."

"Oh, now that's really funny. Keep going, Winter, and you'll find yourself on the night shift for the rest of the week."

"You wouldn't."

"Try me." Jane had held back long enough and began to laugh at the crestfallen face of her assistant.

They were both brought up short by a knock at the door. "Enter," called Jane.

The door slid open and Tapper appeared. "Got any coffee left?" he asked as he came in. "The stuff in my section is like sludge this morning."

Jane handed him an empty cup. "Help yourself. To what do we owe the dubious honor of your presence?"

"Staff meeting in the wardroom in fifteen minutes. Cappy Ash wants to talk about a change in the flight plan."

Belle jumped up. "I'd better get going. I've got to stop in at the comm room to pick up night logs. See you guys later." She dashed out the door.

When she was gone, Tapper dropped a disc on the desk. "Thought you might like to see this," he said, pulling up a chair.

Jane popped the blue disc into her console. Immediately, her mother appeared sitting in her office, not in uniform, but in her favorite sweat suit. Her hair was mussed, but the face was decidedly happy. "I just trounced your Uncle Chick in racquetball, sweetheart. Pretty good for an old lady, huh? I can just see your face lighting up with a big smile" She paused and Jane obligingly supplied the requisite grin. "But it can't be any bigger than the one I had when I listened to Morgan's report on the *Tical* business. You've made both your father and me very proud, Lieutenant S.J.R.Krieg. According to your CO, you handled yourself like the pro you are and, to be truthful, although we expected nothing less, we were a bit worried...parentally so. Dad would have been here with me to tell you himself, but as you probably already know, he's en route from Titan. I talked directly to him last night and he sends his love, as do your aunts and uncles. I saw everyone last night at Cousin Celia's, where you and your brother were sorely missed by the gang of twelve minus two." She leaned back and grinned. "We all talked about you both, so if your ears were burning out in deep space, that's the reason. We heard Jackson is with you. I hope you remember him from the days on Cape Cod. Celia said to give her love to her baby cousin." She paused again. "Well, I'd better get out of here before someone finds me with a crisis. I'm supposed to be having a day off. Take care of yourself, darling, and remember we love you." The screen went dark.

For a moment, Jane was silent. She wished she could have spoken directly with her mother, rather than get a pre-recorded disc, but those were regulations. "Thanks, Tapper," she said, reaching over and patting his hand.

"No sweat, S.J. I was surprised when it came in, but I'm glad it came in as classified, so no one else saw it. Actually, it came addressed to me as 'for your eyes-only.' Clever lady, your mom."

Staff officers were straggling into the wardroom when Tapper and Jane arrived. There was the typical day-after-crisis slowness in all their movements. Lucas was there, saving a seat for Jane beside her. Morgan strode in, ready for business, looking very relaxed and well rested.

"Change of plans, people," he announced as he took his seat at the head of the long table. Yeomate Winter, read the messages from home."

Belle, the only non-com in the room, stood at her place. "This is from the White House. 'Congratulations to all on an exemplary job in a delicate situation. What could easily have become an interplanetary incident was resolved with dignity for all parties involved. The return of the Hamunah Batan to Pitan is viewed as an important piece of diplomacy throughout our galaxy. Speaking on behalf of myself, the Congress, and the Fleet Command, we are pleased to issue a commendation for the entire crew of the *Washington*. Thanks to all of you for a job well done.' It's signed Jacqueline M. LaSalle, President of the United States." Belle paused as a round of applause went through the room. When it died down, she began again. "This one is from our embassy on Titan: "The Admiralty commends the officers and crew of the U.S.S. *Washington, D.C.* for their handling of the incident between the Amitidean vessel *Tical* and the Wa'atsi vessel *Ana'atam*. I am hereby recommending a commendation for the entire crew. You have all participated in demonstrating our intentions of peaceful resolution to potentially explosive situations.' It's signed Edward Rothko, Fleet Admiral." There was a second round of applause.

"Thank you, Ms. Winter," said the captain when the applause stopped. "I think we did all right on this one." His eyes told them how pleased he was with their overall performance. "Now, let's get down to business. There's been a change to the itinerary due to the need to take a slightly longer break on Amitides. The pit stop on Taapusor will be only long enough to pick up a passenger for Lomos, but the stay on Lomos will be extended to two weeks. We've got a base negotiation going on there and they want us to do a show and tell." He looked at Lucas. "That should make you happy, Barb."

"That it does, Captain!" she answered happily.

"Oh, and Barb?"

"Yes, sir?"

"You're on call, but I think we can manage without you bunking on the ship."

Lucas looked as though she was going to jump up and kiss the captain. "Thank you, sir," she said.

He smiled, then continued, "On Kotuchar, we'll be paying a social call, so make sure you all have dress uniforms and full regalia ready to go. I tell you this well in advance, because you're gonna be wearing dress blues more than usual between now and then."

Backtracking, Ensign Davies asked about the passenger coming aboard from Taapusor.

"The Vice-President of the Tri-Planet council." Morgan waited for the oohs and ahhhs to cease. "Contrary to popular belief, Dr. Tatch is not the hard-nosed ogre you've all heard about. He's a perfectly nice fellow with a penchant for drinking large quantities of brine. A typical Taapusorian, you might say. He'll only be aboard four of solar days, but we need to make a good impression. This is his first voyage on a U.S. vessel. Barb, there's a list of preferences for the Veep you can pick up later today."

The rest of the meeting was routine, nothing more. When he finished, Morgan dismissed his staff. Jane hung back, half expecting him to comment on the message from Titan; he did not. With a shrug, Jane went about her business.

Kora Pana-Di and Lalo-Fa had not yet made their usual appearance on the bridge; Jane could only hope that the ambassador or his lovely wife had managed to hold them at bay for a while. Taking advantage of their absence, Jane reviewed the night logs at her station instead of scurrying back to the office. With Barbara, she reviewed the procedures for their arrival on Jeylos. If her luck held, she would not be asked to accompany them to the planet surface. Her bridge duties temporarily completed, she told Joe Newhouse that she would be working in her office.

The number of records to be kept on a command ship, discovered Jane, could be staggering. Methodically, she entered one document after another into the data bank, taking care to correct the few errors she found. Belle stopped in briefly to drop off more reports. The silence of her office began to get to Jane; the San Diego had been a noisy place compared to the well soundproofed *Washington*. Unable to concentrate, Jane pulled a disc from her box and stuck it into the console. The music helped; the tedious work went faster to the beat of her favorite songs.

A sharp rap at her door brought Jane around from her efforts. "Enter," she called and the door slid open, revealing Jackson Cardozo leaning against the door frame. "Yes, Captain Cardozo?" she asked with a polite smile.

He ambled into the room. "Ah was wondering if you'd care to accompany me to lunch, Cousin Krieg?" he drawled.

About to say emphatically "no," Jane reconsidered. She was not in the mood for sitting in the ward room listening to the customary review of what went wrong last night, not that anything ever really did. Nor was she up for Belle's chatter. Imitating his languid Southern speech, she replied, "Why thank you, Cousin Cardozo. Ah'd be most obliged for your company. After all," she added with a twinkle, "Ah have always been dependent on the kindness of strangers." She batted her eyelashes at him.

Blackjack threw his head back and laughed. "A lover of Southern literature! What other surprises do you hide, Cousin Krieg?"

Pleased with his response, Jane looked like a cat who had gotten into the cream. "Oh, lots of surprises, Captain, but I dole them out carefully, one at a time. But here's a little one: Cousin Celia sends her love. Mom saw her last night." She pushed back in her chair and stood. "Shall we go?"

"Thank you. That made my day." He bowed and offered her his arm, which she took. "Chez Coffee, then?"

"My, what an elegant choice. Perhaps Ah should fetch my mink?" she looked adoringly into his eyes and Cardozo laughed once more.

"My dear, you are elegant enough without it."

Jane opted for a salad and an ice tea while Jackson devoured a multi-level cheese sandwich, explaining that good cheese was hard to come by in the circles he travelled. Jane was perfectly willing to listen to him expound on his adventures, some of which were legendary. Blackjack Cardozo was a great *raconteur,* but no braggart, and she found herself asking a great many questions which he gladly answered with good humor. For the most part, the cafe was empty; something especially good must have been on the menu in the mess, but Jane did not mind. Tucked away against the far wall, they were undisturbed until Morgan strolled in.

"I've been looking for you, Blackjack," he said, pulling up a chair to join them. "Your orders have come through."

"And where is the big brass sending me next?"

"Kotuchar." Morgan slid a disc across the table. "You've got a fighter battalion to train. They bought some equipment from us, and you've been elected to teach 'em how to use it."

Cardozo took disc and slid it into his breast pocket. "Hmmmm, sounds like an interesting way to spend a couple of months. Ah take it y'all gonna drop me off?"

"Yep. Think you can stand us for four months?"

He looked at Jane, then at Morgan, and considered his answer. This lady could make the time pass quickly enough but he wondered if Boston had already set his sights on her. They had competed for attention before, but this was Boston's ship; if he was interested in his shirttail cousin, this would have to be taken into consideration. Jane, her parents aside, was not a woman to be trifled with; a liaison with her would, above all else, need be an honorable one. Besides, if Jonathan ever got wind of a breezy affair with his sister, he would come after one or both of them. "Ah suppose Ah don't have a choice, Boston," he drawled, leaning back and locking his hands behind his head. "Ah will need a few things from your ship's store since most of my gear is back on the *Tical*."

"Help yourself, Southern Boy, and charge it to HQ."

"Anyone for refills?" asked Jane, picking up her glass.

"Yes, thank you," said Morgan.

"Me, too," Cardozo said, handing her his empty cup. She took it and headed in the direction of the beverage bar. As soon as she was out of earshot, Blackjack leaned close to Morgan. "Where do you stand with her and don't give me a line, Boston. She's family."

Morgan frowned and did not immediately respond. "If you're asking whether or not I've put the moves on her, the answer is no."

"That's not what I'm asking and you know it."

"The answer is still no."

"She's a beautiful woman, Boston, and with all your picayune requirements. I am surprised you're so slow."

"She's an officer on my ship, Jack, and I don't fraternize." He paused and a slow smile crossed his lips. "But I'll admit, if the situation were different..." He stopped as Jane approached the table.

"She's one beautiful lady," Blackjack said in Ladino, an old dialect they both knew well.

Jane blushed as she overheard the remark. Obviously it was not for her ears. "Here's your coffee," she stammered, setting the tray down.

They both caught the flaming spots on her cheeks, but it was Jackson who laughed, "Is there any language you don't understand?"

Jane thought for a minute, her lips pursed. "Hungarian. I cannot make heads nor tails out of Hungarian. It's a mental block." She sat down.

The two captains chuckled. "Then, we shall make it a point to learn Hungarian," announced Cardozo, looking to Morgan for approval.

Feeling decidedly relaxed, Morgan leaned on his elbows and scrutinized Jane. She seemed at ease, not the way she usually was around him with shoulders sharply back and her head erect. Here she sat, legs extended onto the empty chair to her right, sipping a cool drink, looking like she was at the college snack bar rather than on a military vessel. He could not deny that he liked her better this way. Throwing caution to the wind, he initiated the next conversation with a question. "So what has this good ol' boy been telling you, lieutenant?"

"Oh," she sighed, "he's been telling me his version of things he thinks I don't know about."

"You knew about Venice?" cried Cardozo, slapping his knee in disbelief. "Where would you have heard about Venice?"

"You told her about Venice?" Morgan's eyes were wide.

Jane laughed easily, a pleasant sound. "I heard it from that 'other guy' whose name you tactfully omitted. The one who stole the gondola in the first place."

Morgan's laugh was booming. "So Speed told you, huh?"

"There is very little my brother hasn't told me about his European tour of duty." She paused and looked at Morgan peripherally. "Including the Contessa. I recall it had something to do with a particular piece of silk lingerie."

"Is nothing sacred?" moaned Morgan, shaking his head.

"Absolutely nothing," countered Jane with a sweet grin. Once she knew Morgan was Morgenstern, she realized she probably knew more about him than he could possibly suspect.

Blackjack slapped his friend on the back. "You've been had, Boston!"

⁂

Unable to find Jane on the bridge or in her office, Belle decided to try the cafe. She stepped out of the cage in time to heard Morgan's booming laughter, the type rarely heard on the *Washington*. She came around the corner and spotted the three immediately. For a split second, Belle was seized with jealousy. The two men she admired most, the two she wanted to be with most, seemed to be having a wonderful time laughing with her lieutenant. *Now, Annabelle,* she chided herself, *don't go jumping to conclusions.* She ran a quick hand through her hair before she approached the table. "Excuse me for interrupting," said Belle as soon as she was in earshot, "but Lieutenant, I've got two communiqués Mr. Newhouse says need initialing before they go out." She handed a docupad to Jane.

"Thanks, Belle." Reading them quickly through, she signed each one before handing them back to Belle.

The yeomate half expected to be asked to join them, and waited for a moment in hopes of an invitation, but no one asked her to sit. Sticking the docupad beneath her arm, she saluted and left.

There was a moment of silence before Jackson broke it. "Perhaps we should have asked her to join us?" His voice was filled with honest concern.

Jane shook her head. "Belle doesn't know anything. I'd just as soon keep it that way."

But the conviviality of the moment was lost and Jane was the first to stand. "It's been nice, Captains, but I have to get going." She left them at the table and walked to the cage without a backward glance.

It was almost 1500 hours before Jane emerged from her office and returned to the bridge.

"We'll dock on Jeylos in the morning," Newhouse told her when she asked. "They won't have a parking space for us until then." He nodded toward the closed door to the captain's ready room. "The kora's in there. He's been in there for almost an hour. Any idea what's going on, Jane?"

"None," she replied, mildly curious. "Trouble?"

Newhouse shrugged. "Beats me. The guy marched in and asked, no demanded, to talk to the captain in private."

Just then, the captain's door slid open and Kora Pana-Di emerged, grim faced but calm. He nodded curtly at Jane before stepping into the cage.

"Krieg!" called Morgan from inside, "In here now." His voice was tight.

All eyes turned toward Jane and she shrugged, open palmed. Obviously she was in trouble. Steeling herself for catastrophe, she marched through the open door and was told to sit as soon as it closed.

"The kora has filed a grievance against you personally, Lieutenant," said Morgan, his eyes narrowed. She could not read anything in them and it made her nervous. "You wouldn't happen to know what he was talking about, would you?"

Jane hastily reviewed her contact with the kora and shook her head. "I'm sorry, Captain, but I really don't. All my dealings with the kora have been conduct befitting an officer."

"But he is mightily offended by you, Lieutenant S.J.R. Krieg. Our guest says you have neglected your duties and have been uncooperative toward him and the other Jeylosians. He says you are a bigot."

Part of Jane wanted to burst out laughing while the other part was reeling with shock. In measured tones, she replied, "Sir, I think you know that I am not a bigot. I treated the kora and the other Jeylosians with the utmost courtesy and respect. Should you choose to pursue this matter, an interview with Ambassador and Lady Xinthi-Ang would be in order."

Morgan reclined in his chair and studied Jane's face. He had caught her off guard, yet she maintained her composure. He was sure this had been bred into her by her parents: perfect calm under stress. He was just as certain that the complaint stemmed from Jane's refusal to accommodate the kora sexually; to do otherwise would have required her removal from the ship at the next port. But this was a good test case for the lovely lieutenant; it was merely the first time someone of rank hit on her which probably compounded the reasons Morgan didn't want her on the ship in the first place. Realizing he was getting perverse pleasure out of watching her squirm ever so slightly while he deliberated his next move, Morgan chewed his lip thoughtfully. "I think, Lieutenant, that perhaps the kora is upset because you refused his advances," he said slowly.

"Yes, that might be the reason." Her voice was soft, but very sure. "You were aware that the kora indicated he would like to know me in a way which we both know would be improper..." she hesitated before adding, "under these circumstances." She was on to him. If he wanted to play semantics, he would find no better combatant.

One eyebrow shot up. "And under other circumstances, Lieutenant?"

"Under other circumstances, Captain, I may have been more...amenable." Jane successfully fought the grin tugging at the corners of her mouth.

Ha! thought Morgan. *You wouldn't let him touch you under any circumstances, Sarah Jane Rothko.* Staring directly at her, he caught the glimmer of mirth in her eyes, and narrowed his in response. She sat up a little straighter in her chair. *So, now I've got you confused, do I?* He decided to take advantage of his position. "I will, Lieutenant, discuss the matter with Ambassador and Lady Xinthi-Ang and will then consider what action is to be taken. In the meantime, try to keep this guy happy." Morgan came forward in his chair. "Dismissed, Lieutenant Krieg."

Without a word, Jane left the ready room.

No one on the bridge dared to ask what had happened, but rumor abounded. Jane ignored the questioning glances and set to work at her station until it was time to return to her quarters to dress for dinner.

Officers and passengers gathered for dinner in the wardroom at 1900 hours. Jane found herself seated between Lady Xinthi-Ang and Lieutenant Ryan. The kora sat directly opposite her and throughout dinner tried to make contact with her with his feet. A tiresome game, Jane kept hers tucked beneath her own chair. After dinner, the ship's volunteer jazz band, the Tonians, was scheduled to play down on the recreation deck. The Jeylosians were planning to attend, which meant Jane would, too.

Most of the off duty crew were milling about the area when Jane and the passengers arrived in the lounge. Several tables set at a distance, but not too far from the bandstand, had been reserved for them. Morgan was there, but Blackjack came late, Belle on his arm. As they took their seats, a crewmate serving as a waiter came by for their order. Like her captain, Jane ordered a soft drink while the others opted for beer. Lady Xinthi-Ang expressed her delight at hearing beer was available.

"I must confess," she said in lilting English, "that I developed a taste when we visited your lovely country many years ago.....although I was told it was not considered lady-like at all!"

"Then you were told wrong, Lady Xinthi-Ang," offered Jackson, patting her hand. "Why, my aged grandmother is known to take a glass or two on a hot summer's night. And there is no finer southern lady than my grandmother."

Reassured, the lady went on to ask about the Cardozo family. The conversation was friendly and informal and everyone seemed to be comfortably settled except for Kora Pana-Di, who sat stone-faced beside Captain Morgan. Both the ambassador and his lady noticed his frigid expression, but it was the ambassador who frowned in his direction. Soon enough, the music started and all attention was on the make-shift stage.

The Tonians consisted of a piano, a clarinet, a saxophone, a trumpet, a bass, and drums. The group had been playing together, on and off, for years, and they were better than good. Their nominal leader, a physicist pianist from engineering, also had a degree in musicology. When Butch Kendall found he couldn't make a living playing bars, he signed on for a hitch in the Fleet and never left. Crewmate Dresher, the one who had delivered Jane's trunk to her cabin, played a wicked cornet. The bass player Jane recognized as the trauma specialist from sick bay, and the saxophone was expertly handled by the ship's baker. The drummer looked totally unfamiliar, and Jane made a mental note to find out who he was. The biggest surprise for Jane was the trumpeter, Joe Newhouse, who looked vastly different from the guy on the bridge.

The band played through two sets before a chant began at the back of the room. "Cap-tin, Cap-tin, Cap-tin," the voices rhythmically repeated. Jane looked at Morgan, who looked faintly pink around the edges of his dark beard. The chant grew louder as pounding on the tables added to the beat. At last, Morgan stood and an enormous cheer washed over the room. He strode to the stage and leapt up. Someone produced another clarinet and handed it to him. He looked at the instrument and laughed, recognizing it to be his own. He turned his back to the audience, whispered something to the band. Facing the crowd, he licked the reed, put the clarinet to his lips, and started a rollicking Klezmer number, the kind Jane used to hear as a child. The band, well acquainted with their captain's taste in music, gave him a head start until an appropriate moment, when they all joined in. From Eastern European Klezmer to New Orleans jazz, to Cajun and Zydeco, they played one song after another until a sweaty captain held his hand up.

"Let's take it down a bit, shall we people? Hey Winter, how 'bout a little blues?" Another cheer erupted from the crowd and Belle made her way to the front.

She took the microphone from the stand and warmed it up between her hands. "Ain't Nobody's Business, boys?" She gave them a downbeat and the bass player gave her an intro in return. From the very depths of her came a dark, throaty voice which Jane never would have guessed was Belle's.

The ambassador was totally enthralled, as was his lady. Lalo-Fa looked hungrily at the yeomate as she moved provocatively across the stage. The kora, however, kept his surreptitious glances for Lieutenant Krieg.

The evening's entertainment ended at midnight with a standing ovation for the band. Belle took her bows on the arm of the captain who impetuously hugged her in front of the audience. Wet with perspiration, they left the stage and staggered back to the table where Jane and the passengers were waiting for them.

"Magnificent!" pronounced Ambassador Xinthi-Ang, applauding as Belle took another bow. "Outstanding performance!"

Lady Xinthi-Ang joined her husband with applause of her own, rows of bangles clattering on her wrists. "You must sing and play for us the next time we are together!" she declared. "Between the beer and the music, I cannot think of a better way to spend an evening!"

The crowd was thinning as they strolled toward the cage. "Please, come to our cabin for a nightcap," said Lady Xinthi-Ang to the two captains and the rest of the party. Only the kora, claiming fatigue, declined the invitation.

A couple of chairs were borrowed from Lalo-Fa's cabin to accommodate the visitors. Morgan summoned a bottle of brandy from his personal store and poured for everyone. Mellowed by the wine and the music, shoes were kicked off and everyone relaxed under the watchful eye of Lady Xinthi-Ang who lived up to her inter-planetary reputation as a gracious hostess. Even the ambassador, well known for his insistence on protocol, put his stockinged feet on the coffee table. The conversation was congenial and devoted mostly to music, a subject dear to the lady's heart. Belle, thrilled to death to be included, favored them with a couple of songs she had learned during her travels on the *Washington*.

As the hour grew late, Jane found herself stifling yawns. Lady Xinthi-Ang caught her once, and smiled sympathetically but things were going too well to break up the party. Jane stayed on as long as she could, but finally, exhaustion was beginning to overtake her. As much as she hated to leave, she made her excuses and left the group to keep talking into the wee hours of the morning.

The passageway was deserted as she made her way back to her quarters. Dim night lights cast eerie shadows on the bulkhead, making Jane quicken her step. It was not that she felt in any danger, she was overtired and the sleeping ship seemed a little spooky. At her door, she slipped the card key into the slot and stepped into her cabin.

The kora was sitting on her sofa, reading one of her books. "Good evening, Lieutenant, or should I say good morning?"

"What are you doing in my quarters?" she demanded angrily.

"What, no 'your graciousness humbles me?' Where are you manners, Jane?" He smiled, but it was not a friendly smile.

"Get out of my cabin or I shall call security."

He unfolded from the couch and stood towering above her. "I think not, Jane."

She took a step backward, one hand behind her back groping for the silent alarm, but he was too fast. Grabbing her arm, he yanked her into the center of the room. "No buttons, Lieutenant. Have you no concept of the honor I am offering you, foolish woman?" His eyes bored into hers. "When we get to Jeylos, you would be wise to remain with me. I can offer you pleasures no Terran man can offer. You will be treated as a Kora-Naba, an Imperial princess, with everything a heart may desire at your fingertips!"

"I have no wish to live the life of a concubine, either yours or anyone else's. Your graciousness no longer humbles me, sir, it humiliates me and I find it revolting," she hissed, trying to remove her arm from his iron grasp. "Release me, or ..."

"Or what, Lieutenant? A scream would go unheard in this marvelous vessel. You would be unable to accuse me without sullying your own reputation, I can promise you that. I am not unaccustomed to resistance from females, Jeylosian or Terran." He let go of her arm, but continued to block her path to the door. From the folds of his robe, he withdrew a small stun gun. "I doubt if I will need to use this, Lieutenant. I think you already see the futility of your struggle."

Rubbing the place where he had held her, Jane considered her options. He was right about screaming as he was right about public accusation. On Jeylos, it would be her word against his, and there was little doubt in her mind as to how it would come out. Instinctively, she knew there had to be a way out.

The kora leaned casually against the credenza which held her communications console. With a flick of the wrist, he set it for "alert only," the setting officers used overnight. In the comm room, someone noting a tiny yellow light beneath her cabin number would assume she had gone to bed. The status would not be changed until she entered her password in the morning. "Now, Jane, no one will disturb us." He came toward her and circled her slowly, a wolf about to devour a lamb. "I would have you unfasten your hair. It was quite lovely at the pool the other night."

As her hands moved, something scratched her wrist. *The pager,* remembered Jane, thinking it was the way out of this mess. *Be cool and don't panic. Play with him to gain time.* With unsteady fingers, Jane worked the clip which held her chignon in place. Her hair tumbled down her back.

The kora reached out and touched the long, dark auburn waves. "So soft," he murmured, coming closer to her. He pushed her hair aside and touched the back of her neck with his cool lips. "I will give you great pleasure, Jane," he cooed in her ear. With a deft motion, he tore the front of her uniform, exposing her shoulders and the white lace of her brassiere. He ran his fingers over the tops of her breasts, caressing her buttocks with his other hand.

Jane waited until he stopped to check her reaction. With all the humility she could muster, she bowed her head, averting her eyes, a sign of submission. "Your graciousness humbles me, but I must make myself ready for my lord Kora." Head still bowed, she backed toward the open bedroom door.

"This is much better, Jane. You may go prepare yourself for a feast of delight, but leave the door open. I would have no secrets between us." He was certain he could win her over with passion.

She walked calmly through the bedroom and into the bathroom, making sure to leave the door ajar enough so that he could see the light, but not enough to catch her in the reflection of the mirror on the opposite wall. A green light above the sink told her that the intercom between rooms was on. Thinking quickly, she turned the shower on full blast, and then the sink spigots. She took the pager from her belt, punched in Tapper's number strung together with a second series of numbers set to repeat, and began praying that he wasn't asleep or without his beeper.

Jane stayed in the bathroom as long as she dared. When the kora called to her, she came into the bedroom where he was standing. Slowly she approached him, head still down, until she stood directly before him. His hands felt like ice as they brushed against the exposed skin. Not satisfied with his handiwork, the kora completed the task of ripping open her dress blues. Jane willed herself to stop shaking as he slid his hands beneath the torn material to fondle her breasts. His ragged breath was hot against her ear.

"Great delights," he murmured as he bent to kiss her throat.

Moving her neck, as if to give him better access to the pale, slender column, Jane turned slightly. The kora was too busy nuzzling and caressing to notice the shift in position. Suddenly, she brought her knee sharply up in the direction of his crotch, but the kora reacted swiftly; he jumped away, grabbing her at the same time, crashing onto the floor. Wriggling out of his grasp, Jane crawled toward the desk, from where she could hit the security alarm. The kora, agile as a cat, sprung, landing with a thud atop her body, pinning her down.

"The hunt has always aroused me, but the kill is always most satisfying." With his hand opened, he hit her across the face, snapping her head backward onto the floor. His mouth came down on hers. Jane saw stars, but she continued to thrash until one hand was free and she raised it, ready to strike. He caught it as it reached his face. "You grow hot with the struggle, Jane, but the fires I shall light in you shall make you burn from within." He slid off and pulled her up, only to smack her once again before pushing her in the direction of the bedroom.

Exposed and shaking, Jane allowed him to maneuver her as far as the door before she spun, ready to strike again. She jammed her elbow into his sternum, momentarily stunning the kora. Jane broke his grasp and twisted, kicking upward as she moved, catching the Jeylosian behind the knees. He stumbled, but as he went down, Pana-Di grabbed a hank of Jane's flying hair, bringing her down with him. Jane grunted but refused to scream. The kora laughed, an ugly sound, as he wound her hair around his hand to pull her head toward his. He swung his long legs over Jane, pinning her beneath him while his free hand kneaded her exposed breasts. Jane writhed at his touch; her hands, caught against her body by his powerful thighs, twisted as she tried to scratch him through the fabric of his trousers.

The kora lowered his face to hers. "I shall plow your fertile field, woman, and I shall plant my seed where I see fit. You shall open for me and in the end you will beg me to take you to my bed." He tweaked one rosy nipple and grunted with satisfaction when it peaked taut. "You see, your body already betrays you and longs for my touch."

"You are a fool, Pana-Di," spat Jane, knowing full well her words were dangerous. "I have heard you called many things, but, rapist was not one of them."

"I could have your tongue cut out for words like that, woman," he said, his voice low and dangerous.

"On this ship? I think not. Beware, you know not with whom you play." For once, Jane was glad for her parents' rank.

The kora's eyes glittered; his smile was slow, but smug. "You will make a fine consort, little lieutenant. I will take you with me when I leave the *Washington*. You will prove to be amusing amongst the more docile Jeylosian women." His mouth crashed down on hers, and his tongue assaulted her tightly drawn lips until they parted.

Jane bit down hard on the offending organ as soon as it passed her teeth. The kora roared and he slapped her hard, this time knocking her head into the side of her desk. His hand still wrapped in her hair, the kora jerked Jane upward as he stood. With his free hand, he pulled her to his chest and held her there. "I would have you on a proper bed, woman, where I can comfortably spread your legs to receive me." He pushed her toward the portal leading into the bedroom.

CHAPTER 8

Tapper was neither sleeping nor without his pager. He was sitting at his desk in his office working out an engine adjustment and he had foregone the evening's entertainment to work on the bug. When his pager started beeping, he momentarily considered of switching the damn thing off and letting whoever it was think he was asleep. But his conscience got the better of him and he flicked it on. Instead of a voice announcing the caller, all he heard was a rapid succession of long and short beeps. "What the hell?" he muttered aloud, shaking the little black box. The beeps continued. "SOS.? Who hell is this?" he snarled into the beeper, but the sender was blocking the channel. No answer, except another series of beeps. Only one person would send him an *SOS* and he slammed the thing off, grabbed his stun gun and tore around the corner stopping at the engineering command post long enough to shout for security to meet him on E-deck. Not bothering to wait for the cage, he scrambled up the emergency tube to E-deck, then barreled down the corridor until he reached Jane's door. Tapper listened for a moment, heard nothing, and then shoved his master key into the lock. The door slid quickly with Tapper's help. He burst into the room, stun-gun ready and shouted "Freeze!"

The kora jumped away from Jane and turned to face the intruder. In a deadly calm voice, he asked "What do you think you are doing, Mr. Bear?"

"Move away from the lieutenant" snarled Tapper, his gun pointed at the kora.

As Jane tried to duck into the bedroom, Pana-Di grabbed her arm and pulled her to him. His steely fingers bit into the soft skin of her rib cage. "You can see for yourself that nothing is amiss, Mr. Bear. Now, leave us." He used a voice of command, setting Tapper's teeth on edge.

"Not without the lieutenant, buddy," growled the burly chief tech, noticing her disheveled condition and the clenched look on her face.

The kora narrowed his eyes menacingly. "This is a private matter between the lieutenant and myself, Commander. You're interruption is unwelcome here."

Jane said nothing, but her eyes told Tapper everything he needed to know. "Let her go, Pana-Di."

A sudden commotion in the corridor prevented the kora from answering. Two overly large security crewmates appeared along with Captain Morgan and Blackjack Cardozo.

Jackson took one look at Jane and without missing a beat, crossed the distance between the door and the kora, and punched him squarely in the nose, barely missing Jane. The kora released Jane, covered his face and slid to the floor. Jackson caught Jane, pulled her away from the kora.

"Get the ambassador," barked Morgan. "What the hell is going on in here?"

Jane stood there shaking, unable to talk. Tapper spoke for her. "I got an S.O.S. on my pager, Ash. It looks like our royal guest was foisting his unwanted attentions on Lieutenant Krieg."

"Forget it, Captain, nothing happened," Jane said hoarsely. She tried to hold the tattered remains of her uniform across her chest.

Morgan got a closer look at what was left of her blues and knew something had indeed happened. His jaw twitched dangerously as he stared at the kora who was beginning to come around. "Get up slowly," he ordered.

The kora rose to his feet as Ambassador and Lady Xinthi-Ang arrived. One glance at the lieutenant and there was no need for explanations. "Pana-Di!" shouted the usually unflappable ambassador, his face white with rage. "You have dishonored your father's house!" He turned to Morgan. "Do with him what you will, Captain."

Lady Xinthi-Ang rushed to Jane's side. Putting her arm around her, she ushered the lieutenant into the bedroom and shut the door. Jane stood silently as the woman opened the closet and pulled out a robe to drape over her shoulders. As soon as Jane was decently covered, Lady Xinthi-Ang reopened the door.

Morgan was ordering the patrol to escort the battered kora back to his quarters where they were to stand guard until the *Washington* arrived at Jeylos. Blackjack was apologizing to the ambassador for having punched the prince in the face, but Ambassador Xinthi-Ang assured him that he was not to be held at fault. "Had it been me, I would have shot him and gotten it over with. I would not have merely broken his nose."

"Do you want to come to our cabin, Jane, or would you prefer that I stay here with you?" asked Lady Xinthi-Ang, her arms still around the younger woman.

Jane shook her head. "I'm all right, but thank you anyway."

Despite her motherly inclination, Lady Xinthi-Ang followed her husband and the kora out of Jane's quarters, but not without extracting a promise that Jane would come if she did not want to stay alone.

Tapper, Blackjack and Morgan stood in the center of the room talking softly while Jane stood apart from them. "Any idea how this happened?" Morgan asked the other men.

"None," answered Tapper. "He must have been waiting for her somewhere between his cabin and hers."

"He was here when I got back. *In* my cabin," said Jane sounding stronger than she felt. The three male heads turned and stared at her. "If you will excuse me, I think I shall go to bed. I have a terrible headache" Without waiting for them to leave, Jane started to walk stiffly into the bedroom. She stopped at the door, for the room was beginning to swim.

The last thing she remembered before the darkness was the captain shouting, and then everyone moving in very slow motion toward her.

Jane opened her eyes several hours later. She blinked several times, trying to figure out where she was. It was certainly not her cabin; nothing looked familiar until she turned her head and saw Tapper's ruddy face grinning like the Cheshire cat. "Hi," she croaked.

"Well, look who's back in the land of the living!" He reached for her hand. "How're you feeling?"

She shut her eyes and opened them again, trying to put his face in clearer focus. "I've got a terrible headache."

"As well you should," answered Dr. Vecchio coming over to the bed. She took Jane other hand and felt her pulse. "You passed out in your cabin and the guys brought you here. You took a couple of blows to the head, but I'm not reading a concussion. I've given you a sedative, but it tends to leave a bit of a throbber when it wears off."

"How long have I been out?" Jane tried to moisten her dry lips. "Can I have something to drink?" Tapper held a container with a straw to her.

"About three hours, that's all. Can you sit up?" The doctor watched as

Jane struggled to right herself. "Good. As soon as you feel up to it, you can go back to your quarters."

"Thanks, doctor." She noticed her uniform was gone, replaced by a standard issue sickbay gown. Slowly swinging her feet over the side, Jane took Tapper's proffered hand and slipped off the bed, only to fall back against it. "I feel like I've been hit over the head with a two-by-four."

"Blackjack caught you before you hit the deck, but I'm just sorry we couldn't have gotten to you before that bastard smacked you around," said Tapper. "Pana-Di Neck is confined to quarters until we dock, but Lady X wants to know when you are awake enough to see her."

Jane tried her feet again, this time with more success. The fuzzy feeling in her head was beginning to dissipate. "Can you get me home, Tapper?"

He looked to the doctor who nodded. "Sure, S.J. Just hang on to my arm." Tapper helped her into the robe she had been wearing when they carried her into sick bay.

Luckily, they encountered no one on the way back to Jane's quarters. As they walked, the lieutenant picked up steam until she was walking steadily on her own. Tapper parked himself in the sitting room when she insisted on a shower and getting dressed.

"No way am I not showing up on the shuttle deck to see them off," she said dryly. "He's not leaving here thinking he's won any sort of battle with me."

Tapper knew her well enough not to argue. Once the shower was running, he placed a couple of calls; one to the captain and the other to Lady Xinthi-Ang.

As Jane swept out of the bedroom in a fresh set of dress blues, Lady Xinthi-Ang appeared at the door. She asked for a moment alone with Jane and Tapper stepped out into the corridor to await them both.

"My lord husband and I are deeply aggrieved by the actions of the kora," said the lady gravely.

Jane sighed. "It wasn't your fault, and there was nothing you or the ambassador could have done to prevent it. What will happen to him at home?"

"A great deal, I'm afraid," she answered sadly. "This is not the first time something similar has happened; in the past, his father has turned a lenient eye on Pana-Di's activities. Now, however, there will be no slap on the wrist and a token reproach. Not only has he offended you and the people you represent, he has offended the daughter of someone our Emperor holds in great esteem. I spoke incorrectly earlier; the kora did not know you are the daughter of Admiral Rothko. That has been amended" She paused, as though what she had to say was even more painful.

"Is there something else, my Lady?"

"Yes, Jane. My lord husband will now refuse permission for Pana-Di to marry our eldest granddaughter. The betrothal was to be announced at the next eclipse of our moon."

"Oh," said Jane. "I'm terribly sorry. This must be a great blow to you personally."

Lady Xinthi-Ang smiled, but her eyes were sad. "Our eldest granddaughter fancies herself quite in love with her cousin, but the marriage was more a political union. Now, however, we will not permit her to wed Pana-Di under any circumstances. No Jeylosian would allow a daughter to marry a man prone to violence. It is not acceptable on Jeylos any more than it is on your home planet. There will be great public humiliation for the kora in this."

There wasn't anything left to be said. Jane embraced Lady Xinthi-Ang.

"May your days be filled with the laughter of another generation of happy children," whispered Jane, feeling for the gracious lady.

"And may you find the missing piece of your woman's heart." Lady Xinthi-Ang held Jane's hands in hers. "I know we shall see each other again, Jane Krieg, daughter of the House of Rothko. Until then, be well." She left Jane alone in the cabin to compose herself before going to see them officially off the *Washington*.

On the deck, the Jeylosians' luggage was being loaded into the shuttle. Ambassador and Lady Xinthi-Ang were standing with Captain Morgan talking quietly. The kora stood apart from the others, his nose neatly taped across the bridge, two patrolmen nearby, but not close enough to appear to be guarding him. Jane sailed in, under her own power, but Tapper stayed nearby; she was still unusually pale.

"Are you all right, my dear?" asked the ambassador, the concern clearly visible in his eyes.

Jane nodded. "I wasn't hurt, only shaken." Her cheeks reddened a little.

"Dr. Vecchio said you slept well," said the Captain. "I guess the sedative worked."

Lady Xinthi-Ang looked to her husband, who nodded, and then to

Jane. "We would be pleased, Lieutenant, if you would be our guest on Jeylos when you next have leave. We would like you to see a better side of our nature."

"Thank you, my lady, that would be very nice. I have enjoyed my time with you and the ambassador." Jane smiled. "Your graciousness truly humbles me."

"It is your graciousness in the wake of such a humiliating event which humbles us, Lieutenant," said the ambassador. "You bring great honor to the House of..." he paused, "of your parents."

A crewmate approached and announced the shuttle was ready to depart whenever they were. Captain Morgan was surprised when, after Jane spoke the traditional Jeylosian parting words, both Ambassador and Lady Xin-thi-Ang bowed toward her as a sign of respect and admiration, but she blushed all the same.

Standing with the other officers, Jane watched as the passengers went from one to the next, thanking those who had helped to make their journey a pleasant one. Suddenly, the kora came back to the end of the line where Jane stood beside Tapper. At first, she thought he would apologize for his behavior, but she was wrong.

"Come with me and you shall be an Imperial lady," he whispered as close as he dared. "I offer you delights you can only imagine,"

Jane smiled graciously as if nothing had ever happened. Tilting her head close to his ear, she breathed softly and was rewarded with a smile. "Drop dead, Pana-Di." she murmured in English.

He pulled abruptly back, and then began to laugh harshly. "What a consort you would make, lieutenant." He strode toward the shuttle.

Jane didn't like the sound of his laughter; it was bitter and unpleasant and it made her cringe.

"Did you really say what I thought you said?" asked Tapper when the shuttle was gone and the formation dismissed.

Jane only smiled. "Come on, big boy, how's about buying me a cup of coffee before we hit the bridge?"

Few knew what had happened the night before and those who did weren't talking. There were rumors, most of which missed the truth by a mile, but those in the know were neither verifying nor denying the stories. Blissfully ignoring the tales, Jane concentrated on her deciphering project. When the captain returned from the planet's surface, he would have with him the packet she had requested from Erik Bjorgstrom. Her staff assignments were now complete and she wanted to be ready to distribute the necessary information as soon as it arrived. Belle came to ask her if she wanted to go to lunch, and Jane agreed, so long as they went to the cafe.

The cafe was unusually crowded; Belle explained it was because the cook had creamed chicken on the crew mess luncheon menu and no one actually liked it. They waited for a table to clear before going to the window to place an order.

"I heard there was a security breach last night," remarked Belle, loading her hamburger with ketchup and mustard.

"Yeah?" Jane kept her voice calm and casual. "What happened?"

"I don't know. I was hoping you did. Didn't you hear anything about it this morning on the shuttle deck?"

"Not a word." She wasn't exactly lying.

"All I heard was that there was an alarm on E deck, so I figured, since you live there, you might know. Something must have happened because the kora had a tape on his nose this morning and it wasn't there last night."

"I must have slept through it," said Jane as she took a salad from the crewmate behind the counter. "Well, if it was anything major, I'll hear about it at staff meeting." She let the subject drop.

No mention of the security breach was made at the meeting held immediately upon Captain Morgan's return from Jeylos. Morgan thanked them all for their efforts in making the trip from the *Tical* to Jeylos as calm and quiet as possible before detailing their call on Amitides.

"There will be a reception for the entire crew and everyone except a skeleton crew will be required to attend. I know how good the booze on Amitides can be, but the two drink limit remains in effect. Anyone caught overindulging will find themselves swabbing the shuttle deck. Make that clear to your personnel, ladies and gentlemen." Captain Morgan tolerated no alcohol abuse on his ship and he was not above assigning a ranking officer to swab duty should it be necessary. The rest of the meeting was mercifully brief and he quickly dismissed them.

In her office, Jane's linguistics staff gathered to go over the transmission from HQ. They were excited about venturing into an area which had, for so long, been neglected. Each staffer was handed a packet describing a specific piece of the project and individual deadlines. Armed with their assignments, they went off in different directions to begin work, like children off on a scavenger hunt. When they had gone, Jane set to work on the day's logs and communiqué. Nothing was out of the ordinary, no indication that something extraordinary had happened the night before. She wondered what the captain had recorded in his private log as well as what he had transmitted alone in his ready room prior to leaving for the Jeylos surface.

Newhouse came by, sticking his head through the open office door. "Hey, Jane," he called cheerily, "the boss says to take the rest of the day for yourself. You deserve it and..." he dropped his voice to a whisper, "you probably need it after last night."

She glanced up and smiled. "Yeah, I probably do. Thanks, Joe."

"No sweat, Jane. See you later." He disappeared again.

Jane finished what she was writing and shut down her terminal. *Maybe a swim,* she thought as she gathered up a couple of discs to take back to her quarters.

She never made it to the pool; Jane slept instead. She had underestimated how bone weary tired she was until the bed appeared in her range of vision. Carefully hanging away her one remaining clean dress uniform, she slipped into a robe and lay down, only to be asleep in seconds. She slept through the day, and when she awoke, the clock on the nightstand glowed 1700. Hungry, but not in the mood for company, she pulled out her supply of peanut butter and crackers; it would have to do for now. Maybe later she would wander down to the all-night coffee for something more substantial. At her desk, Jane made up a stack of Skippy covered crackers before sticking a comm disc into the console; she hadn't done a message home in several days and now was as good a time as any to do it. Her parents, first, then Jonathan, then the other sibs. It didn't take her long; her editing of the events was judicial. Because comm disc were private, but unclassified, there was no way to tell anyone about the kora without running the risk of it becoming public domain. And besides, she was fairly certain that her father would hear about it through secured channels.

Letters finished, Jane tried to work on her project, but the long sleep had made her restless. Changing into a loose-fitting jumpsuit, she went back to her office. Waiting for her on the terminal there were several messages Tapper had checked in, Belle needed a question answered about Des-

Marais codification theory, there were a couple of crew announcements including one for Sabbath services scheduled for the morning, and, lying on her desk, was a handwritten message from the captain, asking her to stop by his cabin that evening in the event she even got the message.

Jane had forgotten that on Earth it was Friday night, the start of the Sabbath. Shutting down her terminal, she put everything away. When she could avoid it, she did no work and nothing there required an immediate answer. She left her office and went back to E-deck.

The captain's door was closed, but the small green light glowed beside it, indicating he was awake and a visit was permissible. Jane knocked, and the door slid open, revealing Morgan sitting on his sofa, a large, black book open on the low table in front of him. As she stepped inside, she noticed the tiny *mezuzah* on the inside of the frame. Automatically, she touched the silver casing and then put her fingers to her lips.

The cabin's decor suited Morgan to a tee: clean, modern, yet warm and comfortable. A bookcase occupied one wall, filled with real books, not little disc boxes like most people had these days. The large desk had decidedly old-fashioned Moroccan red-leather accessories, the kind her grandfather had in his chambers. There was a credenza behind the desk, on which sat a number of odd objects as well as a row of pictures in leather and brass frames. The sofa, two armchairs, and the four Breuer chairs at the round table were done in soft, sand colored leather. But what caught a visitor's eye was not the fine furnishings of the cabin, but the short expanse of wall between the bookcase and the bedroom door completely covered in childish artwork, a gallery to the growing skill of one child. There were drawings of people, lopsided with one big eye and one small eye, with sticky-outy hair, the marks of a toddler with his first crayons, as well as painstakingly done renderings of space ships and landscapes. The father had saved it all. The painting which hung on the opposite wall, an impressionist scene of Cape Cod, paled by comparison. Jane stood looking at the conglomeration of color until the captain said quietly, "They're from my son." Reddening slightly, she looked at him.

Morgan was wearing the same djallabah he had been wearing the night he joined Tapper and Jane on the bridge during her first watch. He also had on a pair of glasses, something which, for an unknown reason, surprised Jane. She also noticed he was barefoot. The image he projected contradicted the way she thought of him: all spit and polish in whatever uniform he donned. Instead, this was a man at ease, casual and comfortable in his surroundings. Finding her voice, she said "You wished to see me, Captain?"

"Please sit down, Lieutenant." Morgan pressed a button and the door slid shut. He marked his place in the book and closed it as he waited for her to take a seat in the armchair to his right. He watched as she pulled up her loose hair as she sat; it was almost long enough to get caught beneath her. He noticed how tiny she seemed in civvies, although she was not really short at all; just slender. Her face was clean scrubbed, fresh and glowing, and for a moment, he understood why the kora wanted her so badly. She seemed to be well recovered, judging by the disappearance of the dark circles which had been beneath her eyes when he last saw her at the staff meeting. Realizing he was staring at her, he busied himself moving his book.

"Sir?" asked Jane, tired of waiting for him to say something.

"I wanted to apologize, Lieutenant, for the drubbing out I gave you yesterday. I underestimated the potential danger to you personally."

Jane was immobile in the chair. Part of her wanted to read him the riot act, yet the other part completely understood his position. But she was not going to absolve him completely. "We both underestimated the kora, sir." She stopped and chewed her bottom lip. Jane had questions, but she was unsure of the propriety of asking them. Pulling rank in her head, she decided to fire away. The worst he could do was not answer. But Morgan beat her to it.

"I'm sure you have several questions, Jane, which under normal circumstances I would not answer. However, I cannot dismiss the fact that you are Admiral Rothko's daughter and will find out one way or another."

"What will happen to him?" was the first and most obvious one.

"I believe you already know that Ambassador Xinthi-Ang has called off the betrothal between the kora and his granddaughter. I met briefly with His Imperial Majesty on Jeylos and he was furious with the ambassador's report. Pana-Di is currently under house arrest; rape is a capital offense on Jeylos and the only thing keeping the kora alive right now is that he did not complete the act. Had you been merely a crewmate, how hard the father would be coming down on the son is questionable, but your *yichus* is playing an important role here." He used the Yiddish word for lineage. "I know how you feel about using your parents for leverage, but it could not be prevented." Morgan voice showed honest concern for her feelings. "The ambassador felt it was important your position be made clear to the Emperor."

"Does my father know?" she asked although she suspected the answer.

"By now, yes. I sent out scramblegrams both before and after I went down to the planet. But I made it very clear to him that you were unharmed. I expect you'll hear from him directly at some point. Should he contact us while we're in flight, Tapper and I will arrange for you to take the call privately, on a secure channel." He noticed the way she kept her hands quiet in her lap and her face gave away nothing. *Tough lady,* he thought with grudging admiration.

"What about the crew here? What's the scuttlebutt?"

"Not much, actually. Some know there was a security breach, but no one who was there is talking. We lucked out, Jane," smiled Morgan, trying to get her to relax even a little. "We'd like to keep this as quiet as possible for obvious reasons, since it's being handled on the planet."

"Thank you, Captain. I'd prefer it that way."

"How are you feeling now?" he asked,

Looking away from his steady gaze, Jane shrugged, aware that her cheeks were flushed. She was embarrassed by the question; it indicated that he thought she might have been weakened by the attack in some way. "I'm fine," she mumbled.

Had she been anyone else, anywhere else, he would have leapt across the table and taken her in his arms. He wanted to protect her although he knew that was the last thing she wanted. His concern was not only for a member of his crew who had been injured; he could not deny the growing feeling he had for her. It did not help that she was Rothko's daughter. She was usually in total command, but he could see her mask slipping and it was painful to watch. He wondered if she would cry in front of Tapper and a sharp pang of jealousy raced through him. He wanted to be the one to comfort her. Shaking it off, his voice was a little gruff when he spoke again. "Take tomorrow off, Lieutenant. It's Shabbat; I don't want to see you anywhere near the bridge."

"Thank you, Captain," said Jane, marshaling her strength to the best of her ability. She stood and was about to go, when she turned back to him. She had noticed the book he was pondering when she came in. "I never really appreciated *Pirke Avot* until I took leadership management in Super School." Her eyes twinkled just a little. "*Shabbat shalom*, Captain."

When the door slid closed behind her, Asher Morgenstern chuckled softly. She was going to be, just as she said, just fine.

CHAPTER 9

On a high-backed gilded chair, King Mustafa IX of the Hashemite sat rubbing his hands together in an effort to keep warm while he silently cursed Ali Hassan for insisting that the meeting take place in the middle of the desert. Although it was still October, the night air was bitterly cold. He chided himself for allowing his mind to wander and turned his attention back to Ali Hassan, Syria's President for Life, and his Iraqi counterpart, Gamal Ramadi. Both were droning on and on about the necessity to wipe the Israelis off the map of the Middle East.

"How can you sit there, Mustafa, as silent as a mouse, when the waters of the Jordan are being diverted at this very minute?" demanded Hassan, pounding his hand on the arm of the chair for emphasis. "Your own people are being threatened!"

He picked a non-existent piece of lint off the sleeve of his caftan. "Hardly, Ali Hassan. The waters of the Jordan are well shared between the two nations."

"But do you not pay for the water you take from your own river?" Ramadi barked. "Do you think this is the way it should be?"

"Without the Israeli's dam and their irrigation expertise, my friends, I'm afraid we would be in far worse condition than we are. I have no quarrel with the Israelis." His patience was sorely tried.

"Your father is spinning in his grave and demanding justice from Paradise, Mustafa," sneered Hassan. "He would be ashamed of the weakling he has spawned."

"My father managed only to irrigate the western sector with the blood of his own people. There is no honor in murdering children."

"Only Israeli children," spat the Iraqi.

"NO CHILDREN!" Mustafa was surprised at the vehemence in his own voice and he immediately softened. "For two decades we have had a relatively easy peace with the Israelis. They have offered us much in exchange for very little."

"They still hold Jerusalem," snarled Ramadi.

"And we travel to and from the Holy City with ease. My people are content with the way things are and I see no reason to embroil them in another frivolous war."

Ali Hassan jumped from his chair. "You are worse than a weakling, Mustafa, you are a fool."

The king sighed dramatically. "Again, I must disagree with you, brother. I am not a fool. I am simply a man who must look out for the welfare of his people. Our economy is showing the first true signs of recovery after years of empty coffers and I am not ashamed to tell you that I put that ahead of any endeavor which will empty my treasury. I have no argument with the Israelis and will not manufacture one for your benefit." He stood, feeling the eyes of both men boring through him. "I shall bid you good-night, gentlemen." He left the tent, proud of not being drawn into their ill-conceived jihad.

"We don't need him or his camel militia, Ali," spat Ramadi. "We've got friends in higher places who will provide us with the weaponry we need." He rolled his eyes heavenward.

"Bah! You and your extra-terrestrial friends, Gamal. They will bring us nothing but trouble, mark my words." Hassan took the chair Mustafa had vacated. "They are not all together altruistic, those friends of yours. They want something, and we don't know what it is."

"You are too suspicious, my brother. The only thing they are looking for is a foothold on our planet which they can control without being tied up in knots by the United States. You read too much into it."

Ali Hassan shook his head. "Trouble is coming, Gamal, but it's too late now to stop. How soon can you bring your troops into Syria?

CHAPTER 10

Captain Louakis and his crew arrived only a day before the *Washington* docked on Amitides. The *Tical*, rudimentary repairs underway, was left at the Pitano station with a technical crew shipped out from the home planet. Eventually, when she was space-worthy, the *Tical* would return. Meanwhile, Mitri Louakis was waiting for the *Washington* at the docking platform along with a number of government officials, the League of Planets Consul and the American ambassador.

The crew of the *Washington* attended the memorial for the fallen crewmen of the *Tical*. The Amitidean funeral was a somber, but hopeful event, with families taking final leave of their loved ones with kind words and offerings of fruit. Blackjack Cardozo was asked to speak on their bravery under fire and he did so, eloquently praising the sailors who had fought to return an object precious to a planet not their own. The Pitanese ambassador posthumously decorated the crewmen, giving each family a leaf-shaped medal, the highest military honor Pitan had to offer. Captain Louakis, Blackjack and the Pitanese ambassador together approached the families to express their condolences.

Jane stood with the members of the boarding party trying hard not to cry; it was always painful to watch grief stricken families say goodbye. The Amitideans were no different from families on Earth, and she had, over the years, attended enough funerals to know and understand. Mothers and fathers lost sons, wives lost husbands, and children lost fathers, yet they all managed to keep their heads held high, dignity above all else as befitting an Amitidean. Only when the last body was lifted on the pyre, was the fire set and the hauntingly beautiful elegies were sung by the families alone.

In the evening, when the skies turned lavender with the setting of the

Amitidean sun, a dinner was hosted by the Amitidean government in honor of the *Washington* at the Great Hall of Tyros, the capital city. An enormous structure, the room itself was lined with sculpted columns, each depicting an important event in Amitidean history. The members of the boarding party were asked to sit at the high table with Louakis and the Pitanese ambassador. Jane found herself wedged between Morgan and Cardozo, but she yearned to be at the table where Belle sat with Lucas and Newhouse. Morgan spent most of the time talking to Mitri Louakis while Blackjack was busy with the wife of the Pitanese ambassador who he seemed to know very well. Feeling left out, she picked at the delicacies set before her.

Suddenly, the doors of the hall swung open and the sound of tinkling bells could be heard from outside. The room quieted as a troop of dancers filed in, all dressed in shades of blue, each carrying a basket filled with fruits and flowers. "The Dance of Renewal," whispered Blackjack to Jane, but she already knew. The soft music grew louder as the women began to sway, baskets high above their heads. Slowly, they circled the entire room before separating and circling each table. At strategic points in the music, the baskets were lowered and guests were expected to partake of the proffered fruits.

The faces of the dancers were covered with gauzy veils to represent the indiscriminate nature of death. When the baskets were emptied, the pace of the melody picked up in speed and discordancy; the dancers gathered in the center of the room to begin a complex series of steps and pirouettes. Faster and faster they moved until the music crashed to a halt and the women slid to the floor. In Amitidean fashion, there was no applause, but everyone in the room rose.

One by one, the dancers stood to face the appreciative audience. Then they approached the dais where Jane sat. "We would have her!" said the apparent leader, pointing a finger at Jane.

"Then you shall have her," answered Louakis, noticing the small smile tugging at Jane's lips.

Without a word, Jane left her place and joined the dancers. The leader dropped a veil over Jane's head, took her by the arm, and with the others gathered around her, led the lieutenant from the room.

"Where are they taking her?" hissed Morgan, sounding closer to panic than he would have liked.

Louakis laughed. "Do not worry, my friend; your lieutenant will be safely returned to your ship before you leave." He was amused by Morgan's look of concern. "Judging by the lieutenant's reaction, I think she already knows what she is in for."

"And just what is that?" inquired the captain with a raised eyebrow.

"The ladies have invoked the ancient rite of Pyakos, a sort of sisterhood for women with special talents," explained Mitri. "They will take Lieutenant Krieg to a villa somewhere near the sea and induct her into their society. It is," he added with a smile, "a great honor, especially for an outlander."

∽⊖∽

In the vestibule of the Great Hall of Tyros, Jane's laughter echoed. "Eppi!" she cried, hugging her old friend, "I can't believe you did this!"

"And I can't believe it was you who stepped off the *Washington* this morning, Sarah Rothko, without letting me know you were coming!" She stepped back and looked at the lieutenant. "And what is this S.J.R. Krieg business, anyway?" she asked, pointing to the nameplate on Jane's uniform.

Jane explained and Eppi Spiratai nodded in agreement. "So it works out for the better, this way. No one, or at least most people don't associate me with them and I get to be accepted on my own terms."

"Not an unwise thing, Sarah." Eppi accepted her cloak from one of the other women. "Let us leave this place and go somewhere where we can have some fun." Bundled against the chill of the evening in a borrowed cloak, Jane left the hall amidst the company of dancers.

Belle saw her leave and wondered where Jane had been taken by the Amitidean women. After the dinner was ended, she sought out and found Captain Cardozo standing with a group of men; he seemed engrossed in the conversation, but not so engrossed that he missed Belle's approach. He quietly slipped his arm about her waist as he finished his conversation and as soon as he could break away, he gallantly offered to show her the sights. Captain Morgan went with Tapper, Newhouse and Dr. Vecchio in search of a particular cafe where the music played on until the wee hours of the morning. The rest of the crew could fend for themselves during their brief liberty on the planet surface.

∽⊖∽

The next day, Morgan and the rest of the *Tical*'s boarding party were invited to lunch at the home of Mitri and Amila Louakis. They assembled on the ship and went together, but if Jane's absence was noticed, no one commented. Scuttlebutt was that she was whisked away by the dancers because she was being honored for her part in the makeshift repairs to the *Tical* while others insisted it was because she was the prettiest officer on the dais. In either case, no one was certain why she was selected and the answer to the question would only be known when the lieutenant returned to the ship.

Upon their arrival at the elegant villa, Blackjack swept the very beautiful Amila Louakis into his arms and waltzed her around the vestibule. "Ever lovely, ever tempting," murmured the handsome fighter pilot into her delicate ear.

"Unhand my wife, you cad!" demanded Mitri, although he thoroughly enjoyed the tinkling of his wife's laughter as she danced in Cardozo's embrace. Once, a long time ago, he would have viewed this with great jealousy, but Amila had, after all was said and done, chosen him instead of running off with the dashing Terran.

The lady of the house finally broke away and led her guests into the solarium where a table was laden with native Amitidean delicacies. When everyone was seated, she noticed a single empty place and smiled. "I see that we are missing one, Captain," she said. "Am I correct to assume Lieutenant Krieg is still in Pyakos?"

"I guess so," muttered Morgan. He wished he knew exactly what that meant and where Rothko's daughter was.

Amila patted his hand sympathetically "There is no need to worry about her, Captain. She is in good hands. I should be with them myself, but attending to my husband's rescuers takes precedence." Her eyes twinkled knowingly.

"What can you tell us about the ritual?" Commander Lucas asked; she knew a bit about it, but was hoping for a little more information she could record in her data banks.

"Pyakos is for our women," Amila explained as she began passing the platters around the table. "The dancers you saw last night are called Pyakatyat, and they serve to remind us of the seasons of our lives. I am Pyakatya, although I am growing rather old by their standards. All Amitidean little girls wish to be Pyakatyat, but only the most graceful are chosen. They lead perfectly regular lives, but when the need arises, they go." She glanced at Morgan and smiled. "Much like cheerleaders on your planet, but without the pompoms." This elicited the desired laugh from the guests.

Her curiosity piqued, Dr. Vecchio asked, "How was Jane chosen for such an honor, Madam Louakis? It was my understanding from Captain Cardozo that only Amitidean women were permitted to participate."

"Amila, please," said the hostess pleasantly. "Madame Louakis is the mother of my husband." She noticed Mitri's smile and approved. "Apparently your lieutenant has been here before and has had contact with the Pyakatyat, for no one who was unfamiliar would have been asked."

"Just what will they do to Lieutenant Krieg?" asked Morgan, helping himself to a large quantity of nesta, a wonderful concoction of local fruits long marinated in potent wine.

"Oh, nothing drastic, Captain," laughed Amila. "They'll sing and dance, teaching her what they can in such a short time, and then they'll sit about for hours telling stories and eating. We like the eating part best," she added with a sly wink. The conversation was skillfully maneuvered in another direction; there was only so much Amila could, or would, say about Pyakos.

⁂

The Pyakatyat deposited Jane at the *Washington* shortly before dawn the next morning, leaving her with the traditional gifts of a costume and an enormous basket of fruit. Struggling beneath the heavy load, Jane managed to board the *Washington* with minimal aid from the security guard. She lugged her gifts to her quarters without running into anyone, dropped the basket in the middle of the floor, checked her schedule to make sure she didn't have early bridge duty, and threw herself across her bed, not bothering to remove her clothes. Instantly, she was asleep.

She did not awaken until the powerful engines of the *Washington* were firing up, thrusting against the planet's surface. Sitting upright, she looked at the clock and groaned, holding her aching head in her hands and waited until the ship had passed through the atmosphere and righted itself for steady flight. "Too much nesta," she moaned as she lurched toward the shower.

The hot water, when it finally flowed, helped considerably. She reluctantly washed off the elaborate paintings the women had done on her arms and torso until only a faint blue tinge remained. They were skilled artists and it seemed a shame not to preserve their work, but there was no way to avoid the inevitable. Jane dressed, popped a couple of ibucetaphal to help with the headache, and slowly made her way to the bridge.

"Well, look who's here," announced Barb Lucas when Jane emerged from the cage. "Are you back in the land of the living?"

"I think so," answered Jane, trying to keep her head steady. The pounding, while somewhat diminished, was ongoing.

Morgan stuck his head out of his office door and allowed himself a grin when he saw Jane. On the surface, she looked all right, but the dark circles under her eyes gave her a raccoonish appearance. *Serves you right,* he said to himself. "Good morning, Lieutenant. Did you have fun?" He was teasing and enjoyed watching her squirm.

"Oh, yes, I certainly had fun," replied Jane, forcing a smile. By the way he was looking at her, she wondered how bad she really looked. She took her place at her station and began working on the logs in spite of the queasiness in her stomach. With any luck at all, he wouldn't notice her hangover and she wouldn't end up swabbing the shuttle deck.

A couple of people dared ask her about the dancers; everyone was decidedly curious about where she had gone when she was taken from the Great Hall of Tyros before the dinner ended. Jane answered as best she could, keeping in mind the oath of secrecy she vaguely remembered taking at some point during the Pyakos.

"Pyakatyat make the best lovers," Blackjack told her when he cornered her alone in her office later in the day.

She looked at him curiously. "I take it you know through personal experience, Jackson?"

"A gentleman never tells, especially when a lady asks," he replied with a grin.

"Then why bring it up?"

He took the chair opposite her desk and sat, stretching his long legs before him. "Janie, you are far too serious. Relax, cousin, and enjoy the honor bestowed upon you!"

She wrinkled her nose in his direction. "I am perfectly relaxed, Jackson, if you must know. It's just that I have a headache."

"Still?" He dug into his pocket and produced a small box. Opening it, he handed her two tablets. "Amitidean equivalent of aspirin," he said, "works wonders on the diabolical effects of nesta. You really ought to learn your limit if you're gonna be Pyakatya."

Pouring herself a little water from the carafe she kept on the desk, she gratefully accepted the tablets and swallowed. "Anything to get rid of this headache," she muttered, holding her head in her hands.

He leaned back and laughed, knowing the sound would rip right through her aching head. "Exactly how much nesta did you have, Cousin Krieg?"

"Oh," said Jane, still holding her head, "four, maybe five bowls."

"That's like drinking a fifth of bourbon...straight," he roared despite her feeble effort to quiet him. "Little girl, you have one mighty hangover! Are you still blue?"

"Out!" She picked up her head and glared at him The last thing she needed was someone sitting around watching her be miserable. He was still chuckling as the door slid shut behind him.

Whatever he gave her worked; within the half-hour she was feeling better, well enough, in fact, to try eating something in the wardroom. The cook, pleased to have been given carte blanche at the local fresh air market by the grateful Amitidean admiralty, had prepared a feast of fresh produce for the *Washington*'s crew. In the wardroom, he had a long buffet set up where the officers could help themselves to several different types of salads and a variety of cooked vegetables and meats. Jane took some raw vegetable on her plate, forgoing the more elaborate dishes. As tempting as some of them looked, she was not sure her stomach was up to it quite yet. There was an empty seat between Barbara Lucas and Ensign Davies. Sliding onto the seat, she tried to look as pleasant as possible.

"So," whispered Barb discreetly, "what color is your stomach?"

"Inside or out?" asked Jane, picking up a carrot-like spear.

"Out. I hear they like painted women on Amitides." She suppressed a giggle.

Jane closed one eye while raising the other brow. "Sorta bluish-purple at the moment. But it's fading."

Barb choked on a laugh. "It should wash off in a month or two, if you keep scrubbing."

"Thanks, I'll remember that." She forced herself to swallow even though her stomach seemed to be engaged in open rebellion. Eppi had told her to keep eating at all costs; food would dull the after-effects of the nesta.

Tapper waltzed in, filling his plate high before he took a seat opposite the two women. "Glad to see you up and about, S.J.," he offered. "Jack said he gave you something for the hangover."

"Does everyone on this tub know I have a hangover, or just a select few?" scowled Jane, still chewing on the reddish root.

Tapper stroked his chin thoughtfully. "Everyone," he answered with a nod. "Don't you think so, Barb?"

"Yep." She smiled solicitously at Jane. "Not to worry, dearie, your secret is safe with us."

"Gee, isn't that reassuring?" Jane gave her a wan grin, only to be repaid with guffaws from them both.

Over the next few days, Jane and her staff kept busy with an avalanche of communiqués from various sources responding to the *Tical* incident. Reports to and from home were transmitted at an alarming rate, every department in the Pentagon wanted a different angle explored. In her element, Jane happily manned the communications station, revising and reissuing detailed accounts of what had taken place, what could have been done better, and what might have been done differently. Morgan reviewed everything that went out, giving her the freedom to answer the questions as she saw fit. The only mention of the kora came in a security vidcom from the Jeylosian Emperor himself, addressed to Lieutenant S.J.R.Krieg *for your eyes only*, officially apologizing for his son's behavior and assuring her proper punishment was meted out by him personally. No mention of her parents was made, which perversely pleased her. She took the disc back to her cabin where she threw it in a box with other mementos she had collected during her time in the Fleet.

Blackjack and Tapper made Jane their special assignment, taking turns collecting her for meals and squiring her to rec events. Whenever he wasn't with her, Jane noticed Jackson seemed to be spending considerable time with Belle, which pleased the yeomate no end. By the time they reached Taapusor, Jane was feeling more like herself than she had in a while.

The VIP they were due to pick up on arid the planet turned out to be an elderly professor on his way to the base negotiations on Lomos, not the fearsome official everyone expected. Dr. Tatch was a well-respected authority on land development, but it did not prevent him from being a champion story teller. He kept to his cabin or the library during the day, but at night he held court in the observatory where anyone was welcome to hear his wonderful collection of folktales and legends from planets across in the galaxy. As Vice President of the Tri-Planet Council, his august reputation belied the gentle soul with unruly white hair who came aboard carrying his own luggage. A seasoned traveler, he had been everywhere and participated in almost everything imaginable. When he got wind that someone on the *Washington* had experienced Pyakos, he sought Jane out and plied her with questions, some of which she skillfully avoided answering.

On the last night, Dr. Tatch challenged Blackjack to a storytelling contest in the observatory. Pleased to be asked by a master, Cardozo settled himself in a comfortable armchair waited for the competition to begin

Cardozo's own far-reaching knowledge of folktales and mythology was impressive. As the two men traded tales long into the night, Jane sat riveted to her seat. By midnight, only she, Tapper, and Captain Morgan remained with the storytellers; even Belle had gone off to bed.

Moving from his place against the far wall, Morgan briefly disappeared, only to reappear with a bottle of wine from his private stock and five glasses. The five of them moved to where they could sit comfortably together and talk as friends.

"If my aging memory serves me correctly, Captain Morgan, you began life in the service as a chaplain," he said. "Why did you give it up?"

Morgan allowed himself a sip of wine. "That is true, Dr. Tatch; I found I could serve more effectively as an officer. The chaplaincy is somewhat... limiting."

"How can the pursuit of That which has made us all, what you call God, be somewhat limiting, as you say?" He was not going to let up on the captain.

Jane watched Asher Morgenstern shift uncomfortably in his seat. She wondered how often he struggled with the same question and judging by his reaction, she guessed it was still too often for him. Tapper nudged her in the ribs, and she caught a flash of grin on his lips. Obviously, he was enjoying the debate.

"That which has made us all..." repeated Morgan thoughtfully; "God, no, religion..." he paused again, "can be a difficult taskmaster. There came a time in my life when I believed I could best by putting myself in a position where I could actively practice the principle I believe." Morgan rolled the stem of the goblet in his powerful, yet graceful hands. "As a captain, I have striven to prevent unnecessary loss of life through peaceful negotiation. As a chaplain, I would not be able to do that."

"But surely, Captain, are not religious leaders used for similar purpose on your home planet?"

"Unlike many of the planets we have contact with, religion is not a unifying force on our planet, but I am sure you know that already."

"I know it, but do not understand it. There are still religious wars there, I have heard."

Morgan nodded. "Religion has been the basis for more conflict than we care to admit. With all our advances, some things have not changed one bit."

"As Jews, Dr. Tatch," began Jane, "we are a minority. There are still those who think we are responsible for their misfortune. It is easier to blame others than to look to oneself."

The professor furrowed his brows. "I have met Jews living in odd places throughout the galaxy and I will admit they are different in many ways than other Terran travelers I have met." He looked closely at Tapper, Jane, Jackson and the captain. "You are all Jews, I have concluded, and you serve your nation honorably. Does the fact that you *are* Jews honestly make you different from the others? Is it something you choose to hide?"

Tapper stared at Morgan and when Morgan said nothing, Tapper spoke up. "Some of us hide it more than others, in many different ways. Although our Fleet Admiral is a Jew, it is not always easy for one of us to advance at the same rate as others. It's not intentional, I don't think, but we all recognize that it's there. Admiral Rothko works hard to prevent any sort of discrimination, but he cannot completely change human nature."

"And what nature is that, Mr. Bear?" asked Dr. Tatch.

"To fear that which is not like yourself," answered Morgan with a grimace before Tapper could speak.

"Then perhaps that is why you are so skilled at captaincy, Captain Morgan. You seem not to see the difference between species as keenly as do some others." The understanding in his voice was evident.

"But he does see the differences," countered Jane, "and he applies what he knows to move forward. He's the same way with the crew. You use what you know and apply it judiciously in order to keep life running smoothly. She glanced at Morgan, but his eyes told her nothing. "I'm a good example of the application. I am a woman and a Jew; so in essence, there are two strikes against me. Add to that, that I am the daughter of not one, but two ranking officers, and I become a pariah on any posting. Potentially, I am a spy for the brass; I am of a different faith, sometimes mysterious to the uninitiated, and I am of a gender that is still thought to be better off at home with the kids, not in roaming about in deep space. Obviously I cannot hide my gender, I choose not to hide my faith, but I do choose to protect myself from my family name. The captain knows all of this and respects those choices. It's *how* he uses the information that differentiates him from the pack. I've been in situations where that knowledge is held over me like Damocles' sword, making any attempt to advance on my part almost impossible. He *chooses* to totally ignore who I am, and I'm fine with that."

Dr. Tatch looked from Morgan to Jane. He could see Morgan was taken aback by the lieutenant's speech, but he gave no other indication of how he felt. The burly engineer, on the other hand, appeared thoroughly amused. "I see your point," admitted Tatch, "but I wonder if I were your father, would I allow you to make the same decisions."

"My father had no say whatsoever in the matter. Although he is married to an officer of equal rank, and is fully committed to the equality of women in the service, he set a double standard for me and my sister. For him, a Jewish woman belongs on Earth with a husband, producing grandchildren for him to spoil." She smiled at the last statement, then added quickly, "but even though he's not always thrilled by my choices, he is still proud of me, and I think it's partially because I have done this on my own without him."

"Aahhhh," sighed the professor, "every father's dilemma: the independent daughter." He emptied his glass and allowed Morgan to refill it.

The conversation turned to lighter matters as the visitor began to weave a tale about the goddess Hikabah and the early Taapusori. It was an old, oft-told tale, but one which was a perennial favorite. When they finally called it quits for the night, Tapper offered his elbow to Jane. "My I escort you home, Lieutenant?" he as with a grin. She took his arm, and they bid the others good night.

Blackjack was about to leave, too when Dr. Tatch said, "Captain, if the lieutenant were not a Jew, would that make a difference as her commanding officer? Or, because she is a Jew *and* the daughter of other officers, are you more protective of her?" The old gent paused. "You do realize you are protective of her, do you not?"

Morgan didn't answer right away; it was a difficult question. His initial objection to her posting was, in fact, her family, Speed included, but now the paradigm had changed; her performance under pressure had been spectacular, and he had to admit she was lovely in every sense of the word. But was he attracted to her because she was who she was? "Dr. Tatch," he said seriously, "I can only hope that it would not."

Dr. Tatch sensed he was not completely truthful, but let it go; the captain probably didn't even realize he was not. "Well, it would be unnatural if the thought had not at least crossed your mind, Captain Morgan," he said in an off-handed manner. He turned to Cardozo. "And where do you stand in all of this, Jackson Cardozo?"

Blackjack flashed a smile and shrugged. "Ah'm thanking God at this very moment that Ah am only one of her many relatives and not in Boston's place." The comment got the laugh he wanted, breaking the tension.

"This has been a most interesting evening, Captain and I thank you for you hospitality, but I would ask one last question of you before you go," said the professor as they reached his door.

"Certainly." After an evening of difficult questions, what difference could one more make?

"Would it be a breach of your ethics to confirm who her parents are?" asked Dr. Tatch quietly.

Morgan considered the request, and the person making it. He suspected the good doctor already guessed. "You can ask her, but she would have to be the one to tell you," he shrugged.

"Her facial expressions mirror those of her father, don't you think?" Dr. Tatch smiled, his leathery face creased into a thousand wrinkles. "But much prettier. If I were a younger man, Captain Morgan, I should challenge you to a duel for her." The old man bid the captain goodnight and went into his cabin.

Morgan leaned against the bulkhead and whistled. There was no doubt about it; Sarah Jane Rothko was beginning to get under his skin.

CHAPTER 11

Landing on Lomos proved more difficult than expected. The *Washington* remained in orbit while a typhoon buffeted the coast of Lomosna where they were to set down. From the ship, the bridge crew monitored the storm closely; it was an unusual chance to gather meteorological information which scientists at home would find fascinating as well as useful since a base on the planet was in the works. Lomos, the third planet from their star, was similar in composition and atmosphere to Earth. The population looked remarkably humanoid despite distinct differences in physiology which included a double heart working to pump their pinkish blood in alternating shifts. As a result, the Lomosi were prone to longevity; at one hundred years old, a Lomosean was considered to be in the prime of life.

But unlike Earth, Lomos had a long history of cooperative peace. Six continents represented six distinct nations, each with its own culture. A tri-cameral legislature, the Decta, unified them all. In the first house, the Decta-Nata, sat the hereditary heads of the major clans of all six nations. Once feudal war-lords, the Lomo-natam were now preoccupied with maintaining stable economies within their territories. Decta-Kata, the second house, consisted of elected representatives from individual districts within the nations. A council of sages made up the third house of the Decta. Those in the third house were usually older Lomoseans known for great wisdom in judicial matters as well as great scholarship. A seat in the Decta-pata was a seat for the remainder of one's days. Every three years, a Decta-Batai was selected to serve as head of the congress.

The current Decta-Batai was a handsome woman from Barzot, the smallest of the six nations. A youngster by Decta standards, Leyla Tremna was a feisty supporter of interplanetary trade. Her specialty was economics and she was known in their solar system as a shrewd negotiator who usually got what she wanted through sheer willpower. Although she would have eventually come to the Decta as head of her clan, Tremna's impatience for a seat in the legislature had caused her to stand for election as soon as she reached the permissible age of forty-one summers. Now at seventy five, she was faced with the imminent death of her father, which would force her to give up her seat in the Decta-kata for the hereditary seat in the Decta-nata. The choice of Tremna as Decta-Batai had come as a shock to some on Lomos, but it was a calculated move to further integrate the upper two houses. Until her father passed on to the other plane, she would, by law, be required to maintain her elected seat. Marshaling her support, she accepted the position of Decta-Batai and was already planning how she would use that position when the time came to transfer seats of power.

It was at Tremna's behest that the base negotiations with the Terrans had begun. Lomos needed agricultural advancement if it was to feed its steadily growing population. After a careful study of proposals from an infinite number of places, Tremna selected the bid which would bring the greatest improvements with the greatest speed at the lowest cost. Besides, the topographical similarities between Earth and Lomos appeared to be compatible. She had waited six months for the *Washington* and now she was restless when their arrival was delayed an extra day due to the raging storm.

Leyla Tremna passed an equally restless night, only to awake to perfect skies and bright sunshine. She dressed carefully for the meeting with Captain Ash Morgan; how he reacted upon their first meeting would set the tone for the final stages of these delicate negotiations. Instead of the uniform of Commander-in-Chief of the Lomosean armed forces she was entitled to wear, she chose a less formidable dress of soft native silk in azure blue that set off the blue of her eyes. With deft fingers, she coiled her waist-length hair in a simple knot on top of her head, only to sigh at the grey now showing amidst the copper at her temples. In the looking glass, Tremna caught sight of her husband watching her. "And why are you smiling like a pikki-bird?" she asked half-seriously.

"At you, my dear wife." He came up to her and put his arms around her. "You cannot accept the natural aging process any more than you can accept foul weather on a day you have planned a speech. You have control over neither, yet you fight them."

She laughed softly, resting her head against his chest. "Are you planning on a seat for yourself in the Decta-pata, Resh?"

"No, although my years as your husband certainly qualify me for one," he mused. "No, I think I shall settle for returning to our farm when your term is at long last over."

Turning to him, she asked "Are you missing it more these days or is it that you are anxious to try the new technology the Terrans will bring?"

"Both, I should think. But I am also thinking of our children and our children's children who complain they do not see enough of us. When your term is over and when you join the Decta-nata, we will spend more time at home than here in Kray-Decta. It's a perfectly nice city, Leyla, but it's not home." He gave her a quick kiss on her smooth cheek. "You look lovely, so stop worrying over it."

She checked herself in the glass once more and was satisfied with what she saw. "Then let us go to the port and await the arrival of our guests." Dropping a light cape over her shoulders, she swept out of the room.

At the space port, a large number of Lomoseans had gathered early in the day to watch the docking of the *Washington*. School children in crisp blue uniforms hopped anxiously from one foot to another, winding and unwinding the little flags they had been given by their teachers. The arrival of the Decta-Batai brought cheers, a welcome break from the tedium of waiting. Tremna went to where the children were standing and talked to as many as she could. Like children everywhere, they were shy at first, only to bubble forth with questions for their leader. The time passed quickly as Tremna tried to answer them all. At last, someone pointed upward where a speck could be seen, silver against the deep blue of the Lomosean sky. Spectators craned necks to get a better view while officials scurried to be in proper position for the welcoming ceremonies. Slowly the *Washington*, aided by Lomosean tugs, descended until it hovered over the concrete pylons. With a gentle grace but a great noise, it touched down. The whine of the engines ceased as a gangway was rolled toward the great ship. It seemed to take forever before the hatch was opened.

Captain Morgan stepped out into the bright sunshine. Blinking, he waited until his eyes adjusted to the light before starting down the gangway. He could see the Decta-Batai standing with members of her government and could hear an odd sounding band enthusiastically playing the *Star Spangled Banner*.

Right behind him, Blackjack Cardozo's laughter boomed in his ear. "What a welcome, Boston! This is better than landing in D.C."

Following the two captains was Dr. Tatch, then the officers of the *Washington*. Tremna moved to the bottom of the gangway to shake hands, an odd custom she thought, but distinctively Terran. In lilting, slightly awkward English, she greeted each one as Morgan made the introductions. But when Barbara Lucas appeared, there was a great commotion from behind which caused Tremna to turn around.

"Mom! Mom! Over here, Mom!" shouted two boys being restrained by their father. "Here we are, Mom!"

Lucas winced, but gave a little wave. It was enough to cause the boys to break free of their father's hold and rush toward the ship. With amused faces, the Lomoseans stepped aside to let them pass. Even Morgan jumped out of the way as they barreled past him. Unable to resist, Lucas hurried down the ramp, barely stopping to greet the Decta-Batai, only to open her arms wide to enfold her sons. The crowd roared their approval since to a Lomosean, children come first, last and in the middle.

Tremna was still laughing when Commander Lucas brought her sons to meet the Decta-Batai. Everything stopped while she spoke to them. "How happy you must be to have your mother arrive," Tremna said, shaking their hands in the American manner.

"Boy, are we ever!" answered Theo in fluent Lomosean.

"We haven't seen her in ten months and now we're going to have her here for two whole weeks!" Micah announced, unwilling to let go of his mother's hand even when he shook Tremna's with the other.

Barb blushed in spite of herself. "They are here with my husband who is involved with the negotiation," she said in Lomosean.

"Ah, then you are Mrs. Kipling Lucas," replied Tremna in English, instantly putting her at ease. "I look forward to seeing you at the reception this evening. Will your sons attend?"

"I'll have to make a mother's judgment call on that one, Your Excellency. We'll just have to see how worn out they are by the end of the day."

Tremna laughed. "A wise mother. I will understand whatever decision you reach. Welcome to Lomos, Commander Lucas." She stepped back and watched the officer fly into her husband's arms. Turning to Morgan, the Decta-Batai whispered "Tell your commander that if she chooses not to come this evening, I will understand that, too."

⁂

After the welcoming ceremonies, Morgan, Cardozo, Tapper and Newhouse left Jane to post the liberty lists before joining them at the conference table. Belle had gone with Ngyuen, Olukotun and Chakrabati to observe the proceedings. Back at her station, Jane transmitted a variety of messages to HQ on Earth, and handled a couple of incoming transmissions. There was a vidcom for the captain from his son, a couple of personal messages for Blackjack, and two birth announcements, one for a crewmate in the kitchen, the other for Stewart Ryan, the helmsman. She took a last check on the computer before setting it for transmission directly into the communications room where Crewmate Lewis was sitting, probably playing games on his terminal to ward off boredom while he waited for his turn at liberty on Lomos. She buzzed him to let him know she was leaving the ship and that he was in charge of the comm. "I'm on a beeper if you need me, but try not to call unless it's critical," she said into the intercom at her station.

"No sweat, Lieutenant," answered Lewis with a sigh. "Just don't forget about me."

"I'll try not to. See you later." She picked up an extra docupad and slipped it into her briefcase. A noise coming from the cage brought her head up sharply. The sound of childish laughter seemed out of place on the *Washington*, but at least it told her who was coming onto the bridge.

"Jane!" called Barb, stepping out of the cage. "I'm glad we caught you." Her boys stood beside her, ready to meet yet another colleague of their mother's. "This is Theo, and this guy is Micah. The big one is already at the negotiating table."

Jane went over to the boys and shook their hands. "I've heard a lot about you guys," she said gravely. "I hope you're gonna take good care of your mom, because otherwise I won't let her go with you."

Theo flushed to the roots of his hair, but Micah laughed, the sound echoing about the empty bridge. "I think you have it backward, ma'am," he said in a serious voice when he stopped laughing. "She better take care of us, because Dad isn't very good at laundry and that kind of stuff."

"Or cooking," Theo added, smiling at his mother. "He makes the same things over and over and it gets real boring."

Barb smiled and shook her head. "Children: the great equalizers. It doesn't matter that their mother can command a ship in a pinch; they only care about whether or not I can produce a hamburger on a planet other than Earth. Thank God the cook agreed to carry a hundred pounds of beef in the freezer for me."

"And ketchup?" asked Micah hopefully.

"And peanut butter." Barb rolled her eyes. "Heaven forbid I forgot the peanut butter....or the comic books...or the latest music discs."

Jane suppressed a laugh at the look on the boys' faces. They missed their mother in much the same way she had missed her parents when they were off on official business; she surely sympathized with them. "I know exactly how you feel," she said, explaining that her own parents were in the military. "But in the end, guys, she's still your mom, and you can be proud of the good job she does on the *Washington*."

"We know that," declared Theo, putting a protective arm about his mother. "Not too many guys have moms who look so cool in a uniform."

Jane took the cage with them as far as the boarding deck. She promised to come to dinner as soon as she could, and promised to tell them all about the *Tical* business. As she watched the door slide closed, she was, for a moment, jealous. Although Jane had never given much thought to having children of her own, the thought of not having them left her wistful.

Madame Tremna sat in the center of her people at the large, circular negotiating table. Kip Lucas was standing at a demoboard describing the changes to the proposed base recommended by the Lomosi. The native geologists had made some suggestions which the Terrans had incorporated into the design. Tremna was pleased by that; she had worried that her own people would be overshadowed by the ebullient newcomers. Instead of arguing, the two sides had worked well together, each side learning from the other. And she was enjoying the presentation; the Terrans were able to maintain their sense of humor even in delicate situations, unlike her own people who tended to be overly serious about such things. Their need for green space and recreational facilities on the base itself amused her, but after catching an informal ball game at a local park, she was beginning to understand that peculiar requirement. Most of what Lucas was saying she had heard before, so she let her attention wander as she took the measure of the delegation from the U.S.S. *Washington*.

Captain Morgan, Captain Cardozo and Commander Bear, the one they called Tapper, sat together. The other observers sat directly behind them. But Tremna saw the way Captain Morgan kept his eyes moving, as he analyzed everyone at the table. When his eyes met hers, she saw the quick flash of a small smile, letting her know he was watching her as well. Commander Bear was taking copious notes, passing an occasional one to his captain. Captain Cardozo, however, was a mystery. He sat back from the table, almost reclining in his chair, his eyes half closed, yet there was a tenseness about him which told her he was not dozing. *Quite the opposite,* she thought; *he is listening for nuance in the questions.* That the language officer was not there did not escape her notice for a vacant chair sat beside Captain Cardozo, with *Lieutenant S.J.R.Krieg, Linguist* written neatly on a name plate on the table. Finally, the trim young woman arrived and slipped into the empty chair. The girl whispered something to Captain Cardozo who smiled before whispering it to Morgan. Whatever it was pleased him, for he nodded to her with a slight upturning of his lips. Tremna wondered if these people were as open as they seemed, or if it was their version of politeness.

Tapper slid Jane a docupad and she read it quickly. Sitting erect, she took over the job of note taking. For the moment, the negotiations were in English, but as soon as the Lomosean delegation began asking questions, her ability to translate would be of the utmost importance. Despite the fact that their people wore translators, she would be relied on for nuance, so important to Lomosean linguistics, and clarification.

Finished with his part of the presentation, Kip Lucas turned the floor over to his local counterpart, Dolat Qamtar, for the question and answer period. Qamtar had been instrumental in the original acceptance of the proposal, serving as a go-between for the Terrans and Tremna. With his natural ease, Qamtar easily fielded the questions until Tremna indicated that she wished to speak next.

"We have listened with great interest to the proposed architectural development of the site," said Tremna cautiously, "and I think we can all benefit from its presence on Lomos. But I would like further clarification on the mutual usage portion of the proposal. The payment terms for the land and materials are well within the standards for local development, but we have not thoroughly discussed how we will directly benefit from interplanetary access through your base operations."

The question was aimed at Morgan, but before he answered, he verified the translation with Jane. "Answer as directly as you possibly can; she will not appreciate hyperbole or humor in the answer," whispered Jane.

Morgan nodded, taking no offense at her words, and stood, prepared to answer the question. "Madame Tremna, ladies and gentlemen of the committee, it is well known that Lomos, while being technologically advanced on the planet surface, is not at the same level of advancement in space travel and interplanetary commerce," began Morgan. "With a base on your planet surface, we will be able to work with your scientific community in developing craft which will further open interplanetary trade to you. Through teamwork and shared facilities, you will be able to increase your exports while at the same time strengthen your own planetary defense. As you might have heard already, there was an incident on Pitan which may have been averted had the Pitanese been better able to activate their fleet. Instead, they needed to rely on outworlders for the return of stolen goods. In this period of our history, we are experiencing contact with a wide array of civilizations, not all of whom act honorably according to League of Planets standards. It is therefore imperative that your own people be able to defend Lomos successfully. We view our part in the bargain as one of sharers of technology; we benefit from having a way-station on your planet for our vessels, you will benefit from having our scientists to aid you wherever we can be of service. We are not, under any circumstances, interested in galactic empire building."

Tremna interrupted. "Certainly, Captain Morgan, you are not altogether altruistic, either?" There was a ripple of laughter through the assembly.

"No," smiled Morgan, glad for the break in the tension, "we are not. But the benefits we seek have more to do with trade and a pit-stop than for taking control of a planet. We have enough difficulty controlling our own, thank you very much." The smile crinkled his eyes, and he was pleased to see Tremna's smile widen as well.

"The matter of our security is an important one, Captain Morgan; we do not accept military aid from others," Tremna said, the smile fading.

"We understand that, Madame Tremna; we are not offering military aid. We are offering technological cooperation. If your people choose to use some of that knowledge militarily, that is your prerogative. We would like Lomos to feel secure within its own system, without potential threat from other forces." Morgan could sense the next question.

"And you do not consider yourself one of the other forces." It was a statement, not a question.

"No, ma'am, we do not. The documents which will ultimately be presented for ratification will spell that out in minute detail."

Tremna laughed gently. "You make yourself out to sound like an avatar, captain."

"Hardly that, ma'am," replied Morgan with an answering laugh. "We just have no desire to colonize. It's not our way."

There were a few more brief questions before Madame Tremna rose and signaled the end of the session. There would be an informal luncheon before the committee broke up into smaller groups to continue work on the individual sections treaties. Captain Morgan gathered his people in the lobby outside the main room to assign meeting attendance. "Blackjack, go to the defense committee; that's why you were asked to come along. Krieg, I want you and Winter at the drafting meeting with me, but assign the rest of your staff as you see fit." He handed her a list of committees and locations. "Tapper, you go to technical. I want everyone aboard ship for dinner at 1700 hours." He spotted Kip Lucas talking to one of the Lomosean designers. "I'll catch up with you all later," he said before he walked off to join Lucas.

At the drafting meeting, Jane found her command of the local language better than she had originally thought. She sat beside Twee Hafna, Tremna's personal representative to the committee, and together they hashed out some of the more difficult translations facing the committee. They were about the same age, but Twee had never been away from Lomos. During a break in the proceedings, she turned to her counterpart from the *Washington* and whispered, in English, "I would love to talk to you about the places you've been. Perhaps we can meet for breakfast tomorrow morning?"

Jane was delighted by the request. "Of course, I'd love to." She invited the woman to come aboard the *Washington* at 0730, giving them plenty of time to talk before the meetings began at 0900.

Sitting back in his chair, Morgan watched Jane debate a particularly important clause with the Lomosean head of the committee. He liked the way she diagrammed both languages to make her point, standing at a board as she wrote out the changes which she felt were important. Nuance was crucial in Lomosean and she was not going to allow a statement to be included which could be taken as merely suggestion rather than an absolute condition.

"By writing this," she said, pointing to the chain of words on her board, "we can find ourselves in a position in which you are able to demand that we provide *chihknam*, military manpower in an internal conflict. This is against the directive from our government. The use of *himka chihknam* here leaves too much open. We must specify *chihknam lomosni rifpat,* military manpower when the security of the entire planet is clearly at risk."

"Chihknam is chihknam," shrugged the chairman, trying to downplay the necessity for change. Although internal conflicts were rare on Lomos, they did come up once in a while and additional military assistance could be useful.

"I beg to differ, Mr. Chairman," persisted Jane. "Any use of outside military assistance would be subject to sanctions by the League of Planets. If, in the event that Lomos is at risk, a general call will bring the nearest League member to evaluate and assist if necessary, as happened with the Pitanese incident last week. The *Washington* happened to be closest in the sector therefore we responded to the distress call. The same would apply to Lomos. Since you are already members of the League, these points are clearly delineated in your charter." She was not going to be swayed by the casualness of Lomosean politics.

After quiet consultation with his people, the chair conceded the point and the wording was changed. Pleased with her success, Jane delved into the next questionable phrase. She could feel Morgan's eyes on her back and she hoped he was as pleased with her as she was with herself. When the hour grew late and the session drew to a close, Jane glanced at her commanding officer. He seemed content with the way it had gone, but his face told her nothing in particular.

Walking back to the ship, Morgan strolled alongside Tapper, listening intently to what his tech chief had to say about the architectural plans for the base. Tapper had seen the plans before their arrival, but his opinion following the session was, from previous experience, worth hearing. Nearby, Cardozo escorted Belle. They were laughing, their heads close together, sharing a private joke.

A few paces behind them all, Jane walked alone thinking about the importance of what she had just accomplished. The choice to lag behind was her own. This was a personal milestone; it was the first time she had played an active part in a major negotiation and observations about the experience raced about her head at a furious pace. Too keyed up to talk to anyone, she needed time to review the events of the day in order to put them into perspective before writing her own report. Once she was back in her quarters, Jane changed into a comfortably baggy flight suit and settled down to reread the copy of the treaty she brought back with her.

A sharp beeping brought her attention out of the labyrinth of language in which she had buried herself. "Krieg, here," she muttered into the intercom.

"We're waiting dinner for you, Lieutenant," announced Morgan's voice. "Are you planning on joining us?"

She could not tell if he was amused or annoyed. For a split second, she thought of saying "no," but changed her mind. "Sorry, sir; I'm on my way up."

In the wardroom, everyone was seated around the table, an empty place between Newhouse and the captain. Jane slid into the chair and apologized to the captain as she placed her napkin in her lap. She felt much like she did at home, when her father would look stern if she arrived late from a friend's house. Try as she might, she could not concentrate on the conversation around her. They were all talking about what they would be doing during liberty, but Jane was not in the mood to talk. She picked at her food, sipped her iced tea sparingly, and as soon as she could make a graceful exit, she left the wardroom to return to her cabin. The tension of the day had been draining and if she was to be ready for the next round, she needed to read through the treaties one more time before she went to bed. Jane viewed her role in the process as important, if only to decipher the complexity of the language for those unfamiliar with Lomosean cadence and she knew that her father would be monitoring her performance with a critical eye. She felt the pressure acutely. Still, she wished she could kick back like the others and forget about the negotiations for a while.

"What's eating her?" Morgan asked Tapper after she left. "She did a helluva a job today. She's got no reason to sulk."

"I can only guess," shrugged the chief tech. He wasn't about to tell Morgan that the lieutenant was probably feeling isolated and lonely; that they had ignored her after the meetings when a kind word or two might have helped after everything the kid had been through lately. He recognized the face she had on when she left the wardroom as the same face Jonathan wore whenever being Rothko's son had gotten to him. He made a mental note to himself to find her later on to talk. Tapper studied Morgan's face for a moment, and when the captain was about to say something else, he put up his hand. "Let it go, Boston. S.J. walks a thin line between what she thinks is proper for her and what is proper for everyone else. Unlike the rest of us mere mortals, she's been military her entire life."

"In other words, she needs to relax and you're telling me she can't."

"Something like that." He had said too much already; it was time to shut up. "Wanna play a little racquet ball tonight, Boston?" Tapper asked, pointedly changing the subject.

"Why the hell not?" he agreed, eyeing Tapper carefully. "You look like you could use a good trouncing."

"I was thinking the same thing of you, *mon capítan*. I'll meet you down there in an hour.

Incoming mail had been left in Tapper's box and he took it with him back to his quarters. There were several vidcoms from his family, mostly his mother, one from his cousin and one from Jonathan Rothko. Passing on the others, he played Jonathan's first, anxious to hear what was going on in Israel. He broke open the red seal on the case and popped it into the machine. Jonathan's lean face appeared, tired but well-tanned. After a minute or two of personal news, he told Tapper about his work in the desert. That he was speaking Hebrew, another twist on security, did not surprise Tapper.

"It doesn't look all that good from down here, Tap. There are rumors all over the place that the Syrians are gearing up for an assault from the northeast. We know the Jordanians have met with them, but we don't know what stand they're taking. The pilots I'm training are okay, but they are too cocksure of themselves; it worries me." He paused and smiled a little lopsidedly. "I almost wish I shipped out to Mars...or Saturn for that reconnaissance training, but they needed Hebrew speakers here and there just aren't that many of us around no matter what my parents like to think. Frankly, we could use every Jew in our military out here, because at least another Jew would understand the life and death of another war. So tell me something I don't know...how's S.J. doing on the *Washington*? Is Boston driving her crazy yet? I heard something about some unpleasant business with the Wa'atsi, but no specifics. Was Sarah Jane involved? Aw…come on,

Tap, you can tell me!" He rambled about his sister for a little while longer before finishing off the vidcom with the story about running into Chava in Jerusalem. "No lectures, Tapper; I know how you feel about her, but I guess I have to figure out how I feel. Pretty stupid, huh? Whaddya expect from a flyboy, anyway?" He told Tapper how to vidcom him directly and the screen went dark.

While he changed into shorts for his racquetball game with Morgan, Tapper considered whether or not to show the vidcom to the captain and to Jane. Certainly Jane would want to see it, but the information Jonathan relayed about Israel would concern Morgan as well. Slipping it into his bag, he decided to take it along. The captain could see it in his cabin after the game, and Tapper would cut if off before the comments about S.J. The other vidcoms could wait until later.

Jane toyed with the idea of going to the rec deck to dance, but opted for a swim instead. The hour was late and the pool would most likely be deserted, enabling her to pound laps without having to socialize. Changing into a suit, she grabbed her robe and headed for the pool.

No one was there. Jane pressed the intercom button and waited until the crewmate on duty answered. "Lieutenant Krieg, here. I'll be doing some laps, so if I don't check out in an hour, send the medics."

"Will do, Lieutenant. Have a nice time."

The water was comfortably warm when Jane dove in. She found the lap meter at the end of her lane and set it for five miles. With a deep breath, she pushed off and began swimming at an easy pace; there was no need to rush through it.

Tapper ran Morgan into the wall countless times before the captain threw up his hands in defeat. Sweating profusely, they slid to the floor laughing. "Whatsamatter? Gettin' old, Boston?" teased Tapper, tossing a towel at Morgan.

"Yeah, I think so. When was the last time I beat you, anyway?" he asked, draping the towel across his shoulders.

"About two years ago. For the life of me, I can't see why you keep playing," Tapper grinned, pleased with his continued dominance on the court. "You never win. Better you should stick to Newhouse or Davies for the sake of your misplaced pride."

Morgan leaned his head back against the padded wall. Physical exertion always felt good, especially after a day of sitting around a conference table. But it rankled him that he could not beat Tapper at racquetball. He made a mental note to come down here alone to work on his game; two weeks on the planet would give him a little extra time for recreation. Wiping the sweat dripping off his forehead, Morgan nudged Tapper with the other. "Hey, I don't know about you, but I could use a swim. How 'bout it?"

"Glutton for punishment," muttered Tapper, rising from his place against the wall. "Well, just don't sit there, come on." He grabbed Morgan's arm and pulled him up. "Christ, you are getting old. Just look at all that grey hair," he clucked.

Morgan snarled, but said nothing. He knew all too well how much grey was starting to show, even in his beard. Companionably, they strolled down to the pool.

They could see someone swimming, but it did not stop them from stripping down to their gym shorts. "Race you on the left," shouted Morgan as he sprinted to the far end of the pool, Tapper close at his heels. Morgan made it to the end first and dived in, but Tapper entered the water from the side. Jane's head came out of the water in time to see a body sail over her and slide into the water. Swearing under her breath, she swam toward the edge, ready to haul ashes over the infraction of good behavior upon the return of the two swimmers stroking furiously down the lap lane. As they reached the end where she tread water, she was about to say something when the winner of the race bobbed up and she saw it was the captain followed closely by Tapper.

"Sorry, S.J.," gulped Tapper, shaking the water from his hair. "I hope I didn't scare you."

It was always difficult to stay angry at Joshua Bear, so she settled for a mild rebuke. "Even children know better than to run around on wet tiles, gentlemen," she said sternly.

"Ah, the operative word in *that* sentence is children," laughed Tapper, swimming toward her with his head above the water. "Us boys never really grow up, you know."

"I know," she retorted. "It's gender dependent." Shoving off from the side, she continued her laps.

Morgan and Tapper watched her progress down the length of the pool. "Think you can take her?" asked Tapper, raising an eyebrow at the captain.

He eyeballed her speed and nodded. "Sure. Piece of cake." With a deep breath, he launched himself into the lane, his powerful arms cutting cleanly through the water. Jane could sense movement behind her and began to push herself, not taking the time to see who it was. Because of her head start, she reached the end of the pool first and immediately turned around to go back. The competing swimmer was coming closer at a furious pace, but Jane maintained the advantage. The darkness of the hair told her it was Morgan, and no way was she about to let him overtake her. She pushed herself to the limit, focusing all her energy on increasing her speed. In the end, it was no serious contest; Jane reached Tapper with several seconds to spare.

"Good race!" shouted Tapper gleefully, helping Jane out of the water. "I knew the old man couldn't beat a Rothko, even if it's a girl Rothko!" he added in a conspiratorial whisper.

Wrinkling her nose in distaste, Jane chastised him; "That's a mean thing to say, Tapper! Gender has nothing to do with it."

"Men swim faster than women," Morgan tossed off, hoisting himself onto the side of the pool. "We have greater muscular strength as a rule."

"Sexist! That only applies in cases where people train to swim. Your average person, the kind who swims recreationally, will outswim a person of either sex if they are conditioned to do so."

Tapper laughed, the sound booming off the walls. "That makes no sense whatsoever, S.J." He slid back into the water. "Anyone for another go at it?"

"No problem," announced Jane joining Tapper in the pool. "Captain?"

"Why not? Two complete laps, ending here." He joined them, taking the lane on the other side of Jane. "Ready? Set?" He paused until the other two were ready. "Go!"

They shoved off together, Tapper taking the early lead with Morgan close on his heels. Jane lagged slightly behind, carefully gauging her strength. By the end of the first lap, Morgan and Tapper were battling it out at full tilt, with Jane still behind. At the last turn, Jane noticed the men slowing slightly. Changing her stroke, she started her big push. Soon she was in line with them, but they were too busy watching each other to notice her. With every ounce of her strength, Jane sped up and gradually moved ahead. Stretching her arm as far as it could go, she hit the lap timer at the end of her lane a microsecond ahead of Morgan.

"Men swim faster than women, huh?" snorted Jane, catching her breath against the pale blue tiles of the pool.

Tapper was delighted with the result. "Not your day, is it, Boston?" he grinned, slapping the captain on the back. "First I whup your butt in racquetball, then a girl beats you at swimming twice. Time to turn in the old dog tags, fella."

The captain groaned good-naturedly, and then bowed deeply toward Jane, his face in the water. Coming up, he whipped his head around, splashing her as he said "I concede you are faster in the water. I take it you are buying the first round, Lieutenant?" He smiled expectantly.

Agreeing, Jane laughed merrily. "Coffee's on me... unless someone has something stronger they would like to contribute?"

With a sigh, Tapper invited them back to his quarters. "I just happen to have a bottle of cognac I've been looking for an excuse to open." He pulled himself up and offered his hand to Jane. "Can you manage to get yourself out, old man?"

In his cabin, Tapper played host, pouring amber liquid into fine crystal snifters that seemed almost out of place in the austere rooms Tapper called home. Morgan and Jane sat on opposite ends of the sofa, sipping cognac slowly. They talked about the negotiations before Tapper remembered the vidcom from Earth.

"I figured I'd play it for each of you, but as long as we're together, we might as well get it over with," said Tapper, switching on the comm unit. He put it in the slot and sat in the armchair from where he could watch their reaction comfortably.

Jane's face lit up with the appearance of her brother on the screen. Settling back, she listened to him talk to his friend, almost as though he was in the room. When he began to talk about Israel, she noticed the deep furrow forming between the captain's eyes. Clearly the situation concerned him, as it did her. But it was her brother who was in the middle of a potentially hot zone.

Instead of cutting it off when Jonathan mentioned his sister, Tapper let it run. *Let them hear what he's thinking,* said Tapper to himself, trying to keep a straight face. Morgan laughed aloud when Jonathan asked whether or not he was driving Jane crazy. *Better he should ask the other way around,* though Morgan, glancing at Jane whose face was bright pink. He could only imagine what was going through her mind as she listened to Jonathan's teasing voice.

Both Morgan and Jane groaned when Jonathan spoke of seeing Chava. For all it was worth, Morgan thought he should marry the woman and get it over with, a feeling shared by all the Rothkos, including Tapper. But it was Jane who commented drily on the report. "He's had women hanging around him as long as I can remember," she said shaking her head, "but this is the first time I have ever seen him in such a quandary over a relationship. It'll be a terrible shame if she gives up on him and marries someone else."

"Hear, hear," agreed Tapper, pouring another round of drinks. "But what do you make of this Syrian business, Ash? How serious do you think it is?"

Morgan scratched his beard and considered the question. As a commanding officer, he was privy to a great deal of knowledge unavailable even to Tapper. He looked from one to the other before tackling the question. "Between us, it's more serious than Jonathan lets on. I am assuming that he is aware of recent intelligence which surfaced after this vidcom was transmitted." He looked at Jane. "Your father's last communiqué stated that the situation was hot enough to put us on alert for a fast trip home. Not that we usually get involved with stuff on Earth, but as a command vessel, if a war erupts in the Middle East, we will become part of the monitoring network. For the first time, there is the possibility of outside interference..." His voice trailed off. The rest was understood.

Tapper and Jane were silent, each considering their own assessment of the threat. There were several planetary governments that would be delighted with the opportunity to become involved with a Terran war in order to consolidate a position on the planet. The Syrians were just hungry enough to allow outsiders to ally themselves in an effort finally drive the Jews into the sea. Jane wondered what her parents were doing in light of the potential danger. At home, she would ask all the questions she wanted and her parents would answer as best they could; but out in the middle of space, there was no way to question them without breaking regulations. She would have to rely on Captain Morgan for any information she may get. Taking advantage of the current informality, she asked the captain for further explanation.

"Your father requested, despite Fleet regulation, you be kept abreast of the situation as it progresses. It seems both Admiral and General Rothko feel you have a personal stake in all this." There was an unmasked edge of resentment in his voice. He understood that any military involvement included her family directly, but he was not used to sharing security secrets with junior officers. "Until I tell you otherwise, you are to keep your mouth shut and forget about what we are discussing. Your first responsibility, Lieutenant, is to this ship and your assignments. When something happens, I will tell you."

His use of the word "when" bothered her more than the rebuke. If she read him correctly, he was certain it was a matter of time before they were called home. And she also knew that Jonathan would be in the middle of it all, flying a fighter, risking his life for the one place where he was happiest: Israel. Jane opened her mouth to say something, then clamped it shut. There was no point in pushing Morgan; he could be just as stubborn as she.

When Tapper walked her back to her quarters, he wrestled with what he could say to make her feel better. Understanding what she was feeling was not enough, she needed to know, once again, that he was there for her as more than just a friend. His responsibility was that of a brother, standing in for Jonathan as Jonathan would stand in his stead had the situation been reversed. As they reached her door, Tapper took Jane's hand and pulled her to face him. Swallowing hard, he launched into his speech.

"You know how much I love your family, S.J., and that when I heard you were joining the *Washington*, I was thrilled. But I'm not dense enough to close my eyes and my ears to the problems I knew you'd face as the daughter. I admit it; I didn't expect Morgan's constant grating. He's my friend, but...." He stopped talking when a crewmate came around the corner.

Jane opened the door and waited for Tapper to go in first. She wanted to hear him out; hoping that he would give her a better sense of how to handle Morgan without Morgan being aware of it. As soon as the door slid shut, she turned to Tapper, her eyes bright with unshed tears. "Why is he like this, Tap? Why does he hold my family against me? What's he so damn afraid of?"

Instinctively, Tapper put his arms around her and held her close. It hurt him to see her so frustrated, but he was glad Jane was not too military to hide it from him. The little girl he had known racing around the Rothko house was still there, still demanding to know the answers to questions to which there were no real answers. "He's not afraid of your parents, Sarah Jane, he's afraid of you," he said quietly. "You're smart and determined and you're a terrific officer and he knows it. But you're also very pretty and Asher, for all his bluster and bluff finds that difficult to reconcile." He purposely omitted that he knew for a fact she was everything Morgan wanted in a woman. "I'm sure that even if you hadn't been assigned to this ship he would have met you elsewhere and you two could have danced the night away in each other's arms. But here, on the *Washington*, he's your CO and anything he feels towards you must be strictly professional. So he deals with it by keeping you at a distance, careful not to show you any untoward favoritism even though no one knows you're Ted's daughter. Give him time, Sarah Jane; he'll eventually get past it." He pushed her back and looked into her face. Had circumstances been different, he would have kissed her right there and then, but Tapper was certain her affection for him was only sisterly. Digging into his pocket, he produced a clean but rumpled handkerchief and handed it to her. "Come on, squirt, wipe your eyes and blow your nose. I can't stand to see you cry."

In his own cabin, Morgan chided himself for acting like a jerk. As her commanding officer, he should have been more sympathetic to the plight in which she found herself, understanding of the fact that her brother was in the middle of all this, and that her parents, despite military regulation, felt a responsibility to tell their daughter the truth. If the positions were reversed, he would have wanted his father to bend the rules, and instead of telling her to ask all the questions she wanted, he shut her up with an unkind attitude. In her eyes he had seen the puzzled, hurt look and it had pained him, His mouth was on autopilot and he could not change what came out of it. Muttering, he tossed his wet shorts into the sink and went to bed.

CHAPTER 12

Twee Hafna came aboard the *Washington* right on time. Jane was waiting for her at the gangway and led her through the long passageways to the all-night coffee. Few crewmates were around, leaving a wide choice of tables for the two women. The Lomosean woman asked Jane to select her breakfast, explaining that she had no idea what Terran food was like.

"Not much different from yours," laughed Jane, ordering juice, eggs, muffins and coffee from the crewmate behind the window. "Maybe the preparation is different, but food doesn't vary much from one humanoid planet to the next."

"Kip Lucas always yearns for Chinese food. What is that?"

Jane tried to define Chinese cuisine. "It makes me want some just thinking about it," she admitted. "Perhaps one evening we can get the chief cook to whip up something along those lines. Whenever we're in port and fresh vegetables are available, he tends to give us stuff like that!"

With her first taste of scrambled eggs, Twee grinned. "Oh, these are like chum! Only better!" She dug into the eggs with relish. Pausing between bites, she asked Jane to tell her about Earth and her travels.

It was tough to eat and answer the rapid fire questions Twee fired off, but Jane enjoyed herself anyway. The Lomosean woman was anxious to know how other women fared on distant planets, believing what she read was not always the truth. Jane told her about her home and her family, saying that they were military, but not giving any specifics, especially after Twee mentioned having been assigned to an early stage of the base negotiations where Admiral Rothko had been one of the attendees.

"Tremna was very impressed with that man, I can tell you that!" said Twee, slathering her muffin with butter. "He was so very in command of his team, and seemed to have an answer for everything! But I think Tremna also found him very attractive, because she kept throwing dinner parties for him." Twee giggled at the thought. "Have you ever seen him?"

Jane could not repress her own laugh. Yes, her father was very attractive, and yes, he had told them Tremna had made what he thought was a pass at him, adding but who could tell for certain with a woman in power. They had all found the stories funny, but it was even funnier to hear it from someone else who was there. "I've met the Admiral," admitted Jane, "and I think he's very attractive. All that silver hair!" She took the opportunity to ask Twee about her own family.

"My father is an agricultural engineer and works with Tremna's husband. He was the one who helped me get into the Linguistics Academy. It's very difficult for women here to get out of local work without a mentor and I guess Resh thought I was good enough to get out. I work harder than anyone else because I do not want to shame him," sighed Twee. "But now, I want to go on diplomatic missions, so I work even harder at languages so they will have to take me. I want to leave Lomos and go someplace, your planet, perhaps, where I can study and bring new technology to Lomos. It's the only way we will ever progress past the point we are now at! "

Jane sympathized and told her so. For the remainder of the time, they discussed languages learned and things they both had to do to keep ahead of the pack.

With a promise to meet again for lunch, Jane and Twee parted company in the lobby of the building where the committees were meeting for the morning session. Jane's staff was waiting for her, all of them ready for their next assignment. Pulling out her docupad, she gave them the topics and locations of the sessions in which they would sit, leaving Belle for last. "Brace yourself, Winter, you're coming with me and the big boys. We're doing simultaneous translations for land acquisition. The Lomosean head does not speak any English at all and she's a stickler for grammar. On top of that, she refuses to wear a universal translator, so we have to rely on her personal interpreter to get it right. I'll sit with them, you'll sit with Morgan and Cardozo." She handed Belle an earpiece and small black box. "Wear this one, it's channeled directly into me. That way, we can verify without stopping the discussion."

"What about Morgan? What's he wearing?"

"A UT-61. It should keep him happy."

"What should keep me happy?" Morgan seemed to materialize out of nowhere.

"This," said Jane, handing him a translator. "I know it's bulkier than a UT-47, but it will record any verbal notes you want to make. You can also hear what Belle and I are saying, and if you want to tell me anything, use the c-2 button. But please don't talk to me while we're translating."

Morgan nodded and took the box. "Yes, ma'am. Anything else, ma'am?" His tone was good-natured.

Jane furrowed her brow and thought for a moment. "Yes, as a matter of fact. Keep away from idiomatic expressions. They're hard to translate and the Lomosi almost always get them wrong."

"I'll try to be careful, Lieutenant," he answered, his voice serious but pleasant.

She looked up into the captain's face, puzzled by his friendly demeanor after the previous night's display of veiled hostility. She had expected nothing less than a sharp retort, but this threw her off guard. Shaking her head, she turned to Cardozo and handed him a translator of his own. "This one's a UT-47, Captain Cardozo. I didn't think you'd need a recorder with it." She smiled sweetly and added "I think you can manage with a docupad."

He chuckled and took the small translator from her open hand. "Ah appreciate the thoughtfulness, Cousin Krieg."

"Cousin Krieg?" echoed Belle..

"Ah suppose Ah neglected to tell y'all that the lieutenant and Ah are cousins through a most fortunate marriage." He glanced at Morgan and ignored the scowl.

Morgan muttered as he fitted the device into his ear, "One of you will have to tell me more about it later." Still adjusting the translator, he strode into the assigned room leaving the others to follow.

Belle looked from Jane to Blackjack, and decided to follow Morgan's lead. As much as she wanted to hear what Jane was about to say, the storm brewing in the lieutenant's eyes told her to clear out while she still had the chance.

As soon as they were alone, Jane turned on Blackjack. "Why did you say that?" she angrily demanded.

"Don't get your dander up, Cousin Krieg; it was a perfectly natural response."

"Don't you 'Cousin Krieg' me, you southern snake. You are nothing but trouble and I wish you'd go away!" She spun on her heel and stalked into the conference room, still swearing under her breath, annoyed even further by the sound of Cardozo's laughter behind her.

The meeting droned on for several hours before the chair finally called for a lunch break. Pulling her translator from her ear, Jane momentarily rested her head on her arms. Her ear ached almost as much as her head, but there was little she could do about it. Even with her eyes closed, she could still see the document upon which she was resting. Word by word they had gone over the contracts for land which would be used for the base. The Lomosi wanted every inch accounted for in great detail. The Terrans were prepared for the meeting, but it did not make it any less tedious. Jane was thankful that the only job she had was to keep the translations straight. Morgan had been brilliant in the way he had handled the Lomosean chairwoman. As frustrated as he must have been with the constant nitpicking, he never lost his cool as he reviewed the technical needs for large open space and secured buildings. Kip Lucas, well used to the negotiations, sat back and allowed Morgan to reiterate their position. But something the Lomosean had said stuck in Jane's mind: there were no provisions for comprehensive training of the locals. As Twee had mentioned at breakfast, there were others like her who wanted to study off world.

A pair of hands massaging her knotted shoulders made her groan softly. "I don't know who you are and I don't care; just don't stop what you're doing," she purred.

"Ah'd do this forever," drawled a familiar voice, "but Ah doubt if you'd let me."

"I shoulda known," sighed Jane, reluctantly picking up her head. The fingers worked their way up to her neck. "I'll think about forgiving you if you keep doing that."

Cardozo laughed but kept rubbing. "Ah think you need food almost as much as you need this," he said. "Will you take lunch with me?"

"Where's Belle? I thought she was your in-flight steady."

He laughed again. "She's off with Davies and Nguyen. Something about finding a Lomosean colloquial dictionary."

"Smart people. I hope they find one and share it with me. My Lomosean is a little too literate I think. Sorta like speaking biblical Hebrew. They understand you, but they snicker a lot."

He patted her on the back, signaling the end of the massage. "Come on, Sarah Jane; Ah know a terrific little cafe where we can get something akin to a tuna sandwich and a cup of coffee." He held out his hand and helped her to her feet. "Just lean on me, and Ah won't let you fall."

With a snort, she slipped her arm through his and walked out with him. Captain Morgan was standing outside the room with Kip Lucas. With a polite nod, she strolled past them both.

⸻

Lunch with Jackson Cardozo proved to be a pleasant experience. He did, in fact, know a place where a sandwich could be obtained and, in honor of the temporary residents from Earth, the proprietor had managed to master the art of brewing coffee. Sitting outside beneath a bright yellow awning, Jackson regaled Jane with stories about his childhood and, to some extent, hers. He knew a great deal about the Rothko clan, mostly from family stories and his friendship with Jonathan. His memories of the summer at the beach were far more extensive than hers, but as he related incidents from the long ago summer, she found herself remembering more and more detail.

In her dress blues, Jane looked every inch an officer. Although her hair was pulled back in a chignon, the dark auburn set off the creaminess of her skin. Cardozo was struck by how very beautiful she was, the beauty complemented by a distinct aura of strength emanating from her dark lashed eyes. While she was speaking animatedly of her brother, Jackson idly wondered if she would be amenable to a serious pass from him. She was, as his mother would say, a perfectly suitable young lady, but something held him back. Whether it was the seriousness in which she took herself and her career, or her naturally reserved nature, he did not want to risk alienating her with something which might be automatically rebuffed. Any attempt to court her would have to be done gradually and with great finesse. And there was Boston to consider. Asher Morgenstern might not know it yet, but little Calamity Sarah Jane was as surely getting under his skin as she was under Cardozo's. Thank God for the bubbly Annabelle Winter; she was, at least for the moment, a pleasant diversion.

"I guess I didn't realize that you and Jonathan had trained together," said Jane, sipping her hot coffee. "I always thought of you as being much older."

"Ah am older; Ah'd already been your mother's Air Force five years before I went to Super-School, at her behest, Ah might add."

Jane grinned at him. "I take it her behest was more like an order."

"True, and she paid the price for pissin' me off in the process. Ah deserted her entourage for the Fleet shortly after that unfortunate mishap. Ah found Ah liked space more than Ah expected to like it."

"But Jonathan didn't; he stayed with the Air Force. And then there's the captain....." her voice trailed off.

"Speed and Boston were both in the unit," explained Blackjack. "Boston was assigned as the chaplain because we were supposed to be a full complement. He was busy gettin' certified for interplanetary mission; Speed was just another cadet. The unit was a mixed bag; lots of people with different angles. Sure, we all had a lot in common, but your brother and Ah tended to have radical differences. We did, however, agree on one thing, and that was we were both looking for the Great Adventure. All of us were a little starry eyed, but Speed chose to stay with the fighter force, Ah think, because he wanted more than anything to be attached to the IDF. He was tired of being the token Jew."

"But you and Morgan joined the fleet. I think you're right about Jonathan wanting to go to Israel, though; he saw the Air Force as a way of having the best of both worlds." Her admiration for her big brother was unmistakable. "Mom's very proud of the work he's doing for them."

"That is not at all surprising, Sarah Jane. More than once she's tried to get me and Boston to do a stint with their orbiters."

"But what's your status now, Jackson? Are you officially in or out of the fleet?"

"Half way between the two. Officially, my paycheck comes from the government, but my rank as captain is my own, as an owner of a small ship. The Fleet Command has decided Ah am much more useful to them as a freelance advisor." He paused to pour himself another cup of coffee. "Ah go where they tell me to go, but Ah have the right to refuse as Ah see fit. Not that Ah ever do. Some folk like to think of me as an intelligence officer, but that's not strictly true either."

Jane tried to fit the pieces of the puzzle together, but it was still unclear as to where this cousin-by-marriage actually fit into the military structure she knew so well. "I'm not sure I totally understand," she admitted with a frown.

"You're not supposed to. Ah think the only one who does understand is your daddy," laughed Blackjack, "and he's not sharin' it with anyone else, even me. He's the one who hasn't taken away my uniform; in fact, Ted's the one who insists that Ah even don the ugly thing." He glanced reluctantly at his watch. "Ah think it's time for us to be heading back to the committee meetings, although Ah'd rather be sittin' here with you."

Jane blushed, but smiled. "Ah think you're right, Cousin Jackson," she drawled, imitating his Louisiana accent perfectly. She reached for her wallet, but Jackson stopped her. "Ah'm not in the habit of lettin' men pay for my eatin'."

"Forget it, Cousin Krieg, 'cause this one's on me. Your daddy would find it proper for me to pick up the tab. After all, he pays me a helluva lot more than he pays you." Jackson was pleased to see her blush once more.

When they returned at the negotiations, Morgan was standing in the lobby with several of the *Washington* crewmates. "So nice of you to come," he said, greeting Jane and Blackjack as they joined the others. "Plan on being aboard ship in the morning, Lieutenant. We're having an open house, so to speak, for some of the Lomosi who have never been aboard a large space vessel. You'll be leading one of the tour groups."

"Yes, sir," replied Jane.

"And you, Blackjack, I'd like you to be there as well. Madame Tremna and her husband will be attending the festivities," he added, shooting Cardozo a black look, which Cardozo ignored. "Staff meeting at 0800 before our guests arrive at 0900. Now, ladies and gentlemen, let's get to our meetings." Morgan reached out and grabbed Cardozo's arm, holding him back. As soon as the others were gone, he asked him where he had been with the lieutenant.

"Out to lunch. Is that a problem?"

"Only if you make it one," scowled Morgan. "Did you have a nice time?" The question dripped with sarcasm.

Cardozo was not at all bothered by his tone. "As a matter of fact, yes. Ah highly recommend it, Boston. You might act less like a martinet if you got to know the girl a little better." Without waiting for a reply, he walked away.

As soon as he was seated, Jane motioned to his translator. Morgan switched it on and heard Jane speaking into her own unit. "Sir, if you have the time later, I would like to meet with you concerning an addendum to our end of the treaty." Her eyes met his across the table.

"Certainly, Lieutenant." On impulse, he added "How 'bout over dinner this evening?"

Jane's eyes opened at little wider, surprised by the invitation and at the same time, suspicious. "That would be fine, Captain. Thank you." She did not know what else to say.

"We'll dine in my cabin at 1900." He caught himself foolishly sounding like he had just asked her for a date and hoped his beard masked the redness he felt creeping up his face.

"Yes, sir," replied Jane, still looking at him skeptically. *I'm not making him crazy,"* she thought, *"he's making me crazy!"* With a shake of her head, she focused her attention on the documents on the table.

The session broke up at 1500. Not wanting to hang around, Jane quickly gathered up her notes and left, telling Belle she was going over to some shops she had seen as she walked to the conference.

"Are you actually going shopping?" asked Belle, thinking such a mundane act uncharacteristic for Jane.

"Yes, as a matter of fact, I am," she said a little too sharply and she quickly softened her tone. "On my way to lunch, I passed a bookshop and a gallery. I thought I'd go over and see if I could pick up a couple of local items for my collection of stuff. Want to come along?"

Belle thought for a moment and said yes. "I've got nieces and nephews who love it when I bring back souvenirs."

They walked along a pretty park until the shops Jane remembered came into view. In the gallery, the clerk was delighted to show them Lomosean arts and crafts. She proudly displayed a wide range of local textiles in vibrant colors characteristic of Lomosean taste. Belle found a necklace made from creamy stones found on the beaches around the perimeter of Decta-Pas. Jane picked up a gossamer scarf in the softest material imaginable. The color, a sort of sea blue green, reminded Jane of the Mediterranean and she thought her mother would love it. In the corner of the little shop, she spotted a collection of animal sculptures, similar in characteristics to the Inuit pieces her father prized. The smallest of the figures was a seal-like creature with a baby, and Jane asked the clerk for the price. It was steep, but not out of range for her wallet. Her prep work had told her the Lomosi did not haggle; that a price was the price and it was considered rude to argue, a funny principle coming from a people who were incredibly sharp treaty negotiators. Settling her bill with the clerk, Jane counted out the rest of the Lomosean currency she had picked up at the currency exchange at the landing port. She had more than enough for a trip to the bookstore. "I'll meet you next door," she told Belle who was still looking over the selection of local jewelry.

The bookshop could have been anywhere on Earth, thought Jane as she poked about the stacks. There were a few books in English, mostly travelogues about Earth and a few grammars. Obviously, there was interest in the visitors from another solar system. Jane concentrated her browsing in the literature section. Although some Lomosean works were already available at home, this was a chance to pick up on how they thought in their leisure hours. With the help of the clerk, Jane selected a volume of short stories and a couple of novels. The clerk was showing her the latest offering on Lomosean language structure when Belle came in.

"Ah, Miss Winter! So nice you back come!" cried the clerk.

Belle giggled at the greeting. "Thank you, Mr. Grif. The dictionary you sold us this afternoon is very handy."

Mr. Grif clapped his long hands together. "So glad book well work for you, Miss Winter." He turned thoughtful for a moment, then continued in English. "I be practice English, but it is more difficulter that it looks on paper. You have the strangest word order ever seen."

"That's not the first time I've heard that, Mr. Grif," answered Belle in Lomosean. "But not to worry, you'll get the hang of it after a while." She introduced him to Jane. "She speaks more languages than you can imagine!" she said proudly.

"Then I shall look forward to longer visit about you, Lieutenant." He extended his hand and shook Jane's firmly. In Lomosi, he added, "You speak our language very well, but that is to be expected from an expert translator. Perhaps you would come one afternoon and talk to me in the languages I have yet to hear?"

Jane was flattered and readily agreed. "It would be great fun for me, too." She handed him several coins, certain she had enough to cover the cost of the books.

"You will need two more mehtin, Lieutenant," said Mr. Grif, accepting the coins. "On the price of books, we add an education tax." He noticed Jane's puzzled look and continued. "We believe that if you can afford to buy books, you can afford to contribute to the education of children whose parents are unable to buy books for them. Even we have poverty, Lieutenant, but we do not hold it against those who are less able than others. The monies collected from the education tax are used to buy not only schoolbooks, but storybooks as well. Children should learn the pleasure of reading, not just the task of learning. We believe that every household should have books, not just the households of the affluent."

Jane was impressed with this aspect of Lomosean culture. While she knew they prized education above most things, she was unaware of the more routine ways they provided for their children. "It is a beautiful way to support education," said Jane. "I would gladly pay any tax that contributes to the welfare of children." She handed him the appropriate coins. Promising to come back soon, Jane and Belle left the shop.

The street was more crowded when they emerged. Like people everywhere, the Lomosi were hurrying home at the end of the workday. They passed a grocery store and on impulse, stopped in. There was very little difference in set up from the markets back home, and the two women enjoyed themselves as they wandered up and down the aisles examining the things the natives ate. At the produce section, they giggled as they filled several self-service bags with exotic looking fruits. A kindly woman, fascinated by the opportunity to meet real outworlders, helped them pick the ripest specimens. On the checkout line, a few people surreptitiously stared at them, but Belle and Jane pretended not to notice. Back on the street, they divvied up the parcels. "Do you think they have taxis here?" asked Belle, hoisting the bag in her arms.

"I haven't the vaguest idea," said Jane, adjusting her own packages. "Come on, Annabelle, we're tough, we can make it back to the ship under our own steam."

It was a struggle, but they made it. At the security gate, they saw Dresher coming back from his own excursion. He quickly came to their aid, rescuing the fruit filled bags from their weary arms. "I always tell my wife: *if you can't carry it, don't buy it,*" pronounced Dresher with a grin.

"And do you go along as porter when she wants a new couch?" asked Belle sweetly.

"Nah, she can carry it herself," he fired back without missing a beat. He followed behind the ladies, still smiling.

Dresher deposited the parcels in Jane's cabin where they divided up the fruit, then allowed themselves the pleasure of cutting open a shiny pink globe called fistar. The juice flowed out of the fruit, soaking the napkin

Jane placed beneath it. Greedily, they ate it and were tempted to devour a second, when Jane decided against it. "If I get started I'll never stop," she sighed, licking her fingers. "This stuff is addictive."

"I know what I'm having for dinner," announced Belle, tossing a large pink fruit into the air and catching it like a ball. "What about you?"

Jane debated whether or not to tell her that she was dining with the captain, and decided in favor of truth. "I'm having dinner with the captain."

"Oh?" Belle's eyebrow shot up.

"Business. We're going over some proposals so don't get excited."

"Poor lieutenant; he can't even give you the evening off."

"Good-bye, Belle," said Jane, thrusting a bag into her arms. "I want to shower and change before dinner."

"Well, have a good time and don't work too hard." She freed one hand to take her last package from Jane. "Don't forget, we've got show 'n tell in the morning. I'll meet you on the bridge at 0800."

"Sounds good to me."

Standing in front of her closet, Jane, wrapped in a towel, debated on what to wear. She was not in the mood for a flight suit, and civvies were out of the question. Rifling through the rack, she found a pair of khaki uniform trousers and a sharply pressed white shirt. "Good enough," she said aloud, taking them from the closet and laying them across the bed. Not bothering with the rest of her daily regalia, she fastened her name tag over the pocket and attached her pilot's wings to the collar; absolute standards on any uniform she wore. Slipping on her robe, she went back into the sitting room and picked up the books she had bought from Mr. Grif. Curled up on the couch, she started the novel.

Jane was so engrossed in the saga of a Lomosean woman's attempts to hold her family together despite terrible tragedy, that she almost lost track of the time. It was already 1845 when she reluctantly set the book aside. Hurriedly dressing, she grabbed her leather folio and started out the door, but changed her mind. Coming back in, she scurried into the bedroom and checked herself in the mirror one last time. Her hair, partially gathered in a clip at the top of her head, fell almost to her waist. She ran her hand over the top to smooth it just a little. The rest of her passed her quick inspection; the creases in her trousers were straight, and the shirt, tucked neatly in her pants, was perfectly pressed. She noticed, however, that the trousers were a little looser than they had been the last time she wore them, and Jane made a mental note to herself to stop in at sickbay for a glance at the scale. Satisfied with her appearance, she headed to the door but stopped again. On impulse, she chose two perfectly formed fistars and took them along.

Morgan was sitting in his armchair when she arrived. He stood when she entered the room, and seemed pleased when she handed him the two pink fruits. "It wasn't necessary, but I thank you for the thoughtfulness," he said, holding the fragrant globes to his nose; they were wonderfully sweet-smelling. "Can I fix you a drink, Lieutenant?" he asked, setting the fistars in a pottery bowl on the small end table.

"Yes, thank you," replied Jane, still standing awkwardly in the center of the room. She was a little surprised to find him in a pair of jeans and an oversized raw cotton shirt. In the corner of the cabin, his table had been covered with a snowy damask cloth and laid with china bearing the Fleet emblem and simply blown crystal. Jane recognized it as the same tableware her father used whenever he sailed with the Fleet. Not every captain was provided with such elegant fittings and Jane wondered what exactly he had done to rate this kind of supply.

Morgan took the leather folio from her hand and set it against the leg of his desk. "What's your pleasure? I've got bourbon, scotch, vodka, or would you prefer some wine?" The geniality in his voice did not mask his own nervousness very well.

"Scotch, sir, please. Neat."

The captain poured two shots. "I hope Laphroaig is okay," he said, handing her a glass. "Please sit down, Lieutenant." He returned to his armchair and waited until she sat primly on the sofa. "You mentioned some additions to the proposals as they now sit on the negotiating table."

"Yes, Captain, there was an area in which we can do a great deal of good with very little effort on our part," explained Jane. "In the treaty, there is no provision for exchange of students between the two planets. I think there is sufficient interest here to warrant an investigation of such an inclusion." She went on to relate some of what Twee Hafna had told her at breakfast.

Morgan leaned back in his chair and studied her. The stormy grey eyes widened when she spoke about the need for the exchange. She was, as he had been discovering on many levels, a competent and conscientious officer, everything one might expect from a prestigious military family. In her knife sharp khakis, the lieutenant looked even slimmer, more lithesome, than she did in her flight suit; her tiny waist accentuated by the wide leather belt looped through the regulation trousers. He noticed that she wore no insignia except for her nametag and wings. He was glad she had not worn a dress uniform; she looked less stiff, more comfortable. And the bright, white sneakers were hard to miss. Morgan caught himself wondering what it would be like to be comfortable with her, instead of constantly on his guard. He realized she had stopped talking and was waiting for his reply.

"You're right about an exchange, Lieutenant," he said, quickly recovering, "and I think some inquiries can be made with regard to establishing one within the bounds of the treaty. Why don't you bring it up tomorrow morning at the staff meeting? You can ask Barb to verify the protocol involved and then see if you can get a link to HQ and have them issue an official invitation. I imagine they will. Then you can write it up as an amendment and present it at the next treaty session." Morgan liked the suggestion and hoped his enthusiasm was visible. He was fairly certain HQ would greet the suggestion favorably and it would be a feather in her cap should the amendment be incorporated into the draft of the treaty.

A soft chiming told Morgan the first course had arrived in the dumbwaiter. His was the only cabin with the device and he used it often. "I hope you're hungry," he said, leading the way to the table. "I've ordered a rather unusual dinner for us."

Jane stood and followed him to where he pulled a chair out for her. "I am hungry, sir," she admitted, taking her seat.

Morgan placed a dish of Terran spinach salad before her and smiled when her eyes widened in amazement. "There's a small hydroponic garden deep in the hold. If you are exceptionally nice to the chef, he will turn out a home grown salad on occasion."

The vegetables tasted refreshingly familiar after weeks of local produce and reconstituted iceberg lettuce. Jane tried not to look like a glutton as she finished every last leaf on the plate. Between bites, they made small talk about how she was faring since the Pana-Di incident. Morgan expressed honest concern for her well-being, which made Jane feel a little guilty about her opinion of Ash Morgan the man.

Before the next course arrived, Morgan produced a bottle of Bordeaux. "It's an excellent vintage," he explained as he carefully removed the cork. "I try to keep a decent selection on board, although it's tough to know how much of what to lay in before we leave."

Jane thought a red wine to be a little strange for a man who did not eat meat any more regularly than she did. But the aroma of grilled beef filled the cabin as soon as the dumbwaiter chimed a second time. Morgan jumped up to clear the salad plates, waving Jane away when she tried to take her own to the counter near the dumbwaiter door. With great relish, he placed a steak smothered in mushrooms before her and laughed when she tried to mask her disappointment at his choice.

"I believe, Lieutenant," he announced with an smug smile, "you like yours medium rare."

Jane frantically tried to think of a polite refusal which would not hurt his feelings. "It looks wonderful, sir, but I do not eat meat." She grimaced and waited for his angry reply.

"Not even kosher meat?" he asked, his eyes twinkling.

"Excuse me?"

He was still smiling, enjoying her shocked expression. It was exactly as he thought it would be. "Tapper assured me you were a steak eater...at least at home. And do you think I would offer you *tref*?"

"Oh, Captain!" cried Jane, suddenly allowing herself to take in the delicious aroma. "Real meat! Where did you get it?"

"Captain's prerogative. Surely, you of all people have heard that before." His reprimand was gently teasing. "I keep a small store in the freezer, carefully hidden, to be used when I cannot stand the sight of another ten-grain-and-mushroom patty. And cook has a grill. Again, the joys of being CO." He sliced off a piece of meat and popped it in his mouth. "Eat up, Lieutenant, before I eat yours as well as my own."

She did not need a second invitation. The succulent meat practically melted in her mouth. Even the accompanying green beans and baked potato were a far cry from the normal fare. These, too, were fresh and she suspected that they were from the captain's private stores. For a few moments, they were silent, savoring the familiar flavors long missed. When Morgan finally spoke, it was to ask about her family.

"Tell me about you and Jonathan," he said, taking a moment to refill their goblets. "Back in the old days, whenever he talked about his family, he made it sound like a three-ring circus gone berserk."

Jane nodded; it was an apt way of describing her family: four base-brats with perfectly military parents who needed their comic wildness to relax. "Well," she began slowly, "Bubbe Rose, my paternal grandmother, called us '*der vildes* ' because we were just that, wild. Despite all their efforts, my parents could not instill complete dignity in us until quite late in our childhood, although we always knew when to straighten up and fly right. When I was very little, we lived on base, usually with Mom, with Dad zooming in and out. But we got such terrible reputations that they finally decided we had to settle down somewhere where we could go to school and people weren't afraid of the CO's kids. So we ended up in D.C., and they put us all in the local yeshiva for the rabbis to straighten out."

"Did it work?" asked Morgan.

Jane rolled her eyes and raised a wry brow. "Judge for yourself. Some say yes, others, decidedly no." She laughed lightly at the thought of her and Jonathan in school. "Jonathan was the worst, always in trouble with the *rosh yeshiva*, and I was only a little better. Isaac, he's next in line, is probably the best of the bunch. Very respectable. He's doing his residency in neurology at Johns Hopkins, and Becca, our baby, wants Princeton so bad she can taste it. She's a senior in high school now."

"Does she look like you?" Morgan was unable to resist the question.

"Not a whit. She's taller than me, with big blue eyes and very dark, almost black hair. She's the only one of us to look like a Simon, my maternal grandmother's family. And ooooh, is she smart! Positively brilliant! My father says she's dangerous...absolutely gorgeous and obscenely intelligent....and no fear whatsoever."

And you're not? thought Morgan silently. But he could imagine the Rothkos at dinner and decided it must be a stellar event. "I take it, from what Tapper and Jonathan have told me, that you are all very close."

"Very," agreed Jane, nodding. "When your parents are big shots and other kids tend to shy away from you because of it, it can get pretty lonely. I think that's why there are four of us. We needed each other for companionship."

That was something Asher Morgenstern understood exceptionally well. Suddenly, he wanted to tell her about his family. "I have four brothers," he blurted out. "And I think I would be lost without them, so I know what you mean." He paused, waiting for Jane's reaction to see whether or not he would continue. It was not hard to talk about his family, yet he rarely did. He did not believe in becoming embroiled in other people's private affairs, yet he knew she would understand about them.

Taking the bait, Jane asked "Where are you in the line-up?"

"Number three," he said with a wry smile. "And a terrible disappointment to my parents. They *thought* they were getting a doctor, a lawyer, two rabbis, and a physics professor. They never asked God for a space cadet," he laughed and was relieved to see her smile. "My brothers are all married with kids, all successful. Even Nathan, the next one up, the rabbi, is a success; he chairs the Talmud department at Yeshiva University. I am the bane of my father's existence, but I can live with that. I've given him the one thing my brothers haven't: another son to raise."

"Reuben?"

He raised a surprised eyebrow at her. "Tapper told you about him, huh?" He watched her nod, but she said nothing. "Don't get me started on Reuben; you'll fall asleep at the table listening to me brag about my kid." His voice was full of love and pride, matching the delightful twinkle in his eyes. He pointed in the direction of the artwork gracing the wall beside the credenza. "That is Reuben. All color and grace and exuberance. He lives with my parents while I'm away, and he's given them new life. Of all the grandchildren, he's the odds-on favorite, probably because he is as devoted to them as they are to him. He's a bright, happy kid who plays baseball with the same determination that he studies Torah. Right now, he claims he's having trouble with Mishnah, but I don't believe that for a nanosecond. What's bothering him is that he can't outwit the teacher with his arguments. And all this from a ten-year-old!" As if reading her mind, he suddenly jumped up and went into the bedroom, reappearing with a picture of the boy.

Jane studied the photograph carefully. She could see the father in the eyes of the son, piercingly blue and full of questions. He was wearing jeans and a team t-shirt, a baseball glove dangled from the bat resting on his shoulder, his cap was pushed back on his dark head, and the telltale fringes of the Orthodox hanging out of his waistband on one side. He looked like any other kid, a little smudged but carefree. "He's a cute kid, Captain," said Jane handing him back the picture. "He looks like you."

Morgan held the picture and studied it, a frown creasing his forehead. "A little, but not really. He's more like my wife, of blessed memory." It was the first reference to his late wife and he caught himself sounding a little bit melancholy. Shaking it off, he set the picture on the credenza. Somehow, talking about Tovah seemed all right with Jane. "Tovah was very beautiful, very kind. Reuben is much like her in many respects. They both always know the right thing to say. Something I'm not very good at."

The confession hung between them, making Jane feel as though she had been privy to the most private of thoughts. The mask of captaincy was slipping from Morgan, leaving in its stead a more human, more vulnerable face. The personal nature of the conversation was the complete opposite of what Jane had expected from Morgan. On one hand, she felt as though a friendship might be budding, but she also recognized the danger of feeling too comfortable with him. He had, since she had been aboard the *Washington*, vacillated between hot and cold with her. There were no guarantees that in the morning he would be any different than the way he had been before. Tapper was right; he was not an easy man to know. Despite his momentary openness, he would, she suspected, close right back down the minute she left his cabin. But for the moment, he was affable and expansive and she decided to roll with it.

They continued to talk about their families right through coffee and dessert. The cook had prepared a wonderfully light chocolate mousse which, Morgan explained, had come from his mother's recipe. Leaving the dishes on the table to be cleared later, they went back to the sitting area where Morgan poured cognac into two snifters.

"So what's your assessment of the negotiations, S.J." he asked, using the familiar form of address used only by Tapper. He used it intentionally, silently telegraphing his desire for her to continue in relaxed mode.

"Interesting people, these Lomosi," replied Jane. "They are very skillful negotiators, with a pretty sharp understanding of what's required of them in the event the base is built."

"In the event?" echoed the captain. "Aren't you convinced?"

"Not quite yet. The treaty must be ratified by the Decta on three levels as well as our own Congress. The only way they can get it past their houses is to over-write the treaty in such a way that argument is kept at a minimum. Otherwise it could be locked up here for years."

She was sharper than he expected. Even Cardozo was tiring of the nit-picking over the wording, the need for complete clarification having gone over his head. "What do you know about the Decta?"

"Plenty," she replied candidly. "They are at least as bad as Congress and, to add fuel to the fire, there are a number of reactionaries sitting in the middle house, Lomosi who feel outworlders will pollute the delicate balance they have reached politically. To some extent, they are right, but the other two houses view the treaty as a way to ensure their continued private existence. Until now, Lomos has been basically left alone by other planets. Inter-planetary trade has been pretty much limited to agricultural import-export, but that's only happened when others have come here. As advanced as they are, they have neglected space travel; dangerously so, I might add. Because they do not war, they have assumed others will leave them to their own devices. They are, in that way, very naïve." She paused to sip the cognac. "I think we learned on Pitan that home peace cannot keep away the predators who would steal what they cannot buy."

"And you feel that a base would provide greater security?"

"Don't you? If, say, the Wa'atsi paid a visit here, would they not be less likely to pull another stunt if they know the Lomosi have at their disposal League battle cruisers who routinely pit stop here? The whole issue on Pitan was that they believed they could swoop in and take what they wanted because no one on that planet could catch them in space. They did not bargain for the *Tical* and the *Washington* showing up almost instantly in defense of a poor, technologically backward planet. It was unfortunate that it was the *Tical* who went after them and not a better equipped vessel, but they were still able to stop the raiders. What a shame that Nish died in the battle, though. He was a helluva pioneer and explorer. And basically a nice guy."

Morgan sat upright. "Nish? That pirate?" he guffawed. "How would you know that he was a nice guy?"

A small grin flittered across Jane's face. She enjoyed surprising him with facts little known. "He spent a weekend at my parent's home when we were stationed on Taapusor one summer. That was before the Wa'atsi pulled out of the League. He was a great storyteller. Just another advantage of being an admiral's brat."

Throwing his head back, Morgan laughed. "I suspect only you could find something nice to say about one of the most despised captains in the galaxy! Is there anyone you don't like?"

"Yes."

The lack of clarification told Morgan he had hit a nerve, and he knew that nerve was named Pana-Di. Leaning forward, he reached for her hand. "I cannot tell you how sorry I am about what happened on the way to Jeylos. I should have been more aware of the physical danger to you, personally."

"There was no way for you to know; we both underestimated him, but I told you that already, Captain." She withdrew her hand from his, but it was still warm from his touch. She knew she was blushing and there was nothing she could do to stop it. "No one will blame you, my father least of all, if that's what you're worried about. He's not stupid about those things."

"That wasn't what I meant," he said defensively. "Tapper warned me the kora was circling you like a wolf around a lamb and I should have pulled you off the assignment."

"Don't coddle me, Captain Morgan!" snapped Jane, eyes flashing. "I'm no hothouse flower in need of protection. I did what I had to do; nothing happened that couldn't be stopped and you wouldn't have done anything different if my name was Smith instead of Rothko. I had a job to do and I did it. That's all there is to it."

A part of him wanted to laugh at her vehemence, but his better side kept him from it. Or from snapping back at her. "It's hard, S.J., to separate you completely from your family. The last thing I want to do is bring a broken body back to the Rothkos...or to any family for that matter. But the bottom line was, or rather, still is, that I have a serious responsibility to my crew and I miscalculated. I am still very sorry."

"No apology necessary, sir, but apology accepted if you insist." Jane settled back down, feeling more than a little foolish. Certainly she had gotten some of the anger off her chest, but now, it seemed that he was doing a better job being angry at himself than she was at him. A change in subject was necessary and she took advantage of the silence to get up from her chair and look over his bookcase. In a time when information was collected on discs to be read on screens, it was pleasant to see a wall of books on a space vessel. Morgan's collection could only be described as eclectic; titles ranged from fiction to philosophy, mathematics to murder mysteries. "What was your favorite subject in school?" asked Jane lightly.

"Ambition, distraction, uglification and derision," Morgan said without missing a beat.

She laughed; "'I never heard of uglification," she tossed back. 'What is it?'"

Morgan greatly liked the way she answered. "'Never heard of uglification! ...You know what to beautify is, I suppose?'"

"'Yes, it means----to --make--anything--prettier.'"

"'Well, then, if you don't know what to uglify is, you *are* a simpleton.'"

Thinking quickly, she switched gears. "He took his vorpal sword in hand; Long time the manxome foe he sought---So rested he by the tumtum tree, and stood a while in thought." Eyes flashing, she awaited his reply.

Narrowing his eyes to look at her, Morgan leaned forward prepared to meet the challenge. "And, as in uffish thought he stood, The Jabberwock, with eyes of flame, came whiffling through the tulgey wood, and burbled as it came."

And instantly came the answer: "One, two! One, two! And through and through the vorpal blade went snicker-snack! He left it dead and with its head he went galumping back."

Not to be outdone by a mere slip of a lieutenant, Morgan rose from his chair and approached her menacingly. "*As-tu tue le Jaseroque? Viens a mon coeur, fils rayonnais! O jour frabberjeais! Calleau! Callai! Il corrtule dans sa joie.*" He was close to her, his face bright with apparent triumph.

Jane momentarily considered conceding, but instead, threw caution out the porthole and finished the verse in a third language. "*Es brillag war. Die schlichte Toven, Wirrten und wimmelten in Waben; Und aller-mumsige Burggoven, Die mohmen Rath ausgraben.*"

The triumph was, in the end, hers, for he held up his hands in mock surrender and laughed heartily. "Another Carrollian!" he cried, "I would never have guessed you went in for whimsy!"

"Only by default, Captain," laughed Jane, pleased with the end result of the contest. "My father is the Carrollian and we found, early on, that recitation was a sure way of getting his undivided attention. I can do Jabberwocky in a whole bunch of languages, but English is still my favorite. There's something about the rhythm in the original...." her voice trailed off as she noticed his proximity. Turning back to the shelves, she straightened slightly and studied the other books. "Would you mind terribly if I borrowed a book now and then? You have some here I would really like to read."

Sensing her discomfort, Morgan stepped back. "Any time, S.J. I am always happy to lend a volume to an interested crewmate. Do you see anything you'd like to take tonight?"

"Hmmmm," she purred, running her finger along the row until she found one. "This one, for sure." She pulled a slim volume of poetry from the shelf. "Jonathan is a great fan of Ferlinghetti," she said, her back still toward the captain.

"No surprise there; read the inscription on the flyleaf."

She opened the book and recognized her brother's spidery scrawl. "For Boston," she read aloud, "on another one of your interminable birthdays. This should shed new light on your classical conception of poesy. With the utmost respect, JSR." Jane looked at him thoughtfully. "You're very different from the man you show the world, aren't you, Captain?"

"I suppose," he replied, perching on the edge of the credenza. "But aren't we all?" His brow rose with the question, demanding a reply.

"Perhaps, but I like to think of myself as a little more open than that. I'm far less mysterious than you, sir."

"Mysterious? I wouldn't go that far. Private, perhaps, but not mysterious."

"Have it as you will," shrugged Jane.

He was disappointed that she did not argue the point. Arguing with Jane promised to be as much fun as arguing with Jonathan, but Morgan was unsure as to how to get her to take the bait. "You cannot possibly make a statement like that without further clarification, Sarah Jane," he said, taking another tack, "Come on, defend yourself!"

The gauntlet was thrown down and Jane considered the challenge. For a moment she was silent, weighing the advantages against the disadvantages of repartee with her captain, but it was obvious he knew what he was doing. She raised her eyes to him and straightened her shoulders. "All right then, I'll stand by what I said. You are mysterious to the casual observer, Captain Morgan né, Morgenstern." She caught his eyes flare momentarily. "You seem to be like everyone else, if you discount your rather odd eating habits; that is, odd to those who do not know the rigors of *kashrut*. As captain of a starship, you pose as a man of science, but behind the door of your cabin, you are as much a Talmudist as any other Orthodox rabbi. And a rabbi you are; arbitrating amongst your crew like a *dayan*, stroking your beard and seeking precedents for your replies. You study Responsa with regularity, I suspect, and you mete out judgment much the same way."

"But any captain worth his weight in salt does the same thing." His protest was weak.

"Sure, but not the *same* way. You use your education, and I mean all of your education, to your own advantage, as well you should. But it's more than that, Captain. You belittle me privately because I use my mother's maiden name as a way of protecting myself, but, sir, you are guilty of the same offense. Or is it that Morgenstern was too long to fit on your tags? Frankly," she said, her eyes flashing, "I see no difference."

"And all this makes me mysterious?" he countered, figuring his best defense was offense. "I may not make a public display of my religious beliefs, but when questioned about them, I answer honestly. Can you say the same?"

"Certainly. But my family connections would serve to make others, yourself included, remarkably uncomfortable. I have chosen this way after hours of discussion with my brother who regrets not thinking of it first. We are not ashamed of our parents, but we will not be accused of riding their coattails, either." She paused to catch her breath. "What's your excuse?"

"Rabbi Morgenstern the chaplain is tough to swallow as Asher Morgenstern the Captain. I left the rabbinate because I felt a greater need to do something important in the service of my country. Changing the name was an easy way of indicating a deeper, more complex change in the man." He slid off the credenza and went back to the couch. Sitting, he extended his feet and rested them on the table. "A lot of people still know me as Rabbi Morgenstern; I'm not ashamed of what I was. But what I do now is a far cry from the chaplaincy."

"True. Now when someone dies, you need not administer any form of last rites, regardless of denomination. You merely write to the family."

"FOUL!" he protested, jumping up. "In that case, the chaplain and the captain both have responsibility. I do not serve as chaplain to my own ship, but I can and, unfortunately, have administered last rites for a variety of faiths. The knowledge of how doesn't go away because I choose not to do it full time, and the Fleet knows it. *S'micha* doesn't magically disappear; that responsibility is with me at all times."

She took the rebuke in stride. "Then I shall revise the statement. I think you find it easier to deal with people on a temporal plane rather than a spiritual one. I think you prefer questions with answers rather than questions with lofty opinions."

"Ha!" roared Morgan, gleefully rubbing his hands together, thoroughly enjoying himself. "That's how much you know! Does the thirst for adventure play no part in this, madam?"

"You could have adventure as a chaplain; you could still serve on a space going vessel as a man of God!"

"Yes, but I could not control the adventure, could I? I would be sitting in my chapel watching some other captain make all the decisions I would want to make. Rather than go through life as an observer, I chose to alter my life so I would be a participant. The rabbinate did not offer me that same challenge."

Jane leaned against the credenza and smiled. "Ah, the magic word: control. You do like it, don't you?"

"You bet I do, Sarah Jane Rothko Krieg; and so do you." Now he had her where he wanted her; turnabout was most definitely fair play. "You may have a true talent for language, but linguistics gives you a different kind of control...control over what others perceive when they are dependent upon you for translation. Is true fact?"

"Is true fact," admitted Jane. "Language opens up entire worlds for me.

To be able to communicate successfully with out-worlders on their own terms is a rush *you* can only imagine!" Lights danced in her eyes, her face absolutely glowed. "The power of the spoken word is the ultimate power, for it can fend off war, preserve the peace, make friends out of enemies, and lovers out of strangers."

Her last words hung between them, a prism caught in the sun, midair. In that moment, Asher Morgenstern wanted to take her in his arms and make a lover out of a stranger; it took every ounce of his strength not to do so. To crush her in his arms would destroy the order he had carefully created for himself aboard the *Washington*, yet the temptation was almost too great. This slip of a woman excited him more than any woman since Tovah; she was, in short, that very dangerous distraction. But Ash Morgan, Captain of the *Washington*, D.C., restrained himself, calling on every ounce of willpower to keep the heat he felt rising in his body from reflecting in his face. "But the fact remains, you enjoy the power you have over others."

Jane pursed her lips together, her nose wrinkling as she thought about what he had said. There was a difference between control and power no matter how slight. Power had a connotation that displeased Jane; she was hurt that he would think her power-hungry. Suddenly, the fun of banter was gone. "I appreciate your having invited me to dinner. The steak was wonderful. But it's getting late and I think I should be going."

"I'm afraid I've offended you, S.J.," said Morgan softly. "It was not intentional."

"I'm sure it wasn't." She avoided his eyes. "Thank you again, Captain Morgan. Good-night." She picked up her folio and started to the door, but Morgan crossed the room and took her arm.

With his other hand, he raised her chin, forcing her to look at him. "Never run away from the truth, Sarah Jane. Even if you don't particularly like it, stare at it long and hard and decide how to deal with it. That's the difference between an officer and a good officer."

The grey eyes were bright, too bright, but they bore directly into his. "I'll try to remember that," she said evenly.

Morgan dropped her arm and watched her disappear through the door. "Damn," he spat when she was gone. It was not how he wanted the evening to end. He had hoped to reach some kind of understanding with Jane, some sort of easy peace that would serve to help them work more successfully together. Angrily, he slammed the button on the dumbwaiter, signaling the galley he was ready to have dinner cleared from his cabin.

In her quarters, Jane stripped off her khakis and took a long, hot shower. She was angry at herself for getting into the conversation with Morgan in the first place; angry with him for baiting her. "How could I be so stupid?" she asked herself aloud, the water streaming down her back. "He must think I'm some sort of repressed adolescent!" Her voice echoed off the walls of the shower stall. Then the whole thing struck her as very funny. A guffaw turned into a chortle, the chortle into a laugh. She turned off the water, wrapped herself in a towel, and paused just long enough in front of the mirror to catch her own Cheshire grin. "And he's no better, is he?" she told her reflection.

CHAPTER 13

The 0800 general staff meeting was nothing more than a quick review of open house procedure. Lucas arrived in time to hand out a position roster for each of the department heads delineating where crewmates were needed for the tour. Senior staff would lead the visitors through the ship in groups of eight, with specific people assigned to specific visitors. All Lomosean speaking crewmates were attached to the various groups to serve as translators where necessary. Jane and Belle, however, would lead their own tours.

"As for me," grinned Lucas, "I've got the kiddie corps. The boys are bringing their classmates aboard at 1000 hours, so I'll be with you guys long enough to get you started before I meet the kids at the gangway. Kip'll be with me, but I'll have a pager."

"And I'll catch up with you on bridge at 1030," said the captain. "I want to make sure no one fires up the engines." It got the desired laugh.

"On your sheets, and please familiarize yourselves with them before our guests arrive, I've listed the crew quarters open for inspection. Those lucky people have been forewarned and their cabins should be tidy. Aren't they?" Lucas raised an eyebrow, but that was all. There were a couple of stray groans. "All office doors are to be left open unless instructed otherwise. We are selling openness on this one, folks, so we have to look like we mean it."

"Ah take it that does not include mah cabin?" drawled Blackjack, lounging in the door way.

"Not on your life," Morgan snorted. "Keep your door locked. I wouldn't want them to see how you live. They'd run screaming off the ship."

"Well, that does it for me, Captain," said Lucas as she sat down. "Tour guides meet at 0845 at the bottom of the gangway. Everyone else, at your stations."

Unable to resist, Morgan gave them a quick pep talk himself before dismissing them. Standing outside the wardroom, he watched his staff officers file out, his quick eye checking over uniforms for absolute correctness. As Jane walked by, she flashed him a smile, but did not stop. Morgan, almost sorry but almost relieved that she didn't, allowed himself to enjoy the view of her behind in tailored dress blue trousers.

"That's obscene," whispered Cardozo, nudging Morgan with his elbow.

"What's obscene?" His eyes stayed on Jane.

"Leering is obscene, Boston."

"And of course, you would know." Morgan smiled pleasantly and put his arm around Cardozo's shoulders. "Come on, Blackjack, I'll buy you a cup of coffee before the onslaught."

The two captains strolled to the all-night coffee and found a quiet corner. Morgan and Cardozo, friends for so long, were never at a loss for something to discuss, but it was Morgan who was uncharacteristically quiet. Cardozo regarded him carefully before deciding to pry.

"How was your dinner with Sarah Jane?" he asked casually.

"Fine. Shouldn't it have been?" Morgan replied with a frown.

Shaking his head, Cardozo kept pushing. "Ah can hardly believe that 'fine' would sum up an evening of such import. Speak, Boston, or Ah shall hound you until hell freezes over."

Morgan's burst of laughter caused a number of heads to turn in their direction. He toyed with the idea of saying nothing, but decided that would not serve. "My dinner with Krieg was interesting. She's smart and funny in typical Rothko manner. Well read, full of good ideas, and pleasant to be around." He paused and grinned. "Does that satisfy your prurient curiosity?"

"Close, but not quite. Are you planning to take up with the lady?"

Morgan would not have tolerated the question from anyone else, but from Blackjack, it was to be expected. He opted for the honest answer. "Under other circumstances, I might seriously consider it. But for now, I must decline. It would be un-captainly behavior." The last was drawled, an echo of Cardozo's own patter.

"Ah imagine that attitude will please Mr. Bear. The man is positively protective about the little girl."

Morgan shrugged. "Comes with being an adjunct member of the family, I suppose. Wouldn't surprise me in the least if the order came from the old man, himself."

"Hmmmmm. Ah can't say it would surprise me either." Cardozo chuckled at his next thought. "Then again, you *would* be suitable son-in-law material..." his voice trailed off suggestively

About to tell Cardozo to stuff it, Morgan looked up in time to see Belle Winter, folders in one hand, coffee in the other, approaching the table. "What do you have for me, Belle?" he asked lightly.

"Rough draft of my paper, Captain," she answered, handing him the papers. "I was hoping you'd be able to look it over before we leave port. If there aren't a lot of mistakes, I thought I'd transmit while we're here."

"I'm sure there aren't, Belle. I've never known you to hand me less than anything worthy of an A." He pushed out a chair with his foot. "Would you like to join us for the remaining few minutes before the onslaught?"

"Thank you, Captain." She blushed prettily.

"Ah assume you are doing well in your tutorial with the captain here," said Blackjack, sitting up a little straighter in his chair.

"Better than well. Belle will do us proud at OCS. I just hope I'll be lucky enough to get her back when she's done." Morgan grinned at the yeomate as she turned even deeper red.

"I want to come back, but as a linguistics specialist like Jane. There isn't a language she can't handle." There was a deep snort from Cardozo, and a pursed-lipped grin on Morgan's face. Belle looked from one to the other, wondering what she had said. Feeling the need to defend her lieutenant, she added "She really is a terrific officer to work for. I mean, she's fair and she knows her stuff."

"No argument there," laughed Blackjack, slapping Morgan on the arm. "You see, she's universally loved."

Belle thought she had stumbled into the middle of a very private conversation, one which she did not want to hear. Her feelings for Captain Morgan had been long suppressed, but there was no denying the fact that she hoped he would notice her as woman once she became an officer. On the other hand, Blackjack's recent attentions had been most welcome in spite of his reputation. Now her face, she was certain, was crimson and she practically jumped out of her chair. "I've got to go, sirs," she stammered, wanting to get as far away from them as possible. Leaving her coffee cup behind, she saluted and scurried away, without waiting to be formally dismissed.

"See what you did to her!" demanded Morgan, half amused, half angry.

"What Ah did? Boston, you are thicker than a bayou in weed season! That pretty little girl has a thing for y'all!"

The bare space between Morgan's beard and his brow flushed an uncommon shade of pink. "Don't be absurd!"

"Mah God, Boston is blushing'!" Blackjack's laughter echoed across the mess causing others to again turn in their direction.

"Shut yer trap, Blackjack," he growled, feeling eyes from all directions. Lowering his voice, he leaned toward his friend. "You're the one showing her a good time in port, fella, not me. If she's got a thing for anyone on this ship, it's you!"

Cardozo just kept laughing.

Belle fled to her quarters. Her face was hot and it was all she could do to keep the tears from spilling out before she reached the privacy of her cabin. Mortified, she threw herself across her bunk. They had seen her blush and it had been funny to them both. Even though neither had said a word, the yeomate knew they could see right through her. Sitting up on the bed, it dawned on her that it was Jane who had been the subject of their conversation and it was Morgan who was wrestling with his own conscience. All the baiting and cold-shouldering was nothing more than a ruse on both their parts. At once, Belle was both angry and sad. Jane was pretty, maybe even beautiful she could concede, but she was so obviously not interested in anything but her work. She kept everyone at a cordial but safe distance. And even though they worked together closely, Jane was not at all open about herself. *Maybe it's the mystery that has everyone, even Tapper,* thought Belle, *wanting to be around her.* Wiping her eyes, she had to admit to herself that she was jealous of her lieutenant. She stood up and went to throw some cold water on her face. Being jealous, she decided, was pointless.

Tapper sat in his office alone, waiting for the first tour to hit the engineering deck. In addition to his duties as tech chief on the *Washington*, he served as monitor for classified communications. Due to an odd blip in assignments, Tapper had been handed the job not only because of his little-used rank of commander, but because of his uncanny ability to unscramble cryptology at an alarming rate. Normal communications were routed through the comm desk off the bridge, but anything coming in encoded, went directly to Tapper's office. On this morning, there was a stack of incoming waiting transfer to disc. Three were personal messages from Reuben Morgenstern to his father, all using the classified code Tapper had provided the boy. He slipped them into his pocket to give to Morgan as soon as possible. There was one was for Jane, but the opening greeting from her father was for him as well. That, too, he put into his pocket. But there was another from HQ, marked for his eyes only, which required his full attention. Tapper played the disc, swearing softly at each revelation Admiral Rothko made.

The old man looked grim as he spoke. "The Syrians are mobilizing along the Iraqi border, but they don't seem to be staying there. Latest intelligence reports say that the Jordanians are resisting a safe-passage deal, but we don't know how long they can hold out. Ali Hassan has his eyes on Israel, Tapper, and this time, I think he's got enough fire power to blow through Jordan whether or not Mustafa wants him there. My wife is deploying as many fighters as she can, but we're limited as to how much we can do. As you know, Jonathan is there, but we haven't been hearing much from him lately." The admiral paused and rubbed his cheek. He looked tired, painfully so. "The worst is yet to come. It would seem, via transmissions we have intercepted, Ali Hassan has outworlder friends he's relying on for additional fire power. We suspect there might be Wa'atsi involved, but we're not sure. There is so much we don't know, Tapper! Not that you could find anything else. Share this with Ash, but not with Jane. I'm relying on your discretion to keep this away from her until it becomes a need to know situation. Forgive a father's protectiveness." A small frown creased his face. "She's doing well, judging from what we hear, in spite of the garbage with that slime Pana-Di. Since I haven't heard anything more about that, Liz and I are assuming she is fully recovered. He is officially persona non grata on this planet. Not that it matters much; it doesn't change what happened to an officer on a U.S. vessel." He smiled unexpectedly. "I'd tell you to give her a hug for me, but then she'd know I've been in touch....privately. Keep an eye on my girl, Tapper. And I'll keep you posted." The admiral signed off.

Tapper sat back in his chair, staring at the empty screen. There was no question that the *Washington* would be called home in the event of a war in the Middle East. It wasn't the presence of Jane on board; that was incidental. It was Morgan whom they would call back to monitor the situation from an orbit. Morgan was their best tactician in space. If there was outworlder involvement, he would be the one in command. A noise in the passageway caught his attention and he quickly ejected the comm disc from the terminal.

Jane's face appeared in the doorway. "Permission to enter, Commander Bear?" she asked with a smile.

"Of course, Lieutenant. Come on in." He stood as Madame Tremna and her entourage entered the glass enclosed office overlooking the technical deck. "Welcome to Ship Operations, Madame Tremna. I'm Commander Joshua Bear." He extended his hand to shake hers.

"I believe we've met before. You are called Tapper, are you not?" asked the Premier. "And you usually wear a baseball cap. Correct?"

Tapper laughed aloud. "You've a good memory, Ma'am. We met on Jeylos, at the first negotiation a year ago, when you caught us playing ball between sessions."

Madame Tremna nodded in agreement. "And I've learned a great deal about baseball since then. My husband has taken up the sport with some of our visitors. Now, tell us about your domain, Commander Tapper."

With the chatter out of the way, Tapper began to explain the functions of a tech chief, keeping a careful eye on Jane as she translated for the benefit of those who did not understand English. He fielded the questions, answering those which did not breach security. The more sensitive ones, he deftly diverted to less delicate areas. Tremna seemed pleased with what she saw and enjoyed the opportunity to sit at the computer console with Tapper as he produced a number of graphic displays, showing her how to manipulate the various elements used in fusion reaction.

By the time they left the technical deck, Jane was convinced Tremna was in love with Tapper. She had observed Madame Tremna during the session, when her face never wavered with emotion. But sitting beside Tapper, she was like a little girl playing with a brand new toy. Tapper spoke frankly to her about what a ship could and could not do. The size of the *Washington* was impressive to the Lomosi, who had only smaller, less sophisticated equipment. As the various aspects of the *Washington*'s capabilities were described, the visitor's eyes widened appreciatively. As she escorted the Premier and her party to the rec deck, Tremna chatted to her about how lucky she was to be on such a marvelous vessel.

"We would do well," said Tremna confidentially, "to send some of our people to Earth to study in your academies."

Not one to miss a glorious opportunity, Jane readily agreed. "It would be wonderful if such an exchange could be added to the treaty. There are several off world exchange students already studying in American institutions, including the military academies."

Madame Tremna smiled graciously at the lieutenant. "I suspect you have already had ideas in this direction, Lieutenant Krieg. Have you explored this with your people?"

Jane colored a little, and smiled back. "As a matter of fact, yes. We are preparing an addendum to be submitted later in the week. Would you be amenable to such an inclusion, Ma'am?"

"I would have to study such a proposal and bring it before my cabinet," she said, then added in a warmer tone, "but I could see where my people would find this to be mutually beneficial."

Satisfied with the answer, Jane was still beaming when they reached the rec deck. Morgan was already there, greeting the visitors as they completed their tours. The adults were gathered around several long tables laid out with sandwiches, sweet rolls, coffee and tea. The school children had their own spread at the opposite side of the mess. Jane moved from group to group, chatting with the visitors, occasionally catching the broad smile on Morgan's face. Things were going exceedingly well and the captain was pleased.

Jane found Twee Hafna sipping coffee with several Lomosi delegates to the conference. As soon as the lieutenant approached, Twee introduced her to the group. Jane answered a number of questions, all difficult, but all showing the tour had stimulated positive responses to the future base on the planet. Morgan joined the little group, standing silently beside Jane as she explained their desire to increase cultural exchange with inhabitants of other worlds. Because Jane was speaking Lomosean, Twee translated for the captain.

When Jane paused, Morgan took the opportunity to jump into the conversation. "We are as anxious to study your art forms as we are to study your technology. We enjoy creative expression and value it highly at home. Most civilizations we come in contact with eventually mount exhibitions which are warmly received on Earth." He waited for Twee to complete her translation. “I hope we will be able to see one of your theatrical productions while we’re here,” he added with a warm smile.

The Lomosi were pleased with this and chattered about which play would be best for the visitors to see. It was Jane’s turn to ask questions and at last, a production was selected. Twee would arrange for a block of seats to be held for Captain Morgan.

As the group headed toward the cage, Jane pulled Twee’s arm and whispered “Catch up with me at the afternoon sessions; I’ve got something to tell you.”

“No sweat,” she replied, using a newly-learned expression. She was rewarded with a wide grin from Jane. “Idiom is everything, you know,” called Twee as she stepped into the elevator.

Finally, the last guest disembarked and everyone breathed a sigh of relief. The open house had gone off without a hitch and Morgan told them so over the ship’s PA.

Officers were summoned to the wardroom for a quick debriefing. As they gathered, the talk was of what they had learned from the experience, especially from the questions which had been asked. Morgan sat at the head of the table, listening to his staff review which areas needed further clarification, and what new tacks could be taken during the negotiations.

Lucas breezed in late, having escorted the school children to their transport. “You were a big hit with the kids, Captain,” she announced taking her seat. “They loved the ship and most of them would have stowed away given the opportunity. A sharp bunch, those Lomosi kids; they ask tough questions.”

“What did they like best?” asked Jane, curious about what tickled an outworlder child.

“After the swimming pool, it had to be, of all things, the library. They were fascinated by the number of hard books we carry in flight. And they liked the maps on the wall. They spent a lot of time trying to identify places they’ve all learned about. They don’t use holomaps in their schools.”

“Maybe,” said Jane slowly, “if we have time, some of us could pay a visit to the classrooms. Do you think it could be arranged?”

“Absolutely. Captain?”

“Absolutely,” he echoed. “We should have time early next week. Who would you take?" Morgan liked the idea and hoped she would ask him to go.

"Me, of course," she grinned, "Belle, Tapper, Blackjack, and anyone else who would volunteer.

"I'd love it, Captain, if you would go." Barb flashed him a smile.

"Do it, Barb. Post the results on the bridge board." He looked around the room. "I hope that we have enough brave souls to venture into the schools so we can hit as many as possible. But if kids rattle you, don't feel obliged."

The meeting broke up, giving everyone time at their stations before heading to the afternoon session.

CHAPTER 14

The Syrian army sat waiting none too patiently at the Jordanian border. The men were anxious for battle, even if they were unsure of where that battle was to take place. They could see Israeli reconnaissance jets fly by from their position, but all they were permitted to do was to shout epithets at the pilots. Restless and bored, petty arguments grew into fist fights until the battalion commanders found themselves threatening execution with the next breach of decorum.

Ali Hassan arrived at last, decked out in with chestful of ribbons, medals and insignia, to address the troops. He quelled the disturbances with promises of action, but it was not until a space vessel set down near the encampment that the men believed him. They had heard there were powerful allies from the heavens coming to ensure a victory and now it looked like they had arrived. Strange, reptilian creatures in elaborate battle costume strode off the ship and toward the tent where Ali Hassan and Gamal Ramadi were holding council. Only one humanoid disembarked, a tall, bluish looking man with cold, cold eyes. Those on the tarmac shuddered when he looked at them; there was something about him, a sense of total command which unsettled the Arab troops.

"Ah, Your Royal Highness," gushed Ali Hassan striding across the tent to greet the man. "We are delighted to have you amongst us!"

"Thank you, Ali Hassan. I am pleased to be able to aid in your cause." He did not take the man's proffered hand. "Let us get down to business."

Ali Hassan took his place at the table where General Ramadi sat waiting impatiently to be introduced. The Syrian sat beside him, with Kora Pana-Di on his left. The Wa'atsi commander took the chair beside the prince and ordered the other members of his staff to the table. "On behalf of the Arab

League," began Hassan with great ceremony, "I welcome you to Syria, an ancient land first coming into its own as a world power on Earth."

"If you are such a world power," interrupted Commander Fushar of the Wa'atsi, "why have you summoned us?"

"Because, my friend, we are an emerging power. In order for us to fulfill our destiny, we need assistance not available to us on this planet."

Kora Pana-Di stifled a yawn. "Get to the point, Hassan."

General Ramadi glowered at the Jeylosian. "The point is, Your Royal Highness, that we are in need of expansion. Our mission must be completed quickly and with great stealth. The Israelis are great wizards in technology; they cannot be defeated with the means at our disposal. That is where you come in, my good friends. With the fighter craft you are carrying aboard your vessel, together with your laser capacity from orbit, we will be able to crush the Israelis before they can react."

Commander Fushar studied the map on the table before him. "All of this for such a small piece of land. Surely there is a greater area you wish to conquer?"

"No!" replied Hassan emphatically. "Just Israel. We want Jerusalem above all else and Jerusalem must be delivered to us unscathed."

"And this area," Fushar said, indicating Jordan on the map. "Who is responsible for this area?"

"A weakling puppet king of no consequence," snorted Hassan. "Mustafa will give us no trouble. He is already involved although he is resisting."

"You said there were Americans working with the Israelis, Hassan," said the kora drily. "What will they do in the event of an invasion?"

"Nothing we cannot deal with. They will stomp around and wave their arms, but they will not enter into battle." Hassan smiled knowingly. "The Americans have very strict policies dealing with foreign territorial involvement; they have become impotent. They sell their technology, but do not provide troop support. It is against their way."

General Ramadi slid a folder across the highly polished table. "These are reconnaissance photos taken over the Negev earlier this week." He paused to let the visitors look at the pictures. "We are most interested in taking out this base early in the invasion. From here, the Israelis can launch a powerful air attack. It is from here, Ein Geshem that they monitor the entire region. There are currently two Americans on the base: a technician who is instructing their ground crew and a high ranking fighter pilot, Major Jonathan Rothko, a specialist in F-511."

The kora picked up a grainy picture of a young man, sunglasses pushed back, and studied it carefully. He had seen that face before; there was something unmistakable about the eyes and he struggled to remember where he had seen him. "Rothko...would that be....?" He could not believe that there might be another way to repay the bitch Krieg.

"Yes," interrupted Hassan, already knowing the rest of the question. "His eldest son." His voice dripped with revilement. "It is a tragedy that the Americans have put two military commands in the hands of Jews."

"Two?" asked the kora, glancing at his host.

"Admiral Rothko, as you know, commands their space fleet, a most strategic position, while his wife, the Brigadier General, currently commands foreign assessment and deployment for their Air Force."

"Ah, I see." The kora had not forgotten about the general, but her elevation to a position of strategic importance was somewhat of a surprise. Leaning back in his chair, he looked about the room in an effort to discern the real motives for his being invited. Certainly there was the issue of sheer fire power, something the Wa'atsi could provide. He knew what he wanted from them, but what exactly did they want from him? The voices around him droned on, but all the kora could think about was a pleasant payback to the family which had caused him to lose face before his own father.

CHAPTER 15

The time on Lomos flew by for the crew of the *Washington*. Madame Tremna liked the idea of an educational exchange and a sub-committee was immediately formed to draft the agreement. Jane found precedent treaties from which to draw the language and the amendment passed with ease. Twee Hafna, kept abreast of the developments by Jane, became the first applicant. Morgan shuttled between the various committees, taking with him whomever he thought would benefit from the experience. As the negotiations drew to a close, he was satisfied with not only the terms of the treaty, but with the role his crew had played.

On the *Washington*'s last night in port, chief negotiator Dolat Qamtar threw a party for the participants at his beachside villa. Madame Tremna attended, with her husband, to add her personal stamp of approval to the end result. She had found the Terran captain to be a shrewd negotiator, one well equipped to handle the myriad of details left for his arrival. She knew he was, in essence, the League's stamp of approval and if he had made any personal changes to the treaty, she was unaware. This, she felt, demonstrated the trust and confidence the League had in their team. It would have seemed stranger to her had the negotiations been concluded without some additional presence on the part of the League. That they held Captain Morgan in high esteem had been well documented before the arrival of *Washington* on Lomos. Although in her conversations with him, he had dismissed his presence as a mere formality, Tremna was certain had he not approved of the treaty there would be no ratification from either the League or the Americans on Earth. Additionally, she was pleased by the general demeanor of Morgan's crew. Their appearance at the table had not slowed the process; in fact, in some instances, it had speeded up the negotiations. And the inclusion of an educational exchange had made her especially happy. As she surveyed the crowd milling about the long buffet tables, she smiled to herself; this was exactly the way she wanted the *Washington*'s visit to end: with conviviality.

Stepping out onto the veranda for a breath of fresh air, the Prime Minister found Lieutenant Krieg sitting with Twee. Gliding over to them, she pulled up a chair. "I would join you, if you do not mind," she asked graciously. "I am glad to have found you together."

"The pleasure is ours, Madame," replied Twee, blushing just a little.

"I am curious, Lieutenant Krieg, how you came to request the inclusion of an educational codicil to the treaty. It was an appropriate addition, but an unexpected one." She sipped her drink and awaited Jane's reply.

"It was because of Twee, Madame Tremna," answered Jane. "She said she wanted to study on Earth and I was surprised to find no exchange had been included. It is a natural extension of the treaty."

Tremna nodded. "And you, Twee, have already made an application for exchange. I see no reason why that application should be denied, although I imagine your parents will be less than pleased." Her small smile belied her concerns. "I will speak with them myself if they give you any argument." That Twee was one of Tremna's own people pleased the Prime Minister. She extended her empty cup to the young Lomosi. "Would you mind, my dear?"

"Oh, no, Madame Tremna." She hastened to her feet and went inside the villa.

As soon as she was gone, Tremna leaned toward Jane. "You are an interesting young woman, Lieutenant Krieg. Very bright, very dedicated, and very much like your brother, I should think."

Startled, Jane echoed "My brother?"

Tremna laughed lightly. "Yes, my dear, your brother. He is a delightful boy with a tremendous talent for backgammon." She reached over and patted Jane's hand. "I had occasion to challenge him when he was here two years ago. Anyone who knows Jonathan can see the resemblance between you." Jane's crestfallen looked made her laugh again; she neglected to mention that she had already inquired of Morgan whether or not there was a blood relation between the pretty lieutenant and the handsome pilot, but had been rebuffed. "I take it this is supposed to be a secret. Do not worry, I shall tell no one."

"Some secret. Everyone I meet seems to know my family."

"Such is the plight of children of famous parents, Lieutenant. Ask my own children; they will complain as loudly as I am sure you complain." She looked up to see Twee arriving with a fresh drink. "I wish you well, Lieutenant Krieg." She rose and took the cup from Twee. "I do not wish to separate friends on their last night together, but I must borrow Twee for a little while. I hope you do not mind."

Jane jumped up. "No, it's all right. I'll see you later, Twee." She watched them go and then turned back to the railing. The sea was only a few yards away, looking as much like Miami Beach as the coast of Lomosna. Although their seas were not nearly as saline as earth's, the unmistakable smell of salt still drifted in on the breeze. There was a tiny light in the distance and Jane wondered if it could be a fishing boat anchored for the night. An inveterate beach person, Jane found herself yearning to walk along the sand. Looking about and seeing no one, she slipped off her shoes, glad she had decided not to wear hose. There were a few steps leading down to the short span of lawn and she crossed it quickly, anxious to feel sand between her toes.

The beach was warm and the sand like raw silk beneath her feet. Happy to be alone with the crash of the waves, Jane walked toward the water. Just like home, the damp sand was cool and refreshing against her skin. She danced into the waves until the water threatened the hem of her skirt while overhead, a bright mirror disc of a moon sparkled, shedding just enough light for Jane to see dark splotches of shells in the sand. She plucked one up and held it in the moonlight, marveling at how much it looked like a scallop shell drawn from the Atlantic. Slipping it into her pocket, she wandered a little further until she came to a small rise. Jane sat down, digging her toes into the sand. On impulse, she unclipped her hair and let it fall; she felt truly free, if only for a few precious moments. In the distance, she could hear the sounds of the party going on behind her, but she did not care. Right now, she was alone and content.

The breeze picked up, making her shiver. Reluctantly, she stood; she knew she had to go back and be social; it was part of her job. Suddenly, someone touched her shoulder and she jumped away from the intruding hand.

She spun around and saw his face clearly enough in the light to detect mirth in his eyes. "Don't you know better than to sneak up on somebody when they think they're alone?"

"Looks to me like we had the same idea, Sarah Jane. I didn't know you were down here; I thought I was alone." He studied her for a moment. "You look different...your hair is loose." Jane automatically began to gather it back into its knot, but his hand stayed hers. "Don't." His voice was suddenly gruff. With a single move, he brought her to him and his mouth covered hers.

Jane's first response was to push away, but something inside stopped her. The kiss was tender; his lips tasted of fistar, heady and delicious. He still held one wrist, but his other arm slipped about her. Morgan's arms felt warm and safe, not the way the kora had when he attacked. Molding herself against him, she answered him in kind, allowing herself to be swallowed by the moment.

Holding her close, the scent of her skin mingled with the comforting scent of the sea enveloped him completely. His kisses were demanding, as though he could not get enough. "You," he groaned hoarsely into her ear, "are a dangerous woman."

Jane entwined her fingers in his hair and pushed his head gently back to look at him. "As you are to me, Asher Morgenstern." Jane caught the edge of her lip with her teeth and chewed for a moment. "You know this cannot be."

"I want to try."

"It would never work."

"You're so sure? I'm not." He saw her nod, but it did not prevent him from covering her mouth with his and letting his tongue caress the inner sanctum behind her lips. Raw heat shot through him when she moved against him. Never had he wanted a woman as he wanted her in that moment and he would have taken her there, on the beach, but he knew she was right. With a last, lingering kiss, he forced himself to move away from her. "We need to go back...."

"And behave as though nothing has happened," she added quickly. Shaken, yet not upset, Jane walked along beside her captain, her fingers busy retwining the mass of hair into a passable chignon.

At the foot of the steps leading back to the patio, Morgan held her back. "Before this goes any further, we both have to be sure this is what we both want." His dark blue eyes peered deep into her grey ones. Jane nodded; she understood the gravity of the event, but said nothing. "For now," he added quietly, "we need to act as though nothing has happened."

Jane remained at the bottom of the stairs while Morgan walked up alone. Tapper stood on the terrace watching the separation. Something had happened, but when Morgan strode past, he could not read the captain's eyes. Moseying down the steps, he took Jane's arm and steered her toward a quiet corner.

"What was that?" Tapper asked.

"He kissed me." The simple sentence had an element of surprise in it.

"He kissed you?"

"Yes."

"And?"

"And it wasn't so bad." She shrugged.

"Oh, boy." Tapper saw big trouble looming on the horizon. "I hope you know what you're doing, S.J."

With a sigh, Jane sagged against his broad chest. "I don't."

"Come on, S.J., let's go get a stiff drink and wipe that moo cow look off your face." He linked his arm with hers and guided her back into the party.

Before leaving, Jane made her farewells to Twee and the others from the negotiating team. Since she had bridge duty in the morning, Jane would be unable to attend the closing ceremonies before the *Washington* left Lomos for Kotuchar, their next destination. She assured Twee that she would catch up with her somewhere between Lomos and Earth, and promised that as soon as possible, she would arrange to meet her somewhere. Jane gave Kip Lucas a chaste peck on the cheek and assured him that when Barb returned to the *Washington* in the morning, she would dutifully listen to all the stories she would be more than happy to tell and retell. Tapper waited patiently while she shook hands endlessly. Finally, he was able to maneuver her out the door, but not before they spied Blackjack, Morgan and Belle sitting at a table, heads together, laughing.

"Don't even think about it, S.J.," admonished the man pulling her along. "You have enough on your plate now, so leave them be. You'll talk to him in the morning or whenever you see him."

"Okay, okay, I'm coming." She growled at him, but went docilely along.

Back on the ship, Tapper saw Jane to her cabin, then followed her in. Plopping down on the couch, he told her to go ahead and change while he waited. With a shrug, she did as she was told and came out a moment later in her robe. She sat down on the other side of the couch, propped her feet up on the table and closed her eyes. A finger prodded her in the ribs. "Hey, squirt, don't go to sleep."

"I'm not sleeping; I'm merely resting my eyes. Whaddya want?"

Tapper cleared his throat. "If Jonathan was here, he would have this little discussion with you, but since he's not, it obviously falls to me."

"Aren't you being a little premature, Tap? I mean, nothing has happened."

"No, but it might."

Jane stood and took Tapper's hand, pulling him up. "Good night, Joshua Bear. It's late, I'm tired and I want to go to sleep and I cannot go to sleep if you are here. So, goodnight." She pushed him in the direction of the door.

Tapper draped an arm about Jane's slim shoulders. "I'll go, S.J., but be warned, we will have this conversation sooner or later."

"Preferably later," laughed Jane, kissing his bearded cheek. "You are a dear, sweet man, and I do love you so."

"The feeling is mutual, sweetheart." He returned the peck and disappeared.

Jane was certain Morgan would not show up at her door. With a sigh, she turned in for the night.

Morgan, Cardozo and Winter crawled back to the ship several hours after Tapper and Jane. Like the Three Musketeers, they staggered up the gangway arm in arm, laughing about silly things. Although not even close to being seriously inebriated, they were celebratory. The treaty negotiations had gone better than had been anticipated and now they were ready for the next leg of the journey. The two men escorted Belle to her cabin where Morgan faced the other way when Jackson kissed the fair yeomate good night.

"I don't know about you, Blackjack," said Morgan when her cabin door slid shut. "I'd have figured you'd be spending the night with her."

With a low whistle, Blackjack slapped the captain on the back. "Boston, are you suggesting that Ah break your own hard and fast rules about co-habitation aboard ship?"

"Since when have you paid attention to rules?"

"Since Ah learned better after a particularly harrowin' experience aboard the Intrepid." They both laughed at the shared memory and set off toward Morgan's cabin for a nightcap.

CHAPTER 16

Kora Pana-Di and the Wa'atsi commander took over operations in the desert almost immediately. With confidence that came only from experience in battle, Commander Fushar ordered a regrouping of the forces to be deployed and instructed the battalion commanders in his own brand of strategy. Each battalion was assigned a member of his personal staff who, in turn, taught new techniques to the Arab legions. When the commander was satisfied with the practice maneuvers, he ordered a senior staff meeting.

Ali Hassan and Gamal Ramadi sat in awe as Fushar and Pana-Di outlined the plan of attack. With the Wa'atsi ship orbiting over the area, they could not only monitor all Israeli movements, but they could intercept virtually all communications.

"They will be unable to move without us knowing," explained the kora with a triumphant smile. "You will have your city before the end of the week."

Ramadi snorted. "We've heard that before, Your Highness. Do not underestimate the Israelis."

With uncharacteristic friendliness, the kora patted the general's back. "Do not underestimate your new power, Gamal Ramadi. You worry too much."

Ali Hassan, although wary of the kora's optimism, tended to agree with him. The added fire power of the Wa'atsi, coupled with their new found listening ability, made him think this time the Israeli Defense Force would fall.

At dawn, the first battalions moved out toward the Israeli border. The three chiefs took up position in a mobile command post provided by the Wa'atsi and waited.

The Israelis had been monitoring the activity around the Arab camp and were prepared. In a matter of minutes after the Arab forces established their direction, the IDF deployed their own battalions. At the Negev training base, Jonathan Rothko got the red alert from the base commandant himself. There was a brief, but pointless argument with Colonel BenTzion, during which the Israeli forbade Jonathan to fly. Immediately after he stormed out of the commandant's office, he raced to the hangars.

"Yaniv! Eli!" he called to the two pilots certified for the craft. They ran to him and listened while Jonathan barked a string of orders in rapid fire Hebrew. They disappeared into the hangar and returned a moment later, bringing with them Jonathan's gear. "I'll fly the first bird, Eli, you take the second. Yaniv, you take the lead in the Nesher formation behind us. That way, I've got someone who knows what's what behind us."

"*B'seder*, Major," agreed Yaniv, zipping his flight suit. "We'll wait until you give us the all-clear before taking off."

"Good enough." Jonathan turned to Eli. "You okay with taking the bird?"

"Nervous, but okay." Eli smiled, but there was worry in his clear blue eyes.

"Then let's go." With a quick round of handshakes, Jonathan walked to his jet and climbed up the ladder to the cockpit.

In minutes, the F-511 were in the air, followed in rapid succession by five more Israeli-made Neshers. Climbing to maximum altitude, they circled the base once before heading east.

In Washington, Brigadier General Elizabeth Rothko was on the scramble-line with General Cohen of the IDF. "What you're telling me, Yitzchak, is that Major Rothko is currently airborne and you are unable to call him back," she said in measured, but definitely annoyed tones.

"In a nutshell: yes. He took off despite orders to remain on base. Yoni takes his responsibilities very seriously and would not hear of remaining on the ground while his 'birds' were in the air." Cohen was tired; it had been a long night and there was little hope of a break in the foreseeable future. "I assure you, Yoni is flying in formation with the best."

"It is not the major I am concerned about," snapped General Rothko, although she was indeed worried about her oldest child. "The major is well aware that in Israel he is a training instructor, and is in no way empowered to fly into a battle zone as anything more than an observer. That he is flying a bird tells me, as well as it should tell you, that he is prepared to participate in combat."

"I understand, General." Cohen knew she was right, but he had never met a mother, either in the United States or Israel or anywhere else for that matter, that approved of a child in combat.

"And tell him for me that if his superiors choose to court martial him, there is damn little I can do to stop them! In fact, I'll encourage it!" She broke off the connection and summoned her aide-de-camp. "Get me the Israeli ambassador stat!" Leaning back in her chair, Elizabeth Rothko picked up the picture of Jonathan that sat on her desk. It wasn't him in uniform, it was a very young Jonathan wearing a cowboy hat sitting astride a pony. "Maniac!" she shouted at the picture. "*Vilde*! Your father will throw a fit when he hears this!"

In the first raid, the F-511 and the Neshers took out a small squad of Arab fighters with little effort or damage. Encouraged by their foe's clumsy maneuvering, Jonathan and his band continued their air patrol over the Negev and the northern expanse of the Sinai, then flew north along the Jordan River toward Syria. Israeli reconnaissance planes were spotted several times, each pass with an acknowledgement to the fighters. Yaniv, flying below the other two F-birds, spotted what looked to be major troop movement near the Golan Heights and signaled Jonathan and Eli to follow them. They swept over the border and followed the line of activity to the east. Aware they were well outside Israeli airspace, they continued in spite of warnings from the ground that they should not. At the place where Jordan, Syria and Iraq converged, Jonathan led them back toward the southwest and home base.

The foray into enemy territory did not go unnoticed by Gamal Ramadi and Ali Hassan, with the Wa'atsi ship confirming that seven unfriendly aircraft were cruising their airspace.

"Can you identify?" Ramadi asked the observers.

"Yes, General. Five are what the Israelis call Nesher fighters, but the two in the front are not like the others. They appear to be F-class fighters from the United States."

The kora's interest was piqued. "What does that mean? Are the Americans already involved in flying combat?"

Ali Hassan was quick to reply. "No, Your Highness, it means that the Israelis are already trained well enough to fly the new planes they purchased from them."

"Who is flying, then?" demanded the kora, his hopes rising unexpectedly.

The Wa'atsi manning the telecommunicator relayed the inquiry to the mother ship and waited for an answer. "They are communicating with their base in code, but from what we can decipher, the lead fighter is flown by a non-Israeli."

"How do you know?" asked Ramadi.

"Because he has been the only one officially called back to base. The others have been told to proceed," explained the technician, "but the one is being told to return by a higher command."

Kora Pana-Di started to laugh. "Rothko!"

Ramadi thought he was crazy. "You think so, Your Highness?"

"Absolutely. No question about it. You must order your best fighter pilot to bring him down." He rubbed his hands with delight. "Alive. I want him alive."

Shaking his head, Ramadi acceded to his wishes and gave the order. "It would be nice," he admitted to the others, "to have an F-511 in our possession."

Eight fighters left the Arab base in search of the Israelis. Anxious to intercept them, the lead pilot remained in constant contact with the base rather than rely on visual recognition. It didn't take very long to find them with the help of the Wa'atsi.

The Israeli flying the furthest wing spotted them first. "*Asfourim gamalim* coming up from behind, Yaniv," radioed the pilot. "Six of the camel birds and they look like they want a fight."

"Then that's what we'll give 'em," replied the leader. "Everybody got that?"

"Coming around," called Jonathan, beginning a roll with Eli. No sooner than he banked to come around with the other F-bird close behind, he saw two more jets off to the side. "Looks like we've got us a dog fight, *yeladim*," he clucked into his mouthpiece. "Let's go for it." The formation regrouped with the F-birds hanging back slightly to allow Yaniv and the Nesher fighters to take the front.

Yaniv took out the first Arab jet with ease, but the newcomers only closed their ranks and kept coming. Using some of their newly acquired skills, the Israelis broke formation, causing the Arabs to do the same. With unspoken coordination, each pilot engaged an enemy fighter until a prearranged signal, when they rotated, shifting position leaving the enemy at a distinct disadvantage. One Nesher was hit, but not too badly, and Jonathan ordered him out of the fight after the striking jet had been forced down, leaving the numbers still even. Slowly, but with purpose, Jonathan was inching the battle closer to the Israeli border from where reinforcements could be summoned if necessary. One more Arab fighter was taken out by Jonathan himself before what was left of the formation turned tail. There was a round of applause as the Israelis watched them go before Jonathan ordered them home.

Eli's bird sustained some minor damage in the dogfight. Jonathan ordered him into the middle of the formation where he would be drafted by the other jets. Taking himself to the back, the major flew the rear point of the diamond.

In his cockpit, Jonathan kept his eye on the corner of the HUD indicating what was behind him. Something told him that the Arabs were not quite through with them and if that was the case, he wanted to be ready to turn at the first sign of a second onslaught. He did not anticipate a craft swooping in from the east. Catching sight of the *Asfour gamal* coming in full tilt from the side, Jonathan ducked down to take the lone fighter on away from the others. Despite complex maneuvering, the Arab could not be shaken. Jonathan fired and missed, and the Arab returned the favor, coming close, but missing as well. Rolling away, Jonathan watched the loner follow suit, but not with the same speed. He fired and this time hit the Arab, but not before the Arab fired a round at him, catching his left wing tip. The fighter jerked to one to one side, but Jonathan managed to regain control.

"I'm hit," he yelled, hoping Yaniv would hear him.

"Can you get home?" asked the other pilot who was now heading back toward the wounded bird.

"I'm not sure." He tried to assess the damage, but it was difficult. The jet was not responding well and it quickly became evident that he was losing an engine. The bird lurched, then began another roll. "Go home, Yaniv. I'm going to try to make it over the border and put it down somewhere. I'll see you back at the base." Jonathan sounded a lot surer than he felt. With as much strength as he could manage, he prevented the jet from pitching and began a rapid descent to the desert floor.

The other pilots stayed long enough to see Jonathan disappear beneath the clouds and then sped back to camp.

It was brute strength on Jonathan's part which kept the plane from going nose down into the desert. Unable to stabilize the craft and losing the tentative control he had, he tried to bring himself as close to the Israeli border as he could, without the aid of instrumentation which had, in the last few seconds, become worthless. When the putrid stench of smoking fuel and smoldering plastic reached the cockpit, Jonathan made the decision to eject. With a last look around, he checked his chute, murmured the same prayer he said every night, and pushed the red button between his legs. Immediately, the canopy blew off and he was catapulted into the darkening sky.

"Good news, General," announced the technician with a grin. "We believe the American has been shot down. Our pilot says he ejected and the F-511 has gone down about two hundred and twenty miles south southwest from here. We have dispatched a squad to pick him up, assuming the Israeli's don't get him first."

"Where is this place?" asked the kora, a smug, satisfied look about his face.

"In Jordan, but only about twenty kilometers from the Israeli border. Insh'Allah, we will have him first," replied Ali Hassan, wondering why the Jeylosian wanted this pilot brought in to him directly.

"Make sure that you do." The kora's tone was cordial, but ice cold. Without another word, he left the command post.

On command, the chute opened and Jonathan sailed along, watching his beloved bird spiral nose down into the desert. The sound of impact reverberated through the air, the shock waves jarring him, but he merely clucked in sympathy to himself. The winds were kind, carrying him past the wreckage but when he hit the ground, it was not graceful. A sharp gust caught him, twisted the lines of the chute and caused Jonathan to slam against a bramble bush, then land hard on his shoulder. Pain shot through him like a hot knife; he lay there unable to move while he took inventory of his body parts. Convinced nothing was broken, he worked his leg out of the bush and shucked the chute. As soon as he stood up, his knee collapsed under him. "Damn," swore Jonathan, probing the offending limb with his fingers. He pulled the body of the parachute toward him and went to work with his pocket knife, cutting a length of fabric, then two branches from the bramble bush to make a support for the injured knee. Sucking in his breath, Jonathan stood and this time was able to walk slowly, favoring the right leg.

Darkness was rapidly approaching. There was no place which afforded immediate shelter, but Jonathan was not perturbed. Picking up the rest of the chute, he severed the cords and cut the remaining material into a makeshift burnoose. While the days could reach hellish temperatures, the nights were brutally cold. Satisfied that he had done all that he could for the moment, Jonathan opened the emergency pack attached to the chute's harness and dug out the communicator. For a moment, he debated whether or not to punch in his code, thereby letting the Israelis know his location; he knew the homing signal could be easily intercepted and deciphered. With a shrug, he entered the series of numbers, but with a twist. The last six digits, if relayed correctly to his base, would tell them he had discarded the device and was on foot heading due west

CHAPTER 17

Tapper was asleep, dreaming of days on the beach at the Jersey shore where his grandmother kept a bungalow. In the dream, he was running along the sand with his sister and their dog, racing an incoming storm. They laughed at the lightning, but the thunder was growing louder and louder until Tapper sat upright in his bed. Someone was beeping relentlessly on his pager. Leaping out of the bed, he strode to his comm unit and hit the button. "This better be good," he shouted.

"You've got a red scramblegram coming into the commroom, sir," said the mate.

"On my way, Jeff. Put it on hold 'til I get there." With economy of motion, he pulled on a flight suit and headed out the door.

In the commroom, three crewmates were standing at the board watching the furiously flashing red light. As soon as Tapper flew in, they stepped aside. "Outta here," he barked, closing the door behind them. He entered his security code and the angry red light stopped flashing and Admiral Rothko's face appeared on the screen. "What's the problem, boss?" asked Tapper, noticing the greyness in Rothko's face at once.

"The news stinks, Tapper. Major eruption along the Syrian border. Ramadi is involved, so is that bastard Hassan. So far, Mustafa has kept his nose out of this, but he'll be in before too long."

Although it was important to be kept abreast of these facts, Tapper knew there was something else on the admiral's mind. It didn't take a mind reader to guess what it was. "Where's Jonathan?"

The admiral sagged in his chair. "Down. Somewhere in Jordan."

"Is he alive?"

"The last we know, yes. He transmitted his location linked to a throwaway. He's believed to be on foot heading west."

"The bird?"

"Gone. He took a hit and jumped. According to the IDF, it was a miracle he got as far as he did in the air before he ejected."

Tapper sighed, rubbing his eyes. "How's Mrs. R.?"

"Upset. Angry. He was under direct orders *not* to fly into combat. She's here at the Pentagon, negotiating for emergency aid. We're awaiting an official declaration of war now. This is going to be a hot one, Tapper."

"Where do you want us?" He knew Morgan should be there with him when the question was asked, but there was no time to get him now.

The admiral looked grim as he gave the order to come home. "We want you here as fast as possible. There's a Wa'atsi vessel orbiting us now, and we have every reason to believe they are monitoring for the Arabs. I'm pulling two battleships into orbit from within our system, but I want the *Washington* available. If there were not outlanders in this, I would leave you where you are, but Morgan is experienced with the Wa'atsi and they are not happy campers when he's around. And tell Cardozo; he's to stay with you and not on Lomos or wherever else he was planning to go. Official orders are being prepped now and should be transmitted within the hour."

Tapper scratched his face as he considered the implications. It might be viewed, in some circles, that the admiral was abusing his office by bringing the *Washington* back to Earth when it was on a diplomatic mission. The relationship between Morgan, the Rothkos and himself was well known and not always appreciated; there would be those who said, behind closed doors, Jews stick together, especially when it comes to Israel. But Tapper knew well the reasons why Rothko would bring them back: Morgan was the best strategist in the fleet and his knowledge of the Middle East, coupled with his experience with the Wa'atsi, would be invaluable in the event this exploded into something more than a local conflict. And there was yet another matter to be consider. "Boss?" He didn't have to ask the question.

"Do what you think is best, Tapper. I trust your judgment."

"Not good enough, Ted." Tapper called the admiral by name only on rare occasions and the use of it now was not lost on the admiral. "I need to know what *you* want us to do about Sarah Jane."

"Her mother is of the opinion that the less she knows, the better." He twisted the thin gold band on his left hand, a sign to those who knew him well of extreme domestic agitation. "I disagree with Liz, but not completely. Tell Sarah why you're being hauled back here, but don't tell her about Jonathan until you're within striking distance of home."

"Don't you trust her?"

"Don't be ridiculous; of course I trust her, Tapper. I just see no reason to give her an ulcer yet. Liz and I are that doing quite well on our own without having to worry about Sarah. Isaac is holding down the fort at home, trying to keep Rebecca from running off to join the IDF."

Tapper snorted at the thought. If S.J. was headstrong, Rebecca made her big sister look like an piker. "How much does the media know?" There was always the danger of the news getting through via the news reports which were transmitted to them daily.

"Score one for us; not much. Only that there is a military action going on, but the downing of one of our fighters is only being reported as speculation. The IDF is keeping it as quiet as they can, since it was an American flying outside international law who took the hit. And if it gets out that it was my son in the cockpit, all hell will break loose. The President knows, as do those who need to know, but we're playing it close to the chest."

"Jesus, Ted, what could have prompted him to do something so stupid?"

"You tell me."

"You gonna ground him when he gets home?"

The admiral laughed, the first release of the tension creasing his face. "Yeah, Tapper, I'm gonna send him to his room for a week. And no car keys for a month."

"This I gotta see."

"You and me, both." The smile faded, leaving the admiral with the same gray face he had before. "I'm more worried about a court martial, but if it comes to that, he'll resign his commission and join the IDF. I'm certain of that. Do what you have to do, Tapper. Have Morgan scramblegram me as soon as the orders arrive. I'll be here until I hear from him."

"Will do, boss." When the screen had gone black, Tapper composed himself before going to awaken the captain.

⁂

Morgan took the news about as well as Tapper had expected. He swore repeatedly at Jonathan in absentia, demanding to know what had possessed that complete idiot to do something that irresponsible. "Has he lost his fucking mind, Tapper? What on earth could he have been thinking? I hope they court martial the sonofabitch for this!"

"Be that as it may, Ash, we're going home as soon as we have official confirmation of the boss's orders. And as soon as they arrive, you'll call him." Tapper went to the door. "I'm going back to my cabin to change and then to the commroom. I'll call you as soon as I've got something." He paused and turned back to Morgan. "S.J. is not to know about Jonathan until we get home. Her parents don't want her getting into a lather until absolutely necessary; everything else is fair game."

"She'll figure it out in minute, Tapper," argued the captain.

Tapper shrugged. Rothko had told him to use his best judgment and he knew he would. "Let's play it by ear, Ash."

Left alone in his cabin, Morgan collapsed in a chair. Not only was this more trouble than any of them needed, it also put him in a tight spot with Jane. He understood the reasoning, but he felt she needed to know the truth. Still, the admiral was boss and he would not counter the order. There was nothing left to do but shower and dress for the departure ceremonies.

Due to the impending crisis, Tapper opted to change into a clean flight suit, foregoing the land rituals. Behind a closed door, he prepped a new flight plan and duty roster, taking into account who he thought Morgan would want on deck when they reached home. He summoned Newhouse to his office and briefly explained the situation. The First Officer had a cool head when it came to scheduling and added his two cents before heading out. The others, decided Tapper, could wait until they were en route.

Jane took her place on the bridge at 0600, completely unaware of the events of the last several hours. As she went from station to station checking the logs, she saw a security communication had been received sometime during the night. Noting it in her log, she also made a mental note to ask Tapper what it was about. Her rounds finished, she settled herself in her chair and piped in the action from the base, where Madame Tremna was giving a short speech. On the screen, she could see Morgan sitting on the dais with Kip Lucas and other members of the team. Belle and Cardozo were nearby, but Tapper was nowhere to be seen. On a hunch, Jane called the commroom. "Is Commander Bear around?" she asked the crewmate who answered.

"Yes, ma'am, he is. But his door is closed. Do you want me to get him?"

"No. Just ask him to stop by the bridge when he gets a chance." Jane flicked off the intercom and flicked on the terminal. Pulling up her staff assignment rotation, she began preparing the week's roster.

"Senior staff in the wardroom fifteen minutes after lift-off," called Barb Lucas as she sailed onto the bridge. "Jane," she whispered, "the boss wants you in the small conference room *now*. I'll take the bridge."

"Yes, ma'am," replied Jane, grinning at the other woman who was carrying a large bouquet of fresh flowers and an armload of papers, all of which seemed to be offerings from her sons. Picking up her pager and a docupad, Jane left the bridge.

Morgan was pacing, waiting for Jane. Tapper sat at the table drumming his fingers impatiently. Neither man spoke; there was nothing to discuss until the lieutenant arrived. Before coming, Tapper had arranged to have the next communication from fleet HQ fed into the conference room. While the official change in flight plan had been issued, it had come through with the stipulation that it not be acted upon until direct order from the Fleet Admiral himself.

A rap on the door announced Jane's arrival. "You wanted to see me, Captain?" she asked brightly.

"Come in and sit down, Jane. There's been a change of plans." Morgan waited while she took the seat opposite Tapper at the table. Without mincing any words, he described the situation. "The Admiralty has decided we would be of more use in orbit around Earth than going to Kotuchar," said Morgan, his face grim. "Because of your fluency in Hebrew and Arabic, you will be at your post on the bridge for the duration once we are within range."

Jane looked from Morgan to Tapper and then back to Morgan. There was something else they were not telling her; she could see it in their eyes. Playing the hunch, she directed the next question at Morgan. "Why are you telling me this now? Why not wait until the staff meeting?"

"Because, Lieutenant, this is coming directly from your father," said Morgan gruffly. "It was his wish that we inform you privately."

Without missing a beat, Jane asked quietly, "Where's Jonathan?"

This time, it was Morgan who looked to Tapper and then to Jane. "Your call, Tapper."

"Jonathan's in the middle of it. Where, we're not sure." It wasn't a lie, but it wasn't the complete truth either.

The answer did not satisfy her. "Where is he, Joshua?"

"We don't know, S.J. Somewhere in the desert is our best guess."

"Does my mother know where?"

"No, honey, she doesn't." Tapper did not look her in the eye.

"With or without a bird?"

Tapper looked pleadingly at Morgan, but the captain's face remained immobile. "Without. The IDF's gone out to pick him up."

Jane stood, smoothed her flight suit, picked up her docupad and walked to the door. At the last moment, she paused and turned back to them. "I would like to think that if Jonathan was in serious trouble, you would tell me. Until I hear otherwise, I will assume he is safe." She left the cabin.

"Was that really necessary?" Morgan snarled.

"Did you have a better idea, fella? Just don't tell the boss when he calls."

The red light on the console started blinking furiously. With a single motion, Tapper hit the security code and the admiral's face materialized on the screen. "We're here, sir," said Tapper, moving over to allow room for Morgan to sit beside him.

"At one o'clock Greenwich Mean Time, Syria and Iraq declared war on the State of Israel, gentlemen. Iran and Saudi Arabia have offered military support to their Arab brothers, but so far Jordan and Egypt have remained silent. We expect Jordan to officially support the declaration within the next twenty-four hours, but Egypt should remain neutral. We will, of course, aide Israel within the bounds of previously established treaties, but active military assistance is not forthcoming. The President of the United States, however, has ordered you home." The admiral took a breath, indicating the end of the official statement from his office. "What have you told Sarah?" was the first question he asked.

Tapper stayed Morgan with his hand. "Just that we are being recalled and that Jonathan is somewhere in the middle of it. We did not tell her the rest."

"Thank you. We still have no word on his whereabouts, but the IDF is looking for him. Unofficially, Jordan says if they get to him first, they will slip him over to the IDF and then deny it. Mustafa cannot afford a war right now, but they may be dragged in anyway."

"Will the *Merrimack* be coming in as well, sir?" asked Morgan.

"Yes, they're much closer than you. Where's Cardozo?"

"Sulking in his cabin. We told him the bare essentials, nothing more. He was counting on making it to Kotuchar before the summer festival."

Tapper's grimace was answered with a guffaw from the admiral. "Well, tell him not to get too down at the mouth. I'll have someone bring his jalopy in from wherever he left it after this is over."

Morgan snorted, "That'll cheer him up…assuming he remembers where he left it."

There were a few more details to attend to before the admiral signed off. When he had disappeared from the screen, Morgan let out a low whistle. "This is bad news, Tap."

"You're telling me? Come on, Boston, let's get this crate off the ground and pointed in the right direction."

The *Washington* lifted itself gracefully off the dock and floated up through the pleasant Lomosean atmosphere. As soon as they were airborne, Morgan announced the recall to the bridge crew. In minutes the new flight plan had been entered and the *Washington* was heading home at top speed.

In the wardroom, the senior staff listened in silence while Morgan outlined orders for the trip back to Earth. Surreptitiously, the captain kept an eye on Jane, whose face gave away nothing. No one in the room, outside of Tapper and Cardozo, knew what was at stake for her family; had he not known, he would never have guessed that this was as personal a crisis as it gets for her. Only once did Jane look up from her docupad and meet his eyes unwaveringly; the dead calm of her face was not matched in her eyes; it made Morgan most uncomfortable.

The Pentagon managed to keep the news of an American shot down out of the news. While the reports coming from home were posted as they came in, there was no mention of Jonathan or the missing F-511. The crew rehearsed red alert procedures, all hands making sure everything was in prime condition in preparation for a possible confrontation with the Wa'atsi vessel. At maximum speed, it would still take six days to reach Earth.

CHAPTER 18

Wrapped in the dun colored parachute, Jonathan Rothko blended into the bleak desert landscape. By day he hid in the small caves and craters which pitted the surface. At night, following the stars, he walked westward, hoping that somewhere, at some time, he had crossed over the imaginary line into Israel. Twice he spotted aircraft circling near his hiding place of the moment, but he could not make out their insignia. Rather than risk capture, he remained invisible.

Years of recreational camping in the Negev provided Jonathan with the skills necessary to survive. Plants, scarce as they were, provided enough nutrition, and occasionally he found succulents for water. Tracks in the arid land told him Bedouins had recently travelled along the same path, and that gave him the confidence he was heading in the proper direction; at this time of year, with winter approaching, the nomads often crossed the border to where wells were maintained for them by the Israeli government. With any luck, he might run into a band making their way to winter pasture.

On the fourth night of his trek, Jonathan heard the sounds of an encampment. Flattening himself against the ground, he crawled up onto a ridge to scope out the area. Three large tents were silhouetted against the darkness; camels and horses were tethered to the side and guarded by two men sitting beside a campfire talking animatedly. The smell of cooking was redolent in the desert air, and Jonathan's stomach audibly rumbled. Two robed figures, women he decided from their movements, emerged from the center tent bearing food for the men at the campfire. They stayed only long enough to leave the trays before returning to the tent. Jonathan estimated the band to be a small one, of no more than three families, probably six to eight adult men. A single man, coming out of the desert on foot, would pose no threat and they would be obliged to offer hospitality. Wrapping the chute tightly around him, Jonathan stood and walked toward the fire.

The two men jumped, weapons drawn, as Jonathan approached. He held his hands up, displaying no firearms, and shouted "*Salaam Aleikem!*"

"*Aleikem Salaam!*" they answered, still brandishing their old-fashioned laser rifles. "What do you want?"

"I seek shelter for the night, my friends." Jonathan was thankful for his mother's insistence that he master Arabic. "I have been walking in the desert for several days and seek a friendly face."

The older of the two came forward. "How have you come to be in the desert? Are you a mad man or a holy man?"

Jonathan laughed grimly at the joke. "Neither. I am a lost man."

The younger man spoke rapidly into the ear of the other in such a way that Jonathan could not hear him. The older man grinned, revealing a mouth of gold, and opened his arms to Jonathan. "If you are the lost man everyone is seeking, then you are welcome at the tents of Achmed ibn Suleiman!"

Jonathan accepted the embrace and then salaamed his thanks. "I may be that one, but I do not know for certain."

"Have you lost a large bird, my friend?"

"What have you heard, Achmed ibn Suleiman?"

"There are many who comb the desert for you. The IDF is out in force, but so are the Syrians. And the Syrians have some strange looking creatures in tow." He looked at Jonathan carefully, as though taking the measure of the man in the makeshift burnoose. "But here, you are among friends. Come, we have talked enough; you must be hungry and tired, not to mention very, very thirsty!" He shouted for the women to bring more food and drink. "Sit by the fire and warm yourself. You will be safe with us......so long as we burn your parachute and uniform and lend you some decent clothing!"

❧

The other men were interested in hearing what Jonathan had to say about the Syrians and the Iraqis. Although they were Arabs, they hated anyone who would disturb the tenuous peace of their desert existence, one which relied heavily on the Israelis insistence that the Bedouin avail themselves of good pasture and medical supplies.

"Ali Hassan is a pig of the worst kind," spat Achmed's eldest son. "He cares nothing for his people, only for what can fill his own coffers."

"Allah be praised that Mustafa has distanced himself from Ali Hassan and his friend Ramadi. The little we have heard says that the Hashemite wants no part of this war. It will benefit no one in Jordan, least of all him."

Jonathan listened to the grumblings of the other men. None of them displayed any loyalty to the warmongers, preferring to sit in the middle of the desert, out of harm's way. "Tell me about the 'creatures' travelling with the Syrians," asked Jonathan, wondering who they were.

"Disgusting looking beings, more like lizards than men, with beady eyes and evil faces," said Achmed with a shudder. "Do you know what they are?"

"From what you say, they sound like Wa'atsi, from a system not too far from ours, called Wa'atnam. Not a very nice group, more like the Barbary pirates of olden days. Usually they keep to themselves, so this is a little unusual. I wish I could tell you more, but I don't know much else."

The men clucked sympathetically. Finally, Achmed's son asked the stranger a direct question about himself, something usually not done. "I would want to know who you are," he said almost apologetically, "for you bring with you danger."

"A fair question," added Achmed, relieved someone else had asked. "Why are they looking for you?"

Jonathan looked from one face to the next, trying to gauge how to answer the question. "I am an American; I was flying a fighter when I was shot down. As to why they are looking for me, I would guess the IDF is trying to bring me home 'cause that's what they're supposed to do. But I cannot imagine why the others are searching. By rights, I should be dead." In truth, he had a gut feeling the Syrians knew it was a Rothko they had knocked out of the sky, and that alone was reason to find at least the corpse.

The question answered, the conversation turned to other things. The Bedouin were concerned about any number of issues, most of which would not have been imagined by people who lived in houses. Feeling safe for the first time since he had taken off from Ein Geshem, Jonathan, his hunger and thirst banished, drifted off where he sat.

When he awoke, the pilot found himself in a tent, buried under a mound of sheepskin covers. Some had removed the burnoose Achmed had given him, leaving him to sleep only in a pair of briefs and his dog tags. The powerful aroma of Turkish coffee wafted under the tent flap, a perfume he could not ignore. Finding the robe at the foot of his bed, Jonathan dressed and left the tent, but not before properly folding his bedding.

Four men in Syrian uniforms were arguing with Achmed near the place where the campfire still smoldered. Women, completely covered from head to foot, sat near the other fire, tending the food and thick Turkish coffee. Adjusting the kufiyah Achmed had given him, Jonathan draped the cloth, Bedouin fashion, until it all but covered his eyes. He strolled casually around to the other side of the tent, made his way to the horses. A fine lot of Arabians, Jonathan took one by the reins, and then limped toward Achmed and the soldiers.

Achmed's men saw Jonathan, but did nothing as he came closer. Achmed himself began waving his arms in Jonathan's direction, while saying "My idiot nephew! Mute son of my sister! A more foolish curse a man could not have on his family. And as blind as a mole! And lame! Why don't you take him and tell them he's the American? It would relieve me of this burden!"

The soldiers laughed. One of them came toward Jonathan and began shouting in his ear, but Jonathan made no move. The horse, however, began to rear, and the soldier backed off. The captain of the group, satisfied that the American was not there, turned to go, the others following. As soon as they were in their hovercraft and on their way out of the camp, Achmed rushed over to Jonathan and took the reins of the jittery stallion.

"Allah be praised that you said nothing, American!"

"And I thought my Arabic was pretty good," laughed the pilot, glad to have the horse taken from him.

"Good, yes, but your accent is Israeli! They would have taken you on principle!"

~

In the hovercraft, the captain was watching the activity behind him through the mirror. Although the horse blocked a clear view, he was convinced Achmed was talking to the man. "I am not convinced that was the idiot son of the dog's sister. Keep an eye on them."

~

The Bedouins were not, as Jonathan hoped, heading toward Israel; they were en route to a market on the Jordanian side of the border. Achmed begged Jonathan to travel with them, but the pilot declined, explaining that he would be better off moving on alone.

"I cannot even offer you a horse or a camel, American," sighed Achmed, "they are already spoken for."

"I could not accept one, my friend," replied Jonathan. "Although one would speed my way, I must travel in darkness and I would be unable to hide it during the day. But I thank you."

"Allah be with you, American," said the Bedouin, embracing his new friend. They were only about ten kilometers east of the border. Achmed outlined a map in the sand to show him where shelter might be found along the way, then erased it with his foot until no trace remained. "May you reach you destination with no interference from the dogs of the north."

With food in his pack and a skin of drinking water, Jonathan set off in the direction Achmed said would be the shortest route. A few kilometers away he would find caves in which he could hide until nightfall. As he reached the top of the ridge, he turned and waved to them one last time.

The Syrians found a crater in which to hide the hovercraft. One of the soldiers, sitting on a small hill, alerted his captain as soon as he saw the small band of nomads moving to the south. "Sir, I can see them clearly. There are six men, four women and two children. No change in the number of animals."

"Six men?" echoed the leader, pointing his own binoculars in the same direction.

"Six, sir."

"That's it. That was the American pilot." He slapped the soldier on the back. "You have sharp eyes, Hussein. We'll wait until the sun begins to set and then we shall go west. There we shall find the pilot."

Alternating between sleep and restless wakefulness, Jonathan remained in the tiny cave until the sky had turned almost black. Stars dotted the sky; there was not much of a moon, but it was bright enough to shed long shadows on the cracked earth. Jonathan ate a piece of bread and cheese before pulling his laser pistol from his pack. The Syrians were out there somewhere and the gun made him feel less vulnerable. He checked his compass, hoisted his pack onto his shoulder, and set out toward the west.

In the distance, a hyena howled at the moon. Jonathan welcomed the sound, for as long as he heard the normal nocturnal noise of the desert, it meant nothing was amiss. He stayed as close to the ridges as possible; there were caves and other forms of shelter which could be used if necessary. To walk upright on the flat land would make him an easy target; it was preferable to see first rather than be seen.

The Syrians used a scanner to hunt for life forms in the darkness. An animal read differently on the screen from a man, and so far, they had only seen animals. Slowly making their way west in widening circles, they stalked the pilot. It was only a matter of time before they found him.

With unofficial permission from King Mustafa of the Hashemite, the IDF sent a small search party over the border. Yaniv and Eli went with them; they had a better idea of where the plane had gone down and the landmarks would be more familiar to them than to the others. Using four hovercrafts, they started their search on the Israeli side, hoping Jonathan had gotten that far on foot. The only homing signal they had from him indicated his course from where he had touched down and they could only assume that he stuck as close to it as possible. Still, there was the chance he had met up with Bedouin and taken refuge with them. For four days they had combed the desert, looking for signs of the American and had seen nothing.

In the north, the fighting had begun in earnest. The IDF was holding their own against the combined forces at the Syrian border, but it was not without cost. Always ready for war, the Israeli army kept the enemy at bay, uninterested in making territorial gains into Syria. The United States, true to its treaties, immediately delivered ten F-511s the IDF had ordered the year before. In addition, Brigadier General Rothko arranged for military advisors to join the IDF at headquarters, along with the latest in surveillance equipment. An official warning to leave the area had been issued to and ignored by the Wa'atsi visitors. The League of Planets, through their office in New York, had issued similar injunctions, and as a result, the Wa'atsi legation withdrew their consul from the council. The United Nations censured the action with no response from the Arabs. In an unusual gesture of support, the Russians recalled their ambassadors from Syria and Iraq at the same time as the United States, Great Britain and France. In answer to this, several other Arab states issued statements of support for the instigators. Libya sent troops and supplies, the Saudis released additional amounts of refined oil, and the Arab Emirates provided cash for additional arms.

In Washington, Brigadier General Rothko was locked in meetings 'round the clock while the admiral held down the fort at home. During the joint meetings of the Admiralty and the Air Force, they sat together, trying to put aside the desperation they felt for their son while doing the best for both the United States and her allies. There was no question of divided loyalties when it came to the Rothkos, but everyone there, including the President, at one point or another, expressed their sympathies.

"He deserves a court martial for this," General Rothko told the President after thanking him for his kind words.

"Be that as it may, Liz, we'd rather have him safe in a stockade than lost in the desert. How much longer until the *Washington* arrives, Ted?"

"Two days," replied the admiral. "We believe that when the Wa'atsi see them, they will have second thoughts about floating around up there."

"I hope you're right. That last thing we need right now is an interplanetary incident."

When the President had gone, Admiral Rothko took his wife to the private dining room reserved for top brass. Sitting at a corner table away from prying eyes, they held hands and prayed for their children.

The Rothkos were finishing their salads when a young officer approached the table carrying a battered brown leather case. Snapping a salute, he handed it to the general and said "A courier just brought this, ma'am. I'm to wait for a reply."

She opened the case and withdrew a sealed envelope. Breaking the seal, she read the document and handed it to her husband. "End of lunch, Admiral. Let's go." Taking the single sheet back from him, she turned to the lieutenant. "Tell General Adamson we're on our way. And thank him for us."

A hovercar waited at the entrance for the Rothkos. Getting into the back seat, General Rothko slid the privacy window shut, preventing the driver from hearing any conversation. "Teddy, why do you think the Xinthi-Angs are here? They were not scheduled for a visit until January. Do you think this has anything to do with Sarah?"

"It might," said the admiral, taking her hand in his, "but there could be a hundred reasons why they have come now. Let's meet them at the field and not speculate. In the meanwhile, there is little we can do except wait."

Ambassador Xinthi-Ang sat in the cabin waiting for his ship to land outside Washington, D.C. Normally, his wife would not accompany him on such a delicate mission, but his lady had insisted, saying that she wanted to speak with General Rothko herself, in person, rather than rely on transmissions and vidcoms.

The decision to come to Earth had been made quickly and without waiting for a formal invitation. The emperor was furious when he learned Pana-Di had escaped from his luxurious prison and had shuttled out to a renegade ship orbiting Jeylos. Where he had gone, no one was certain, but the emperor was convinced he was en route to Earth. Transmissions to the kora had been intercepted, and they all pointed to the planet in the next solar system. In a rage, his Imperial Majesty declared Pana-Di an outlaw and pronounced the death sentence upon his third son before his entire court. Armed with official letters to both the Rothkos and the League of Planets, Ambassador Xinthi-Ang was immediately dispatched to Earth.

The sky over the desert was softening to velvet gray when Jonathan decided it was time to seek shelter. The air was already growing warmer and the sounds of the night had all but ceased. With the rising of the sun, even the bravest of animals would disappear from the barren landscape. Standing atop a small hill, he scanned the horizon for the edge of the crater which Achmed had described in his map. In the distance, he could make out a darker line against the lightening sky. As he started toward it, he heard an unnatural sound. Squatting, he put his ear to the earth, but heard nothing. When he stood, the sound seemed to have increased and he recognized the gentle whoosh of a hovercraft. In spite of the throbbing in his leg, Jonathan began sprinting toward the crater.

CHAPTER 19

As the *Washington* approached her home system, activity sped up. Jane was found in either her office or on the bridge, never far from a console, and almost never in her cabin. She monitored all transmissions from Earth assiduously, refusing to leave them to the staff. If Morgan had heard directly from the admiral, he did not tell her, and Jane refused to ask.

Four days out, Jane called a staff meeting of her own. Handing out assignments, she brooked no disagreement from her people. "All of you speak a number of languages, but I want to know now who is totally fluent in Arabic and Wa'atsi. In addition, I want 'round the clock monitoring of all transmissions outbound from Earth. Nothing is to escape notice. What sounds like a regulation trade transmission might very well be encoded information for outlanders. I want hourly reports on what's been heard and I want them complete. Do I make myself clear?" She looked around the wardroom, closely gauging their reactions.

Tom Peters and Prakesh Chakrabati both volunteered to work the Arabic. Ho Ngyuen took the first monitor shift, and Belle opted for the second. Adela Olukotun's abilities in Wa'atsi language and code had been established during the *Tical* incident and she took that end. Satisfied that everything was covered, Jane dismissed the meeting and went in search of Morgan. She found him in his office on the bridge going over satellite maps with Newhouse and Blackjack. Jane rapped on the door post and waited for permission to enter.

"Are your people in place, lieutenant?" asked Morgan, looking up from the charts.

"Yes, sir. I would like to requisition another station on the bridge for the duration. It would be more efficient to have both my station and a second operational as we monitor, rather than using one on the commdeck."

"That can be arranged, lieutenant. Anything else you need?"

"Yes, Captain." She paused, then added, "I would like to send a scramblegram to HQ as soon as possible requesting any additional information they might have collected in the last twenty-four hours."

Morgan knew she was asking for more than information; she was asking for permission to call her parents. It was not an unreasonable request. "That can be arranged as well." He hit a button on his console. "Tapper, Lieutenant Krieg wants to scramble a line to the home office."

"Aye, aye, Captain. Send her down."

Morgan looked up at Jane, trying to read her eyes. Like father and brother, she had the ability to drop a steel mask over her face and he could discern no trace of emotion except for the slight tightening of her jawline. "Go ahead, Jane," he said quietly, then added, "and keep me posted."

"Thank you, captain." For a moment, the mask slipped and she seemed almost vulnerable, but it was quickly gone. Turning sharply on her heel, Jane left the bridge.

Tapper was waiting for her in the commroom. "We can do this in the office," he offered when Jane arrived.

Belle was sitting at a console watching text roll by on the screen. "Can I listen in?" asked the crewmate with a smile.

"No!" Jane's retort was sharp, too sharp, and she felt a pang of regret when Belle's face fell. "I'll tell you about it later." She preceded Tapper into the office and the door slid shut behind them. She watched the console light up, indicating that Tapper was transmitting, and was surprised when the door opened and the Chief Tech exited, leaving Jane alone inside.

"What's with her?" asked Belle, a slight annoyance in her voice.

"My guess is that she is tired, Belle," Tapper said kindly. "Leave her be."

Belle was not put off. "Why is everyone so protective of her, Tapper? No one sends scramblegrams around here except the Captain and you. There's something going on and I know I'm not the only one who's noticed."

Sitting down on the edge of her desk, Tapper put a friendly arm around Belle's shoulder. "The lieutenant has a lot more at stake in this than most people realize, but it's not for me to tell you."

"Oh." The answer did not satisfy the yeomate, but there was a certain finality in his comment.

Inside the office, Jane waited while her father was located. When he finally appeared on the screen, he looked older and more weary than she could ever remember seeing him. "Dad, are you all right?" were the first words out of her mouth.

"Hello, sweetheart. It's so good to see you." He smiled, but it did not relieve the tension around his eyes. "To what do I owe the honor of a scramblegram from my daughter?"

"I want to know what's going on, Dad. I would have called Mom, but there was no way to get through to her without going through too many channels. Tapper said it appears less strange to call you."

"Listen to that boy, Sarah Jane, he knows what he's talking about."

"Dad?"

"How much do you know?"

"I know the official stuff, but I think Jonathan went down hard and Morgan isn't confirming. All he said was that he was in the desert without his bird and the IDF's gone to get him."

"That more or less sums it up, Sarah Jane." The admiral seemed to sag in his chair. "Your brother was flying outside orders and was shot down close to the border, but over Jordan. He transmitted his location once, coded that he was moving west on foot, but he dumped the damn device because he knew it could be compromised."

"Will they find him, Dad?"

"Your mouth to God's ear. The IDF made contact with a band of Bedouin who seemed to have helped him out, but he refused to travel with them, opting to keep heading toward the Israeli border." He studied his daughter's face and felt guilty for not allowing Morgan to tell her in the first place. As it was, Liz would be angry that she knew anything at all. "Look, sweetheart, Jonathan is a pretty resourceful guy and knows the desert as well as he knows the back yard. We have no reason to believe that anything else has happened. Besides," he added with dismissive wave of his hand, "they've got the search area pretty much narrowed down."

Fighting back tears, Jane struggled to retain her composure. It was conduct unbefitting an officer to allow her emotions to run amok. "We're monitoring all transmissions out from Earth and once we're in orbit, we'll begin listening over the Middle East."

"That's all we can ask." The admiral allowed a fatherly smile to be transmitted several thousand light years into space. "Now go blow your nose, splash some water on your face and get back to your post, Sarah Jane. Mom and I need you to be at your best. We know you'll make us proud."

When Jane left Tapper's office, she was in complete control. She had a job to do and she would do it with finesse. Belle was still sitting at the outer console with Tapper.

"Anything to report?" asked the Chief Tech.

"Nothing you didn't know already." Jane shot him a look fraught with meaning peppered with no small amount of fury at having been kept in the dark. "I'll be in my office and then on the bridge." She stopped at the door and turned back to Belle. "I'll take your logs in half an hour."

"Aye, aye, ma'am." Belle gave her a quizzical look, but it was lost on Jane; she had too many other things on her mind.

In her office, Jane collected a few things she thought she would need on the bridge. It was taking every ounce of her strength not to cry and she thought if she stayed where she was, the tears would come. Better to be in the middle of people and activity; it would take her mind off Jonathan. She was ready to leave when Blackjack showed up at her door. "What do you want?" she asked, not moving from behind her desk.

"I came to see if you were all right." His drawl was all but gone.

She eyed him carefully, deciding whether or not he had been party to Morgan's attempt to keep the truth from her. "How much do you actually know, Jackson? About Jonathan, I mean."

"Morgan told me before we left Lomos. That's why I'm still here. Otherwise I would have jumped ship there." He sat on the corner of her desk, preventing her from leaving. "How much do you know?"

"All of it now. Why didn't you, of all people, come and tell me the truth?" There was no anger in her voice.

"Your father's orders. I think he wanted to spare you worrying as long as possible. It's a daddy's prerogative, you know."

Jane shrugged; there was little room for argument. "He's alive, Jackson; I know it. I would know if he wasn't."

On impulse, Blackjack reached for her hand and she did not snatch it away. "Sarah Jane, all of us, I mean Boston, Tapper and me, we all want to hear Speed is alive and well; and I don't think I have to tell you that we're here if you need a shoulder. No one is expecting you to carry this by yourself."

Although her eyes were stinging, Jane would not permit tears. "Thank you, Cousin. I appreciate it." She slipped her hand from his. "Would you care to escort me to the bridge, Cap'n Cardozo?"

"With pleasure, Miss Sarah," he replied gallantly with a warming grin. Jackson offered his arm and she took it.

Morgan was sitting in the command chair when Jane and Blackjack made their entrance. For a split second, he thought she had been crying, and if not that, she was definitely supporting herself against the southerner's rangy body. Without comment, he watched as Blackjack deposited her at her station and then leaned forward to whisper something in her ear. Jane's response was a smile, albeit sad, but it seemed to him that Blackjack was caring for her in a way he could not. Suffering a not-so-small pang of envy, Morgan focused his attention on the screen displaying their location.

Things were unusually quiet on the bridge. Everyone went about duties, but it was with palpable tension, waiting for the inevitable confrontation. The air was somber, giving the bridge an eerie quality as crewmates and officers spoke in low tones and no jokes passed from station to station. Morgan found this oppressive and wished someone would say something ridiculous to break the tension.

Cadet Peters, sitting at the console Jane had requisitioned, suddenly sat up in his chair. Quickly transcribing a transmission onto a docupad, he shouted "I've got something, lieutenant! I think you'd better see this!"

Jane flew across the small space separating them. Hitting the speaker button, a crackly voice was heard on the bridge, speaking rapidly and in the same code they had heard before running into the *Tical*. "Are they stupid, or what?" asked Jane. "You'd think they'd change the code after we breached it the last time!" She looked at what Peters had written, made some adjustments, and smiled. "They're not as stupid as they seem. This was made to be intercepted."

"How do you know?" asked Morgan, coming close to where she

was standing. Tapper flew onto the bridge and skidded to a halt behind the captain.

"Here, look at this. The message is destined for another Wa'atsi vessel, one that must be somewhere in the area, probably hiding behind a moon or something so we can't see it. Normal Wa'atsi communiqué will hail according to who's captaining the ship, but this one is not encoded that way. See? There's no mention of specific recipient. That tells us that they want whoever is listening to know there's another ship out here." Jane handed the pad to Morgan. "There's a non-Wa'atsi with them on Earth, but they are careful not to say who. Whoever it is, though, must be pretty high up in someone's organization."

"Nothing here we don't already know," said Morgan, handing her back the pad.

"There's more, Lieutenant," said Peters, holding his hand up for silence. The language had changed subtly, but it was still verbal transmission. Abruptly, it stopped, then it was followed by a long string of what sounded to be gibberish. "Are they finished, do you think?"

Jane waited while the computer put the last section on the screen. "Hmmmm, yes. This last piece is the all clear, but there is no responder code. It's a one-way only job. This however...." She nudged Peters out of his seat and took his place at the terminal. She stared at the screen and then began writing. Slowly, the message began to take shape. "They're still using a Hatma base, but this is more sophisticated than the other." She pointed at a string of words. "This is classical Hatma, sorta like Shakespearean English.... no, more like Old Church Slavonic. Old English we can get easily, but O.C.S. is almost indecipherable to the average Russian speaker. Some Hatma dialects can be like that." Jane punched a series of keys and waited for the computer to respond. When the screen filled with strange characters, she began sorting through the transmission until she hit upon the right combination. "Here we go, fellas."

Everyone on the bridge gathered around Jane as she translated the gibberish. Belle arrived on the scene and squirmed in beside Peters, who was verifying the Hatma from the computer. "No, Lieutenant," said Belle, pointing to a word chain, "this has to be an event in the past."

"You're right. Okay, then this is a progression. Okay, this is..." her voice trailed off as she kept writing. Slowly, Jane turned whiter and whiter, so much so that everyone noticed, including Morgan. Leaning over her shoulder, he read the translation. Gently, he put his hand on her arm and stopped her from writing any more. "Let's go into my ready room." With Tapper and Cardozo following, they took Jane away from prying eyes.

"What the hell was that?" asked Peters, looking the translation copy he had made.

"'First success in battle. Fighter down. Pilot Rothko located and will be intercepted. There will be no challenge here.' What fighter went down? Anybody know? Is that the admiral's son?" asked Belle.

"Probably," said Peters.

Joe Newhouse kept his mouth shut. After what he had learned from the captain earlier in the day, he saw no reason to comment.

In his office, Morgan tried to reassure Jane that Jonathan was alive. "They said 'intercepted,' not dead. If they have him, at least he's out of the desert."

"And just what do you think the Syrians will do to him, Captain Morgan? Feed him lunch and drop him off at the border?" Jane was shaking but her words were razor sharp.

"S.J., he's far more valuable to them alive than dead!" shouted Tapper in frustration. "They're not stupid and they obviously know who he is. He'll be a pawn, if nothing else." He glanced over at Morgan and knew the captain felt no more confidence than he did. But Jane had to believe them, that was the main issue.

"We'd better get the admiral on the horn. There's no guarantee they have this," said Morgan, his mouth in a tight, grim line.

Tapper called the commroom and had a secured line opened. It took longer to reach Admiral Rothko than they would have liked, but finally he appeared on the screen. Tapper stepped aside to allow Morgan full view.

"Ted, we picked up a transmission from Earth to an unspecified Wa'atsi vessel." In a few brief sentences, he outlined what they had learned and Rothko confirmed they had reached the same conclusion.

"Dad?" Jane leaned over so that he could see her. By the look on his face, Jane knew this was the first word he had gotten. "Is there anything you or Mom can do?"

"I wish there was, but we've had no communication from the Syrians at all. We cannot send our own people in, as you well know, and there is still the question of what Jonathan was doing there in the first place. The news that an F-511 went down was leaked several hours ago, but so far, they haven't said a thing about the pilot." Someone entered the admiral's office and handed him a docupad, then left. "I just got a copy of the complete transmission." He looked it over, then at the screen. "Same as yours, almost verbatim. Ash?"

"Yes, sir?"

"I know you're pushing the *Washington* now, but how much more can you push her?"

Tapper moved into range. "Not much, Ted, but I'll see what I can do."

Admiral Rothko looked away, as though he was private debating with himself about something. Jane knew that look well. "What aren't you telling us, Dad?"

He looked up. Rather than tell her what he had learned from the Jeylosian Ambassador, he said, "I guess I'm just trying to think of a way to tell you...and I'm glad you're with people we trust." The *we* in the statement was not the Fleet; he was speaking for his family. "He'll be okay, Sarah Jane. Jonathan is tough and he's been in scrapes before. He'll be just fine."

Reluctantly, Morgan changed the subject, requesting a second set of orders that would include combat. "There's at least one other vessel out here," explained the captain, "and I am not averse to taking it out if necessary."

"If you deem they pose a security threat, I will rely on your judgment, Ash. You'll have orders within the hour."

Jane wasn't really listening to the rest of the conversation. Lost in her own thoughts, she remained ramrod stiff in her chair.

By the time they emerged from Morgan's office, the bridge was back to normal. Jane took her seat at her station and filed the communiqué in her log. She stayed there as long as she could, but it was not helping. Anger was welling dangerously inside her and when she could no longer control it, Jane rose stiffly from her chair and went back to the Captain's ready room.

"Come," called Morgan as the door slid open.

Tapper was there, leaning against the bulkhead. "Feeling any better?" he asked her kindly.

"Get out, Tapper," replied Jane, her mouth set in a tight line.

Two pairs of eyebrows shot up, but Tapper moved quickly. "Call me when you're ready, Ash," he said as he went thought the door.

Jane waited for the whoosh of the sliding door, but even then she remained silent.

"Do you have something to say, lieutenant?" asked Morgan, "If not, I've got a lot on my desk right now."

That was all it took. Jane's hands balled into tight fists as she took a step toward the captain. "I don't know what the bloody hell game you think this is, Morgan," she started in a low, tightly controlled voice but it built to a shout. "You've got one helluva nerve treating me like I was some sort of porcelain doll. Goddamn it, I'm an officer. If I were a man, you'd have told me Jonathan was MIA right off the bat. When are you going to get it through that thick skull of yours *breasts don't make a difference*?"

Morgan was stunned by the outburst. He had, after all, followed orders issued from her father. This was exactly what he didn't want on his ship: to be caught in the middle between parent and child, no matter who the parent was and how competent the child. "I was following your father's directive!" he shouted back at her.

"What are you, some kind of Nazi? *I was only following orders?* What kind of Fleet bullshit is that? Since when do you follow orders to the letter? You think I don't know? Your reputation was built on doing whatever you goddamn well pleased when you goddamn well felt like it. Everyone knows that! It isn't exactly news."

"One more word, Krieg and you'll find yourself confined to quarters."

"Yeah? And then what? Court martial me for insubordination?"

"Don't tempt me, Lieutenant."

Jane planted her hands on the edge of the desk and leaned forward, her eyes narrowed dangerously. "Just you try it, Captain Morgan. The only thing I've ever asked for is to be treated like an officer. If you can't see your way clear to that, I'll request a transfer off this ship as soon as we reach port. If you think my presence compromises your integrity, then sign the goddamn transfer." Jane spun on her heel and slammed out of the office. Managing to maintain outward control, she left the bridge.

Left alone in his office, Morgan almost put his fist through the bulkhead. Never had a woman, not to mention an officer, angered him to this extreme. Morgan prided himself in his ability to never lose his cool, but this pushed his patience farther than he realized. In one breath, he wanted to call ship's security and toss her in the brig, in another he forced himself to admit she was dead to right. He was trying to protect her and that was wrong. If positions were reversed, there was no question in his mind that Jonathan would have immediately been informed his sibling was missing in action. Instead of following his gut reaction and ignoring the admiral's decision to shield Jane, he went along with it and now, there was no question that he regretted the decision. Add to that the sinking feeling he was beginning to care for her more than was healthy for either him or his career, Morgan sullenly sunk into his chair while he tried to figure out how to undo the damage.

∞⊖∞

Belle Winter went in search of something to eat and found Blackjack pouring over a chart in the all-night coffee, alone. Taking a sandwich from the bar, she joined him at the table. "I would like to know what is going on around here, Cardozo."

"We're preparing for battle?"

"You know what I mean. What was in that message, besides the mention of a Rothko, that would make her turn white as a ghost? Does she know him or something?" Belle was tenacious, if nothing else.

"Something," replied Cardozo grimly.

She put her hand over the chart, preventing him from looking at it. "Okay, Blackjack. Let's cut to the chase. There's nobody around and I want to know. Is Pilot Major Rothko her guy?"

Blackjack laughed, but it was a bitter sound. "Shit no, Belle. You're not even close."

"Answers, Blackjack. I'm not moving until I get answers. She's been a bitch since Lomos and it's getting worse. I like Jane; she's a good officer and up 'til now, we've been straight with each other. What is going on?"

Cardozo sat back in his chair and rubbed his tired eyes. He had been up for almost seventy-two hours and he was not up for a continuous harangue from Belle. "Ah guess she never told you what the 'R' in S.J.R.Krieg stands for."

Belle's mouth fell open. "She's a relative? She's related to the admiral?" she stammered.

"As close as you can get."

Without another word, Belle jumped up from the table and went to the bridge. Jane wasn't there, but Peters told her the lieutenant was in her office.

∞⊖∞

At her desk, Jane was trying to read copies of other transmissions sent to the *Washington* from HQ. The console crackled, but nothing was coming over. Angry and frustrated, she wished the ship to go faster.

Belle didn't knock, but once she stepped through the open door, she slid it shut behind her. "Permission to speak freely, lieutenant," she said, snapping a salute.

Frowning, Jane looked up, wondering what the hell the crewmate was doing. "Is this important?" she asked, annoyed at the interruption.

"You bet it is. Permission to speak freely, lieutenant," repeated the crewmate.

The frown deepened and a furrow appeared between Jane's brows. "Sit down and cut the crap. What's on your mind?"

Belle sat down, reached over, and took the picture that sat on Jane's desk. "This is you, and this guy must be Major Rothko. And that, I'll bet, is the admiral." She slid the frame back across the desk.

"Who told you that?" demanded Jane, almost shouting.

"I thought we were honest with each other, Jane. But you…you must've thought I was a complete jerk at the Titan conference when I made that crack about the admiral. You've been walking around here like the Wicked Witch of the West for days, and no one knew why. But you, and I guess Tapper, too, and Blackjack all knew about your brother days ago and never said a word."

"It wasn't germane."

"Yeah? So you took it out on everybody else? Why didn't you tell me, at least?"

"Would you have been so friendly when I first came on board if you knew I was his daughter? Wouldn't everybody have treated me with kid gloves...like a spy or something? I got *into* superschool without my parents' help. I got *through* most of superschool without most people knowing I was a Rothko. I got *here* based on a number, not on a name; my father didn't even go to candidates' review because he knew he might slip and say something. The last thing I need are people treating me differently *because* of my name. My brother lives that life and does not highly recommend it." She stopped and collected herself. "Jackson told you, didn't he?"

"Yes. And I'm damn glad he did."

"When?"

"Just now. I made him tell me." It sounded lame even as she said it.

"Whadja do? Threaten not to sleep with him?"

Hands flying to her face, Belle reddened violently, as though Jane had slapped her. "If you weren't an officer, I'd punch your nose to the other side of you face, and don't think I can't do it!"

"Get out of my office!" Her voice was cracking.

"I will not." Belle ran around the desk and gathered Jane into her arms. Holding her close, she stroked the dark brown hair. "Come on, Jane, don't be stupid. It's okay. Shhhhh." Like a mother comforting a child, she rocked her back and forth, trying to soothe away the pain while the lieutenant just sobbed it all out.

After a few moments, Jane picked up her head and accepted the handkerchief Belle dug out of her pocket. "Thanks," she sputtered, wiping her red eyes. "I'm sorry about what I said."

"Forget it, Jane, it's unimportant."

"I feel like a jerk."

"You're under a whole lotta pressure."

"That's no excuse. It was a terrible thing to say." She blew her nose loudly and then laughed. "I guess I owe you a handkerchief."

"Yeah, but don't worry about it. You okay?"

"Yeah, as okay as I can be at the moment." She took Belle's hand. "Will you promise me not to say anything about this?"

"About who you are or that you actually broke down and cried?" asked the yeomate with a wry smile.

"Both. I wouldn't want to ruin my reputation as a hard ass."

"I'll promise, under one condition: that you get out of here and go take a swim or something. There is nothing you can do right now except wait, and a swim will do you some good. If anything happens, I'll come get you."

Jane promised, but Belle insisted on walking with her to her quarters. "Thanks again," said Jane when she reached her door.

"No sweat, lieutenant." Belle headed back to the bridge where she would take over at Jane's station.

⁂

Belle stopped at the captain's office, "The lieutenant went to take a swim," she told him, then admitted to knowing what the "R" stood for. Judiciously omitting the rest of the conversation.

Morgan nodded. Any anger he was feeling toward the wayward lieutenant was private and not open to scrutiny from others. He was not unhappy that Winter had cajoled Jane into doing something physical; it might ultimately help diffuse her own frustration. On one hand, he was relieved Blackjack told someone who had at least some small influence on Jane; he never could have gotten her to leave her post. On the other, he was annoyed that the Southerner had breached the confidence. Still, Belle was known to keep her mouth shut. She was about to leave when Morgan called her back. "Belle, you're doing well in your tutorial, but we're going to have to put things on hold for a while, until this business is settled."

"I sorta figured that out, sir." With a quick salute, she was gone.

CHAPTER 20

The hovercraft moved faster than Jonathan could run. They played cat and mouse with the pilot until they tired of the game, then forced him against a ridge with no real place to take cover. Not willing to go without a good fight, Jonathan pulled out his side arm and with lightning speed, fired, hitting a Syrian soldier. His next shot at the hovercraft went wide, but his third found its way into the propulsion system. The craft bucked, dumping the wounded soldier out onto the desert floor. Taking advantage of the surprise, Jonathan sprinted along the ridge, ducking in and out of the coarse brush growing out of the barren rock. The Syrians pulled out of the buck, slowed somewhat, but followed the prey. At the end of the ridge, the pilot leapt over the top, rolled to the other side, and managed to crawl into a small cave. As they came around, he could see them, but they could not see him. He waited until the craft was almost directly in front of him, then fired, hitting the driver. The hovercraft lurched, skimming the side of the hill and flopped over. For a moment, everything was quiet except the whooshing of air from the overturned craft.

Two Syrians crawled from beneath the wreckage and dove for cover in the brambles. Jonathan could hear them, but they were well secreted in the thorny branches. Suddenly, one emerged firing in his direction. A laser blast caught Jonathan in the arm and he fell backward. Righting himself, he aimed at the cave entrance and as soon as the Syrian appeared in silhouette, he fired at point blank range, killing him instantly.

Once again, quiet settled over the desert. As best he could, Jonathan staunched the bleeding and gave thanks that it was only a flesh wound. He knew another Syrian was out there, but he was certain the soldier would not come into the cave based on what he had done to his partner. Curling himself into a niche in the rock, he steadied his laser and waited.

There is no place darker than a cave in the desert. Through the opening, Jonathan could see the stars, but he was not about to go out into the night. Sleep longed to overtake him, but the pain in his arm kept him easily from dozing off. Although the wound wasn't deep, he had lost a considerable about of blood and he was beginning to feel light headed. As the night deepened, Jonathan felt himself losing ground. Every time he moved, he bled more until finally he slumped forward, unconscious.

Jonathan awoke because of the tremendous heat and bright sunlight bathing his already sweaty body. Gone was his burnoose, leaving him in his shorts and dog tags only. His arm, still aching, was wrapped in a white bandage. Blinking to better focus his eyes, Jonathan noticed the bars on the window. He struggled to sit up, unable to use the injured arm for support. "Anybody here?" he called out in Arabic.

A face appeared through the barred door. He stared at the prisoner, and then smiled a wide, gap tooth grin. "Mahmud! He's awake!" called the guard to someone else outside. He turned back to Jonathan. "General Ramadi is waiting for you, American," he said with the same smile.

Jonathan smiled back and the guard laughed. Somehow, he didn't think this was to be a social call. Leaning back on the metal bunk, he waited, but it was only a moment before the door was opened and he was escorted to a large, sparsely appointed tent in the middle of the compound. A guard pushed him toward a single chair and when Jonathan sat, his hands were bound behind his back. Wincing with pain, he thanked the man politely in Arabic.

"I thought you were American," said the soldier, taken aback by the prisoner's command of the language.

"I am," Jonathan smiled pleasantly, "but I speak Arabic. Do you speak English?"

The soldier was about to reply when General Ramadi entered the tent and ordered the guard to stand away from the prisoner. Coming closer, Ramadi inspected his catch. "How is your arm, Major Rothko?" he asked.

"Healing nicely, thanks to your medic, General." Jonathan studied the man and decided the general was under stress not necessarily related to the war. There was a quality of tension about the way he moved, a quality Jonathan had not seen in Ramadi before even though he had had occasion to see the man in action long before today. A commotion outside the tent caused them both to look to the flap. Four others came in, but only one was human. Jonathan recognized the tall man as a Jeylosian by his skin color although he was wearing clothes more appropriate for the climate than native Jeylosian garb. The other two, both saurian, were obviously Wa'atsi. The Jeylosian seemed to be the one in charge.

"So," drawled the Jeylosian in English, "this is Major Jonathan Rothko." He sauntered over to the chair. "I would have preferred to meet you under happier circumstances, Major."

"And what circumstances would those be, sir?" asked the pilot, wondering who the guy was.

The kora laughed, but it was not a pleasant sound. "I recently had the pleasure of meeting your sister." He paused, waiting for a reaction.

Jonathan knew at once, the only outward clue being a slight twitch in his clamped jaw. "My sister? Where would you have encountered Rebecca?"

The kora's hand shot out, smacking Jonathan across the face. "Don't play games with me, American. Your sister may have caused my father's anger, but you will pay for it."

Shaking his eyes back into his head, Jonathan pushed on. "My sister is seventeen years old and I cannot imagine what she could have done to anger the Emperor."

The hand shot out again. "You are not a fool, Rothko, so do not play the idiot son."

Narrowing his eyes, Jonathan considered his reply carefully. "I am not an idiot, but I think you know something I do not. Would you care to tell me what you are talking about or are you going to keep hitting a man who cannot defend himself?"

The kora sneered, positioning himself to Jonathan's side. Leaning closer to him, he said, "Your sister has a lovely body, but she is unschooled in how to use it. I would have taught her many things, but we were… interrupted."

"My sister is as flat as a pancake and has no interest in boys, let alone men."

General Ramadi observed from a distance. He was aware of the kora's fall from grace on his home planet, but he could not understand the current exchange between the two obvious adversaries. Although the discussion was pruriently interesting, Ramadi was more interested in what the American knew about Israeli installations along the Syrian border. He glanced at Ali Hassan, who stood at the entrance of the tent, and shrugged. The Iraqi was less patient. Crossing the space between him and the Jeylosian in a few long strides, he interrupted the kora.

"Get on with it, Your Highness. This may be of some importance to you," he said, controlling the anger in his voice, "but we have more important questions to ask."

The kora was tempted to lash out at Ramadi, but instead, stepped away from the prisoner. "Suit yourself," he replied with a sweeping gesture.

Ali Hassan took a chair and sat opposite Jonathan. "You will describe the new armaments on the Golan in great detail," he said in Arabic, knowing he was understood. "If you do not, we will not kill you, but we will send your body to your father piece by piece."

Jonathan watched the Iraqi's eyes and knew he was not bluffing. He wondered how much they already knew and how much leeway he had in giving them bogus information. "There isn't much I can tell you, Hassan," he said looking directly at him. "I've never been there."

"I find that difficult to believe, Major," Hassan sighed aloud. "You, of all people, have toured the northern installations repeatedly, I would venture."

With a snort and a laugh, Jonathan shook his head. "Your information is lacking, sir. I was assigned to the desert and in the desert I stayed. I have no reason to travel in the north."

Hassan knew beating the prisoner would gain him nothing. Standing up, he waved in the direction of the flap. "Perhaps a few days of incarceration will change your mind, Major." He stepped aside while two soldiers got Jonathan roughly out of the chair. "We will speak again, Major Rothko."

When they were gone, Kora Pana-Di raised his voice at the Iraqi. "What are you hoping to accomplish by letting him alone in a cell, Ali Hassan? Do you think a few days will change is mind?"

General Ramadi knew AIi Hassan well enough to know what the Iraqi indeed had in mind, but he remained silent. Hassan seemed unperturbed by the outburst. "You have little experience with us, Your Highness. There are ways of wearing him down until he tells us what we want to know. For now, we will continue maneuvering to the south, where the Israelis are weakest." He left the tent.

Ramadi smiled at the outlander. "He is right, you know. We will get what we want and you will get what you want. Leave these details to us."

"Are you certain you want to speak at this thing, Liz?" asked her husband as he watched her pack an overnight bag. The news that Jonathan had been taken prisoner was fresh and the admiral was not happy about his wife leaving Washington when so little was known.

"Can I afford not to, Edward?" she replied, carefully folding a clean uniform shirt. "They know one of ours is down and a prisoner. So far, we've been lucky, they haven't mentioned Jonathan by name. If I go to the Security Council and answer them directly, we stand a chance of not being drawn farther into this mess than we are already. Besides, Mustafa is sending representation and the word on the grapevine is that they want a meeting with me personally."

"Do you want me along? There is no reason why I can't go with you and fly back tonight."

The general stopped what she was doing long enough to kiss her husband. "No, Ted, you stay here. If the *Washington* calls in, you're going to want to talk directly with Morgan or Joshua. I'll be fine." She closed the suitcase and lifted it off the bed. "Do you really think," she began slowly, "that Pana-Di is here...in the Middle East, I mean?"

"Hard to say, Liz." He rubbed his stubbly chin. "We've had no reports of anything except Wa'atsi in the area, but if he's gone native, he would be hard to spot. Xinthi-Ang thinks it's a pretty good bet."

"And his wife thinks if he's there, he knows Jonathan and Sarah are brother and sister. I don't like it, Ted. I don't like it at all."

For three hours, Brigadier General Rothko fielded questions about the American involvement in Israel. Repeatedly, she reassured the Council that the pilot acted without sanction from the government and that in all probability, they were on a routine reconnaissance mission due to the red alert in the area, and the dog fight was simply a response to danger. The lone Wa'atsi representative insisted that they were observers in the area only and had no part in either destroying the F-511 nor in the search for the downed pilot. The general noticed and did not like the sneer the Wa'atsi shot in her direction at the mention of the pilot. She kept her cool, but made a mental note to put him under tight surveillance after he left the United Nations.

In the lobby, General Rothko spoke informally with several members of the Security Council. All were concerned that this might escalate into an interplanetary incident, but they were equally certain that the esteemed general was telling them the truth. As she spoke to the representative from Great Britain, General Rothko spotted a swarthy, but familiar face lingering against the wall of the lobby. The general's assistant spotted him, too and casually went over and engaged the man in conversation, nonchalantly escorting him toward the exit before returning to the general's side.

In the waiting car, Lieutenant Villard confirmed his boss's suspicion. "I told him to come to the hotel in an hour, Ma'am," he said with a grin.

General Rothko returned the smile. "Thanks, Chuck. You did that very nicely."

"Let's hope no one else noticed him."

⁂

The swarthy man knocked on the general's outer door at precisely six o'clock as instructed. When he was admitted, he allowed the aide to pat him down for weapons and then was shown into a large, well-appointed sitting room. As soon as the general entered, his handsome face was split with a wide smile and he rushed to greet her. "So good to see you, Madame Rothko!" he laughed, kissing her on both cheeks.

"Selim, you are a welcome sight for these tired eyes. How are your parents?" The general looked him over, admiring how much he had matured in the years since she last saw him.

"Father is upset, but Mother is downstairs in a suite waiting to learn whether or not you will see her."

"Fatima here?" cried the general. "Of course, I want to see her." She waited while the young man picked up the house phone and summoned his mother.

In a few moments, there was another knock at the door and a beautiful woman wrapped in an exquisitely embroidered vermillion robe swept into the room. She was covered from head to toe, her face hidden behind a gauzy veil. Lieutenant Villard, upon cue from the general, left the room, closing the doors behind him. As soon as he was gone, Queen Fatima of the Hashemite Kingdom whipped off the head covering. There was a warm embrace between the two women, one which the son watched with amusement.

"I am risking a great deal by being here, Elizabeth, but Mustafa and I agree there is even far more at risk if I do not speak with you directly," explained the queen, a worried look in her almond-shaped brown eyes.

"You would not be here without good reason, my dear friend, because it is well known that you do not leave Amman without your King. Not even to visit old friends in London."

The queen laughed lightly at the barb. "I wanted to see you and Ted in London when you were here last, Elizabeth, but both Mahmud and Sufiya had good, old fashioned colds! How we mothers must put aside our own wants!"

The general laughed with her. How many times she had cancelled trips because one or the other of the children was ill, she could not count. Leading the way to the sofa, she sat beside the queen. "So, what's on your mind, Fatima?"

"The news is not good, Elizabeth." The queen took the general's hand. "It's Jonathan." She paused long enough to read the terror in the other mother's eyes. "The boy is alive, but in terrible danger. We think we have a way to help." She felt a hand tighten on her own. "Mustafa is against this war, but our politics are so wrapped up with our Arab neighbors that we are going to be dragged in whether we want to or not. Mustafa visited Ramadi and Hassan in the desert several weeks ago and told them both he wanted no part in this."

This confirmed what they already knew. The general had been briefed by an emissary from the king after the meeting, but was warned that it might be the last direct contact they were able to manage. "How long can you hold out?" she asked.

"Not much longer, but before we are too far in, Mustafa wants Jonathan out of their hands." She looked at her own son. "We have known Jonathan since his prep school days with Selim and we are fond of him. That they have him does not sit well with us."

Selim joined them, taking the opposite chair. "I am expected to observe from the command post next week. Right now, they think my mother and I are in Amman attending to the preparations for my father's birthday celebration. But I think I know a way to get Jonathan out."

General Rothko weighed the offer. She was not willing to put Selim in danger, even for her own son. Selim, a progressive and intelligent young man, would one day succeed his father as King of the Hashemite's and his ascension to that throne would ensure the continued drive for permanent peace between Israel and Jordan. "I cannot allow that, Selim," she said reluctantly.

"I don't care whether or not you allow it, Madame Rothko. It will be done." He pulled a folded piece of paper from the pocket of his burnoose. "Let me show you what we have in mind."

Elizabeth Rothko sat back and listened, knowing it might be the only way she would see her son again.

CHAPTER 21

Behind closed doors, Morgan conferred with Tapper, Blackjack and Newhouse, reviewing transmissions received over the last forty-eight hours; still thirty-six hours away from Earth, strategic planning required finalization before beginning orbit around the planet. Jane returned to her post on the bridge where she monitored all interspace communication with Belle at her side. There were nuances they picked which so far had provided both the *Washington* and Fleet Headquarters with invaluable insight. The Wa'atsi were not particularly popular through the galaxy, but that did not prevent them from having friends in space.

Two transmissions were of particular interest to Morgan. The first was to another ship in a sector close enough to Earth's to pose an additional threat. The transmission had been oddly encoded and had taken Jane several hours of diligent arguing with the computer's logic banks to crack it. The essence of the message asked whether or not the vessel would be interested in participating in a skirmish with local ships. The receiver was not registered with the League of Planets, leading Jane and the others to believe that it was a privateer from the K'natcha system outside the League's influence. Pirates at heart, the voyagers from K'natcha enjoyed a little target practice wherever they found it. Not only were they admirable warriors, they were also known to hijack the unwary freighter now and then. Using the same code, Morgan sent his own message warning them away from the area. There had been no response, but there appeared to be no other communication from the Wa'atsi to the unidentified ship.

The second transmission was perhaps the stranger of the two, since it came from the Syrian/Jordanian border on Earth. Although the sender was not readily identified, the author of the message was a person of obvious rank, judging by the tone of command in the transmission. This one, also in a highly complex code, was easier to crack, however. Scrambled, but directed at the Stellar-3 system, the transmission was a call to rebellion on an unnamed planet. Try as they might, the linguistics crew on the *Washington* could only decipher the text of the transmission, not the address. It was a relay message, designed to be picked up and repeated from interceptor to interceptor until it reached the end of a long, prearranged chain. The first link was a moon of the eighth planet, a trade colony, but only the receiver would know where it was to go next. A common way to send highly sensitive material, it left Jane bothered.

The text itself was also strange. "Mission in progress," it began, "expect success. Have gathered additional support. That which should be will be ours. Organize phase three as soon as possible." It was signed "Kroushma."

"Isn't 'Kroushma' something like 'exalted leader' in Hatma?" asked Belle, studying the translation.

"It's also king, emperor, prophet, or messiah in most Stellar-3 dialects," replied Jane, wondering why Belle had asked such an obvious question.

"Wouldn't it mean, then, that the sender is someone of serious rank," offered the crewmate, "someone with a pretty big ego?"

"Got anyone in mind?" asked Jane, reconsidering her initial assessment of the comment.

Belle was quiet. She had someone in mind, but only because of a little conversation she had overheard when she had been waiting for Captain Morgan the day before. "I'm not sure, but I'll let you know if I come up with anything."

At the terminal, the screen displayed a series of possible destinations for the transmission. Several planets were experiencing civil unrest, situations the Wa'atsi might find inviting under the right circumstances. Jane, however, was convinced the sender was not Wa'atsi, but rather a traveler with them. Carefully reading and rereading the transmissions from Fleet HQ, she looked for any information which might provide some clue as to the identity of the sender. Although HQ had been working on the same set of transmissions, they were no closer to fully understanding them than was Jane. If they knew who was transmitting, they had not shared that information with the *Washington*; Jane kept that thought in the back of her mind.

Morgan stepped out of his office in time to hear the last exchange. He glanced at Tapper and Cardozo, but kept silent. Admiral Rothko had come in earlier, confirming that Jonathan had been found and taken prisoner by the Syrians. Coupled with it was the possibility that Pana-Di might be involved. For the moment, Jane was not to know. Morgan had argued with the admiral but, in the end, acceded to his wishes against his better judgment. Watching over her shoulder, he was impressed with both Jane and Belle's technique; the women worked well together, and from what he could gather from observing them, they had become friends. Unexpectedly, Jane looked up into his face, her eyes searching for some sort of answer to the questions she asked. He met her gaze but his eyes gave nothing away. "Krieg," he muttered gruffly, knitting his dark brows, "take a break. Go do something else for a while; you've been on the bridge too long."

"Is that an order, sir?"

"Yes," Morgan replied without missing a beat. "You're dismissed until 0700 hours."

Jane slid back in her seat, then paused, as though she expected someone to protest. When no one did, she gathered up her things and stood. "I think I'll take a swim," she muttered as she headed toward the cage.

Morgan watched her go and then disappeared into his office, closing the door behind him, leaving Tapper and Blackjack on the bridge. "Anyone for a dip in the pool?" the burly commander asked the tall Southerner.

"Ah was just thinkin' the very same thing, Joshua." Cardozo bowed gallantly from the waist. "After you, suh."

For a few wonderful moments, Jane luxuriated in the empty pool, swimming leisurely along the far lap lane, working off some of the tension she had been harboring seemingly forever. The water felt good, sluicing along her body, almost as good as the relative quiet of the natatorium. But the peace was short lived. Suddenly, the door opened and two bodies came hurtling through space, towels flying in every direction. With a great, resounding war cry, they leapt across the last few feet of pristine white tile and landed in the pool with an enormous splash, water sloshing over the sides. With furious effort, they swam toward Jane, shouting with each breath of air.

Jane, divided between abject anger and total amusement, started her own race for the end of the pool. They caught her mid-way, one on each side, and pushed her to the limit. As they neared the edge, a male voice shouted "One more time," and with a single touch, the three reversed and sped in the other direction.

By the time they finished the lap, Jane was winded but laughing until she held her sides. "Unfair!" she cried, taking a swipe at the nearest intruder.

"All's fair in love and water, S.J.," countered Tapper, draping an arm over her shoulder. He gave her a loud smacker on the cheek, tickling her face with his beard. "Feeling better?"

"I was, until you two animals arrived. Can't a girl get *any* privacy around here?"

They answered in unison "No!" and convulsed at their own humor.

"You guys are sick, you know that?"

"Ah should hope so, Cousin Krieg," sputtered Blackjack, shaking the water from his hair. "We would not be nearly as much fun if we were decidedly normal."

"Nor would we be floating around space in this tin can," Tapper added with a grin. "We'd be sitting in our recliners reading the latest stock prices."

Jane swam away with a snort. Somehow, she knew they were going to follow her. The truth was, she didn't really mind, but she'd be damned before telling *them*. Scrambling out of the pool, she scampered to the diving board, pausing at the edge long enough to give the rear of her suit a provocative snap, and then yelled "Three full laps, I get a dive for a handicap, loser buys a round of soda!"

"Aw right!" hollered Tapper, racing Jackson to the end beneath the board. "On your mark, get set... *GO*!!!!!"

The board gave a resounding slap when Jane took her running dive off the end, giving her almost a full half-length head start. She could hear the splashing behind her, but she was not about to check how far. She reached the first turn well ahead of the men, pushing cleanly off the tile in the opposite direction. It was easy to maintain the lead for a while, but at the end of the second lap, Tapper was right on her heels with Jackson only a split second behind him. With a great gulp of air, Jane submerged, using every bit of her strength in a powerful breaststroke. She beat them both at the turn, but not by very much. Betting that the men had pushed hard all the way through the race, she figured they would be less likely to power push the last lap. She could feel water churning behind her, but it seemed to be less close than before. Pushing herself just a little harder, she touched the finish line and emerged in time to see Tapper pull ahead of Jackson to finish second.

"Ah concede to the fair lady," announced Jackson, struggling for air as he hoisted himself out of the water. "What's your pleasure?"

"Ooooh, it's so hard to decide," she sighed, leaning against the cool tile wall. "Ah think a mineral water with a wedge of fresh lemon would be evah so lovely, don't you think, Cousin Cardozo?" Her drawl was a perfect imitation of his.

"*Fresh* lemon?" groaned the Southerner. "Where am Ah going to find a *fresh* lemon?"

Jane smiled demurely, "Why, Cousin Cardozo," she drawled on, "Ah was under the distinct impression that y'all were a man of infinite resources. Are y'all sayin' that y'all would be unable to find little ol' me a little ol' wedge o'lemon?" She added a little ol' eyelash batting for effect.

Tapper smirked and Cardozo groaned. "Ah shall return," he muttered, grabbing a discarded towel from the floor.

"Hey, Southern Boy, what about me?" Tapper yelled after him.

"Ah shall get you your usual, Mr. Bear." Leaving a trail of water, Cardozo disappeared through the door.

While he was gone, Jane and Tapper swam companionably about the pool. Respecting her need for not talking, the burly commander, took turns diving off the board with her until Jane, with one final dunk of the head, announced she was ready to get out. He followed her to a table at the end of the room, plopping down in a chair beside her. "You okay, S.J.?"

"As okay as I can be under the circumstances, Tap. I'm worried, tired, and frustrated, but there's damn little I can do about any of it. I can't sleep and I can't march into Morgan and demand answers to questions he can't possibly know the answers to. My father isn't telling me everything…that much I'm sure of, but whether or not he's telling Morgan...I guess I'm not so sure." She shrugged and went back to toweling off her long hair.

"There isn't much you don't know, Sarah Jane, and the stuff you don't know has no bearing on your situation." He paused and took her hand. "Look, I know it's not much comfort, but we're worried about Speed, too."

Jane leaned over and kissed his bearded cheek. "It is a comfort; at least I'm not alone in this. I guess I'm lucky that I ended up on the same ship as you and that's the truth."

"Things have a way of working out. We all have to believe that."

A commotion at the door caught their attention. Cardozo came in, carrying a large tray of drinks and assorted delicacies. "It would seem, Cousin Krieg, that you have friends in the galley. There was no possibility of a fresh lemon until Ah mentioned that a certain lieutenant would be mightily disappointed without one."

Jane clapped her hands in glee. "See, boys, it pays to be nice to the chief steward!"

"They're in the pool, sir," reported the crewmate in the security office when asked by the Captain for the location of Tapper and Cardozo. "With Lieutenant Krieg. Do you want me to beep them, sir?"

"Thanks, no. Captain out." Morgan leaned back in his chair and wished he was with them. Any place but on the bridge. He looked up at the screen and watched the Wa'atsi ship maneuvering in space. The *Washington*, still too far away for a clear shot of the Wa'atsi vessel, was being supplied with the picture via transmission from the Intrepid, orbiting Earth at close range. The markings on the Wa'atsi ship denoted its class as a cruiser, but the configuration of the engine housings were unfamiliar to Morgan; he wondered if this was a new design of their own, or one which had been pirated from another source. "Winter," he called over his shoulder, "how 'bout a status report on who else is floating around out there?"

"Rush hour, sir. Other than the big guy you're watching, there's a Russian freighter in orbit not far away, a British research bell-pod, two lunar shuttles, both ours, one going, one coming, and a couple of our patrol skimmers," said Belle, counting the blips on her screen to make sure she accounted for them all. "And the *Merrimack* is incoming."

"Can you get Coleridge on the horn...or is he out of range?"

"I should be able to reach him. Scrambled, sir?"

"Natch." Morgan leaned back and waited for Clay Coleridge to appear on the screen.

"We've got to stop meeting like this, Ash!" boomed Coleridge as he materialized.

"Yeah, no argument there." Morgan liked the other captain, counting him as a good friend in all circumstances. "What do you know, Clay?"

Coleridge laughed, "Probably not nearly as much as you do. We were already in docking mode when we got diverted back here. The Wa'atsi are maintaining silence in our direction, but they are receiving and responding to communiqués from the hot spot. What the hell are they doing, Ash?"

"Beats me, but I don't think I like it whatever it is. The transmissions aren't telling us a damn thing, but I get the impression they're waiting for something." He was about to add another comment when he caught Belle's hand waving in his direction. "What's up, Winter?"

"Another Wa'atsi ship is coming into our sector from Quad-17K. It looks like the *Pu'unoti*."

"Uh-oh," grinned Coleridge, having heard the news. "P'nucha is not very happy with either of us, Ash."

"P'nucha may not be happy with us, but he isn't stupid. I'll call you back."

"Do that, would you? *Merrimack* out." Coleridge disappeared.

Morgan waited while Belle opened a hailing channel to the newcomers. Flicking on the translator on his console, Morgan greeted the Wa'atsi in a friendly voice. "To what honor do we owe this visit, Admiral P'nucha?"

Unexpectedly, the fierce, reptilian admiral appeared on the *Washington*'s screen, an unusual occurrence for Wa'atsi who preferred voice links only. "We come in peace, Captain Morgan."

"Like your sister ship orbiting Earth?" he countered pleasantly.

"Not like that renegade ship," P'nucha spat, tension visible in his scaly face. "She is out of jurisdiction, here without permission from the Supreme Command, and I have been dispatched to discover why."

Eyebrows were raised across the bridge. This was not the anticipated response. "You have no idea why she is orbiting, Admiral?"

"The Rasha'atam is a Wa'atsi vessel, but privately owned. We received word that a Wa'atsi warrior was in your sector and our Supreme Command has issued a formal statement to your government disavowing ownership. What information do you have, Morgan, which might serve us both?"

Morgan flicked the mute, allowing him private conversation with his crew. Turning his back to the screen, he faced Newhouse. "Assessment, Joe?"

"He's not lying, Captain. He would not allow us to see him if he were not deadly serious."

Morgan turned back to the screen. "I accept what you say as truth, Admiral P'nucha. Are you able to share intelligence with us, or are you under a command of silence?"

The Wa'atsi snorted. "We would be most willing to share intelligence with you, Morgan, provided you will do the same."

Considering the response, Morgan carefully reviewed the options. Since they were heading in the same direction at approximately the same speed, there was little time to spare in coding transmissions for secrecy, nor was he about to give them the ability to use an American scrambler. The best of all possible means would be to meet face to face. "Admiral, would you be willing to come aboard the *Washington* to discuss this in person?"

"What guarantees of safety will you provide?" shot back P'nucha.

"You may bring a security team...or we can send someone to you for safekeeping." Although he thought it, he did not say *hostage*.

The Wa'atsi turned his back for a moment and then spoke. "We will shuttle over to the *Washington* in one hour, Captain Morgan. It will not be necessary to send us an officer in exchange; I believe we have the same goal to accomplish and I will trust your offer of hospitality. P'nucha out." The screen went blank.

There was a smattering of applause on the bridge, and Morgan acknowledged it with a courtly bow. Clapping his hands twice, he smiled at the bridge crew. "Okay, you swabbies, we've got an hour to get this tub cleaned up. That means workstations pristine and emptied of all non-essentials, and dress uniforms all 'round. I want the humidity adjusted so that we're all reasonably comfortable. And coffee. I hear they like coffee. Black and thick." He hit a button on his console, linking him into the ship's p.a. "This is your captain. We will be visited by Admiral P'nucha of the Wa'atsi Supreme Command at 17:45 hours. This is a formal occasion. Let's look sharp, people!"

In the natatorium, Tapper, Blackjack and Jane nearly jumped out of their seats. "What the hell?" shouted Tapper, running to the intercom on the wall.

"Oh, shit!" moaned Jane, wrapping a towel around her wet suit. "I've got to get a shower!"

Blackjack leaned back and just laughed.

Hair still wet, Jane flew onto the bridge in under a half-hour, her fingers tucking the last damp strands of her braid into a knot. Sliding into her seat, she punched up the transmissions received since she had last been at her station and began reading while she anchored her cap over her wet head.

Belle appeared, also in dress blues, and immediately handed her a docupad with the notes she had been processing.

The bridge was alive with activity; everyone was rushing about, making sure the area was in perfect order for the Wa'atsi visit. It was, to anyone's knowledge, the first time one of them had ever been on a Fleet vessel. By the time Morgan breezed out of the cage, his staff was ready for him. The captain made a quick tour, nodding contentedly at the quick change from chaotic crisis to tidy workplace. Standing in the middle of it all, he commended them on their quick response and smart looks, and announced a senior staff meeting in the conference room. "It will be short, ladies and gentlemen, for we have precious little time to waste."

The officers filed in and quickly took their seats. Morgan reviewed the procedure for non-allied visitation, and then handed out assignments. "I want all of you on the shuttle deck with smiles on your faces. I want no mention of the Pitan incident, no lizard jokes, no smirks, giggles or anything else that will make our guests even remotely uncomfortable. The Admiralty is thrilled that a Wa'atsi of high rank is coming aboard and they want nothing to jeopardize what might be the beginning of more friendly relations with them." He looked at Jane and Tapper. "We will give them what information we have about the transmissions, and you will be expected to answer any questions P'nucha might ask, except in the area of code breaking and scrambling. Lieutenant Krieg, I assume you are fluent in Wa'atsi?"

"Reasonably fluent, sir," answered Jane with a wince. It was not one of her master languages.

"Do we have anyone else who's got the lingo?"

"Winter, sir, and both Peters and Ngyuen can manage. Will you be using a UT, Captain?"

"Yes, but I want you with me. Assign the others to whomever else P'nucha brings along. How do you say 'welcome aboard' in Wa'atsi?"

Jane smiled; it was a nice touch. "*Himnacha kruptna, Gacham P'nucha.*" Morgan repeated the words and Jane corrected the pronunciation. "Roll the R's a little more," she suggested "and less accent on the cha's. It's a softer sound than that."

Satisfied that he had done it right after a second repetition, Morgan continued the assignment roster. When the light on the wall flashed blue, he stood up. "Okay, people, let's go do our thing on the shuttle deck."

All available crew assembled on the shuttle deck to greet the Wa'atsi. Excitement was running high; few had ever seen a saurian in person. A constant whisper ran along the length of the ranks, but rather than hush them into fidgetiness, Morgan relaxed and let them carry on, enjoying the break from recent tension.

A warning buzzer sounded when the outer bay doors opened to admit the Wa'atsi shuttle. On the shuttle deck, the crew snapped into sharp formation, eyes front, in perfect stance, ready to salute the moment Admiral P'nucha stepped onto the *Washington*. The alien craft, a sleek silver pod with fanciful markings denoting it as the personal craft of a high ranking Wa'atsi official, slid gracefully into the moorings anchored to the floor. Six crewmates ran out to secure the pod, an awkward moment as they sought to figure out how to slip the locks over the nose. As soon as it was managed, they returned to line as the door of the craft lifted open and Admiral P'nucha made his entrance.

Tall, yet broad of stature, P'nucha was the epitome of a Wa'atsi warrior. His chest was covered in colorful ribbons and highly polished medals, each denoting his role in battle. The cloth of his tabard was fine quality black Toran silk, as was the bright white shirt beneath. His leggings, barely visible under the long over vest, were tied with purple ribbons, yet another sign of his exalted rank on his home world, Wa'atir. Unlike the four others in the Wa'atsi party, P'nucha was capless; his scaly head glistened brown-gold in the bright light of the shuttle deck. With an uncharacteristic smile, the admiral strode toward the captain, his hand extended. "At last we meet, Ash Morgan," said P'nucha in accented English.

Morgan was a little surprised, but maintained his own smile. "A feeling we share, Admiral." He sucked in his breath and carefully said "*Himnacha kruptna, Gacham P'nucha.*"

"Ho! What a kind greeting! I am pleased!" P'nucha's brusque laugh echoed through the deck.

"Allow me to present my senior officers, Admiral," said Morgan, indicating the patiently waiting people behind him.

P'nucha followed his host and greeted each member of the senior staff. When they reached Lucas and Krieg standing together toward the middle of the line, P'nucha hesitated before touching either of them. Touching Morgan's sleeve, he leaned close to the captain and asked "You have females to serve you on your command, Captain?"

Morgan suppressed a grin and answered gravely, "They serve me as competent officers, Admiral P'nucha."

"Hmmm, only as officers?"

"In no other way." He glanced at Jane whose eyes danced at overhearing the exchange; it was hard not to laugh at the implication.

"Our females stay home with our hatchlings, but I have heard females serve in other fleets, as well." Tentatively, he reached out to shake Commander Lucas's hand, then the lieutenant's. "A pleasure to meet you, Madame officers."

"*Nihk ma tantam ni akhshap, Gacham P'nucha*," replied Jane, surprised by the satiny coolness of his hand.

P'nucha laughed again, obviously pleased by her remark. "*Lahk ni akhtar humit t'napta chilmas.*"

Jane blushed prettily and caught the look of approval in Morgan's face. With his translator functioning, he understood when the Wa'atsi Admiral called them the prettiest human officers he had ever seen.

Once the review was over, Morgan led the way to the bridge and gave P'nucha a quick tour. The Wa'atsi were obviously impressed by the ship's equipment, asking a few probing questions which Morgan answered and Jane translated for the other guests. They moved from the bridge to the wardroom where docupads and appropriate refreshments had been laid out on the long table. P'nucha seemed pleased when Jane sat beside him at the end of the table where Morgan took the head.

"Let us get down to business, admiral," began Morgan, pouring a cup of coffee for the visitor who accepted it graciously. From all his contact with the Wa'atsi, Morgan would never have guessed that the famous First Admiral P'nucha, one of the most feared warriors in space history, was an easy-going, thoroughly likeable guy in person.

P'nucha opened the portfolio one of his men had carried onto the *Washington*. Taking out a sheaf of paper, he slid it toward Morgan. "This is transcription of the messages we have intercepted in the last four days. I must assume you have also intercepted these."

Although the English translation was rough, it had been an honest effort, judging by their own versions, accompanied by the original texts. Morgan read them over and gave them to Jane. In turn, Jane passed their edition to P'nucha who studied them closely.

"Sir, we have a difference in the second message," said Jane. "Your translator identifies the sender as Jeylosian. We do not make that assumption. Is there a piece of code you have which we do not?" She did not see Morgan and Tapper exchange worried glances.

"Perhaps, Lieutenant, perhaps. We have had other communications which indicate the Jeylosian in question is a renegade from his home planet and unwelcomed on yours." P'nucha brought out another piece of paper. "Here, this was received two of your weeks ago by our listening post on Trodentia, near Jeylos."

Jane read the document and looked up, her brows knitted together. "Did you know about this, Captain Morgan?" she asked quietly.

He took the message and read it, then pushed it back to her. "We had an unsubstantiated report, Lieutenant, but not enough to trust the source." His eyes tried to telegraph a silent message to her.

"Are you certain that it was the Kora Pana-Di who was picked up, Admiral?"

"Reasonably certain, Lieutenant. There is a death warrant on his head issued by the Emperor himself."

"I see." Jane's jaw muscle twitched as she reread the transmission.

Morgan jumped into the silence. "Where does the Supreme Command stand on this, Admiral?"

Thinking for a moment, P'nucha carefully constructed his reply. "What we want, Captain, is to get our people out of there before there is an interplanetary incident. We have no wish to be involved with your domestic affairs. As for the Jeylosian, he is of no consequence." He looked from Morgan to Jane and back to Morgan. "The pilot, however, is of great importance."

Jackson Cardozo appeared at the door in the dun colored uniform of an American Air Force officer. "Ah should hope so, *Gacham P'nucha*," drawled the Southerner leaning against the doorframe.

"I heard you were on board, Jackson, but thought you must be hiding yourself." The Wa'atsi's voice was not enthusiastic. He held out his hand, palm up.

Digging something from his breast pocket, Cardozo sauntered around the table and dropped it in the admiral's open hand. "Ah believe this belongs to you, P'nucha."

"And this must be yours." P'nucha removed a medal from his chest and handed it to Cardozo. "Peace is made, Jackson."

"Peace is made, Gacham P'nucha." Blackjack pinned the medal to his uniform where it fit snugly into a blank space, obviously belonging there.

"So, P'nucha, are you really here to get your people off Earth, or are you here to get Speed out?"

Jane's mouth dropped open. Morgan turned red. "What is going on here, Cardozo?" he demanded, rising to his feet.

"Clear the room." P'nucha's voice was low, but the tone of command unmistakable. Everyone, including Jane, rose, leaving Morgan, P'nucha and Cardozo in their places. Tapper remained at the door, unwilling to let Jane leave with them.

"Sit down, Jane," ordered Blackjack, his hand shooting out to capture her arm. "You, too, Bear."

"Why is the female remaining?" asked the Wa'atsi. "We do not need translation."

"She stays." Morgan looked grim, angry at Cardozo. This was just one more case of Blackjack withholding primary information and springing it theatrically at the wrong time.

Blackjack held Jane's chair and stood behind her when she sat. "P'nucha, meet Speed's sister, Sarah Jane Rothko-Krieg."

He looked at her with new eyes. An admirer of Admiral Rothko, P'nucha was unaware that there were children other than the son. "You are of fine lineage, Lieutenant. Your brother is equally respected."

"He damn well should be, P'nucha." said Cardozo. "It seems to me he did you a rather large favor several years ago."

"Would someone tell me what is going on?" repeated Morgan angrily.

P'nucha suddenly looked tired, slumping slightly in his chair. "The Rothko son was on Kotuchar when my eldest hatchling was on his first exploration. There was an incident in which my son was wrongly accused of cheating in a gambling game. His life was not to be his own, but the Rothko son took it upon himself to remove Thram from the situation and return him to his ship. I am indebted to him for the life of my son."

"It wasn't such a big deal, Ash, but it was sticky. Speed just did what Speed does best." Cardozo took the chair beside Jane and held her hand. "But we have another axe to grind, Gacham P'nucha. We want Pana-Di."

"Why? Is he offensive to you?"

"He is offensive to the daughter of Rothko. He attempted to force unwanted attentions on the lieutenant." Cardozo's face was grim.

"And this is why he was held prisoner by his father?"

"Yes," answered Morgan. "We don't know why he is where he is, but we want him out of there."

"You *did* know, didn't you?" Jane asked Morgan, still holding onto to Jackson's hand.

Morgan shook his head. "Your father told us that it was a *possibility* he was with the Wa'atsi, but it was unconfirmed."

Her voice was deadly calm. She yanked her hand from Cardozo's. "Damn you all. Were you saving this for a surprise?"

Ash Morgan regretted looking into her eyes; there was such terrible anger there. He could pass the blame to the father, but realized that would serve no purpose. He knew he would get no help from Cardozo. He saw Tapper move to Jane, his arm protectively about her shoulders. Feeling decidedly alone in this, Morgan clamped his jaw shut.

"It was your dad, S.J.," said Tapper quietly. "We all disagreed with his decision to keep this quiet, but the source was not reliable and we had way too much doubt to trust the information as it was given."

Jane cut him off. "Since when have you listened to anything my father has said to you about me?"

"Since none of us wanted to be the one to tell you the bastard was on the loose when we didn't know for sure," Cardozo offered limply.

Jane was about to say something, but changed her mind. Looking up at Tapper, she placed her hand over his and squeezed it. "Okay. This is going to have to be a battle I fight with them, not with you." She turned her attention to P'nucha. "Do you, Gacham P'nucha, have any sort of plan to get my brother out of there?"

"Yes, daughter of Rothko." He began to outline what exactly he could do with his own people.

The two odd companion ships moved toward Earth at a steady pace. As they approached scanning range, the Wa'atsi vessel employed a cloaking device to shield it from unwanted detection. Admiral Rothko transmitted to the ship at a prearranged time and was satisfied with the progress being made by Morgan and the Wa'atsi Admiral. He officially sanctioned the joint maneuvers. In turn, he agreed to meet Morgan and a small expeditionary force at Ein Geshem as soon as they could arrive there. Morgan allowed Jane a few private words with her father, and it was further agreed that she would remain on the ship monitoring the action on the ground.

"It's not that I doubt your ability to manage a ground base listening post, Sarah," explained Admiral Rothko after seeing his daughter's frustration. "It's that both your mother and I feel that because Pana-Di is involved, your physical presence may draw additional fire. You are a potential pawn."

She accepted the answer, opting not to fight about it now. The important thing was to get Jonathan out of the middle and if her being there might make it worse, then she would stay behind. On her recommendation, Ngyuen was sent in her place. Standing on the shuttle deck with several others, she watched as P'nucha left the *Washington*, followed immediately by their own landing party.

CHAPTER 22

In his cell, Jonathan, barely conscious, lay on a filthy mattress, dumped here after his last session with the Kora Pana-Di and General Ramadi. Unlike the rest of his peace loving people, this Jeylosian took great pleasure in watching the pilot writhe in agony each time he refused to answer a question. When slapping him around had no effect, the kora resorted to other, more sophisticated forms of torture. One by one, he had ordered Jonathan's fingers smashed with a flat sided paddle. On his orders, Syrian soldiers had had their own fun with him, beating the pilot until he was nothing more than a bloodied body on the carpet of Ramadi's tent. Still, despite their efforts, they could get no information from him.

Only a bucket of brackish water dumped on him brought Jonathan around. Gritting his teeth, he braced himself as two Iraqis dragged him from the floor and back to Ramadi. They tied him to a chair; his head slumped lifelessly against his chest. Jonathan could hear their voices, but he lacked the strength to pick up his head to see them. There was a new voice in the tent, one he knew well. Struggling, he tried to focus on the men standing at the desk, but he could only see a stranger in a long, snowy white burnoose and black checkered kufiyah.

"My father is a woman when it comes to the Israelis," said the new voice. "I prefer not to sit by and watch our people be tantalized by unattainable wealth. This seems a better solution than waiting for the Prophet to come to our aid." There was some laughter from Ramadi and Hassan, but it was short lived.

"I will admit I am surprised by your support, Your Royal Highness," countered Ramadi, allowing a small smile. "I had been led to believe that you support your father's foreign policy."

Prince Selim snorted indelicately. "What son would be insane enough to defy his father publicly, when the father has the power of life and death?" He slapped Ramadi companionably on the back. "When I succeed my father, General, then you shall see the true son of Achmed, not the weakling he spawned and called his heir."

Ramadi caught the sly grin inching across Ali Hassan's lips. The Syrian firmly believed Selim was not of a similar mind as Mustafa and had insisted the Prince be allowed to visit the installation as soon as the request had been made. Ramadi, however, was not convinced. Before this sudden interest in the war now being waged against Israel, Selim had always been a voice for moderation, echoing his father's policies. Still, if his own family was typical, one of his own six sons adamantly opposed this war until he had to order the boy to be placed under house arrest as a last resort to silence him. "Does your father know you are here, Your Royal Highness?" asked the general.

"Hardly. He would have me ordered to prison before he allowed me to come here, General." Selim strolled in the direction of the prisoner. "So, this is the American pilot. Have you gotten anything from him?" The Prince positioned himself directly in Jonathan's sightline.

"Not yet, Selim," admitted Pana-Di, permitting himself familiarity of similar rank. "But it will not be long before he is broken."

Jonathan raised his head slowly, unable to believe both his eyes and ears. He heard the name Selim, but the face was hidden beneath the drape of the kufiyah. Through swollen eyes, he watched the newcomer raise his hand to push aside just enough of the cloth and touch the end of his nose. A glimmer of hope ran through Jonathan; there was no doubt that it *was* Selim standing before him and that the Prince had given him the all clear signal from a long ago soccer field. There was no way to return the sign, but he slowly blinked his eyes, hoping that the makeshift signal was not lost on his friend.

Selim reached out and pushed against Jonathan's chin, raising the prisoner's head as high as it could go. "American Yehudi swine," he spat but his touch was reassuringly gentle. He let the face fall. Turning his back on Jonathan, he faced the other three men, thankful that the kufiyah hid his effort to swallow his own bile. "What are your plans for this piece of garbage?"

"One more session with my intelligence officers should bring us the desired results, Your Royal Highness," answered Hassan pleasantly.

"Your methods are crude, gentlemen. Let's hope you get answers before you kill him." Selim was feeling nauseated.

Ramadi laughed bitterly. "We cannot kill him, he is worth much more alive than dead. Our methods may be crude, but they are not slovenly."

"Come, sirs," suggested Hassan, "let us have lunch before we begin the next interrogation."

From his ship, P'nucha hailed the Wa'atsi vessel orbiting Earth. The crew was not expecting the summons home to come from a top member of the Supreme Command in a ship less than two hours away from them. After the first transmission, they raced to reach their captain who had accompanied the Kora Pana-Di to the surface. A shuttle left the mother ship in a matter of minutes while the communications officer repeatedly tried to hail the officers on the planet. Admiral P'nucha's order was to withdraw immediately, but they were loath to do so without their commanding officer, even if they were not directly under P'nucha's military jurisdiction.

For his part, as soon as the shuttle left the ship, P'nucha blew it out of space with a laser missile. He had been explicit in his orders and this was a breach he would not tolerate. It also sent a signal he meant business and that no interference would be tolerated. The *Washington* remained silent as P'nucha told Fleet headquarters he would handle his people in his own way.

From his own position, Morgan had been actively monitoring the whole of the Middle East. Several battles were already in progress in the area of the Golan, but the Israelis maintained their original position. A small force was making its way toward Jerusalem from the northeast, but again the IDF was keeping them at bay. The battles were little more than skirmishes, a test of the waters by the invading forces. Behind the Golan Heights, half way to Damascus, the joint Syrian and Iraqi army was preparing for a major offensive. The Jordanians, led by King Mustafa, had refused to participate in the venture, but no trespass warning had been issued by the government, thereby allowing access to Jerusalem through territorial Jordan. Although he believed Jonathan was being held in Syria, Morgan opted to land his shuttle craft at the Negev installation. From there, they could, with permission obtained from Jordan, make their way into Syria without being detected by conventional monitoring devices.

The IDF commander at Ein Geshem welcomed Morgan and his small landing party when they arrived shortly after dawn. Admiral Rothko, en route from Tel-Aviv, was delayed, but would arrive before they left the base. Although General Boruch BenTzion spoke English reasonably well, Morgan found it was easier to communicate effectively in Hebrew. Tapper and Blackjack, sitting in the Quonset hut, listened carefully as BenTzion detailed the course they would need to take to reach the Syrian camp well before dawn.

Morgan had chosen his people carefully. Along with Tapper and Blackjack, neither of which would have countenanced being left behind, he had taken Crewmate Bean, well known for his brute strength and ability in hand-to-hand combat, Wes Larkin and Vic Moreno from security division, and Ngyuen, the linguistic specialist. The others would come from the IDF. Satisfied with the make-up of the party, Morgan focused on what BenTzion was saying, asking questions as they came to mind.

The fan whirring softly in the ceiling did nothing to dispel the oppressive heat building in the hut. As the sun rose higher in the sky, they could all feel the tension creeping up their spines; there would be no relief until the fireball disappeared once again from the horizon and they could leave Ein Geshem.

When the briefing was over, Morgan went to the door of the Quonset hut and looked out over the bleak landscape. Apart from the camouflage netting covering the craft parked on the tarmac, there was no cover. Brown, parched, desert rock stretched forbiddingly for miles in all directions. Shielding his eyes from the intense glare, the captain scanned the horizon. Nothing seemed to move in the wasteland; as though every living thing with any sense had taken cover from the heat. Morgan wondered what the odds were that they would succeed. He knew Selim should already be with Jonathan, but there were no guarantees, nor any way to confirm, that the Prince had been able to convince Ramadi and Hassan his sympathies were with them. *Too many unknowns,* thought Morgan with a grimace. There were too many aspects to the mission that could not be preplanned or controlled. It left him with a vaguely unsettling feeling in the pit of his stomach.

As if he could read his friend's mind, Tapper came up behind Morgan and put his hand on the captain's shoulder. "Forget the doubts, Asher. We will do what we have to do."

"Yeah," snorted the other man, "we always do what we have to do."

"And so far, we've come out of it all in reasonably good health."

BenTzion joined them at the door. "Come, my friends, we've got a commando who needs to say *Kaddish*. Let's make the minyan."

Morgan, Tapper and Blackjack followed the Israeli to where several men had already gathered to pray.

At BenTzion's insistence, the landing party from the *Washington* had been given cots in one of the barracks. While the others slept, Morgan lay on his back reviewing the plan, looking for possible loopholes and potential problems. He dozed a little, and was sleeping when a hand shook him awake. "It's time," said Blackjack, already dressed in a black flight suit. "Ted's here and wants to see you before we take off."

Wearing the same type of black flight suit, Morgan strode into the Quonset hut where they had met earlier. Admiral Rothko was sitting at the table with Tapper and BenTzion, looking over the map. As soon as Morgan came in the door, the admiral stood and extended his hand. "I wish it were under better circumstances, Asher," he said quietly.

"I wish it were, too, Admiral," replied Morgan feeling great sympathy for Jonathan's father. As a parent, he could only imagine what lengths he would traverse if it were Reuben in this same situation. "Are you satisfied with the plan?" he asked.

Rothko nodded. "It's as good as we're gonna get. Let's just hope it's good enough."

Sixteen Israeli commandos filed silently into the Quonset hut. Taking seats as they found them, they were the toughest, meanest looking lot of men Morgan could ever remember seeing. Each one was a specialist in terrorist activity, each ready to risk his life in what was considered to be an almost suicide mission into Syrian territory. BenTzion went over the details one last time and ended with a small prayer for their success.

Outside, on the tarmac, they divided into smaller groups and boarded their hovercraft. It would take almost six hours to reach the camp in Syria; six hours of complete silence. There could be no transmission between craft and no transmission to base camp. As they maneuvered into travelling formation, Morgan could see Ted Rothko standing with BenTzion. And for the first time in as long as he could remember, he was scared.

Selim checked his watch for the thousandth time. If all went according to plan, the IDF commandos would be less than thirty kilometers away by now. Silently slipping from the warm sheepskin bedding, he dressed in his dark blues and began preparing his gear. A noise outside his tent startled him and he dived back beneath the covers. A man in a flowing robe stepped inside and stood, poised at the door. In the weak light of a tiny lantern, Selim could not quite make out his visitor. The figure moved closer until he stood directly above Selim.

"Are you awake, sir?" asked the gruff voice in a low whisper.

Selim breathed a sigh of relief. "What are you doing here, Ishmael?"

"I am never far from you, sir." The older man crouched beside the Prince. "They are very close, but the security here has not picked them up."

"How did you get into camp?" asked Selim, never failing to marvel at the old man's ability to move in and out of the shadows like a ghost.

"It was easy, my prince. The guards are very lax on their perimeter. They took no notice of an old man on a camel." He paused and sighed aloud. "I am not sure you know what danger you are in, sir."

Selim crawled out of the bed again, stood, and smiled at Ishmael. "The danger is unimportant, my friend."

Ishmael was still frowning. "What have you told them, sir? Why have they allowed you to stay?"

"I told Ramadi that in exchange for my support, he would see that I succeed my father on the throne. Immediately."

Eyes wide, the old man stifled a chuckle.

Selim whispered, "Now, you go out the way you came and I shall see you when this is over." He watched the tent flap open and close once again before he set to work preparing his gear.

The commandos halted their progress behind a ridge twenty kilometers from the camp. Yaniv Evron scooted over to where Morgan stood near his hovercraft. Pulling a reconnaissance photo from his jacket, he laid it on the hood and shined a tiny light on it. "Here is the lock-up we think the Major is in." He indicated a single, makeshift building near the center of a circle of tents. "There are guards, but, according to our sources they tend to fall asleep." He moved the light to the left. "These, however, are listening posts and are constantly manned. And this tent is where the outlanders have been staying."

"If we go in from the north, we can get to Jonathan and still bypass the posts. Assuming, that is, that Selim is able to disarm the perimeter alarm."

"Right, but we can short circuit the alarm with one of these." He pulled a small black box from another pocket. "We slip this under the wire and it will give us about two feet in which to move. If Prince Selim is successful, he will be waiting for us at the appointed place."

Morgan signaled to Tapper and Blackjack. "Are you ready to split up?"

"Yep," said Cardozo, studying the picture. "We're ready when you are."

"*B'seder,* let's go." Evron and Morgan jogged back to their craft.

The hovercraft moved as a graceful, silent armada invisible against the black night sky. At five kilometers, the craft carrying Tapper and Ngyuen veered off to one side and settled on the desert floor. The other five craft hovered nearby until a tiny flash of light from Tapper told them to proceed. In seconds, they vanished over the last ridge before the Syrian outpost.

Tapper adjusted the tiny receiver in his ear and set the device for bilateral scramble. The messages would come across as a thin stream of high pitched noise, fed into the main unit, and translated into understandable language. The language, on Ngyuen's insistence, would not be an Earth based tongue, but a dialect few would be able to decipher. A prearranged system of beeps would be the only way Tapper could communicate with the commandos en route. One Israeli remained with the crewmen from the *Washington*; he would track the other craft with a similar homing device. Settled beneath a dun colored tarp designed to blend into the landscape, the three men sat in silence watching the first hint of day creeping over the eastern horizon.

A single, flickering fire was the only sign of human habitation on the flat plain of a desert depression. As had already been decided, based on the photos of the area, each hovercraft landed in a sheltered area creating a semi-circle around the camp. The commandos along with the *Washington* crew checked their weapons one last time. Morgan transmitted safe arrival to the outpost and immediately received the go-ahead from Tapper. Stealthily as mountain cats, they crept toward the encampment. Morgan took his team to the northern side of the tents. The others flanked them on both sides, ready to move inside the perimeter as soon as the alarm was disabled. As they neared the edge of the camp, a lone figure emerged from the shadows.

Morgan breathed a sigh of relief and transmitted news of Selim to the outpost. Within minutes, he, Cardozo and Evron crouched beside the Jordanian while the others remained secreted in the brush. The Prince indicated where the alarm wire ran through the ground. Using a pocketknife, Evron dug a small channel into the hard packed earth. "It's here," he whispered as he began to slide the black box into the hole. They held their breath when Evron activated the device and passed his hand through the space and waited a moment to be sure no alarm had been sounded.

An arm motion brought the others to the opening. Still moving close to the ground, the first ten invaders entered the Syrian-Iraqi Command Post, led by Selim, Prince of the Hashemite Kingdom.

The first order of business, at the command of the IDF, was to take out their communication system. With two large armies within easy hailing distance of the camp, the Israeli high command insisted that the raiders cut off any possible communication with hostile forces. Selim led the way to an area secured by an electrified wire fence. While Morgan and the others hid behind the nearest tent, Selim roused the dozing guard and insisted that he be allowed into the area. "I must contact General Basam at once, soldier," he announced, his eyes boring into the man. "Open the gate."

"But I have no orders, Your Highness," stuttered the man, unsure of what to do.

"Would you have me awaken General Ramadi?" He waved a hand in the direction of the general's tent.

"No, sir, but this is not regulation." The soldier was muttering.

"Open the gate, man, and I shall see that you are rewarded for your devotion to your duty. This will only take a moment." Selim stepped closer to the fence.

Reluctantly, the man reached for the lock. "You will have to sign in, Your Highness."

As soon as the gate was opened and Selim stepped in, Morgan and Evron raced out from the hiding place and tackled the soldier to the ground. Without a second thought, Evron fired his laser at point black range, stilling the struggling body. Another soldier appeared at the door of the building and went down with a second laser silent blast from Evron's weapon. The rest of the team emerged from the black night and in minutes the communications building was under their control.

Across the compound, a lone Syrian wandered out of his tent in search of a place in which to relieve himself. Glancing toward the fire where several of his comrades were sleeping, he noticed several shadows moving quickly along the perimeter. Immediately hitting the ground, he crawled back to his tent and awakened the others.

Selim motioned to Morgan and Cardozo to follow him back into the darkness. Leaving three commandos at the communications building, they met up with the others outside and scurried to the stockade. Bean and Moreno made quick work of the two soldiers dozing in front of the shack while Morgan blasted the lock off the door. The Iraqi inside drew his weapon, but Blackjack fired first. Stepping over the body, they broke through the door to Jonathan's cell.

The tiny room smelled of imminent death; Morgan gagged, but managed not to vomit. A single light from the hallway shed enough illumination so that Morgan could see the curled form, motionless, on the floor. Crouching next to him, Morgan put his hand on the pilot's shoulder and heard him moan. "Jonathan, can you stand?" he whispered.

His eyes were swollen shut, but he managed to open one. His lips, cracked and swollen, moved, but no sound came out. It was only the faintest hint of a smile which gave Morgan any comfort. "Can you stand, Speed?" he repeated.

"I must be dead...or this is one helluva hallucination," croaked Jonathan. He tried to right himself. "I need a hand, Boston."

Morgan slipped an arm around his battered torso as gently as he could. "Come on, fella, we don't have a helluva lotta time." Using his own body as a brace, he drew Jonathan up. "Selim," he called softly, "give me a hand with this lug."

When Selim came into the tiny cell, Jonathan picked up a broken hand and touched his nose. "Got the message, buddy."

"Shut up and let's go, American Yehudi swine pilot," Selim chuckled as he lifted Jonathan's arm and put it around his shoulder. Half dragging him, they left the stockade.

From behind the flap of a tent, a dozen Arab soldiers watched as the prisoner was brought out. The sky, barely turning grey, helped to highlight the black clad figures as they moved toward the perimeter. With a whoop and a shout, the Arabs exploded from their tent firing at the invaders.

"Take him and get out of here!" shouted Morgan, passing Jonathan's weight onto Selim. He began firing in the direction of the soldiers, covering Selim's escape.

Lights suddenly flooded the compound, causing everyone to freeze momentarily. A burst of laser fire caught one of the Israelis and he went down, still firing in the direction of the hit. Cardozo, covered by another commando, ran in, scooped up the downed man, and ran like hell out of the camp. A phalanx of soldiers surrounded three tents clustered together near the center of the camp, the ones housing Ramadi, Hassan and the kora, who appeared at his flap brandishing a Wa'atsi photon rifle.

Morgan saw him first. Standing near the smoldering fire, he caught Pana-Di's eye and automatically fired his laser, catching the Jeylosian in the shoulder. Buckling at first, the kora returned the blast, but it went wide, missing his target. Two Wa'atsi leapt in front of the Jeylosian, shielding him with their bodies. A third Wa'atsi warrior took aim at the captain, but was shot from behind by an Israeli commando. Morgan ran for cover, diving behind the communications building. Crawling on his belly, he made his way to the break in the perimeter where he could see Selim and several others moving away from the encampment. Slowly, the other invaders began heading in the same direction, still firing at the oncoming soldiers. Grenades were lobbed directly into the fray and the ground rocked with the explosions. Syrians and Iraqis alike fell under the heavy laser fire. From above came a momentous noise, and then dust began swirling about the compound like a swarm of locusts. "Move out!" shouted Morgan to his men.

The noise grew louder until the silver underbelly of the Wa'atsi shuttle filled the sky. Before it even touched the ground, the door slid open and warriors began jumping out, lasers drawn. The newcomers showed no interest in the battle going on in the center of the camp; they immediately headed toward the tent that held the kora and the Wa'atsi he had brought with him. In moments, there was nothing left of the tent but smoldering sheepskin, filling the air with a nauseating stench. The few aliens able to stagger out were immediately cut down by laser fire from the heavily armored warriors.

By the time Morgan reached the last Israelis, the center of the encampment was littered with bodies. A hovercraft swooped in and the invaders boarded. Morgan, riding with Evron and two others, could not see either Selim or Jonathan. Looking over his shoulder, he could, however, see Iraqi marked craft heading out in pursuit. He pulled a grenade from his jacket and yanked the pin. Waiting for just a moment, he hurled it behind him, and held on when it hit, shattering the desert stillness.

Another craft fanned off to the east and sped up after a single Israeli craft. Rapid fire hit the hovercraft, causing it to buck and then smash against the desert floor. From his position, Cardozo launched a grenade and the Iraqis took the hit square on. He ordered his driver back for the downed men. The Wa'atsi shuttle, airborne again, managed to fire on and hit at least three more of the pursuing craft before disappearing.

Ali Hassan stood amidst the carnage. From every corner they could hear the groaning of the wounded, a pitiful sound he could not bear. He offered comfort wherever he could, masking the growing anger he felt at the destruction around him. In the communications building, soldiers worked to repair the damage the Israelis caused in the raid. While Ramadi and his men pursued the raiders, Hassan had dispatched a single craft to the bivouac closest to them to get medical assistance. Stepping over what was left of an Iraqi soldier, he went toward the stockade where his last security man was questioning the man who had sounded the first alarm.

"I only saw them once they were in the camp," wept the man as a medic bandaged his arm. "I awakened everyone I could, but we were too late." He paused when Hassan approached. "I have failed my people, Abu Hassan," he said, falling to his knees. "We have been shamed by them."

"You are not shamed, soldier. You were the only one alert enough to do something. We have shamed ourselves." Ali Hassan felt sick to his stomach, but not sick enough to take his anger out on the poor bastard who stumbled out of his tent to urinate. The others, however, those who should have been on patrol, if they were not already dead, they would be soon. He glanced to where the kora's tent had stood. "Where are the outworlders, Akim?" he asked the officer standing beside him.

"Dead, sir, as near as we can tell. The reptiles were shot by other reptiles who came in the ship."

"And the tall, blue man?"

The officer shook his head. "We have not found his body."

"Find it." Ali Hassan spun on his heel and strode angrily toward the communications building.

The Kora Pana-Di managed to wrap his own shoulder with fabric ripped from a corpse. There was no point in returning to the encampment; Ali Hassan would kill him on sight, of that he was certain. He skirted around the perimeter until he found what he was looking for: a desert sweeper craft the patrols used to cruise the area during the day. A quiet machine, he thought it would be the fastest means of escape, faster than one of the strange humped beasts the Arabs kept for their amusements. The sweeper started up easily and after a moment, the kora was silently skimming along the far side of the ridge toward Damascus.

Morgan lost sight of the other hovercraft as they raced toward the Israeli border. It bothered him that he could not see them, but each knew where to go and he had to trust their instincts. Settling back against his seat, Morgan folded his arms across his chest and closed his eyes; there was nothing he could do now except murmur a prayer and wait.

The first rays of morning sun were spreading thin light across the desert when the hovercraft crossed over into Israel. Past the blue grey line of the River Jordan, the startling green of Israel's irrigated fields could be discerned in the near distance. Suddenly, several hovercraft appeared on the horizon, coming toward them at great speed. Morgan's transmitter, still nestled in his ear, came alive. Hitting Evron on the shoulder, he motioned to him to switch on the unit in the craft.

"*B'ruchim habayim, yeladim!*" said a jubilant voice. "We have come to escort you home." They formed a semi-circle around the incoming hovercraft.

"Where are the others?" asked Morgan in Hebrew into the transmitter.

"There is one not far behind you and three are already on their way to base."

Evron turned far enough in his seat to see the look of relief on Morgan's face. "Are you satisfied, Captain Morgan?" he asked solemnly.

Morgan nodded. "For the moment, I am satisfied."

They slowed long enough for the last two incoming craft to join them and then picked up speed as they skimmed the surface back to Ein Geshem.

Aboard the *Washington*, a crowd was huddled around Lieutenant Krieg's station waiting for word from the Israeli base. Admiral P'nucha had already called in a successful mission from his end and it was only a matter of time before they heard from their captain and the others. Belle positioned herself directly behind Jane, reassuringly gripping her tense shoulder. They listened to the Arab transmissions from a jerry-rigged unit to main camp, but there had been no mention of the pilot; only of massive destruction at the hands of the Israelis and unidentified outworlders. Ali Hassan was calling for the complete destruction of Israel, but his troops were less than enthusiastic when they heard spacecraft had been involved at the secret camp. General Ramadi had not returned from following the Israelis and a search party was being assembled to go out looking for the missing commander. Cadet Peters, at the other monitoring station, picked up something other than Arabic and quickly switched over to the central system.

"Mechinah Ein Geshem calling the *Washington*," crackled a voice on the speaker system.

"*Washington*, here. Go ahead, Ein Geshem," replied Jane, her knuckles turning white as she grabbed the desk before her.

"*Washington*, your Captain Morgan and his party are expected here any moment. Missions accomplished."

A shout went up on the bridge. Gathering her wits, Jane waited for the noise to subside and asked the terrible question. "Is Major Rothko with him?"

"No, *Washington*, he is not with the Captain; he is with another craft coming in from the east. We are expecting them shortly."

"Is the major alive?"

A new voice, one familiar to most people on the bridge, replaced the accented Israeli speaker. “Major Rothko is wounded but alive. He will be stabilized here, and then orbited to Bethesda Naval Hospital immediately. Once your monitoring is wrapped up, head to Andrews, *Washington*. Admiral Rothko out.” The transmission ended.

Jane lowered her head against the cool surface of her station. Belle patted her back gently while Barb Lucas leaned over and whispered “Go to your cabin, Jane,” in her ear. Without another word, Jane left the bridge.

CHAPTER 23

Almost 18 hours crawled by before the *Washington*, guided by a dozen tugs, touched down at Andrews Air Force Base. As soon as the gangway was attached, Jane, using every ounce of her reserve, walked slowly down the carpeted tunnel and through the security checks. She passed through each procedure, keeping her impatience intact, until the MP gave her the all clear to exit the area. Outside, one of her mother's aides was waiting for her and she followed him to a waiting hovercar. "Can we go directly to Bethesda?" she asked, getting into the vehicle.

"Yes, ma'am," replied the aide, knowing how anxious her parents were to have their daughter by their side. He started the hovercar and turned on the flashing blue light.

At the hospital gate, they were waved through without the usual delay. Jane nearly jumped out of the hovercar before it stopped and raced into the lobby. Flashing her ID, she asked where to find Major Rothko.

The woman looked at the lieutenant with a none-too-pleasant frown and punched a series of numbers. After a lengthy conversation, she glanced at Jane and proceeded to give her directions to the intensive care unit.

When the elevator opened, Jane rushed out and into her mother's open arms. "When did he get here? Is he okay?" she asked, hugging the general tightly.

"Last night, around midnight. He's alive and he's home. The rest is out of our hands." Taking her daughter by the arm, General Rothko led the way through the maze of technology to where Jonathan lay hooked up to a myriad of machines. She remained at the door while Jane went in. His eyes fluttered open.

"Hey, squirt," whispered Jonathan hoarsely through his tubes. "Howdja get here so fast?" He tried to smile, but it came out more of a grimace.

"We docked at Andrews." Impulsively, she leaned over a brushed a light kiss on his forehead. "You look awful," she said, grinning as best she could under the circumstances.

"Thanks," he croaked. "Shoulda seen me a few hours ago."

"No thanks; it's bad enough looking at you now."

Jonathan shifted slightly, the pain evident on his face. "You're hanging around Tapper too much, squirt; you sound like him."

"Shut up, Speed, you talk too much." She took his hand in hers and stroked it. "Go back to sleep, Jonathan. I'll be back later." She gave him another kiss and watched his eyes slide close again.

Outside the room, her parents were standing together, watching their two oldest children through the window. Isaac and Rebecca hadn't arrived yet, but it would be only when they were all together that either Rothko would begin to relax. Jane hugged her father and then, linking her arms with both parents, they walked to the small room where they could speak in private. "What did the doctors say?" asked Jane as soon as the door closed behind them.

"There's serious internal bleeding, but they cannot perform any kind of surgery until he stabilizes from the trip here," explained Admiral Rothko looking older than Jane had ever seen him.

"They hope sometime tonight, tomorrow morning the latest." General Rothko sat beside her husband holding his hand. "The important thing is that he is awake and alert. The IDF trauma team did all the right things to get him here, so now we wait."

Jane turned to her father. "How long can I stay, Dad?" she asked, almost dreading the answer.

Stroking his stubbly, unshaven chin, he considered the question. "I am holding the *Washington* here for at least a week. Morgan'll have to be at the initial inquiry about the raid and his contact with P'nucha." The admiral managed a wan smile. "In spite of the positive things which might very well come out of the joint venture, we bent a few rules by allowing the Wa'atsi on the ship without complete authorization."

"But, Dad!"

"But nothing, sweetheart. I authorized it, but we still have to have an inquiry in order to establish whether or not we will be opening treaty negotiations with the Wa'atsi. P'nucha has made motions in that direction and should it come to pass, I want Morgan on the team." It was a perfectly logical first step. "In the meanwhile, Sarah Jane, we will be granting shore leave for the crew."

Jane looked hopefully at her parents. "Can I come home for dinner once in a while?" she asked.

"Your father and I think you will be best off staying on board the *Washington* until Jonathan is out of the woods," said her mother. "Then, we would like you to go up to the cabin.

It sounded suspiciously like she was being shipped off to boarding school. "Why can't I stay at home?"

"Because, sweetheart," began the general, "the kora is missing. Neither we, nor, it seems, the Arabs know where he is. On the ship, there is ample security, but we know you and you're not gonna stay put. If you go up north, with no one knowing where you went, he cannot find you hanging around here." He paused, sighing. "This was your brother's idea and we think it's a good one."

"It's a ridiculous idea, and I'm not going."

The parents looked at each other. "This is not a choice question, Sarah Jane. You need to be removed from the area and tucked away someplace odd. The cabin has excellent security, as does the park."

The cabin, on a secluded lake in the Green Mountains of Vermont, was not far from Bennington. Her Krieg great-great-grandparents built the rustic lodge the family used a retreat. Because the locals were naturally reticent, a stranger would be unlikely to locate her up there.

"Not happening."

"So, you're willing to put your shipmates in additional danger with your presence." It was not a question.

"Suddenly my presence is a threat to the *Washington*?"

Admiral Rothko shook his head. "Listen to me, Sarah Jane. Who you are has put everyone in a bizarre position and we trying to figure out what's best. We don't want to throw you in a brig, although we can if you keep this up. Your choice."

"Dad and I thought the cabin might give you a little time to sort through the last few months. You've been beaten up pretty badly not just as an officer, but as your father's daughter. We're talking about a week, just enough time to get you out of the equation."

"Getting Pana-Di to show up is gonna be tough enough. We will not use you as bait," said her father. "Go to the cabin. Take a week to regroup. By then, this should all be over."

"Excuse me, but I have a captain to consider...or is he already informed?."

"Morgan will do as he is told."

"Just following orders?"

"Sarah Jane," snapped her mother, "That was uncalled for."

"Fine. I'm taking Spike with me." Jane knew her parents would be all too happy to let her take her bounding golden retriever along for company. Besides, Spike was completely devoted and would tear apart anyone who threatened her.

Jane stayed at the hospital with her parents through the long night. At two in the morning, the decision to operate was made, and the Rothkos were led to the surgical waiting area where a guard was posted outside the door. Someone arranged for refreshments, and when they arrived, so did Tapper.

"How is Selim?" asked General Rothko, kissing the burly commander on the cheek.

"I left him in good hands at Hadassah Hospital at Ein Kerem." He glanced at his watch. "By now, however, he should be back in his father's palace recuperating amongst his lovely sisters." It was tacitly understood that he had been taken to Hadassah and then home wrapped in complete secrecy. "It was the least the IDF could do for their closet hero," he added with a grin.

An attaché from the Pentagon arrived and handed General Rothko a thick folder. She broke the seal and read the documents, a smile crossing her tired face. "The IDF has destroyed the road between Damascus and Al Qunaytirah, successfully preventing the combined army from movements to the south. The Iraqis are withdrawing from the Jordanian border." She handed the document to her husband. "The war is not over, people, but has been seriously altered in the IDF's favor." Leaning back, she closed her eyes and rested for a moment.

The noon sun was already lighting the hospital's windows before a woman in blood spattered surgical greens knocked softly on the waiting room door. "Admiral, General, Lieutenant?" she said, waiting a moment for them to rouse from their semi-slumber. "I'm Dr. Hutchinson. Dr. Finkel asked me to give you the latest progress report on Major Rothko." If the profusion of ranks surprised her, she gave no indication. "The major has made it through the most difficult part of the surgery," explained the doctor. "We have taken his spleen, appendix and one kidney. The other kidney appears to be functioning normally so the loss of the one should pose no problem for the moment. We took a wide tissue sample from the damaged kidney to create a new one to be transplanted at a later date. Dr. Finkel has also performed some repair work on the rupture in the Major's stomach and a temporary colostomy has been put in place." She paused, waiting for any questions, but no one spoke. "Right now, Dr. Chaney is setting the left leg, which is fractured below the knee. The team at Hadassah did a fine job, but there was some new swelling in the area Dr. Chaney felt should be addressed and this required that the leg be reset. His fingers, while badly broken, will mend, but he will require some physical therapy if he is to regain full use of his hands. But the bottom line, sir, ma'am, is that your son should recover, barring any unexpected complications. He's a very lucky man."

General Rothko stood and went to the doctor, her hand extended. "Thank you, Dr. Hutchinson, for coming to see us. Are you going back to the OR?"

"Yes, ma'am, I am. We just thought you'd like to know how it was going. We expect to move Major Rothko to the recovery room within the hour. Dr. Finkel and Dr. Chaney will come and see you as soon as they are out."

When she was gone, Elizabeth Rothko broke down and cried. Edward led her to the sofa and sat beside her, stroking her back and speaking softly in her ear. Jane wandered over to the window and stared outside, wondering how people managed to come and go to the enormous building without being physically drained each time. Hugging herself tightly, she wished she had someone, anyone, to throw her arms about and cry.

Suddenly, the wide door flew open and Isaac and Rebecca ran into the room, followed closely by Tapper. "Is Jonathan okay? What's happening?" demanded Rebecca, throwing herself into her big sister's arms while Isaac went to their parents.

"He's going to be fine," offered the admiral, putting an arm around the boy who stood almost as tall as he.

"I found them chasing around the ICU looking for you people." Tapper went over to the general, bent down for a hug. "Are *you* okay, Liz?" he asked holding onto her hand.

"I'll live," she answered, managing a small smile. "I cannot thank you and Captain Morgan enough for what you did."

Tapper grinned sheepishly. "Aw, shucks, ma'am," he drawled. "'Tweren't nuthin' we would'na done fer a good dawg." The laughter in the room said it all. "There are a couple of guys in the hall who would like to pay their respects to the brass if you're up to it." At the admiral's nod, Tapper opened the door and motioned to the men outside.

Morgan and Cardozo, still looking scruffy and in need of a good bath, came in. "He's okay?" asked Morgan, almost afraid of the answer.

"He's okay," announced the admiral. "We owe you a great deal, Ash, and you, too, Jackson. As for Selim, his father will relay our gratitude." Rothko's voice was filled with unspoken emotion.

The two men stayed near the door. "We only wanted to stop in for a moment," muttered Morgan, feeling as though he were intruding in a private moment for the Rothko family. He fidgeted with the cap in his hands.

Jackson agreed and added, "We need to head back to the ship to clean up. Ah'll come see y'all later, when the dust settles."

"Call your mother, Jackson," said General Rothko, "she already knows you were there."

"Not exactly a surprise, Tante Elizabeth." Jackson saluted the Rothkos. "Give Speed our best."

"Thank you, both, for everything." Admiral Rothko returned the salute.

As he left, Morgan caught Jane's eye. The resemblance between mother and daughter was unmistakable, but Jane's mannerisms mirrored her father's. There was much he wanted to say, but this was neither the time nor the place. Anything he would say could wait until they were back aboard the *Washington*.

For a moment after they were gone, when the room was silent, Jane wished Morgan had said something, anything, to her.

Morgan, Blackjack, and Tapper walked through the corridor in silence. It was only when they were standing on the apron outside the hospital that Blackjack finally spoke up. "Ah will be the first to admit that it is hard to see that family standing there sufferin' together. And Ah will also be the first to admit that seein' Sarah Jane with her parents makes me wonder why Ah didn't guess at first sight that she was Liz's girl."

"Yeah," agreed Tapper with a grin. "Liz's girl with Ted's penchant for stubbornness. He glanced at Morgan who remained quiet, seemingly staring off into space. Ignoring his captain, he turned back to Cardozo. "Where are you off to now?" he asked, knowing full well Cardozo's sea-bag was stowed in the hovercar he'd driven over.

"Just over to Silver Spring. Ah have an aged aunt who's offered to put me up until we know what's what, but Ah still have a battalion awaitin' on me on Kotuchar." There was a decided twinkle in his eye.

"Aged aunt, my Aunt Bessie!" laughed Tapper. "More like you're going over to some poor female's house who's going to put up with your snoring."

Cardozo shrugged. "Ah'll be in touch, gentleman...and Ah do use the term loosely." With a lazy salute in Morgan's direction, he sauntered off.

Tapper waited until the southerner had disappeared before he threw an arm around Morgan. "Come on, Boston, I'll buy you a drink somewhere quiet where we can both sulk in peace."

Driving into Georgetown, Morgan was still broodingly silent. Understanding his need for no conversation, Tapper drove with only the radio on for noise. There was a brief news report about the rescue of the American pilot, still nameless, from Arab hands, and an update on the war in the Middle East; nothing they had not known before. There was no mention of the part the *Washington* had played, nor of P'nucha's assistance. It was exactly how the Rothkos wanted it. Eventually the news would leak, but for now, their privacy was safe. Tapper found, after some hunting, a parking place near a small grill he used to frequent while he was living in D.C. At three o'clock, the lunch rush was over but the dinner crowd had not yet arrived, making it uncommonly easy to secure a quiet table in the back. Tapper ordered a pitcher of beer and commenced waiting for Morgan to start talking.

The first words were long in coming, but they were not surprising to Tapper. "What the hell ever possessed Speed to fly that mission?" asked the captain, scratching his bearded cheek. "He broke every rule in the book. And this time, being the general's kid isn't going to bail him out."

"He'll be damn lucky if his mother doesn't personally court martial him," said Tapper, refilling the glasses. "What I don't understand is how we got dragged into it. Calling us back didn't make a lot of sense. There's got to be a piece missing from the puzzle."

"It's not missing if you look hard enough, Tap; we just haven't looked yet. We were too busy trying to save that bozo's hide." Morgan took a long draught of the icy beer, relishing the taste. "Let's look at this thing from another angle."

"Okay. Start with the *Ana'atam* business. P'nucha was there at the last minute, but he made no effort to contact us. We also know that the late Captain Nish was not one of his favorite saurians, and neither is Yeynum. Although the *Ana'atam* is a military vessel, they were out there alone, ostensibly on a trading mission."

"Which tells us that both Nish and Yeynum must've yanked someone's chain but good to be shipped off to a non-military assignment." Morgan allowed a small smile. "Do you think we did P'nucha a favor by catching them red handed?"

"Yep, and what's more, we opened up an interesting door which allowed P'nucha to come to our aide. What is it that Intelligence Section ain't telling us, Boston?"

Morgan leaned back in his chair and considered the question. A thousand thoughts flew by in rapid succession before one jumped out as a distinct possibility. "The night after the *Tical* business, when we were all sitting around the observatory trading war stories, Xinthi-Ang mentioned something and then covered it over as mere speculation." Morgan changed his position so that he was closer to Tapper. "He said that the Wa'atsi economy was collapsing under the weight of its military obligations..."

"You mean the high cost of colonization," sarcastically interjected Tapper.

"Exactly. Were the Wa'atsi traders out looking for *markets*?"

"Markets? As in trade? Now there's an uncharacteristic thought."

"But that would explain why Nish was on Pitan in the first place. We never gave that much credence, but maybe it was actually true," suggested Morgan. "In any case, P'nucha is pretty close to the top and having him come personally to pull a bunch of renegade Wa'atsi off Earth would also put us in the host position."

"And would require that, as long as the old boy was in town, that we get to wine and dine him, all the while chatting up the mutually beneficial aspects of the League of Planets."

"Give the man a cigar." Morgan rubbed his hands together gleefully. "Which, in turn, puts us exactly where the Wa'atsi want us. They tell their people they are doing us a favor and we get them guaranteed trade routes. Not too bad, for a bunch of former black hats."

Tapper nodded, agreeing completely with Morgan's analysis, but wondering about one unanswered question. "But how did Pana-Di get hooked up with them?"

"Elementary, my dear Bear. The Wa'atsi are known for besting each other. If, as I suspect, the commander of the other ship was looking for a way to beat a senior officer to the punch, as it were, and the kora knew from some of his less savory connections that this was the case, he provided the hapless Wa'atsi captain with a reason to become involved in our international politics. The kora bet on the wrong horse, however," Morgan grinned. "He figured that any toehold was a good toehold and this one was as good as any. He did not understand third-worldism in the Terran sense. Pana-Di only saw a chance to be an intergalactic hero, but he did not do enough research to figure out that even if he had assisted Hassan and Ramadi successfully, he still would have been stuck in a backwater no better than if he had been sentenced to life on Jeyloti Lunar-4."

Tapper whistled low and appreciatively. "Pretty good theorizing, Boston, but there are an awful lot of 'ifs' in there."

"Be that as it may, I think that I'm right. What Intelligence Section isn't telling us lowly flyboy types is that they want the Wa'atsi name on the dotted line so that they can trade for certain military secrets, like, say," Morgan waved his hand in the air, "their new work on orbital cloaking?"

Tapper's booming laughter filled the room, and then he whispered. "I'll be damned!"

Draining the last of his beer, Morgan stood. "Come on, Tapper, let's go home."

Once Jonathan was out of the recovery room and sufficiently awake to smile wanly at his parents and siblings, the Rothkos decamped, en mass, across the border to Virginia. Although they had kept an apartment in Washington for years, it was the house in Fairfax County they all called home. Situated on three acres of beautiful rolling hills, it sat well back from the road behind a secured brick wall. The house itself was an old Palladian two story, with ample room for them and the never ending parade of family and friends who came to stay. Spike, the killer retriever, howled with glee when his beloved mistress emerged from the hovercar.

Jane, Spike at her heels, climbed the stairs to her room tired, but relieved to be allowed to come home at least for dinner. She shucked her rumpled uniform and took a long, hot bath before dressing in jeans and a sweatshirt, an outfit which would no doubt raise her father's silver brow. Tying her hair into a free swinging pony tail, she skipped down the steps and found her parents sitting in the library in similar attire.

"What'll it be, sailor?" asked her father, wearing an Annapolis sweatshirt she thought he reserved only for the cabin.

Jane glanced quickly at her mother who smiled and held up her own drink. "Gin and tonic?" she answered tentatively, a more than a little surprised by the question.

"I'll have one, too" chirped Rebecca, bouncing into the room.

Edward Rothko looked disapprovingly at his youngest, the eyebrow raised high over his eye. "Forget it, you're under age, young lady. You'll have a Coke." A bemused smile twitched at his lips as he watched Rebecca flop in his chair, her legs immediately thrown over the arm. He handed his lieutenant the drink. "After dinner, Sarah, I'll drive you back to the ship." No dissent would be permitted.

"Yes, sir." Sarah took the glass and went to her own favorite chair. Spike, not to be left out, climbed halfway into her lap. "Sophie's not here, so who's making dinner?" She raised an eyebrow in her father's direction. He sighed audibly. "Good. I'll go start the grill."

On the long ride back to Andrews, father and daughter finally talked at length about her service on the *Washington*. Satisfied with her answers to the routine questions, the admiral brought up the more difficult questions about the incident with the kora. He was silent as she told her side of the story without tears or theatrics, careful to include details she thought he might find useful. There were things they laughed about and other things that left them in momentary silence. But by the time the base loomed ahead, Jane felt as though most of the hard parts were thoroughly dissected and ready to be stowed away.

The guard at the gate, more than a little shocked to see the Fleet Admiral drive up in the middle of the night, waved them though. The *Washington* sat on its pylons, a gleaming white behemoth lit from the underbelly by floodlights where ground crew did routine maintenance on the hull. The guard at the fence surrounding the docking platform checked the admiral's credentials and then snapped a salute. "Go ahead, sir," he said as he stepped aside to let them proceed through the gate. Driving slowly toward the gangway positioned beside the *Washington*, Ted Rothko could not help but be impressed once again by the beauty of the vessel. He rolled gently to a stop.

"Don't get out of the car, Dad," Jane sighed loudly. "I don't want you to embarrass me with any of this weepy parent stuff."

The admiral laughed as he leaned over to kiss her goodnight. "Don't forget your uniform," he admonished, handing her a khaki bundle.

"Thanks, Dad. See you tomorrow."

"Be careful, Sarah Jane."

"Dad!" She stood at the bottom of the lift and waved, but he would not leave until she was recognized by the crewmate allowed to step inside.

~

There were several messages waiting for Jane on the comm-panel in her quarters. She listened to them, making notes where necessary, and then, flicking the thing off, got ready for bed. Admittedly, she would have preferred to be safely tucked into her own bed in her own room, but the cabin would have to suffice for the moment. She was about to climb into her bunk when a soft beeping told her someone was at the door. With a long suffering sigh and a wide yawn, Jane slipped on her robe and padded to the door to release the lock.

"I've been waiting for you for hours!" cried Belle as she breezed into the cabin. "How's your brother?"

Jane followed the yeomate back into the sitting area, letting the door whoosh shut. "He's in pretty tough shape, but he's a pretty tough guy. They say he's going to be okay."

"And your parents? How are they holding up?"

"As well as can be expected." Jane wandered over to her desk and pulled a bottle of Laphroaig from the drawer. "Want a drink?" she asked the Belle, knowing that more than sleep, she needed a little friendly conversation.

Belle accepted the offer and curled herself into a ball on the sofa. "I wanted to go to the hospital in case you needed anything, but Tapper said no."

"It's just as well, because we were all kinda stressed out. The guys only stayed for a couple of minutes." She did not add how disappointed she was.

Handing Belle the glass, Jane took the easy chair, wrapping her robe under her feet. "Anything happen while I was gone?"

"Nothing of great interest, except that the captain wants us to work on that code book while we're here. He said that he'd talk to you about it in the morning, but we should avail ourselves of the facilities in the area." Belle sipped her scotch, a little surprised the peaty taste of the scotch.

"How was the rest of the visit? Did you get to go home?"

"I went home for dinner. My father made hamburgers on the grill and we sat around for a while. Everyone was tired, but they were pretty set on my coming back here tonight."

"Why? Why couldn't you stay at home?"

Jane debated whether or not to tell the crewmate what she knew, and decided, for the moment, against it. "Regulations, I guess. Everyone else has to stay on board, so I do, too. But I'll be able to go back to the hospital tomorrow and then, if we get shore leave, I can go home for a couple of days."

"I heard we might get leave, but no one was sure how it was going to work. Any thoughts?"

"No," shrugged Jane, "not really. Whatever the captain decides, that's what we'll do." She yawned again.

Belle took the hint. Setting the empty glass on the table, she stood and stretched. "I'd better get going. Peters and Ngyuen want to go to the Pentagon tomorrow to look at new codification stuff. I figured I'd go and work on my end."

"Sounds like a good idea." She walked Belle to the door. "Thanks for stopping by. I guess I needed the company and the drink."

"No sweat, Looie, my pleasure. Good night." Belle disappeared into the corridor, the door sliding shut behind her.

For a moment, Jane considered going in search of Tapper whom she was sure was sitting in the commroom reading newspapers on his screen. It was an old habit she remembered from when he was hanging around their house in the old days. He and Jonathan would sit in her father's library after a long day devouring the news from as many sources as possible. They would swap tidbits and oddities until dinner was called. Standing beside the door, Jane considered going down there, but, stifling another yawn, she opted for bed.

Tapper was in the commroom, but he was not alone; Morgan sat beside him, his eyes glued to a second screen, reading library files on news from Wa'atsi while Tapper scanned transmissions intercepted by the Fleet over the last year. Little news from Wa'atir filtered through the system; most of it was second hand from the few planets who traded with the warrior race, but little was known about the inner workings of the Supreme Command and the interplanetary government it maintained to control the colonies. Generally, League members stayed away from the Wa'atsi, preferring not to have access to their few exportable resources rather than risk having them establish a presence.

Suddenly, Tapper sat upright and studied the screen carefully. "Here, Ash," he called out, sliding back to allow the captain closer view of the screen. "Look at this. Assuming the unnamed personage of rank was indeed the Kora Pana-Di, then there is a lot that the Jeylosians aren't telling us."

The article on the screen described in sketchy detail a meeting held on Nimth Wa'atir, the colonized outpost closest to the Jeylos system. According to the report, a Jeylosian of rank met with and began to establish a trading link with a member of the Supreme Command. Neither system, when asked to ratify the contract, did so, each claiming that the other was not to be trusted. "But it does indicate that trade routes are being considered, otherwise why would they have even approached the Pitanese in the first place?" asked Tapper, chewing on his lip.

"Because they were the ones out fishing for expanded markets," replied Morgan, sliding back to his own console. "The Kora had the most to gain from a successful deal with the Wa'atsi. He's fighting a losing battle for succession with his older brothers. Additional fire power provided by the Wa'atsi would help him to consolidate his position, as well as make him out as a pioneer in economics should he succeed in securing independent treaties."

"The whole thing sounds pretty damn stupid to me." Tapper stretched and yawned widely. "So what happens now, Boston?"

"We find the kora. His father wants him dead, P'nucha wants him alive, and God only knows how Hassan and Ramadi want him, but you can be sure that they do. Speed said he talked incessantly about Jane, so there might be the possibility that he's going to come after her." Morgan shrugged.

"How hard can it be to find a seven foot blue man?"

"Pretty tough, if he knows the planet as well as I think he does. But it's Jane that worries me; Ted wants her either on the ship or someplace she can't be found."

"Can he pull her off duty without causing a lot of questions?"

"Sure he can. He can send her anywhere he wants on a transfer. On paper at least."

Tapper studied Morgan's face for a brief moment. "And where do you want her, Boston?"

Morgan returned the glance, his face gone hard. "Anywhere she would be safe."

In the morning, Jane saw her staff off to the Pentagon with a promise to join them as soon as the captain released her from the bridge. When they were gone, she returned to her station to begin filing the night log, wishing that she could get off the *Washington*. Lucas stopped by on her way to a meeting at the State Department's protocol section. She assured Jane that most questions had been easily deflected and that her secret was still just that.

"I don't know for how long, Jane, but I won't say anything until the Captain tells me the cat is officially out of the bag." Barbara gave her a quick hug. "I hope everything is all right at home, sweetie. Beep me if you need me."

Jane thanked her and went back to work. It was exceptionally lonely on the bridge when no one was around. The helmsman and the navigator were both doing logs down in engineering, while everyone else who normally populated the bright room seemed to drift in and out, wondering what was going to happen next. Other than standard maintenance, there were no orders published to indicate how long they would be detained on the surface. Jane considered calling her parents' house, but changed her mind, knowing that they must have already left for the hospital. Restless, she left her station and wandered into the conference room where the huge portal looked out over the field. She did not hear Morgan's footsteps on the carpet as he came into the room.

"Did you sleep?" he asked gently, causing her to jump at the sound of his voice. "I didn't mean to startle you."

Jane shrugged lamely. "I guess I'm a little jumpy, Captain."

"Shore Patrol is outside with a car to take you over to Bethesda. I take it you want to go over to the hospital."

"Thank you, Captain." She walked slowly toward the door, hoping he would say something else. When he didn't, she stopped and turned back to him. It was hard to read anything in his eyes, yet they were neither cold nor forbidding as they had been lately. "I appreciate you coming to the hospital yesterday. It was a nice thing to do."

"Jonathan is my friend."

She smiled and for a moment, she saw his eyes warm. "It was more than that, you know. The admiral wanted people whom he could trust. I wouldn't take that lightly, if I were you."

"I don't." He made a move toward her, but caught himself. "Be careful, S. J. Don't do anything foolish." His admonition was as gentle as his voice.

"Yes, sir." Jane saluted.

At Bethesda, the lieutenant found her mother sitting outside ICU deep in discussion with another officer. Her mother waved her into the room and Jane automatically saluted. The officer looked up, said nothing, but the general paused long enough to introduce the newcomer.

"Pleased to meet you, Lieutenant," said Major Quinn, his voice as bland as his face. The man had an ashen complexion and watery blue eyes set wide over a flattened nose and pencil-thin lips. He glanced at General Rothko as if he expected her to end their conversation. Instead, she asked the lieutenant to sit down.

The talk seemed to center around military aid to Israel and Jane listened closely although she feigned disinterest. There was something about Quinn that made her uncomfortable, as though he lacked the respect the general normally commanded. Although she kept her voice even and quite low, Jane could tell her mother was exasperated. He was adamantly arguing against sending additional training personnel to the Negev when four more F-511s were shipped out, while General Rothko had already made the decision with the obvious backing of the Pentagon and an endorsement from the Congress. The growing tightness in her voice was evident; Jane had heard that tone before and rather than add to Quinn's obvious distress, she excused herself from the room and went in search of her brother.

Jonathan lay on the bed connected to a new set of tubes, but his eyes were open and seemingly focused on the television over his bed. He was somewhere between a grimace and a smile as two people argued on a daytime drama. Seeing Jane at the door, he slowly pressed the control and shut it off. "Hey, squirt," he rasped, his mouth twisting into a more obvious imitation of a smile.

"Hi." Jane tiptoed over and kissed his forehead. "How are you feeling?"

"Horseshit, but I'll live. At least they took some of the damn tubes out." The effort of speaking seemed to exhaust him, but he kept going. "Did you see that wart Quinn with Mom?"

"Yes. They were fighting about the birds."

"Yeah, I know... Mom'll win.... She always does."

Jane grinned, glad to see Jonathan back in the land of the living. "Who is Quinn, anyway?"

"A bozo who thinks we should stand back and let them drive Jews into the sea." There was a flash of anger in his eyes before he closed them for a moment.

"Maybe I should let you rest, Jonathan," offered Jane.

"Don't leave. I wanted to talk to you without anyone around." He motioned to the intercom on the unit beside the bed. "Tell the nurse you're gonna turn it off for a few minutes, and then close the door."

She did as she was told, assuring the duty nurse that she would call if they needed her. Pulling a chair up close to the bed, Jane sat down and took her brother's hand. "What's on your mind, Speed?"

"You... And that kora guy." He pointed to the cup of ice chips and when Jane gave it to him, he slowly chewed one. "Heard you had a run in with him. Why is he after your ass?"

Jane sighed and told him, if not in great detail, what had taken place on the *Washington*. Jonathan listened, asked a couple of questions, but mostly just watched her face. When she was through, Jane leaned back and waited for Jonathan's assessment.

"He's out there... and he's looking for you. He figured out who I was.... he was more interested in ragging on you than on getting IDF movement out of me. Even Ramadi asked me what it was about." He paused to suck on another chip. "By the time the cavalry showed up, I think Ramadi and Hassan thought he was crazy." Jonathan waited for a wave of pain to pass before he continued. "Wouldn't let them use drugs on me, kept saying he wanted me awake enough to scream."

"Did you give them anything?" Jane asked, almost afraid of the answer.

Jonathan frowned. "Hell no, squirt. Without drugs, the best they could do was get me to moan and give 'em a couple of bogus numbers." He looked pained by the memory; he was neither as strong nor as resilient as he wanted to believe. "Truth was, outside of Ein Geshem, I didn't have anything they could use." His lips turned slightly upward. "Was a terrible waste of their effort."

"At least they didn't kill you," she said. "Do you remember anything about the rescue?"

"Only seeing Boston's ugly puss. He looked like God." Shifting slightly in his bed, Jonathan pulled himself up as far as the tubes would allow. "Make me a promise, Sarah Jane."

"Sure. Anything."

"Mom said you're arguing about going up to the cabin. Take Spike and go. Get out of town. That prick is alive and he's gonna come looking for you." He stopped for another ice chip. "Take my speeder; it doesn't have SJRK on the license plate." Jonathan flopped back against the pillows and groaned at the exertion.

A knock at the door made Jane turn around. Her mother's face popped in. "Is this a private party or can any officer join?" she asked, pleased to see her children alive and together.

"Come on in, Mom," said Jane, nodding her silent agreement with her brother's request.

"Your father is bent on having a few people to the house for dinner this evening, children," frowned the general at the absurdity of the thought. "I suppose I shall have to be there, playing military wife, passing drinks on a silver tray in my hostess pajamas." When Jonathan managed a chortle, she was satisfied. "He's asked Jackson and your captain, Sarah, as well as Joshua, Commander Lucas, and a few other notables."

"Who's the main course?" rasped Jonathan, instinctively knowing there was one.

"Triple whammy, kids. Admiral P'nucha, and Ambassador and Lady Xinthi-Ang. Wanna come?"

"Sure, Mom, let me get my wheelchair." He grinned in spite of his disappointment at having to miss such a fascinating crowd.

Jane furrowed her brow, unsure of whether or not she was expected to attend. He mother noticed and patted her daughter's hand. "Attendance is optional, sweetheart."

"I'll have to think about it. I thought I might leave for the cabin tonight."

The general looked at Jane quizzically. "So soon? I thought you wanted to stay in town for a little while."

"I know. But I think I'd be better off up there. Dad can transfer me off the *Washington* temporarily, can't he?"

"Of course he can. When do you want to leave?"

"How about I show up for drinks and then take off. I don't want to stay for dinner. Tapper can give me a ride to the house and then I'll take his speeder." She pointed at thumb at her brother. "It's newer and faster than mine."

"Better sound system," croaked Jonathan, the teasing unmistakable in his voice.

Elizabeth Rothko looked from one child to the other. She knew, without being told, that the decision had been made while the door was closed. And she also knew that once they made a joint decision, there was no point in arguing with either of them.

The linguistics team was already back when Jane boarded the *Washington*. She stopped on the bridge just long enough to file the day's transmission log before heading to her cabin to pack a bag. There would be time enough to see the captain when the senior staff convened for their meeting at 1600 hours. From her quarters, she left messages for Belle and Tapper, hoping one or the other would get back to her shortly. Optimistically, she did not pack all her gear. She left the duffle beside her console and went to her office to write a schedule for her staff in her absence. As Jane sat at the desk wondering how long she'd be gone, she almost missed a light knock at the open door. "Come on in, Belle, and close the door."

The yeomate did as she was told and took the chair opposite Jane's desk. "We made some progress at the Pentagon, Jane, but we're going to need a note from our CO to get into the inner sanctum of their library tapes." She ran a hand through her errant curls. "Not even this adorable carrot top made much dent in the stuffed shirt running their system," she sighed.

"You're losing your touch, Belle," laughed Jane, knowing well how difficult the Pentagon could be. "How 'bout I get a letter from the admiral giving you guys access to the files?"

"That would be great," Belle replied with a sheepish smile. "I was hoping you'd offer because I didn't feel I could ask."

Jane returned the grin but then grew serious. "Off the record, my parents are shipping me out for a couple of days. There seems to be some concern for my safety."

"Your safety? I don't get it."

"Pana-Di is unaccounted for. My brother thinks he might be coming after me." Although she tried to make light of it, Jane was disturbed at the thought.

Belle sensed her discomfort, the smile disappearing from her face. "Where will you go?"

"My family has a cabin. Everyone agrees that will be the safest place to be."

"Want some company?" The question may have sounded off handed, but it was far from casual. "I'm a crack shot. Maybe you shouldn't be alone."

"I know, Belle; I've read your dossier. I'll be okay and with any luck, I'll be back before you know it." Jane slid the docupad across the desk. "Here's the duty roster for while I'm gone. If anyone asks, and I'm sure they will, you are to tell them I am on special assignment for the Admiralty. Any other questions should go to Morgan."

Belle glanced at the docupad and then at Jane. "When are you going?"

"After the staff meeting. I'm going home first and then I'll leave from there." Jane paused before sliding a comm disc to Belle. "You might want to take a look at this in the privacy of your own quarters later on, Yeomate."

"What is it?"

Jane flashed a wide smile. "It's my recommendation that you be passed on the languages section of your equivalency, you should go right into second year OCS, and start Super School the following term."

"You're kidding!"

"Would I kid about a thing like this?" She leaned over and whispered conspiratorially, "Both the captain and my dad concur, and will support the application. The hotsy-totsy admiral was very impressed with you at the conference."

Belle's eyes widened. "You didn't tell him what I said about him, did you?"

"No," grinned Jane, "but my mother thought it was really funny."

There was no stopping the red flush springing over Belle's face. She stood up and slipped the disc in her pocket, walking numbly to the door. Suddenly she turned back to the lieutenant. "I don't know whether to thank you or punch you out," sighed Belle.

"Thank me and leave it at that. You're dismissed." Jane was still laughing long after Belle left the office.

Tapper gave Jane a ride home. They laughed a lot about going to her parents' place in dress blues rather than the ratty clothes they usually wore around the Rothko homestead. Tapper had stopped at the hospital only to find Jonathan arguing with the nurse. "Obviously he's going to be fine," said Tapper, finally believing it was true. "I wouldn't have given you a plugged nickel for his life when we pulled him out of that hell hole."

Jane was quiet for a moment, trying to find a way to express what she was feeling. As though he read her mind, Tapper reached over and took her hand. "There's nothing you can say, S.J., so let it go. We did what we had to do, but it was only worse because it was Speed. Had it been a stranger, we would have done the same thing, but," Tapper considered how to say what he was thinking, "it was tenser because it was Speed, not because it was some high ranking Fleet brat. Understand?"

"I think so. But it's hard to separate, Tapper. There's a part of me that knows why we were brought back to pull him out, and another part of me that is really angry that the *Washington* was recalled. There were any number of commandos in both branches that could have done what we did."

Tapper mulled it over. He had wondered the same thing, but was convinced it had been the correct decision on more than one level. "I think, S.J., that your father had the involvement of the Wa'atsi in mind when he called us home. It was very possible that an invasion of sorts might have been in the offing, in which case, we would have been too late to do anything about it except come home and join the fray. Trust your dad on this one, squirt, he knew what he was doing. But I wish I was driving you up to the cabin." Tapper turned into the private road which ended at the Rothko house. "Now slap a smile on the face of yours, sailor, and try to act like an officer."

His brusque tone didn't fool her and Jane began to giggle. "Yes sir, Commander Bear."

~

Admiral and General Rothko were still upstairs when they arrived. Jane and Tapper headed straight for the kitchen.

"Anything to eat, Sophie?" called Jane as she poked her head through the door.

"Sarah Jane! Joshua!" Sophie wiped her hands on her floured covered apron and went to give them each a kiss. "Or should I salute first?"

Throwing her arms around the diminutive housekeeper, Jane told her a kiss was just fine. "I was sorry you weren't here when I came home last night."

"So was I, but the grandchildren come first. You should see that little Robert; he's got his fingers in everything!" Although Sophie had been with the Rothkos for years, it was an unspoken agreement that her own family always came first.

"You like the toddlers best, Sophie!" teased Jane, giving her another hug. "Mmmmmm, everything smells wonderful! What are you making?"

"Your father's favorites for alien folk: smoked salmon mousse, tossed salad, a selection of roast capon, rack of lamb, and, for the non-meat eaters, lentil curry with all the trimmings. Something for everyone." Sophie bustled back to the stove and began spooning curry into two small bowls for her visitors. As they took their usual places on stools at the end of the long counter, she proudly accepted their compliments to the chef. "Are you taking good care of Sarah Jane, Joshua Bear?" she demanded of Tapper, her face a mockery of sternness.

"Yes, ma'am. She eats regular and everything."

Sophie's pink face turned dark. "And just what are you eating regular that you look like a toothpick?"

With a half-choke, half-swallow of the savory curry, Jane replied "Lots of salad, not too many eggs, and tons of spinach lasagna. None of which is as good as yours."

"Harrumph. You should be eating better than that, Miss Skinny Minnie. Before you leave, I'll have the admiral authorize a private stock for you with the cook on that ship." If anyone could manipulate the admiral, she could, especially when it came to food and the children. She had been keeping house for the family for twenty-two years and her word in the kitchen was law. "Eat up and get out of here, you two. I've got work to do!" They did as they were told, leaving Sophie to her pots and pans.

They retired to the library where Jane poured a couple of drinks while they waited for her parents. No sooner had the Rothkos stepped into the room then the chimes rang.

Captain Morgan was shown into the library by the butler General Rothko requisitioned from the staff roster at the Pentagon. His first sight of Jane standing beside the fireplace with her father struck him as perfectly natural, although he felt vaguely uncomfortable. Morgan let the admiral pour a stiff scotch, and settled himself into one of the armchairs near the bay window. The conversation centered on Jonathan's progress.

Cardozo arrived next, followed immediately by Ambassador and Lady Xinthi-Ang. Admiral P'nucha, along with his first officer, came next, escorted by Rear Admiral Harlan Duffy and his wife, Meredith. Senator Patricia Collins, chair of the Senate Interplanetary Relations Committee and her husband, James, were the last to arrive. As soon as the Senator was introduced to the outworlders, the discussion, although light in tone, shifted to the reasons for P'nucha's visit. From her corner, Jane watched the senior Rothkos manage the interaction skillfully; it never ceased to amaze her how well they operated as partners. She was almost sorry she was not going to stay for dinner, but she wanted to be on her way before dark.

Excusing herself when the butler called dinner, Jane went upstairs. With Rebecca and Isaac back at school, the house seemed empty even with guests sitting down to dinner. Jane changed out of her dress blues and into a pair of ratty jeans and a sweatshirt. She found socks in her drawer and a pair of beat up old sneakers in the closet. Pulling a bag down from the shelf, she threw a few things in.

"Mind if I come in?"

Jane jumped; the voice did not belong in her room. Recovering herself, she said "Sure," and kept on with what she was doing.

Morgan stood in the doorway. The room was much different from what he expected. The walls were covered with a cheery print of spring flowers interwoven with yellow ribbon making the room pop like a profuse spring bouquet, the antithesis of the lieutenant herself. A bookshelf crammed with math, science, and linguistics texts belied the whimsical atmosphere. A brown, velvet helmet hung jauntily from a hook beside several pictures of a young girl on horseback. There was an overstuffed chair in one corner, a worn teddy bear nestled in the cushions. Other mementos of a girl's life were scattered about, a far cry from the austere surroundings in which she lived on board the *Washington*. As she moved between the dresser and the bed filling her bag, she looked as though she belonged nowhere else. And if that was not enough, the room smelled just like she did: fresh scrubbed and a little like the lavender that grew in his mother's herb garden. It was all disconcerting.

Morgan pulled an envelope from his inner pocket. "These are for you." He tossed it on the bed. "No need to open it now," he added when she did not pick up the packet. "Those are your temporary transfer orders. They say you'll be assigned to the Pentagon until further notice."

"How long will that be, Captain?" she asked, still not looking at him.

"As long as it takes to find Pana-Di." She picked up the envelope and dropped in the bag. Morgan's hand shot out and grabbed her wrist as she passed him. "I didn't want you to disappear, Sarah Jane, before I had a chance to talk to you."

She looked down at his hand on her wrist. "Y'know, I've already had a stranger in my quarters man-handling me. Don't make it twice."

Morgan released his grip.

"Here's the thing," she continued, "You're in *my* room, in *my* parents' house, so I don't really think you're the captain here even if you want to be. I don't even know what to call you…in private. I have no idea what you're thinking, and truthfully, I don't know if I want to know. How does that sound?

"I'm not sure."

"What are you looking for me to say, Captain? What aren't you asking or telling me?

"I'm sorry we botched that end of the operation. I'm sorry you have to leave." His face was close to hers.

"I am, too. It appears I'm a threat to the safety of everyone on the ship."

"I wouldn't go that far."

"Yeah, well, my parents did, and since they outrank you, I guess they get the deciding vote on the matter."

"I wish to God I was going with you."

"You and everyone else," Jane snorted, "I'll be fine. There's no place safer than the cabin."

"I wish I believed that."

Jane stuffed another sweatshirt into the bag with a vengeance. "You wish an awful lot of things, Asher Morgenstern, but you don't have to wish for me. I can do it perfectly well for myself." The vehemence in her voice surprised her.

He felt like a teenager taken to task. "I meant what I said at the beach on Lomos," he said quietly.

"So did I."

"And I am sorry about what happened on the ship."

"For God's sake, Captain, stop apologizing. You had no more control over the last few weeks than I had. Just forget the whole thing." Jane stuffed some clothes into her bag and closed it with a snap. "Maybe we can start over when I get back. If I get back."

"No." The word was simple enough, but the power behind it was not. Crossing the space between them in a couple of long strides, Morgan spun her around to face him. "I will not forget the whole thing and neither will you. And neither of us will forget what happened on the beach." He silenced her protest with his mouth on hers.

All Jane's defenses crumbled. Her first response was to smack him, but instead her arms went about his neck. When she finally pushed away from him, the words she spoke were not in anger; they were sheer frustration. "This is not the place either. If anything is to be between us, it will happen away from here, away from the ship, away from my parents. I won't allow myself to be swept away like some idiot adolescent." Jane slung her bag over her shoulder and walked to the door. "Maybe some other time, we can work this out, but I can't do it now." Without a backward glance, Jane ran down the stairs and into the kitchen.

Her parents came out to say goodbye. Both elicited a promise to call as soon as she reached the cabin. Her mother was still standing with her when the butler approached.

"General Rothko, Major Quinn to see you."

"Send him in here, please," she answered. "Sophie, when Martin comes back, have him carry the cooler out to Jonathan's speeder, please." She turned back to Jane. "Don't go yet."

"Sorry to disturb you, General, but this just came in." He handed her a sealed courier pouch and waited while the general opened it and read the contents. "They would like a response from you directly."

General Rothko took a pen from Quinn and handwrote a reply. "Interpol spotted Pana-Di in Zurich," she said with a frown. "They think he might be on his way here, travelling under a forged passport listing him as a delegate from Jeylos to a mining conference in Pittsburgh."

"I'll be all right, Mom."

"I'd be happier if you had an escort at least as far as Connecticut."

"I have an escort; I'm taking Spike. Besides, the Cabots will keep an eye on me."

The general finished writing, returned the document to its pouch, and handed it to Quinn who stood impassively near the door. "We can't arrest him, but we can detain him. Alert INS to closely vet all incoming Jeylosians until they have a working bioscreen for the kora. I'll discuss this with the ambassador privately. I'm sure he will agree. Process this as a direct order. Dismissed, Major." She waited until the officer left the kitchen. Putting her arm around Jane, she added, "Come on, sweetheart, let's go get Spike out of dog jail and get you on your way."

Outside, the air was sweet with new mown grass. Jane and her mother walked the short distance to the kennel where Spike was patiently awaiting his mistress. As soon as they were in sight, the dog jumped up, barking joyously at their approach. Jane opened the gate and let Spike out, at the same time letting him jump all over her. "Down, boy," she laughed as he tried to lick her face.

Liz Rothko watched her daughter and the dog. She found it hard to believe Sarah was already twenty-nine, the same age she was when Jonathan was born. Equally difficult to absorb was that Sarah had become an officer, not the linguistic professor she had expected. There was no denying her pride in her daughter's accomplishments, but at the same time, she wished Sarah had chosen a less difficult arena in which to display her incredible talent for language. *It's our own fault,* the general chided herself; *we were the ones to give her a taste of the galaxy.*

"What are you thinking about, Mom?" asked Jane when she caught her mother's gaze.

"Oh, just mother stuff, dear."

"Like?"

Liz Rothko smiled and took her daughter's hand in her own. "Like I was your age when Jonathan was born. Like I wonder what will happen to you in the next years...things like that."

"Don't let it get to you, General Mom. I'll be okay."

The crickets were chirping loudly, just as they always did this time of year. Their song seemed to fill the air but they could not distract Liz from asking the next question. "What about you and Morgan?"

The question took Jane by surprise. "What about him?"

"You and Asher, dear. It's obvious from the way his eyes follow you around the room that there is something under the surface. Have you been…" Liz stumbled for a moment, "intimate with him?"

"Are you asking if I have slept with him, mother?"

"No. You know intimacy and sex are two very different things. I am asking if you and he are having some kind of relationship other than that between captain and subordinate."

Jane sighed; there was no point in lying to her mother, although there was precious little to tell. "We had an *incident,* but nothing has come of it."

"Do you want something to come of it, Sarah Jane?" She brushed an errant lock of hair from Jane's forehead.

Thin shoulders rose and fell. "I don't know. It's all very complicated."

"How does he feel?"

Jane smiled and gave a short laugh. "I think he's just as confused as I am. He's a widower, you know. And he has a son."

"I know all these things, Sarah, and so does your father. Morgan is what, ten years older than you?"

"Eleven. But that shouldn't really matter, should it?"

"Does it matter to you?"

"Hard to say, Mom. I haven't decided." Jane looked up at the moon hanging full in the sky and almost wished she were there instead of talking to her mother in the back yard. "He's strong willed, attentive to detail, nothing escapes him..." her voice trailed off.

"Sweetheart, you're describing a captain, not a man."

"They're not synonymous?" snickered Jane.

"Hardly."

Jane sighed again. "Okay, he's handsome, has great table manners, a terrific smile, a good sense of the ridiculous, can quote Lewis Carroll at will...what more could a girl want?"

Liz put her arm about her daughter and squeezed. "Your father can quote Lewis Carroll and look where it got me."

CHAPTER 24

On the road, Jane began to feel better. She quickly maneuvered the speeder into the upper level, express-flight lane of the freeway and, with the help of light traffic, made excellent time. Beside her, Spike curled up in a ball and slept, his gentle snoring barely heard over the music coming from Jonathan's prized sound system.

It took only a couple of hours to reach New York City, and then, rather than take the sterile Throughway up north, Jane opted for the more scenic Taconic route. Skimming along, she followed the curves of the Catskills as they grew into the Adirondack Mountains. The ride was pleasantly familiar as she recalled all the other trips she had taken along that path, most of which had been with her entire family packed into her mother's extended hover-wagon, the rear stuffed with luggage, books, toys and hampers of picnic food. Whether they were going to the cabin or to the beach house on Cape Cod, the journey always included a portion of the Taconic. At Saratoga Springs, Jane stopped long enough to eat a sandwich and let Spike answer the call of nature. It was already after eleven and she knew, if she got to Branch Pond Access Road too late, she would have to awaken Ben.

⁂

The Krieg family retreat actually sat on the edge of the wildlife sanctuary sector of the Green Mountain National Forest and was normally closed to the public. Jane used a card key to open the gate to the private road which would take her to Ben and Hester Cabot's house at the bottom on the road leading to the cabin. Old friends of the family, Ben kept his eye on the place during the year, making sure nothing untoward took place when the family wasn't there. A typical Vermont Yankee, he and his wife were taciturn people who did not take kindly to strangers wandering around their rural habitat, preferring the locals to the summer folk. The Krieg clan was the exception to the rule. When Great-great-great Grandpa Krieg went in search of a quiet place to send his family for the summer, he found Lemuel Cabot and a long standing friendship was born. Five generations of Krieg children had grown up wandering down the road to the Cabot place in search of excitement. Even Spike was a Cabot; he was the offspring of Ben's prized retriever bitch.

The porch light glowed, the only break in the deep woods darkness, when Jane turned into the Cabot's drive. The front door was open and before she could hop out of the speeder, Ben was standing there, hands on hips, a wide grin on his narrow Yankee face. "Yer late, missy. Yer mother's called twice in the past hour wondering where the dickens you are!" His reprimand was colored by good humor. Spike bounded out of the speeder and ran full tilt toward the old man who stooped to scratch the large dog. "Go on, Spike, yer brothers are in the back." As if he understood perfectly, Spike tore around the side of the house, barking all the way.

"I stopped in Saratoga to let Spike run and to eat something," admitted Jane apologetically. "Sorry I'm so late, Ben." She looped an arm about his shoulders and gave him a buss on the cheek.

Hester appeared at the doorway, wiping her hands on a flour covered apron. "Well, if it isn't Ted's wandering girl!" she laughed opening her arms to Jane. "You come in here while Ben goes up the road to open the cabin. And call your mother!"

Within the hour, Jane had spoken to her mother, eaten a homemade bread and jam sandwich at Hester's table, caught up on all the local happenings, and was ready to follow Ben up the road. Spike opted to run along behind the cars, his ears flopping as he checked out every inch of the way to the cabin. Driving slowly down the narrow, twisting road with her windows open, Jane relished the rich, woody scent wafting on the autumnal breeze. It was too long since she had last been at the cabin and now, as they approached the rambling log cabin, she realized how much she had missed it. No other place she had been during her travels in space could compare with the simple, natural beauty surrounding Branch Pond.

"Hester's loaded the refrigerator with all the essentials," said Ben as he opened the door with his own key. "Everything is up and working, including yer dad's comm system. The canoe is stowed on the dock and there's fuel in the motorboat, too."

"I can't thank you and Hester enough, Ben," grinned Jane, dropping her bag on the floor. "I'll be fine up here, just knowing you are down the road."

"Spike'll take care of you, Sarah Jane. But if there's a problem, you can hit the console and it'll ring down at the station."

The last words, coupled with the concerned look in Ben's eyes, told Jane that he knew why she was there alone. "I'm not expecting any trouble," she replied seriously.

Ben frowned. "No one expects trouble, Sarah, but sometimes it shows up anyway." He strolled over to the door. "In any case, I'll be back to check on you in the morning."

"Thanks, Ben." She joined him at the door. "See you in the morning." She watched until he drove off in his ancient hovercraft.

Automatically, Jane locked the door and headed to the other side of the room where the adjacent deck overlooked the pond. It wasn't really a pond at all; it was a small lake fed by several quick running creeks with a narrow, sandy beach encircling it all. A few other houses dotted the shore, but each was accessible only from well-hidden private drives off the main road through the forest. The Krieg cabin was perched on top of a steep hill with a path cut down to the water. In her great-grandfather's old age, one of his sons had added tidy steps and a railing to aid the old gentleman's trips up and down to the beach. Beneath the deck, there was a small grassy area where numerous volleyball games had been played over the years. Grandma Krieg's day lilies still lined the edge of the grass, separating the cultivated area from the woods. Taking a last deep breath of delightfully fresh air, Jane went to unpack.

Rather than sleep in the usual narrow bed in the back loft, she opted for bunking in the big guest room right off the living room. By the time her clothes were put away, Jane was more than ready for bed. Spike dragged in his favorite throw rug and curled up on the floor beside the bed as his mistress snuggled beneath the warm feather comforter and quickly fell asleep.

∞⊖∞

Major Quinn arrived at the Pentagon earlier than usual. Foregoing the morning ritual of coffee with the other aides, he went immediately to his office to prepare for the general's staff meeting. He didn't like working for Elizabeth Rothko, believing his talents were wasted on the woman who seemed to have a driving need to control everything around her. Nor did he care for her personal politics, not a well-kept secret in the tight world of military personnel. Periodically, he would look about for another position, but Rothko's office was considered too plum a place to leave without exceptionally good reason.

A noise in the outer office caught Quinn's attention and he went to investigate it. At the central desk sat Sergeant Whiting, the general's secretary. "You're in early, Whiting," said Quinn affably. "What's up?"

The young man shrugged. "The boss wanted a bunch of documents set up for the meeting and I didn't finish everything last night. I figured I'd better get here before she does."

Quinn's laugh was sharp. "The last thing you want to do is get on her shit list. She can be real pain in the ass if she doesn't think you're up to speed on your job." Parking himself on the corner of the desk, Quinn bantered casually with the recently assigned sergeant. "Have you got her psyched out yet?"

"To some degree," Whiting admitted with a shrug. "She's taking this Middle East business as far as she can without alienating the entire brass, but at the same time, they're all walking on eggshells around her because of the major. How is he, by the way?"

"Seems to be doing better. I was over at the house last night. She and the admiral were hosting a dinner party for that reptile P'nucha."

"Yeah?" Whiting was definitely curious about the party, but waited for Quinn to take the hint.

"The Jeylosian ambassador and his wife were there and a couple of hot shots from the Hill." Quinn caught the widening of the aide's eyes. "I met the Wa'atsi; he seemed like a nice enough fellow if you can get past his ugly face and all the booby prizes on his chest." He leaned forward and spoke in a conspiratorial whisper. "I tell you this, though, I wouldn't want to meet him in a dark alley."

Whiting snorted in agreement. Lowering his voice, he asked "Was the daughter there? I mean the lieutenant daughter. She's a piece of work, if you can go by the picture on the general's desk."

"Yeah, she was there; she's one hot number." Quinn could tell Whiting was more than simply curious about her. "They shipped her out somewhere last night; it seems the old man thinks she's at risk with Pana-Di running around loose. Rumor has it the blue boy wants her for his very own."

"Where did they send her?"

"Beats me," shrugged Quinn. "All I know is she was heading out in her brother's speeder. Very hush-hush."

Whiting brightened; he knew something the Major didn't. Considering how valuable the information was, he debated only briefly whether or not to tell him. He decided in favor; a little good gossip could be exchanged for a favor later on. "Probably went to Bennington, Vermont," he said casually. "The family has a summer place up there and the old lady has been calling there a lot lately."

"Yeah?" This was what Quinn was hoping for. "I didn't know they had a house up there."

"More like a cabin, I guess."

"Well, she couldn't have gotten better weather." Quinn slid from his perch. "Lucky kid, having big brass for parents. Who else could pull strings like that?"

"I wouldn't want them for parents," shuddered Whiting. "Could you imagine having to look at them every morning over breakfast while you're growing up?"

"You might be right, Whiting." The Major glanced at his watch. "Well, have a good time, fella. You've got about an hour before the old lady shows up." Quinn strolled off, hands deep in his pockets, looking as unruffled as possible. Knowing where they had sent the lieutenant was, in no small way, the bargaining chip he had been waiting for. Barely able to contain himself, Quinn cleaned off his desk and grabbed his coat before walking calmly out the door.

The office of the Chief of Fleet Operations reflected the simple taste of its current occupant. The outer office held two desks, one for his administrative assistant; the other for his liaison officer, and comfortably seating area. The inner office was furnished with antiques, many of which had come from old, long-retired, sailing vessels, each with a story of its own.. A series of windows overlooked the Pentagon inner yard, almost directly opposite another set of windows belonging to his wife. More than once signals had been flashed across the lawn, much to the dismay of the tight security team who would have preferred more conventional means of communication between brass.

Pacing before the windows, Admiral Rothko complained to his visitors about the length of time it took a congressional committee to convene. "You would think they were deciding the fate of the damn planet," he nearly shouted, "instead of considering whether or not inter-planetary extradition can be arranged without a damn congressional vote! How long can it possibly take?"

"Probably as long as it takes the Supreme Command to decide what to eat for lunch," mused Admiral P'nucha with a wry glance at Morgan who sat on the opposite end of the sofa.

Morgan stifled a laugh. "Possibly longer. You don't know our Congress and if you did, you might seriously regret it." Morgan appreciated the way the alien rolled his eyes in agreement. "Admiral, why can't I just issue a three day shore leave for my people before they climb up the fuselage out of boredom?" he asked hopefully.

"Because until I hear from Collins, I can't do a damn thing. Hell, I can't even release Jackson until they say so. If we are infracting interplanetary law, there is no point in holding you here; you may as well take off and head back to deep space. But if they decide we are within our jurisdiction on this kora thing, then you have to sit tight until he surfaces. In any event," he added, stopping at his desk long enough to drum his fingers, "all we can do is wait." Rothko stared at the window for a moment, and then turned toward the desk. "Buzz, damn it!"

As if the machine understood, the vidcom unit emitted a low buzzing. Sliding into his chair, Rothko hit the console. "Go ahead."

A clearly feminine voice was heard. "Ted, is that you?"

He hit another button and Pat Collins appeared on the screen. "Yes, Pat. Whaddya got?"

"Tell Morgan to schedule shore leave for the *Washington*, but retain Cardozo here until further notice. And Joshua Bear, too. The committee wants to talk to them directly about the raid." She paused for a moment. "Is Morgan with you?"

"I'm here." Morgan moved to be in view of the screen.

"Interpol thinks your friend Pana-Di is out looking for *you*. A communiqué was intercepted indicating that he has you on his hit list." She paused and took a deep breath. "And Sarah, too, Ted."

"Sarah's safe." Rothko's voice was sharp with anger. "Does Interpol have any suggestions?"

"Yes. D'Agostino in Rome thinks that if we leak word of shore leave for the *Washington*, Pana-Di might surface more quickly looking for Morgan. He thinks you, Captain, should take yourself away from here, maybe somewhere up north, where there are more Jeylosians; he would be less conspicuous and more likely to be sloppy."

"Any suggestions?" asked Morgan.

"None, so long as we know where you are and you stay in touch. But it has to be someplace where you would want to go. It seems the kora knows quite a bit about you." Pat Collin smiled sweetly, but the message was clear: anywhere away from Washington, D.C.

"Anything you say, Senator," replied Morgan amicably.

"And one last thing, Captain. Do carry a sidearm and take a scrambler with you. I know you have a habit of not carrying those items, but we would like you to make an exception in this case. While the committee would like to see the kora apprehended, we have no desire to lose a perfectly able captain in the process." She paused. "You might consider Boston, Morgan. Jeylosians are fairly common up there."

Morgan stifled a chuckle; the lady knew him well. "Yes, ma'am."

Senator Collins sighed and shook her head; she knew she was being humored but trusted that if Morgan agreed to the two items, he would indeed be carrying them. She straightened up a little in her oversized leather chair. "Admiral P'nucha?"

"Yes, Madam Senator," he called from his seat, "I am present."

"The committee would take it as an honor if you would attend a meeting here on Capitol Hill this afternoon."

"I would be delighted, Madam Senator. I am at your complete disposal." A trip to the Hill would be an interesting adventure, even for such a well-seasoned traveler as a Wa'atsi admiral. He could only imagine the questions they would be poised to ask.

"Then I shall leave you gentlemen to your deliberations," said the Senator, and then she paused. "Oh, Morgan?"

"Yes, Senator?"

"Don't do anything heroic."

The men laughed congenially, fully understanding the last comment. "I'll try not to," replied the captain with good natured patience.

Admiral Rothko asked if there was anything else, and the Senator asked him to pick up the handset. Morgan noticed the admiral hit the scrambler button. The vidcom screen went dark. For a moment, he listened to what she had to say, his face grim, his mouth setting itself in a taut line. He thanked Senator Collins and replaced the handset. Without a word to either man, the admiral stood, took his jacket from the coat rack near the door, and indicated that they should follow him. When he finally spoke as they waited for the elevator, his voice was soft. "I think it's high time Admiral P'nucha saw our famous gardens."

P'nucha looked at Morgan, but the captain merely shrugged; he had no better idea of what was going on than the outworlder, but he said nothing. They walked outside the building and toward the artfully arranged flower garden hidden on the side of the Pentagon's inner courtyard. They walked in complete silence until the admiral stopped at a bench where they could sit comfortably.

Morgan spoke first. "What's up?"

"I can't repeat everything Pat told me, but this portion is a 'need to know.'" He looked at P'nucha. "In a roundabout way, this affects you, too."

P'nucha weighed his response cautiously. "Anything you say to me under these circumstances will remain strictly confidential, Edward Rothko," he said, using the admiral's name for the first time. "I believe we have a common goal and sharing of valuable information is a foundation for future trust."

"Pat thinks, along with several others, that there is a high level leak here, in the Pentagon," said Rothko quietly, studying P'nucha's face for any sign of a reaction. "One has to decide whom to trust and how far to trust. In this case, there has obviously been misplaced trust."

The Wa'atsi grimaced in what might have passed as a human smile. "I hope you are not suspecting me, Edward Rothko; I would have far more to lose by breaching your confidence than I would have to gain."

"No," replied the admiral, "I am not even remotely concerned about that. I am afraid that the leak would have to be one of our own people."

Morgan shifted on the bench. "Any clues?"

"Yes and no, but none that I can go into right now. Internal affairs is looking into several possibilities, but this is a time we can ill afford to be cleaning house. What the kora was trying to do by establishing a foothold on this planet is far more dangerous than just the harm which can be done by a misguided fool." He did not need to mention the danger to his own family, but Rothko gave the impression that was not the overriding concern. "Frankly, I'm not completely sure why Pana-Di has embarked on such a bizarre course and neither is Xinthi-Ang.

The three men sat in silence, each considering his own view of the kora's motive. When Morgan finally, spoke, his words were slow and well chosen. "Admiral P'nucha, I have been wondering why, if you would forgive my curiosity, you came here. I understand your desire to repay a personal debt to Jonathan and at the same time address your people's concern that one of your ships was participating in an unsanctioned military maneuver, but what is the actual connection between the Wa'atsi and Pana-Di?"

Rothko winced at the directness of the question, but he held his tongue. P'nucha, however, barked a short laugh. "Your speech is certainly refreshing, Captain Morgan. It is well past the time for polite inquiries." His tone reassured the other admiral that no offence had been taken. "The connection is quite simple. There is none."

"None?" echoed Morgan in disbelief.

"None that is official." The Wa'atsi stood and walked a few yards before coming back to the bench. "You handled the situation with the Ana'atam quite well, Captain. But what you could not have known was that Nish and Yeynum were acting independently from the Supreme Command. At no time did we sanction the theft of the Hunam Batan from Pitan, but someone wanted it. That someone, we suspect, was the Kora Pana-Di."

"That confirms what Ambassador Xinthi-Ang suspects," offered Admiral Rothko, the corners of his mouth pulled down. "The ambassador said Pana-Di was unreasonably upset about our unwillingness to allow him to negotiate the return of the thing, and of the Pitanese to take it back without some sort of reparation."

Morgan was puzzled. "But why would he want the Hunam Batan in the first place?"

"Because, my friend, it was a test of his ability to command. He wanted to be hailed as a hero of great finesse. The kora, we believe, entered into an agreement with Nish and Yeynum, both of whom are considered *limchat,* renegades, amongst our people. The point of stealing the Hunam Batan was not to keep it, but to make a great display of its restoration to the Pitanese. Nish and Yeynum were on a trading mission, a punitive action for certain unsanctioned activities, when this took place, but the Ana'atam was not alone; there was a second ship with them."

"And the second ship was the Ripa'atam."

"Correct, Captain. First Officer Yeynum thought he was being very clever when, after we escorted the Ana'atam to a repair station, he shuttled to the Ripa'atam, ostensibly to complete the mission when, in fact, he was joining Captain Krosh to continue on the path Nish had set for them."

Instead of going to a Stellar-3 market negotiation, explained P'nucha, they had gone to Bimwar, the furthest of the Jeylosian moons. When Pana-Di opted to take his punishment at the Imperial Palace on Bimwar, they intercepted his shuttle, killed the crew, and headed to Earth. It was several days before the Imperial Guard learned of the kora's disappearance, giving him ample head start to join with Ramadi and Hassan. "Thus," continued the admiral, "he was able to be involved."

"Which would explain only part of this, Gacham P'nucha," said Rothko, only partly satisfied with the explanation. "But why isn't the Supreme Command more enthusiastic about this breach of Earth's security?"

"Because, Edward Rothko, between gentlemen, I will tell you that the Wa'atsi Empire is in dire straits." He paused to consider how he could continue without losing face before his potential allies. "The economy is crumbling under the weight of our own colonization program; several of our highest ranking military leaders are already strained beneath the economic burden and now preach a coup behind closed doors. The Supreme Council of State is convinced that without expanded trade routes, we will be unable retain control of our home planet, let alone the colonies." P'nucha seemed to sag a little, as if the weight of his mission suddenly became unbearable. "The Supreme Command has no interest in challenging League of Planet members, hence the anger with the Pitan escapade."

"And where exactly does the kora fit into this?" asked Morgan, still puzzled.

"Your friend, the kora, sees no hope of acceding to his father's throne; therefore, he is a man without true occupation," stated P'nucha. "He was at a trade negotiation with a number of outer systems and found a sympathetic ear in Nish. Together, they began to formulate a plan to set in motion the overthrow of one, if not both, governments. In order to obtain the support of my people," sighed P'nucha, "Pana-Di had to prove himself in battle. He was the one who identified the Hunam Batan as a potential target."

"You're not serious?" asked the captain.

"Deadly serious, Captain Morgan. Pana-Di was in on this debacle from the start. Nish need a backer, a money-man as you Terrans call it, and Pana-Di had plenty of capital at his personal disposal. It was an ideal set-up. Jeylos is a wealthy system, gentlemen. Merging their economic power with Wa'atsi military strength could, conceivably, produce a galactic power never before seen."

Rothko sat quietly trying to sort out what to do with convoluted mess P'nucha had described. That the Wa'atsi economy was in distress was an open secret, but mutiny in the ranks was another matter completely. As feared as the Wa'atsi were, they were considered a stable planet, one slowly approaching a time when they, too, would join the League. "Off the record, Gacham P'nucha, I will see what I can do about getting the League to extend an official invitation of membership to you, but it will be up to your people to decide whether or not to accept. It would require the Supreme Command to consider autonomy for a large number of you more unwilling outposts...."

"That would not be a problem, Edward," interrupted the Wa'atsi Admiral. "We are looking for a graceful way to liberate several of our outlying colonies. Unfortunately, they became colonies because they were unable to govern themselves. They were what you might call easy prey."

A khaki clad officer entered the courtyard and stood a few paces from the three men, waiting for a signal to approach. Rothko saw him and waved.

"Ambassador Xinthi-Ang has arrived and wishes to speak with you, sir."

"Escort him here, Miller," replied the admiral.

"Yes, sir." The aide trotted off and returned a moment later with the ambassador.

"I am glad to find you together. I have had word from His Imperial Majesty on Jeylos." The grim look in his eyes held the men silent. "His Imperial Majesty sends this message to you, Admiral Rothko, Admiral P'nucha and you, Captain Morgan. He says: 'Pana-Di is no longer my son. Find him and show him no mercy.'"

Ground crews were crawling over the fuselage of the *Washington*, checking for any damage during its last flight. Tapper, standing to one side, was going over structural plans with the head of base maintenance. He spotted Morgan as the dun colored speeder pulled onto the tarmac.

Morgan gave Tapper a run down on the meeting with Rothko, P'nucha and finally Ambassador Xinthi-Ang. The tech chief concurred with the decision for Morgan to leave the ship, but argued whether or not Boston was the right place to go.

"I know how much you want to see Reuben, Ash, but you run the risk of exposing him to danger if Pana-Di finds you there," insisted Tapper heatedly.

"But if there's a leak and he knows where Jane is, Boston is the most convenient place for me to draw him out," Morgan countered; "besides, Mass Fleet's intelligence sector has always been the sharpest outside Washington, and I know the people up there."

There was truth in his last statement which Tapper could not argue. "Want me to come along?" he finally asked when he knew there were no arguments left.

Morgan shook his head. "Go to New York and see McGee at Interpol. I'll be in touch through him." Tapper walked with him as far as the gangway. "Finish up here and come on board. I'll call a senior staff meeting before I leave. Newhouse can run things while I'm gone, and I'll leave you to straighten out a duty roster with him. You can leave for New York after Congress is done with you."

Tapper watched him walk up the gangway, whistling under his breath. He wondered about Morgan' sanity, but he had never known the captain to do anything without examining every option.

From his cabin, Morgan ordered a sub-orbiter for the flight to Boston, and a civilian speeder to be waiting for him upon arrival at the base outside Boston. He called a quick staff meeting and hurried to finish packing. Time was tight; he wanted to be home for dinner. *Home.* The mere thought of sitting in his mother's kitchen made him smile. For a brief moment, he debated calling his parents and decided against it; better to surprise them rather than have them sit around waiting in case he was delayed at the base. Quickly changing his clothes for fresh khakis, he brought his duffle to the bridge and from there summoned a crewmate to take it down to hovercar waiting to take him to the sub-orbiter.

Winter was waiting for him in his office. "Are you going to see Jane?" she demanded as soon as he closed the door.

"Should I be?" He made light of the question although her face told him she was concerned for her lieutenant.

Belle would not be put off. "If Jane is in danger, and I think she is, then you should be going up to wherever she is to protect her, Captain."

His laughter surprised both of them. "I think the lieutenant can take care of herself, Annabel. But if you are so concerned, I think I can manage to check in on her."

"Then you know where she is."

"Do you?" Morgan's eyes studied hers, curious as to how much Jane had told her.

"More or less." Belle met his stare dead on. "It doesn't matter whether or not I know; what matters is that you know." She sank into the nearest chair, holding her head in her hands. "It's not like I'm psychic or anything like that, Captain, it's just that I have a really bad feeling about all this. I can't put my finger on it, but it's there."

"Hey, it's okay, Belle. My best advice to you is to get involved in the encoding project so when the lieutenant does return to the *Washington* you've got your end done." He gently steered Belle toward the door.

"Be careful, Captain," she added quietly before the portal slid open.

The staff meeting was brief and to the point. A few questions about Lieutenant Krieg were asked and general answers given, but no one pressed for details. Barb Lucas would assist Newhouse; Morgan felt confident leaving them in charge; it was not the first time they had acted as command team and they were damn good at it. Morgan issued his last orders before departure and then met briefly with Lucas and Newhouse. Assured everything was in place, he and Tapper walked down to the hovercar.

"Give my love to Reuben, Ash," said Tapper as they reached the car.

"Will do. I'll call you as soon as I know anything. And check in with Mass Fleet when you get to New York." He got into the vehicle and opened the window. "Don't do anything stupid, Tap."

"Same to you, buddy," laughed the tech chief. He stayed long enough to see the hovercraft exit the security gate.

CHAPTER 25

Major Quinn stood on the steps of the Lincoln Memorial, sweating beneath the weight of his coat. The weather was much too warm for such a garment, but he wanted his uniform hidden. The last thing he wanted was to be an object of curiosity by either tourists or the D.C. police casually strolling around the mall. His contact was late and for the umpteenth time, Quinn checked his watch.

"Excuse me, but could you tell me how to get to the Justice building?" asked a plain-looking woman with short, blunt-cut dishwater hair.

Quinn was about to tell her when she casually tugged on her left ear. Only then did he notice the earring, a long, dangling thing with a little silver charm hanging from it. "I'm afraid I'm just as lost as you are, miss," he replied slowly.

"Perhaps we can walk together for a bit and find it on our own." She smiled, revealing an uneven row of yellowish teeth.

Quinn did not offer her his arm. Sticking his hands deep into his pockets, he followed her down the steps. "I wasn't expecting a woman," he said in a hoarse whisper. "Where's Rega-Dop?"

"All in good time, Major Quinn." She moved at a good clip, weaving in and out of the pedestrian traffic with considerable skill. As they neared the Vietnam War Memorial, the woman spoke again. "Wait at the far end; someone will come to you there." The woman melted into the crowd.

Quinn stuck out in the throng of short sleeved people milling about the long, black wall. He felt stupid in his coat; he was acutely aware of the stares due to his overdressed condition. Quinn needed a diversion from his own discomfort and he began studying the people around him. Most were from this planet, but he easily picked out the outworlders. It certainly wasn't the way they were dressed; many wore t-shirts emblazoned with one slogan or another. Alphans were obvious; their flattened heads gave them away even when they wore hats. There was a couple from Kotuchar with a young child strapped to the mother's back. A group of Asian businessmen were openly staring at a group of saurian types, definitely not Wa'atsi, but most likely from one of the planets in their system. Several Jeylosians also milled about, but none of them looked familiar to Quinn.

A tall, blue-skinned man made eye contact with the major. He nodded slightly, just enough to tell Quinn his presence was noted. Quinn wanted to follow him when he walked around the side of the monument, but he resisted the urge; he had been instructed to wait and he would do as he was told. There was far too much at risk. Finally, a different Jeylosian appeared at his side.

"Can you tell me where our lady friend has gone?"

The question caught Quinn. Did he mean his escort or Krieg? He looked blankly at the stranger. "Who the hell are you?" spat Quinn. "And where the hell is Rega-Dop?"

"The less you know the better. Where has she gone?"

The tense tone clarified the question. "She's at a cabin in Vermont, near Bennington."

"Specifically?

"Somewhere in or around the Green Mountain National Forest."

The Jeylosian looked annoyed. "Surely you can do better than that, Mr. Quinn. Vermont is not a large state, but we can hardly go searching for a cabin in the woods."

"What are you going to do with her?"

"Nothing that concerns you," replied the stranger.

"I beg to differ. I want to know what you are planning."

The Jeylosian sighed dramatically. "We have no interest in her; we want the captain."

"But he's not with her."

"Our sources assure us he soon will be."

Quinn snorted. "If your sources are so damn good, why don't they know where the kid is?"

The Jeylosian bent over, bringing his face close to Quinn's. "Let me remind you, Major Quinn, you are in this to a point where you can be identified by any one of a number of people who would gladly see you court martialed. If you have any desire to protect your rather thin hide, I would suggest strongly that you provide the information for which you are being handsomely paid."

There was something so threatening about the Jeylosian that Quinn felt his mouth go dry with fear. Somehow, he managed to croak out "Branch Pond."

The Jeylosian allowed himself a thin, unpleasant smile. "Very good, Mr. Quinn. Now go back to your little desk and we will be in touch." He watched while Quinn scuttled away as fast as he could.

"Well?" asked Hum Rega-Dop, stepping out from behind the monument.

"His usefulness is ended. Silence his mouth before he compromises the mission

CHAPTER 26

Morgan's sub-orbital flight to Boston took barely an hour, giving him precious little time to consider how he was going to explain his sudden appearance to his family. A crewmate from the motor pool met him at the shuttle to take him to where a hovercar stood waiting. Morgan signed for the vehicle, then set out in the heavy afternoon traffic. By the time he reached the tree-lined street he knew so well, Morgan had decided that the truth was the best explanation to offer his father; to concoct a complicated story would serve no purpose. Hoisting his duffle onto his shoulder, Morgan walked around to the back, pausing at the window just long enough to see his mother standing at the stove tending a large pot. Rapping sharply at the window, he called to her, "*G'naidik Fräu*, got some food for a hungry sailor?"

Feigel Morgenstern spun around, the spoon she held clattered to the floor. "Asher!" she cried and ran to unlatch the screen door. The tall man had barely dropped the duffle before his mother was covering his face with kisses.

With her beloved boy at her kitchen table, Mrs. Morgenstern fairly flew about the kitchen loading plate after plate with the things he loved to eat after a long day at school. When he finally convinced her to sit, the conversation immediately centered on Reuben. "He's such a good boy, Asher," beamed the grandma. "A joy to have around. You should spend more time with him."

Between bites, Morgan agreed. "Where's Dad and Reuben now?"

he asked, wondering why his father's car was in the drive, but they were nowhere to be seen.

"They went for a walk to the park," laughed his mother, "and I would think Rueben had a baseball in his pocket. If I know them, they went to play catch."

As if on cue, two voices were heard outside. "Come on, Zayde, that's a motor pool car. Something must have happened to Dad!" There was terrible fear in the boy's voice. "Bubbe!" he called as he yanked open the screen. Reuben's eyes widened to take up half his face and he charged across the room into his father's open arms.

"Careful, you'll knock him down, Reuben," admonished Mrs. Morgenstern, trying to keep from crying at the sight of her son and grandson.

"How long can you stay, Dad?"

"As long as I possibly can, champ. I'm on call up here and I do have Fleet business in town, but I'll stay here with you here instead of at the base, if it's okay with your grandparents."

"Of course you'll stay here, Asher," said his father, speaking for the first time. "Welcome home." As much as he disagreed with his son's profession, there was no question that Asher would stay at home where he belonged.

After dinner, the Morgensterns trotted off to watch Reuben's team play against another yeshiva. Ash watched with pride as the boy deftly handled short stop, each throw, each tag made with surprising speed and sharpness. Almost as much fun was watching his father shout and cheer in a way Ash remembered warmly from his own childhood. The time the old man had spent playing endless games of catch with Reuben had paid off grandly; the kid was good, very good, and with a bittersweet tug, Morgan admitted to himself that he was jealous of the relationship between the boy and his grandfather.

Feigie Morgenstern noticed the setting of her son's jaw, a look she recognized as "the wrestling face." Silently, she bided her time until the end of the game when they walked over to the school to wait for the victors. Her husband was busy talking to one of his friends a few steps away, allowing her to take Asher's arm as they walked. "It's good that your father spends so much time with the boy; it keeps him younger than if he had nothing better to do than to go to the office and come home to read the paper like his friends. But, Asher, I know you must wonder who Reuben thinks of as father, in the real sense," she said quietly, glancing up to see the sharp line between his brow. "You should know that Reuben understands the difference and makes the best of the situation. There are times he wants only his father, but those are fewer than they used to be. And yes, he still cries for his mama on occasion."

"There are times I feel that I have deserted him, in a way far more cruel than if I had been the one to die, Mom. Tovah couldn't stop what happened to her, but I could be here."

"Could you? Could you be here and be happy? Life isn't all happiness, Asher, but being miserable here would do Reuben no good." She squeezed his hand and smiled. "He's so very proud of what you do and how you do it."

The boys were starting to come out and Morgan and his mother joined the others near the door. Reuben sauntered into view, a lopsided, nonchalant grin on his still damp face. Looking up at his father, he controlled his exuberance. "So, Dad, whadja think?"

Morgan stroked his beard slowly, savoring the moment, memorizing the clear blue eyes staring into his. "Well," he drawled, "not too bad for a little kid."

Reuben's mouth opened to protest, but the twinkle in his dad's eyes turned the retort into a clear peal of laughter. He threw his arms around him and was not surprised when Morgan lifted him into the air. The elder Morgensterns watched them, each loving the sight of father and son clinging together.

The Morgenstern house had settled down for the night. Reuben went reluctantly to bed, but sleep quickly overcame the tired boy. Feigie sat in her favorite chair working a crossword while father and son studied each other over a chessboard. Strains of Mozart drifted over the audio system Feigie had finally convinced her husband to buy. Every so often, she would glance up, smile and quietly sigh, pleased to see the two men playing their favorite game so amicably. It hadn't always been like that, and certainly not in recent years. When the hour grew too late for her, Feigie kissed them both good night and went to bed.

Ash watched his mother climb the stairs, noticing how her once brisk pace had slowed considerably. As if he could read his son's mind, Aaron waited until his wife had disappeared before he spoke. "She's getting old, Asher. The doctor says she needs to slow down."

"What else does the doctor say, Dad?"

The old man shrugged. "That if she takes care of herself and takes her medication, she'll live to be a hundred and twenty."

"And you?"

For the first time, Aaron Morgenstern truly smiled. "Me? Reuben keeps me young. I can't afford to grow into an old man with the boy around." He reached over and patted his son's hand. "Besides, there's too much fight left in this aged body to give in now." He looked back at the board and with an even broader smile, moved his queen. "Checkmate."

Asher began to laugh. It was testimony to the other things on his mind which allowed the father to so easily maneuver the son into a corner for in an easy checkmate without even a simple check first. Standing up and stretching, Ash smiled at his father. "Glass of tea, Dad?"

"Are you making?"

"Naturally. You can't boil water."

"Then I accept." Aaron followed his son into the kitchen and sat at his place at the table. He watched Asher move easily about the room, as though he had never left, first filling the kettle, then setting out the appropriate equipment for a proper glass of tea. When the tall, barefooted man took his traditional place at the table, Aaron asked the question he had waited all night to ask. "Why are you here, Asher? You don't show up without a reason and since you were not scheduled to be home until next year some time, I must assume there is a reason."

"There is always a reason, Dad." He retold the story of Jonathan, the role of the *Washington*, and the desert mission. There was no point in being circumspect with his father; the old man would have seen right through him.

"So you are a hero to the Rothkos and you have served your own people as well. This is good, Asher; you have played an important role in the preservation of Eretz Yisroel. You make us very proud; Tovah would have been proud, too."

With pursed lips, Asher nodded. This was the highest of praise from his father, unexpected, but very dear to his heart. "You're right, Tovah would have been pleased."

"So, tell me why this has brought you home. A call, yes, but to come to Boston tells me the mission is not over."

"No," admitted Asher, "the mission is not over. Pana-Di is missing and the admiralty believes he might make an attempt on one of my officers....a lieutenant."

Aaron studied his son's face, noticing the tightness at the mention of that name. "Who is this lieutenant and why would that man be going after him?"

"Her. Lieutenant Krieg is the daughter of Admiral Edward Rothko and Brigadier General Elizabeth Krieg Rothko.....she uses her mother's name. The lieutenant is Jonathan's sister."

"Ah. I see." He paused and weighed carefully his next statement. "And you have feelings for this woman?"

Asher nodded slowly. "Yes."

"Does she have feelings for you?"

"I believe so."

"Where is she now?"

"In Vermont, at her family's cabin. The admiral wanted her out of town, somewhere away from the *Washington*. Their cabin seemed to be the most logical place to stash her for the moment."

"And this why are you here? Are you going to join her?" The questions were not accusatory.

Asher shook his head. "Interpol says we are both on Pana-Di's hit list. I can't run the risk of drawing him to her, but they want me out in the open where we'll be most likely to see him. Boston has a pretty big Jeylosian community and one more Jeylosian on the streets won't be noticed. Tomorrow morning, I have to go to the intelligence sector at Mass Fleet and check in. I will stay here as long as I pose no danger to you, but as soon as he's spotted, I'm outta here. I figure I have about twenty four hours before that happens."

"Can you explain all this to Reuben?" asked Aaron. "He needs to be told something."

"I will tell him as much as I can in the morning. Meanwhile, if anyone... anyone one at all calls or comes here asking for me, you don't know who or what they are talking about. Under no circumstances, should a Jeylosian show up, even speak English." He leaned forward and covered his father's hand with his own. "Pana-Di is a dangerous man. I have taken a risk by coming home, but if you take what I tell you seriously, nothing will happen here."

"Tomorrow morning, we will all wake up early and we will sit down together. You will tell your mother and your son what they must do. Then we will go to shul for morning minyan. There's a pair of *t'fillin* in cabinet."

"I have mine in my bag, Papa."

~

Intelligence at Mass Fleet was ready for Morgan when he showed up. Agents from Interpol were already in place at strategic locations in the city, convinced it was only a matter of hours before the kora would be spotted. Morgan listened carefully as they outlined a plan worked up with the team on the base.

They wanted him to be visible. Henry Sewell from Intelligence had made contact with two Jeylosians on Xinthi-Ang's payroll, both of whom wanted to see Pana-Di shipped back to Jeylos in a box. They were more than happy to cooperate with Interpol and Mass Fleet. A meeting had been arranged for the next day at a cafe where Jeylosians studying at the various colleges hung out drinking *carespa*, the Jeylosian equivalent of coffee. "Wear your khakis, Ash. Let 'em know you're military," suggested Sewell taking in the jeans and sweatshirt the captain currently donned. "Nothing too formal, just your bars and nothing else. No cap."

"How about a flak jacket?" laughed Morgan.

"Nah, nothing that obvious," smirked Sewell, and then added, "but you should wear a body liner under your shirt."

Morgan hiked up his sweatshirt, revealing a thin, silver undershirt. "I'm no stooge, Henry." The others in the room laughed with him. "How will I know my contacts?" he asked when the laughter died down.

"They'll know you. Thamal Hicha-Pa you might recognize. He's the one you met last year in Florida. His buddy, Dimdan Lotari-Nang, is our nomination for alien of the year. He knows more about this planet, I think, than we do," said Henry. "He's made Earth his life work and he is one very popular dude with the Jeylosians in town. At the moment, he's a guest professor at Harvard in interplanetary relations. Very young, very handsome by Jeylosian standards, he's also one of Lady Xinthi-Ang's nephews and totally devoted to her. Rumor has that he wants to succeed Xinthi-Ang as ambassador at large and stands a good shot at it if he catches the eye of the Emperor."

"Why," asked Morgan, "are they on the outs with Pana-Di?"

Henry shrugged his broad shoulders. "Family feud, from what I understand. Lotari-Nang apparently knows about the Krieg business and wants his ounce of flesh for the humiliation of his cousin, the one who was supposed to marry the bastard. He is also Pana-Di's cousin. Apparently, this is a bigger family deal then we realized."

"Yeah, but are they reliable?" Morgan asked.

"Exceptionally."

One of the agents from Interpol slid a folder across the table to the captain. "Here's everything we have on them both. Xinthi-Ang has given them top marks in reliability."

Morgan scanned the dossier. He also recognized Lotari-Nang; they'd met briefly at lecture on negotiation. Dimdan was considered by many to be a whiz kid and was greatly respected by his uncle. "Okay with me," he said when he had finished. "I'm going home for now. As soon as you have something concrete, call me there and I'll move to the base."

Dinner at the Morgensterns was a subdued affair. Reuben had thought of a million questions while at school and asked them one by one as his grandparents listened carefully to the answers. After dinner, Tovah's parents stopped by for a visit, helping to take Asher's mind off the problems at hand. They spoke of various relatives, catching their son-in-law up on the latest family news. As they were leaving, the vidcom unit in the kitchen began beeping. Feigel went to answer it and returned a moment later to summon Asher.

When the Steins had gone, Asher asked his family to sit in the kitchen while he explained what was going to happen next. "Reuben, under no circumstances are you to talk to strangers, especially if they are outworlders," said Asher as calmly as he could. He asked his parents to escort Reuben to and from school for the time being, explaining that he felt there was no reason to take any extra chances. "I have no idea how much he knows about me, or whether or not he knows where I am. But the boys at the base are going to make me highly visible to draw him out and I don't want to run the risk of having Pana-Di show up here." He could see the worry in his mother's eyes despite her effort to keep her face unlined by concern. "This won't take very long, Mom. The kora is sloppy and we'll have him quickly. Just be careful and I will stay in touch."

CHAPTER 27

Tucked into a corner of Cambridge, Jeylasm Cafe was an unassuming little place popular with outworlders of all types, but especially the Jeylosians. Morgan noticed four humans, probably students, sitting at a table near the door. At the counter, Morgan ordered a cup of carespa and a muchna, a thin native pastry sprinkled with a cinnamon like substance imported from Jeylos. As soon as a table became available, he took it, glad its position was to the side, yet in full view of the entrance. His back against the wall, Morgan opened the book he was carrying and appeared to be absorbed in its contents.

Few patrons took notice of the military man sipping carespa, but Morgan knew he was noticed. From the corner of his eye, he watched a pair of Jeylosians lean closer together to talk. When the door opened and a third Jeylosian entered, Morgan caught an exchange of glances between those at the table and the newcomer before the newcomer turned around and left. He wondered who they were, making a mental note of the oddly tailored jacket of the one who left. He had seen clothing like that before, but not on a Jeylosian, and he wracked his brain trying to remember where. The door opened again, and this time Morgan recognized the Jeylosian who entered the cafe. Dimdan Lotari-Nang spotted Morgan and immediately approached him. Before he sat, he signaled the counterman for a cup of carespa. The respectful nod told Morgan that the guy behind the counter knew exactly who Lotari-Nang was.

"Captain Morgan, I presume," said Lotari, extending his hand. "I hope we can be of service to each other as well as to our mutual friends." His English had a distinctively Bostonian accent.

"One can hope, Professor," replied Morgan with a hint of a smile. He liked the man when they met the first time and he had the same feeling now. "Have you any news for me?"

"Dimdan, please. Would that I did," he sighed as he looked about the room. "But, I suspect we soon will." Focusing on Morgan, he spoke softly. "See those two sitting beneath the painting of the Emperor? The one on the left is Pogna Katam-Enog, one of Pana-Di's buddies. He's considered a bit of a hothead at home and the only reason he is studying in the United States is because his parents needed to get him off Jeylos before there was a scandal." Dimdan allowed a sly smile and added, "If you know what I mean."

Morgan chuckled at the universality of indiscretion. "Who's the other one?"

"A man of little breeding and even less sense. Chi Hapa-Lin is a student at B.U., with big dreams and dangerous ideas. Another supporter of the kora, but he has no position at home. Chi likes to think that if the kora takes the throne, he will become high ranking," said the young Jeylosian. "A fool at best, because should the kora ever succeed, he will discard those without connections. He will need every bit of aristocratic clout he can muster, and giving a powerful position to one like Chi will gain him nothing."

Morgan described the Jeylosian who had come and quickly left. "I've seen clothing like that before, that metal band across the chest and silver cuffs. Too fancy for a regular student," said the captain.

Dimdan grimaced. "Right on the money, Captain. He is Jeylosian by birth, but grew up on a Wa'atsi lunar colony. His family has strong ties to the Wa'atsi and your own government would like a reason to deport Hum Rega-Dop. Hum is known to be a negotiator for the Wa'atsi black market." Dimdan stopped talking when the counterman delivered his cup of steaming carespa. Between the cup and the saucer was a napkin which the Jeylosian removed and set of the table. "Ah," he said brightly, "I see we've been spotted. Tikka behind the counter says Hum came in the back and used the vidcom. Successfully, I might add." With a deft motion, Dimdan used the napkin to wipe a spot of spilled carespa and the ink magically disappeared. "If the kora is the heart of their operation, Hum Rega-Dop is the brain."

"What do you suggest I do now?" Morgan felt Dimdan would be the best judge of the next move.

"Our mutual friend, Thamal Hicha-Pa, is across the street, standing in the window of the Friendly Planets Book Emporium. There are many places the kora may be hiding, but we can be certain that he knows you are here with me and, in turn, he believes you will lead him to where his target hides. He did not ask Morgan to identify the quarry, but suspected it was the woman lieutenant his uncle had mentioned in passing. But whomever the target, it did not matter to Dimdan; only the capture of the kora was important. "You must finish your carespa and we shall leave. Together we shall stroll to Harvard Yard where I shall bid you good-day. You shall then go to the Harvard Coop and browse. I am certain you will see Hum Rega-Dop following you. Once you see him on your tail, you will know you are being sought by Pana-Di."

"Then it's only a matter of time before he'll come out into the open," said Morgan, understanding Dimdan's intent. "How can I contact you?"

Dimdan shrugged. "Call my office, I suppose. But most likely we'll contact you should we obtain any further information." He drained the last of his carespa. "Let's go now. I have to teach class in half an hour."

The two men ambled out of the cafe and headed toward Harvard Yard.

The Yard was a place Morgan knew well. He could not count the number of times he wandered around waiting for Tovah. Images of the slender, intense Tovah filled his mind's eye and he could almost feel her presence beside him. He remembered how he would run from class at MIT to meet her here, her eyes shining, her long hair flying behind her as she would hurry toward him. Dimdan's pleasantly accented voice kept a steady stream of information flowing into Morgan's ear and the captain tried his damnedest to pay attention. Students swarmed around the two strollers, passing with intent and speed as they moved between classes. Occasionally one would raise a hand in greeting toward the Jeylosian, and Dimdan would acknowledge, but his deep purple eyes never stopped scanning the crowd.

"Students here are as students everywhere," commented Dimdan drily, "they all know more than their elders and each is certain he.....or she holds the key to universal happiness. It is for this reason I enjoy teaching. I find great personal satisfaction in pushing the infant intellect to its limit."

Morgan smiled; he understood and fully agreed. "How did such a young guy like you get so smart?" he asked with good humor.

The Jeylosian blue blush crept along his smooth cheeks. "Dogged determination, much like yourself, Rabbi Morgenstern." He liked the way the captain's jaw dropped, then snapped neatly shut. "I know a great deal more about you than you might realize, Captain. His Excellency, my uncle, holds you as an example to the rest of us."

"I'm afraid I would disappoint him if he knew the truth," countered Morgan with honest modesty.

Dimdan shook his head. "I beg to differ, Captain. Your career began in one area of expertise, transferred to another, and finally settled into a position which demands a combination of the two. Your scientific knowledge joined with your spirituality has instilled in you a finely honed sense of what is needed combined with what is wanted. Somewhere between the two, one finds a basic truth. A working truth. You, Captain Morgan, strive to achieve that truth, thus you are trusted by many."

"And despised by an equal number." Morgan stopped walking and looked carefully at Dimdan Lotari-Nang. "Don't let the education fool you; ninety percent of what I do relies on gut reaction, not some high blown theory hammered into practice."

Dimdan's laughter caught Morgan off guard. "That, my friend, is the secret of happiness. You know, Captain, when this is over, I would like to spend some serious time with you. I suspect there is a great deal we can learn from each other."

Morgan was pleased with the offer and grinned boyishly. "Tell me, Dimdan, do you like baseball?"

"Like it? I love it! I am a diehard Sox fan."

"Next spring, let's go to a game at Fenway. We can sit in the bleachers and solve the problems of the galaxy while we boo the umpire."

Dimdan shook Morgan's hand vigorously. "You are on, Ash Morgan. I shall look forward to it with great relish."

The Jeylosian decided it was time for Morgan to head over to the Coop. He had kept his eyes open while they walked, but he had not spotted the Jeylosians they had seen at the cafe. They were about to part company when something Morgan heard made his blood freeze in his veins. "Are you all right, Captain?" asked Dimdan.

The captain did not respond, nor did he move.

"Ashi! Ashi!" yelled a clearly female voice from some distance behind him. The voice persisted. "Ashi! Wait up!"

Morgan spun around. A woman with shoulder length dark hair was sprinting toward him, waving frantically with one hand while her other clutched a load of books against her chest, skillfully dodging the foot traffic as she ran. At first sight, Morgan thought he was hallucinating, but then, with a great shout, he opened his arms wide just in time to catch her. The woman squealed, books dropped everywhere and she kissed him loudly on the mouth.

"Ashi, what are you doing here? I mean, my folks said you were in Boston, but what are you doing on campus?"

"Fleet business, Basha." Morgan held the girl at arm's length and gave her the once over. "You look terrific, Basha. I can't believe my eyes." What he didn't say was *I can't believe how much you look like Tovah.*

Dimdan was busy picking up the fallen books, at the same time, trying to figure out what just happened. "I believe you dropped these, miss," he said, handing her the books.

"Thanks, Dr. Lotari. I hope I didn't scare you or anything."

"Do you know each other?" asked Morgan.

"I know Dr. Lotari by reputation, but we've never met." She extended her hand to him. "Hi. I'm Basha Stein, Asher's sister-in-law."

Dimdan looked a little surprised. "I was unaware you are married, Captain."

"Widower. Basha is my late wife's youngest sister."

"I'm a law student," added Basha with a quick grin. "I wanted to take your philosophy of ethical communication, but I got shut out."

This time it was Dimdan who grinned. This sister-in-law was a beautiful young woman and the sparkle in her eye hinted she was quick witted. "Come to my office before the next registration, Ms. Stein, and I will be more than happy to sign your card."

Basha pumped his hand with enthusiasm. "Thank you, Dr. Lotari. This is great."

Dimdan made farewells and promised to be in touch with Morgan through Mass Fleet. As soon as he was gone, Basha turned her bright eyes on Morgan. "So, where are you off to, sailor?" she demanded in a tone he knew so well.

He told her he was going over to the Coop, fabricating a need for a new MIT sweatshirt at the store shared by both august institutions. While he did not want to put her in any danger, Ash easily admitted to himself it was nice to have her along. Tovah had been very close to her sister and if Basha wasn't Tovah, she was the closest thing to hearing his wife's voice come alive once more. "Can you spare a couple of minutes for an old worn out brother-in-law?" he teased. "At least walk with me to the Coop."

Basha laughed, a sound so like Tovah's it sent shivers up Morgan's spine. "Sure thing, Cappy Ash." She slipped her arm through his proffered elbow.

From a safe distance, Hum Rega-Dop watched Morgan with the woman. He did not know who she was, but he judged by the captain's surprise at her appearance, she was someone of importance to him, possibly the woman they sought. When they started to walk, he followed them, taking care not get too close. He motioned to Hapa-Lin and Katam-Enog, to join him. "Chi, find out who she is," he instructed Hapa-Lin, "and you, Pogna, you follow the captain."

At the Coop, the woman separated from Morgan, but not before another embrace. She went on her way and Morgan went into the store. The Jeylosian waited a couple of minutes and then he, too, went into the Coop.

Morgan was standing near the back, browsing through a rack of sweatshirts. He seemed intent on the task, but Katam-Enog was certain he was waiting for someone. When Thamal Hicha-Pa joined him at the rack, Katam-Enog was not surprised at all; Hicha-Pa was the Emperor's lackey and therefore an enemy to Pana-Di. Katam-Enog inched as close as he dared, but it was not close enough to overhear their conversation. Disappointed, he left the Coop.

"Did you see him?" asked Hicha-Pa as soon as Katam-Enog left.

"How could you miss him? He's a terrible spy." Morgan pulled an MIT sweatshirt from the rack and held it up. "For my son," he said when his companion noticed the disparity in size.

Hicha-Pa smiled in understanding. "All parents are the same the galaxy over, Captain. When I was a child, my father always brought me hats from wherever he travelled." He touched the brim of his Red Sox baseball cap. "It is a habit I have yet to break."

They wandered over to the counter where Morgan tried to pay for the sweatshirt with cash. The clerk stared at him. "Don't you have a card?" she asked, not touching the money.

"No, ma'am. Sorry. Can't you make change?"

"I'll have to see." She opened the terminal and took her time deciding whether or not she could break a fifty dollar bill. "If you don't mind singles," she told him. "Nobody uses large bills around here, y'know."

"That'll be fine." He opened his hand and waited while she counted out the change. He took the bag, then turned to Hicha-Pa. "What's next?"

"We shall walk for a time, then we shall part company. If all goes according to plan, I shall know within the hour whether or not we have been successful."

"How will I know?" asked Morgan.

"Go back to Mass Fleet. I shall contact you there."

Chi Hapa-Lin had no trouble following the woman. She was obliviously unaware she was being tailed, and when she finally entered the Law School's library, Hapa-Lin went in after her. The woman stopped to talk to the man behind the desk, then went into the main reading room.

Hapa-Lin stopped at the desk. "Excuse me, but could you tell me if the young lady who spoke to you was Jane from the Law Review?"

The librarian shook his head. "There's no Jane on the Review this year."

"I must have her confused with someone else. Do you happen to know her name?"

"Stein. Batsheva Stein. Everyone calls her Basha. Do you want me to get her?"

"No. That's not necessary. It is the wrong woman." Hapa-Lin left the library, but he did not go far. He wanted to know more about Basha Stein and the only way to find out was talk to her directly.

Mass Fleet was quiet when Morgan arrived. Henry Sewell was sitting in his office with Paul Jeffries, one of the liaison operatives to Interpol. As soon as he saw Morgan, he waved him in and introduced him to Jeffries. "The news is not good, Ash," said Sewell. "General Rothko's aide-de-camp, Harlan Quinn, was found dead under the Arlington Bridge."

"Suicide?"

"Nope; murder. Shot at close range with a laser pistol. The MP's are sure his body was dumped there."

"What does the general say?" asked Morgan.

Jeffries answered the question for Sewell. "The general hasn't said shit. She's too busy trying to determine whether or not there is a leak in her department."

"And whether or not the leak was Quinn," added Sewell with a grimace. "Major Rothko told the general the Arabs knew ahead of his capture that they were looking for him specifically, not just any pilot."

Morgan whistled softly. "Only the general's staff knew for certain it was Jonathan up there."

"Exactly. Which makes her believe her office was compromised." Sewell leaned back in his chair and locked his hands behind his head. "Quinn was not a happy camper, according to the admiral."

"The admiral?" repeated Morgan.

"Admiral Rothko is of the opinion that Quinn had a chip on his shoulder. A very big, very ugly chip. Morgan, you ever hear of a group called *Inworld*?"

"Sure. They're isolationists. Was Quinn part of them?"

Jeffries rolled his eyes. "His father, Avery Jamison Quinn, was a founder. But Harlan doesn't talk to him; he prides, or rather prided, himself on his open-mindedness when it came to aliens. He was so open-minded, it's pretty damn likely he was on the kora's payroll."

Morgan looked confused. "I don't get it. Would someone like to explain all this to me?"

"Sure, Ash. It's really very simple. The kora needed inside information to find an opening on the planet. He found it in the newspapers, or at least enough information to make a few discreet inquiries about the volatility of the situation in the Middle East. Once he had a potential location, he needed someone on the inside to feed him data so when he made his approach, he sounded as if he had obtained this stuff with outworld listening devices."

"So where does Quinn come in?" pushed Morgan.

"They met several years ago when both Quinn and the kora were in London. Quinn made a big deal of showing Pana-Di around, sort of sticking it in his father's face," said Sewell. "The general, if you recall, was representing us at the nuclear disposal talks in London, about the same time, and that was the first time Quinn was attached to her staff. He proved himself to be resourceful, so when an opening occurred at HQ, she recommended Quinn and he jumped at the chance."

"You'd think he'd want to keep his job, not throw it away with his career. But I still don't understand what caused him to defect."

Jeffries round face split with wide smile and he leaned over to pat Morgan on the back. "You've been out in space too long, Captain Morgan. Quinn wanted to be in the center of things, but he did not want to be working for a Jew. Is that simple enough?"

Morgan almost leapt from the chair. "What? That's absurd!"

"Sorry, Ash, but Paul is right," said Sewell quietly. "We like to believe shit like that doesn't happen anymore, but you know as well as I do it does. It was bad enough for Quinn when the general requested him for her aide-de-camp, but it got worse when she became involved with the IDF's training mission. Quinn was vehemently against it, so much so, he railed against her to her face at a staff meeting. The general was furious."

"Why the hell didn't she cut him loose right then-and-there?"

"Because, as the admiral pointed out, as her aide, she thought had control over him. If she cut him loose, as you suggest, he would have been a loose cannon with too goddamn much information. Keep your friends close and your enemies closer. You know that as well as anyone would."

Morgan stood up and gathered his gear. "That's it, then. I'm going up to the cabin. There's every reason to believe if he was on the kora's payroll, the bastard knows where Jane is."

Feigie Morgenstern stood wiping her hands while her son threw some clothes back into his duffle. She had never seen him so rattled; not even when Tovah was dying, when every minute counted, did her son move with such hasty abandon. As if he could read her mind, Morgan stopped and reached for her hand. "I couldn't do anything to keep Tovah from dying, Mom, but I can stop someone from killing Sarah Jane. It's different, Mom, this time I have at least some control."

"I understand, Asher and I pray that you can help this girl." She stood on her toes to kiss his dark bearded cheek. "Go, Asher. I will explain everything to your father and Reuben. They will understand."

"I'll be back as soon as I can, Mom," he said, returning her kiss. Morgan grabbed his bag and flew down the stairs.

CHAPTER 28

Late in the afternoon, Basha Stein emerged from the law library. With her arms full of books, she mentally reviewed her schedule as she walked along a quiet side street, paying little attention to anything around her. So engrossed in her thoughts was Basha that when the tall man bumped into her, she almost fell and it was a pair of seven fingered hands which prevented her from hitting the sidewalk.

"I am so sorry," said the stranger as he righted Basha. "Can you forgive me?"

"My fault. I wasn't paying attention." She looked up at his bluish face and smiled. "Have a good afternoon." Basha started to walk away.

"Wait," he called after her, "may I at least buy you a cup of your coffee to make amends?" The stranger was now walking beside her.

"No, but thanks; I'm in kind of a rush."

"At least allow me to escort you to wherever it is you are going, lest more harm befall you."

Basha stopped walking. "Thanks, but no thanks. Okay?"

"Do you not like outworlders?" he asked

This was getting weird. "Look, I know you're trying to be kind, but I'm already running late and need to get to my next meeting."

Hapa-Lin's narrowed dangerously as he fastened an iron grip around her arm. "I don't think so. I think you will come with me." He pushed the blunt end of a laser pistol into her side.

"Let go of my arm, buster," hissed Basha through clenched teeth. The stranger said nothing as propelled her back up the empty street. She moved with him, but as she did, she glanced down and measured his stride, matching hers to his. Two guys were coming toward them, both wearing jackets, but also the kind of khakis Asher wore. *Uniforms?* thought Basha. She could have sworn the shorter of the two nodded directly at her. The corner was a few feet away and Basha decided if there was any hope of breaking away, it would be when the two strangers were within pushing range.

Hapa-Lin maneuvered her to the left and slowed his pace slightly to let the two strangers pass. Basha counted three more steps, then raised her foot slightly higher than normal and brought it crashing down on the instep of the stranger. He cursed as he stumbled and Basha, using all her weight, hip checked him into the nearest tree. She twisted, but as she turned, new hands reached out and pulled her away from her assailant.

The second man grabbed the alien. There was a struggle and Basha heard the whine of the laser as it fired a single blast. The would-be rescuer struggled to maintain his hold, but he was hit and the alien used his large hands to down his attacker. Instead of grabbing Basha again, the Jeylosian fled. Neither man went after him.

"Are you hurt?" asked Basha, rushing to his side.

"No, ma'am, only a flesh wound." He smiled and held out his arm where the laser had put a crease in his sleeve. "Are *you* all right?"

"Yeah, but...." Basha started to shake. When the shorter man put his arms around her, she did not pull away; instead she let him hold her. She stood that way for a moment then looked up into a red beard and ruddy face. "Who are you.......and who was he?"

"Just think of us as the Lone Ranger and his faithful companion, Tonto," drawled the tall one. He picked up her scattered books and held them out to her. "And he is someone you want to steer clear of."

Basha separated from the red beard and shook her head. "This is just too weird for words." She took the books and started to walk away, then turned back. "Do I know you?" she asked the red beard.

Tapper had seen her at Tovah's funeral. "Would that you did, ma'am."

"Or are you following me because I was with a fleet officer earlier?"

"No, ma'am, but if you were with the captain, he should have arranged some surveillance for you." Tapper realized he might have said too much. "Can we escort you somewhere?"

"Sure," said Basha, certain she'd seen the red beard before. How he knew who she'd been with, was a little unsettling, but somehow seemed okay at the same time. "I live over on Mellen, not far from here." She touched the burn mark on the tall one's sleeve "Maybe you'll let me at least give you a Band-Aid for that cut."

Blackjack and Tapper saw Basha to her door, but did not go in. They assured her there would be no repetition of what happened, while telling her as little as they could. She thanked them again before she ran up the short set of stairs to her door.

"Talk about seeing a ghost, Blackjack," whistled Tapper when she was inside.

"No argument there; she's like a miniature Tovah, complete with gestures. Did you see the way she waved her hand?"

Tapper nodded. "I think I'm in love."

"Don't tell Boston; he'll have a hissy fit." Blackjack laughed all the way back to the rented hovercar they left near Harvard Yard.

"You missed him by an hour," Henry Sewell told them when they arrived at Mass Fleet.

Cardozo let loose a string of expletives. "Did he say where he was going?"

"Up to the cabin in Vermont." He filled them in on the investigation into Quinn's murder. "He's probably right, you know. If Quinn knew where she was, that prince does, too."

Tapper told Sewell about their run-in with Basha Stein. "It was pure dumb luck," he admitted; "if I hadn't taken a double take when she came out the door of the library and gone after her, we would've missed the Jeylosian completely. Pure dumb luck." He asked that surveillance be established in the vicinity of Basha's apartment on Mellen Street.

"No problem. Any idea who it was?" snorted Sewell.

"Tall, blue, seven fingers....young for a Jeylosian," offered Blackjack with a shrug.

"I'm guessing it was Hapa-Lin, one of the local flunkeys. Morgan said he was in the crespa shop where he met Dimdan Lotari. He's an idiot more than anything else, but I'll put a probable cause warrant out for him. You guys going to head up to that cabin?"

"You know how to get there?" Tapper asked Blackjack. "I've been there, but Speed's always driven."

Jackson shrugged, "Sorta. I haven't been up there since I was a kid Take us about a couple of hours to get to Branch Pond, assuming we don't hit traffic on the way out of town?"

"Ay-eh," said Jeffries. I'll call ahead and let the ranger station know you're coming up. Whatever you do, don't bypass the ranger station. That place is a retreat for a bunch of bigwigs and it's armed to the gills."

"What are we waiting for, Tap? Let's go."

All the way to Vermont, the Kora Pana-Di sat in silence, gnashing his teeth. He was angry with Pogna Katam-Enog for ordering the termination of Major Quinn; he was even angrier at Chi Hapa-Lin's clumsy attempt to intercept the woman with Morgan. "Obviously she is not the Rothko daughter, you fool!" he screamed when told about it. "You could have been taken prisoner by those two pigs had they caught you. It is only by the grace of the Tamta that you are not in their hands!"

Hapa-Lin had nothing to say. He hung his head in shame, unsure whether his Kora would allow him to live. But Pana-Di was not about to leave another body around for the authorities to find. Instead, he ordered shamefaced servant to drive him to Bennington.

They reached the outskirts of Bennington by nightfall. Armed with routing from Katam-Enog, Hapa-Lin headed toward the Green Mountains Forest.

By the time Morgan arrived at his contact point, he was tired, edgy and uncommonly nervous. He found the park's ranger station easily enough, but the ranger wasn't there. A note taped to the door directed him further up the road, inside the gated perimeter, to the ranger's house where he was supposed to park himself on the porch until someone got there. As instructed, Morgan used his military ID to open the gate; it closed as soon as he drove between the two posts. At the house, Morgan did as he was told. Parking himself in an ancient rocker on the porch, he stretched his legs while his fingers drummed an endless tattoo on the chair arm. The night air was pungent; the scent of damp autumn and pine, heady, and for a moment, Morgan relaxed enough to savor the smell and the constant clicking of the season's last crickets. Above the canopy of trees, stars were coming out, tiny specks of light which still filled Morgan with a sense of wonder.

Soft crunching on gravel made Morgan jump; he left the comfort of the rocker for the shadows; until he knew who was coming, he was not about to expose himself. He listened closely to the sound; it was not a hovercar or even an old four-wheel vehicle; the steady crunch, crunch, crunch resembled footsteps, heavy footsteps, but it was the unmistakable whinny which caught Morgan off guard. A lone rider on horseback emerged from the woods and only the outline of a ranger hat in the dim moonlight let Morgan breathe easy.

The ranger waved at him. "You Cap'n Morgan?"

"Yes, sir." Morgan stepped off the porch and walked toward the horse. The animal nuzzled his outstretched palm.

The ranger dismounted down with a groan. "I'm getting too old to spend more than a couple of hours in a saddle," he snorted, patting the horse on the face. "She likes you, though; count your blessings, or you'd be counting your fingers. Orphan Annie here is a biter."

Morgan grinned at the touch of the horse's velvety nose against his cheek. "Orphan Annie?"

"Her dam died right after she foaled. She sorta adopted me as her mother."

"Am I gonna have to ride one of these things to get to Branch Pond?"

"Nah, you can drive over there." The ranger walked the horse to the tie rail and threw the reins over the log. "Pete Cabot," he said, extending his hand. "My cousin Ben takes care of the Rothko's place when they're not up there. I think that's why you were sent to me." He walked toward the house, waving Morgan to follow.

Inside, the cabin was rustic but comfortable. Old furnishings made the room cozy, if very old fashioned. Morgan felt considerably better once he heard Cabot was familiar not only with the area, but the family as well. "You may as well relax, Captain, because you won't able to get over to Branch Pond tonight. When you 'tweren't here by nightfall, I turned up electronic surveillance on the road in." He poured two cups of coffee from a pot on an ancient wood-burning stove. "Ted Rothko's hosted some hush-hush meetings up at the cabin in the past, and the surveillance is a little perk from the feds. Ben knows about it and went up to tell Sarah she was locked in for the night. I can keep the wires hot until dawn, but then I gotta shut it down; it's still camping season up here." Cabot caught the flash in Morgan's eye. "Not to worry, Captain; there's a double perimeter up there. One covers the road; there's no other way in on that side. There's a second around the ground of the cabin; Sarah knows enough to keep Spike in tonight. The thing's got a real high pitched sound so the animals tend to stay away, but anything larger than a raccoon crossing the secondary beam will set off the alarm."

"And what happens if the alarm is tripped?" asked Morgan. "Who can get to her and how fast?"

"Anything that trips that beam is dead before it hits the ground. Does that do the trick?"

Morgan was honestly impressed and, at the same time, much relieved. Picking a fat, overstuffed chair, Morgan parked himself, coffee in hand. He watched Cabot go about the business of starting a fire in the stone hearth, and soon the room was filled with the aroma of burning apple wood. A gentle chiming from a dark corner disturbed the rustic tranquility. "I think you're being paged," said Morgan when Cabot made no move to answer the call.

"That's Ben; I was waiting for his call. He's back at his house." Cabot flicked on a light and most incongruously, the height of modern technology appeared, filling the far corner of the room. A highly sophisticated control panel complete with comm unit was built into the log wall. Cabot hit a button and Ben Cabot's face appeared on the screen. "Sarah okay, Ben?"

"Snug as a bug. Did he show?"

"Ay-eh," answered the ranger in typical Yankee fashion, "you didn't go tell her he was coming up, did you?"

"Nope."

"Good. Anything on the road?"

"Nope."

"Good. We'll be up at first light, Ben."

"Good enough, Pete. I'll wait 'til you get here."

"'Night, Ben."

"'Night, Pete." The screen went dark.

"Don't waste a lotta words, do you?" asked Morgan with a grin.

The ranger shrugged. "What's the point? He knows what's what. Besides, the less we talk the better. You never know who's listening. We like to think we're secure, but who knows?"

"You got a secure channel on that unit?"

"Ay-eh, but you're not to call Mass Fleet unless it's an emergency. Their rules."

"How long have you known the Rothkos?" Morgan asked, trying to sound casual.

The ranger shrugged. "Longer than I can remember. Well, the Kriegs, anyway. This is their place. They actually own part of the forest."

"I thought this was federal land."

"It used to be. A long while back, the government decided to sell off land they didn't think was used. Well, the folks up here thought differently. Six families banded together and bought the whole east side of the forest at the auction. That's why there are cabins in there…like the Kriegs' place. The Cabots, the Sewells, the Kriegs, the Sanders, the Tobiases, and the Finkels. Working with the state, they put the land in a trust, leasing it back as protected environment. To do that, each family had to build a house. And that's how the cabins came to be here. The six still own their houses, passed down from one generation to the next. Lizzie's brother is the oldest grandchild, so he's titular head of family but everyone uses the place and calls it home."

"Are you part of the six?"

"Ay-eh. So I've got a vested interest in keeping it going. Ben's the real ranger, I only fill in. I'm really a professor over at the university. Forest management, of course." Pete stood up and stretched. "Hope you don't mind sleeping in a loft; I've got it all set up for you."

"That'll be great. Thanks," Morgan replied, warming up to Pete. He understood why the family trusted him. "Can I still get my gear from the car?"

"Sure. My perimeter extends to the barn." Pete Cabot liked the captain; there was an air of confidence, not cockiness, about him, the same kind of no-nonsense pragmatism he valued in a man. No question about it; this was the kind of man Lizzie would trust. "It's a fine night, Captain. Come on out while I stable Annie and I'll show you around a bit."

It was too good an offer to refuse.

⁂

There was a chain-link fence across the road leading into the area where Branch Pond was marked on the map. The kora jumped out of the car, followed quickly by Pogna Hapa-Lin. At the park ranger's kiosk, they stared at the sign:

ROAD CLOSED. ABSOLUTELY NO ENTRY AFTER DARK. FOR MORE INFORMATION, CALL 711.

Hapa-Lin picked up a handful of sand and tossed it through the chain. When an erratic stream of sparkles fluttered in the darkness, the Jeylosian swore aloud. "We cannot cross, Highness; this is impenetrable."

"Then let us return to Bennington and secure a room for the night. We will deal with this in the morning."

"I thought you said you knew where you were going?" growled Cardozo as they drove further into the Green Mountains.

"You're the one who missed the damn turnoff, Jackson. I told you to take Old Highway 103."

"According to the map, Old Highway 103 is a dirt track."

"You got a better idea?" snapped Tapper as he furiously pushed pads on the hovercar's GPS. Finally a new possible route appeared, redirecting them back forty miles to Route 7. "We'll make Sunderland by ten, if we're lucky."

"Lucky my ass, Joshua Bear. Next time, get a program from someone who knows where they're going."

CHAPTER 29

Spike nuzzled Jane awake, ready to go out. Stretching languidly beneath the thick down comforter, she swatted at Spike's cold, wet nose, but the dog would not be put off. He pushed against her with his paws until his mistress rolled over and opened her eyes. "Okay, okay, I get the message." Jane slid her feet into a pair of sheepskin lined moccasins and wrapped herself in a Hudson Bay blanket retrieved from the chair. It was barely dawn, but she knew the Cabots would be up and moving even at this hour. Thumping her way into the living room, Jane went to the comm-panel and pushed the Cabot's number. Hester, already dressed, with a spoon in her hands, answered the call.

"You can let Spike out, Sarah; perimeter's already been cleared. Just don't go down the road yet."

"Thanks, Hester. See you later." Jane switched off the unit and let Spike out through the glass doors overlooking Branch Pond. Jane stood there for a while, staring at the glassy surface of the water catching the early morning light. The trees along the shore were already ablaze with color, deep ambers, crimson and gold making the forest look as though it was a woman dressed for a night on the town. A flock of geese was gathering in the center of the pond, their honks constant as they called to each other to ready themselves for the next leg of the journey south. Jane watched Spike bound toward the stairs leading down to the waters' edge and wondered at what made him repeat this exact same routine every morning he was at the cabin. At her parents' house in Virginia, Spike had a completely different ritual, yet whenever he arrived at Branch Pond, he followed the same circuitous route around the garden then down to the water. It was hard to tear herself away from the window, but she was cold and wanted coffee. Here, there was no dispenser.

When Spike returned ten minutes later, his bowl was full and his mistress ready to inspect him for any burrs and ticks he might have picked up along the way. The dog sat quietly while Jane ran her hands over his glossy coat, removing the weeds clinging to the long, golden hair. As soon as she was finished, Jane gave him a loud kiss on the top of his head and he returned the favor with a sloppy lick before attacking his food. Jane took her coffee and sat down at the comm-panel and summoned up an electronic newspaper.

The aroma of eggs and bacon caused Morgan to awaken from his deep slumber completely confused. He lay, for a moment, under a pile of woolen blankets and tried to figure out where he was and why he was there. It all came back to him in a rush and he leapt from the bed, knocking over his bag in the process.

"Good morning, Cap'n Morgan," called Cabot from below. "I hope you're hungry."

He was, but the hearty fare being prepared on the stove was anathema to him. "Thanks, but no thanks, Professor Cabot. I need to get up to the cabin as soon as possible." Morgan dressed hurriedly and came down the ladder from the loft with his bag in hand.

"Don't tell me," laughed the ranger, "you eat like Ted and the rest of the clan?"

Morgan grinned sheepishly and nodded. "I'll take a cup of coffee if you have some made," he said.

"Sure. And I can toast you some bread. There's no lard in it. Sit yourself down; Ben hasn't opened the road yet."

At the table, Morgan accepted the offer of toast. The morning air was brisk, even in the house, and the captain pulled a lightweight jacket from the bag at his feet. "You like living up here?" he asked offhandedly.

"If I didn't, I wouldn't. It was easier when my wife was alive and the kids were still home."

"I know what you mean," replied Morgan, gratefully accepting the steaming mug.

"You married?"

"Widower." It seemed he'd been saying that word a lot these days, and he was no more comfortable with it than he was the day after Tovah died.

"Kids?" asked Cabot.

"One. Lives with my parents in Boston."

"Must be hard on him. Mine were grown when Betsy died, but it didn't make it any easier on them.....or me." Cabot sat down opposite Morgan, his plate filled to overflowing with scrambled eggs and bacon. "Ted must think highly of you, if he sent you to keep an eye on Sarah," offered the ranger, changing the subject. "That girl's the apple of her old man's eye."

"I've noticed," replied Morgan drily.

Cabot's chuckle was more like a low rumble. "I hear she goes by Krieg in the service; not like that girl to ride on her pater's coattails. She's an independent one, that Sarah Jane, a little headstrong but smart as a whip. A lot like Lizzie when she was a girl." Morgan's eyebrow shot up; he had never heard anyone call the General *Lizzie* until last night and it seemed strange. Pete caught the look and chuckled. "I've known Lizzie Krieg since she was born, Captain. I'm four years older than the general and for a long time, she was my best buddy. If you think Sarah is stubborn, and I bet you do, Lizzie makes her look flexible."

Morgan couldn't resist asking what they were all like as kids. Although he had seen Jonathan with his parents once, he never had the opportunity to meet the rest of the Rothko clan. He heard enough stories from Jonathan and Tapper, but this was different. "Tell me about them," he asked.

"They're a family like any other, I suppose," started Cabot, "with squabbles and all, but I gotta hand it to Lizzie's granddad Hersch. He was a U.S. Supreme Court justice, y'know. One solid old gent. That old man gave those grandkids kids a rock solid foundation; every one of them is successful, and from what I can see when they're up here, pretty satisfied with life. Lizzie's dad was on the federal bench. Her brother Dan is a physics professor at Yale; he uses the cabin the most. Lizzie's sister Helen is sculptor; she and her family have a place on Cape Cod near the Rothko's beach house, but she comes up at least twice a season. Add to that Justice Krieg's other grandkids and families, and come July Fourth, you can get quite a crowd up at their place. Jonnie and Sarah are the oldest of the cousins and were the organizers of Pond Patrol, aka the Krieg family militia."

Morgan could just imagine his lieutenant commanding an army of kids like herself. She was a natural; that much was evident from the way she handled her staff aboard ship. Finishing up his coffee, Morgan rose and stretched. The sky was already bright blue and as much as he would like to sit with Pete Cabot, it was time to go. "How far is it to the cabin from here?"

"'Bout eight miles in. When you go down the road, you'll pass three smaller roads on your right. Keep going two miles past the last road and you'll see a turn off to the left. Take that and follow it 'til you pass a white clapboard house on the right. That's Ben's place. I'll let him know you're on your way up and he'll lead you down there. It's a twisty road and tough to navigate even in daylight. He'll take you right up to the front door."

Morgan shook the ranger's hand and thanked him for his hospitality. "I can see why the family hangs on to this place, Professor; with friends like you and your cousin Ben, they probably feel safer here than anywhere else."

"We like to think so." Cabot paused thoughtfully for a moment. "It's not exactly regulation, but I think I'm gonna keep the wire on the eastern perimeter live for a while. That way, I'll know who comes in and goes out of this end of the forest."

"Thanks, I'd appreciate that."

The chain across the road was gone when Chi Hapa-Lin drove up to the ranger's kiosk at the entry to the forest. A young woman dressed in uniform khakis and a Smokey Bear hat was sitting inside; she waved him over and slid open her window. "Good morning, sir! How can I help?" she called brightly with a wide smile.

"Is the park open today?" asked Hapa-Lin.

"Yes, sir. I see you don't have a permit sticker on your windshield. Is this your first visit to a National Park?"

"Yes, it is. How do I obtain such a sticker?"

"A day pass costs ten dollars, a yearly pass cost fifty. If you are planning to visit any of the other National Park sites, your best bet is a yearly pass," explained the ranger as she passed Hapa-Lin a packet of park information.

"I shall have a year pass, then," decided the Jeylosian, giving the woman a smile. "I should like to see many parks while I am a visitor in the United States." He handed her a fifty dollar bill, then waited while she affixed the sticker to the window.

"Enjoy your stay!" she called as Hapa-Lin drove down the road. She watched him drive away. When he had disappeared into the canopy of trees, she hit the miniature comm-panel and waited for Pete Cabot to answer. "A Jeylosian just entered the park, Pete. He's alone and heading east toward the big pond."

"Thanks, Mary. Keep me posted."

"Will do, Pete." She entered the communication in her log and sat back to wait.

⊖⊖⊖

On the kora's command, Hapa-Lin had come out to the park alone. He was to drive as far as he could on the far side of Branch Pond to see if the house could be reached without taking the direct route. All the information they had gathered indicated the cabin was quite isolated, but after last night, the kora was certain the woman was being guarded. There were precious few signs along the road, but Hapa-Lin had the map the motel clerk had given him and Branch Pond was clearly labeled. According to the paper map, the east side of the Pond was restricted access, but the west side had public facilities.

Hapa-Lin navigated the miles of thick, dark forest slowly, memorizing each road intersection and route marker. Finally, the road veered to the right and through the thinning trees, he could see the water. He found a small public parking area and left the hovercar. Once on foot, he was able to walk along the sandy edge of the pond. He could see the other side; three buildings which could be houses sat well above the water's edge. Other than a flock of geese floating on the water, the entire area seemed completely deserted and Hapa-Lin wondered if this was indeed the right place after all. Then, something moving on the water caught his eye. It was a lone figure in a canoe, about halfway across, moving at a steady clip. Binoculars to his eyes, he watched for a moment. He did not know what Lieutenant Krieg looked like, but the person in the boat was a dark haired woman.

⊖⊖⊖

The cabin was the most perfect home Morgan had ever laid eyes on. Nestled in a clearing, the rambling log house was tailored to fit into the space. Huge pines flanked the long, wrap-around porch, with endless clumps of lingering tiger lilies in startling orange lining the flagstone paths around the house. Birdsong floated through the trees and there was no other noise. Morgan went up to the door and knocked, softly at first, then louder, but no one answered. He walked around to the back, following the line of lilies that gave way to a hedge of late summer roses.

Ben let Morgan into the house. “She’s out on the lake. You can probably see her through the spyglass on the deck,” he said, pointing to the glass door leading to the deck. “The house is wired; there’s even a telephone for inside the park. There’s a full console in the alcove next to the kitchen, and remotes on scattered around. Make yourself to home. Sarah Jane’ll come up when she gets tired.”

The telescope mounted on the railing beckoned to him; when he pointed it in the direction of the pond, he spotted the canoe gliding on the water. Focusing on the little craft, he watched Jane gracefully plying the paddle. Morgan smiled; she looked so beautiful, so carefree as she propelled the canoe toward the center of the pond.

Inside the cabin, Morgan felt like an intruder, but he made no move to leave. Like Cabot’s lodge, this one was rustic and old fashioned. Bentwood furniture with plump, plaid cushions created a space in which people could sit and talk to each other comfortably, a three-sided square with the fourth side dominated by a wide, fieldstone fireplace. Books and magazines on every conceivable topic were scattered on tables strategically placed for maximum ease of reach. The walls were decorated with pairs snowshoes and skis, poles canoe paddles and fishing rods. Upon closer examination, Morgan realized every piece of equipment was well used. He wandered into the kitchen, a much more modern affair, and he spied an empty mug sitting beside a coffee machine, the carafe still warm and half-filled. On the counter beside that was an open docupad. Morgan glanced at the screen and grinned; it was a section of ciphering code. Morgan helped himself to a mug from the hook above the coffee machine and filled it with the strong brew. It tasted bitter, but good, just the way he liked it.

Back in the living room, Morgan continued meandering. He looked at the collection of music discs stacked neatly beside the audio system, then at the framed collection of photographs lining the shelves nearby. Some of them were quite old, others more recent, but it was obvious they were in chronological order, all taken at the cabin. Some were large groups of people in summer clothes, with tan, happy faces, others were of individuals buried beneath winter gear, skis and skates in hand. Apparently the admiral and the general were married at the cabin, for there was a very young, very handsome couple in wedding clothes standing on the deck overlooking the pond. Morgan was unexpectedly touched by the picture; it was a side of the admiral and the general he had never considered. Close to the wedding picture was a wonderful shot of the admiral sitting with a skinny little girl, long pigtails tumbling down, her face turned adoringly up to her father. Jonathan was standing beside his father, his elbow resting on a broad shoulder. There was such a strong resemblance between parent and children that it surprised Morgan for a reason he could not fathom.

Soft chiming from the comm-panel's screen-less extension invaded Morgan's reveries and he automa*ticall*y answered with a simple "Hello." He noticed the little red light flashing, indicating the call was coming in on a secure channel.

"Who the hell is this?" bellowed a man's voice.

"Since you called, why don't you tell me who you are first," Morgan replied.

"Is that you. Morgan?"

The captain swallowed a laugh. "Good morning, Admiral. How are you today?"

"What the hell are you doing in my house at this ungodly hour of the morning, Captain?"

This time, Morgan laughed out loud. "I just got here. Ben let me in. Your lieutenant is out on the pond; she doesn't even know I'm here."

There was a "harrumph," followed by calmer conversation. "You spent the night at Pete's, I take it?"

"Yes, sir."

"And everything was quiet?"

"As quiet as the woods."

"Three Jeylosians were seen in Bennington last night. Based on the descriptions, it sounds like the kora and two of his buddies."

Morgan felt peculiarly relieved; at least they knew where the bastard was for the moment. "Well, I guess the fun's about to begin."

"Yeah, I think so. Jackson and Tapper are in the vicinity; they should be making contact with you sometime this morning." He told him about their encounter with Basha Stein. "Do you want anyone else?"

"No," answered Morgan after thinking about it for a moment. "I fewer the better, I think. When he gets here, what do you want me to do with him?"

"If he's manageable, bring him to Washington." The admiral paused. "If he's not, do what you have to do to make him manageable."

Morgan was glad the admiral could not see his eyebrow shoot upward. Rarely did the admiral issue a shoot to kill order, but in this case, he almost expected it. In any event, Ambassador Xinthi-Ang had said the same thing. "I understand, sir," said Morgan simply.

"Good...and Captain, this is Sarah Jane's father talking: try to keep my daughter out of harm's way. I know that makes it sound as if I think she's inept, but she's not. She is a damn fine officer and I don't want to lose her."

Standing in this man's home, looking at his personal possessions, and fully understanding that this was a parent talking, Morgan glimpsed Rothko in a different light. He wasn't about to tell his boss he was falling in love with the boss's daughter, but he suspected the admiral might already know. "She'll be just fine."

"Call me when it's over. The general and I will be waiting."

Morgan disconnected and took his coffee outside. Jane was still on the pond, but she was closer to shore now. Through the telescope, he saw something swimming near the canoe. Morgan felt for his sidearm but stopped when he realized it was the dog. Settling into a weathered Adirondack chair, Morgan leaned back and enjoyed the calm before the storm.

~

The kora's arrival at Green Mountains National Forest did not go unnoticed. The pleasant young ranger in the kiosk welcomed the visitor, then called Pete Cabot with her report. "Same car, different outworlder," she told him.

Cabot saddled up his horse, but this time he slipped his laser gun into his holster and a trouble-pack into the saddlebag. Usually, the ranger carried an open channel pager, but he replaced it with a mini-scrambler. Before taking off, he checked the perimeter controls one last time, satisfied with leaving the wire on alert. Any movement in the park would be spotted and recorded through the sensor monitors, giving them a hard record of the Jeylosians' progress. Hoisting himself onto Annie's back, Cabot trotted off toward the western shore of Branch Pond.

He found the abandoned hovercar parked in the visitor's lot closest to the pond. Cabot relayed the license number to the police in Bennington and asked them to find out if the number was registered at a hotel. "If you come up with a winner, post surveillance, Roy," he told the chief of police, "but don't do anything until you get the word from me or someone higher up the food chain."

"Will do, Pete. Keep us posted."

Cabot directed Annie toward the beach. There were few footprints in the soft sand, but his tracking experience told Cabot the most recent prints were heading north. "Damn," swore the ranger. That route around the pond was the most difficult to follow on horseback, but rather than leave Annie tied to a tree, he decided to see how far he could take her.

Spike came bounding up the stairs but slid to a halt when he saw someone sitting on the deck. Baring fangs, he growled menacingly at the stranger in the chair. Morgan knew enough not to make any sudden movement; the knotting of Spike's muscles warned any motion at all would cause the dog to attack.

From below, Jane heard her protector's growl and set her laser on stun. She crept up the stairs, prepared to take out whomever or whatever had Spike on full alert. When she saw the captain sitting stock still, she flicked off the gun and called to the dog. "Sit, Spike!" The dog's rear end barely touched the wood of the deck, but his fangs remained exposed. Leaning casually against the railing, she let Morgan sweat.

The sight of Jane in shorts, a sweatshirt tied over her shoulders covering the top of her bathing suit, her long hair hanging free beneath a camp hat, was enough to send Morgan careening toward the edge of reason.

"What the hell are you doing in my house?" demanded Jane.

"Good morning, Lieutenant. Can I move?"

"No. What the hell are you doing in my house?"

"Your father had pretty much the same reaction when I answered the com," grinned Morgan.

"What the hell were you doing answering my com?"

"It beeped; I answered. Sorry."

Jane let a long sigh escape. "Why are you here, Captain?"

"Because Pana-Di is somewhere in this park."

"Oh. That's not good." Jane went to the dog and stroked the golden fur. "He's all right, Spike," she said softly into his ear. The dog stood up and padded over to Morgan, his nose ready to sniff the stranger. Convinced the human in the chair was friend, Spike shook out his long coat, spraying the captain with pond water. Jane, leaning against the rail again, grinned when Morgan raised his hands to ward off the shower. "That's enough, Spike. Go lay down." With a final snort, Spike trotted over to another chair, pulled the cushion off with his teeth and curled up on it.

"Great dog you've got there."

"Yeah, well, he's all mine. If I didn't call him off, he'd have gone for your throat."

Morgan knew she wasn't kidding. Now that Spike was settled, he dared to get out of the chair. He joined Jane at the railing and looked out over the silver blue water now sparkling in the early morning sun. "It's hard to imagine there is real danger hiding somewhere out there." He gently placed his arm around her shoulder and was relieved when she did not move away.

When Jane spoke, her voice was soft as the breeze rustling the trees nearby. "I've always felt safe up here. When I was little, this was the place we would come as soon as we returned planetside. My grandparents would always be here to welcome us home, my cousins would help us get back into real life. You have to understand, we were different. Still are, I guess. They all had…still have… very normal lives in very normal places while my family was zooming around the galaxy. Before she was a general, Mom used to organize training programs for populations just emerging into interplanetary trade. If we were lucky, she and dad were sent to the same place. That's how I knew all those women on Amitides; we lived there. And on Jeylos for six months and even on Kotuchar. All those places are more than names to me, they are places I went to school, made friends, spoke the language. I learned to move in and adjust fast, otherwise it was very lonely." She paused and looked up into his eyes. "So this place is different. When I come here, I come home, more so than the house in Virginia. This place is constant; it never changes. I don't want the kora to come here, because it might change how I feel about being here. Can you understand?"

"I wish I could tell you he won't come here, but it's too late. Quinn was the leak, and we're pretty sure he told the kora exactly where you are. Quinn is dead, but Pana-Di is somewhere out in those woods and unless we have a master stroke of luck, he'll find us before we find him." As if on cue, Morgan's pager buzzed in his pocket. "Morgan here."

"Captain, this is Pete Cabot. I'm on horseback across the pond from you, heading north. I don't think you can see me, but I see you both standing on the deck. Sarah Jane?"

"I'm here, Pete."

"I'm setting the outer ring perimeter on monitor. Can you keep Spike up top?"

"Sure thing, Pete."

"I've got the residential roads closed. But your stalker seems to be making his way around the pond on foot, so he's gonna be hard to follow.

I'll check in with you every half hour on the quarter hour. If you need me, use channel 2A."

"Will do, Pete. And thanks."

"Call you in a half."

Morgan took the pager from Jane and slipped it back in his pocket. "How long would it take to come around that side of the pond on foot?"

"About an hour, give or take a little. We've got time. Wanna eat something?"

"He meant well. He didn't know you."

She started into the house, but Morgan reached out and took her arm. He drew her to him and as he did, he tilted her face up to meet his. When he kissed her, it was slow and lingering. He savored the sweetness of her mouth against his; he did not want to let her go.

His kiss was sweeter than anything Jane could imagine. She felt herself melting into him, as though he would completely consume her. Any resistance was gone, in its place only the burning need to be part of him. "I thought you were hungry," she whispered, catching her breath.

"I'm hungry for you." His lips trailed upward to her ear. "I want you. I want you now and forever."

"Oh, God, Asher, you don't know what you're saying," groaned Jane.

He continued whisper into her ear. "I do. I know exactly what I'm saying, what I'm doing, what I'm feeling. I'll go slow, I'll be patient, but let me love you." His voice was ragged, reaching into the very essence of her core. "Let me give you what I have refused to give anyone else in so very long."

Jane placed her hand over his heart; she could feel the steady rhythm. "Then give me time, Asher. If this is to be, if it's to last, you have to give me time to get used to it. I never bargained for falling for anyone, much less my C.O." This time, she kissed him.

When they separated, Morgan gazed into her deep, grey eyes. "And I never bargained for falling for a lieutenant. We'll take it one day at a time." He brushed a stray lock of hair from her forehead. "Will you feed me anyway?"

Jane, in that moment, fell in love with the twinkle in his eyes, that spark that had been missing these past weeks. "Yes, Captain, I'll feed you. After you taste my cooking, though, you'll change your mind."

It was past nine before Tapper and Cardozo found their way to police headquarters in Bennington. They were tired after having spent the night wandering around Vermont until exhaustion overtook them both and they found a motel willing to admit two scruffy strangers at four in the morning. After a couple hours sleep and some strong coffee, they were on the road again, this time with accurate directions. Chief of Police, Roy Aitkin, was less than willing to believe they were from Fleet Headquarters and he made them cool their heels on a hard wooden bench while he ran a check on their credentials. Finally he emerged from his office, handed them their identification cards, and asked them to come on inside.

"You man is in the park," said Aitkin. "So's your captain. According to the ranger on duty, he's up at the Kriegs' cabin now."

"How far are we?" Cardozo shot Tapper a black look.

"'Bout fifty miles give or take, but it's fast this time of year. Not many tourists, so there's not much traffic into the park."

"Can you give us exact directions?" asked Cardozo.

"Sure thing." He took a piece of paper and carefully wrote out the necessary information. "When you get to the park, you'll see a sign, then a road off to the right. Don't try goin' up that road. The perimeter's monitored and I don't know how hot Pete Cabot's got it set. It'll be blocked off, so don't go gettin' any ideas. Go through the main gate. I'll call ahead to Mary and she'll let you on through and tell you how to get up to the cabin."

Back in the car, Tapper entered the new location into the GPS. Unlike the last set, Aitkin's version of how to get to the park was heavy on the plat designations rather than *a couple o'miles.*

"If there was something going on up there, he would've told us," announced Tapper to Jackson as they headed toward the freeway.

"Let's just hope if there was something going on, he would know about it. I'll feel better once we're there."

⁂

The kora became aware of someone following him when he stopped to rest at an abandoned camp site. Secreting himself in thick brush away from the shoreline, he listened as the footsteps came closer. At first, the rhythm threw him, but after concentrating on the sound, he decided it was one horse. He waited for what seemed like an hour, but eventually the horse and rider came into view. He could hear the rider speaking to the animal, a habit he thought peculiar to humans and one he did not completely understand. Fairly certain he left minimal tracks once he left the soft sand, he was glad he had taken the hard mud track. The rider stopped no more than twenty yards from where he was hidden.

"Just checkin' in," he said into the air. The kora could not make out the reply obviously coming from a pager. "I'm now heading east along the shore, about three miles from you. I'll keep you posted."

The kora smiled coldly as he watched the rider dismount. He knew from the hat that the man was a ranger; by the way he scouted along close to the ground, the Jeylosian recognized an able tracker. Sliding his laser gun from his pocket, the kora prepared to fire.

"Did you go home?" Jane mopped up the last of her fried egg with a piece of bread.

The question surprised Morgan; he wasn't used to being asked about his personal life. Immediately, he chided for the reaction. He had just declared his love for this woman and of course she would ask questions. It had been so long since anyone had bothered; there was no denying it felt good. "My mother was thrilled to have me under her roof," He faltered, not knowing quite what to say next.

"And Reuben must've been equally happy." She watched the smile grow beneath the thick, dark beard.

"I see my son so infrequently that I'm always amazed at how fast he grows. He's almost to my shoulder," said Morgan with undeniable pride, "and strong. He's a good athlete."

"Probably smart as a whip, too," added Jane with a grin. "Does he look like you, Asher?"

He liked the way she said his name; it was a soft sound and he wished she's use it more often. "Yes and no. He's got her...Tovah's eyes." He paused; it felt strange to speak that name, but he made himself continue. "When he's concentrating, his eyebrows knit up the same way hers did. You'll like Reuben; he's a good kid."

Jane reached across the table; she put her hand over his. "I'd like to meet him." Morgan didn't say anything but the distinctive pink creeping up over the edges of his beard spoke volumes. "Come on, let's clean this place up."

They worked in tandem. Morgan cleared while Jane washed the few dishes by hand. Their banter was light, mostly about the ship and its crew, but most importantly, it was comfortable. They were fresh in the newness of this relationship and each tested the other. She splashed him with water when he snapped a towel at her derriere, and when he held her wet palm to his lips, she stroked his cheek with her other hand.

"What time is it?" Jane asked lightly as she put away the last of the dishes.

"Twenty after ten."

"Pete's late."

Jane didn't have to say it for Morgan to be acutely aware the ranger had not checked in. Going out onto the deck, Morgan trained the telescope on the area in which Cabot should be riding. He saw nothing but shoreline and trees, no movement other than leaves moving in the breeze. He didn't like the silence; it was eerie and it was making him uncommonly edgy. Morgan pushed 2A on his pager and waited for a response. Nothing came back to him. He hit the numbers again, and again, there was nothing. Unwilling to worry Jane, Morgan whistled to the dog. "I'm going to walk down to the water," called Morgan. "Go inside and set the house alarm."

"I'm coming with you," answered Jane, grabbing her sweatshirt.

"Forget it, Lieutenant. Stay here. That's an order."

Jane frowned, and threw her sweatshirt on the chair. "Go down then stay on the flagstones or you'll trip the perimeter. She followed him outside and watched as Spike followed Morgan down the stairs.

⁂

She stayed outside until they disappeared into the trees and then some. A cold, creeping dread permeated her bones until Jane finally turned back to the house. Carefully, she slid the locking bolt into the doorframe. Inside, it was quiet, too quiet for comfort. Slipping the sweatshirt over her head, she went over to the com panel and started enter the code for the house alarm.

"There is no need to do that," said an all too familiar voice from the hallway leading to the bedrooms.

Jane froze, her back to the intruder. "If you value your life, get out of my house," she hissed.

The kora crossed the distance between them and spun Jane around. His fingers gripped her arms until she squirmed. "Does my touch please you so that you tremble with anticipation, Lieutenant?" The kora laughed harshly when she said nothing. "Where is the demur Lieutenant Krieg ordered to see to my every whim? Have you changed so much, Rothko's daughter?"

"We are not aboard the *Washington*, we are in the house of my father, the ally of your father Ampat-Di, his Supreme Majesty, Kaila of Jeylos. Leave now, and I will keep my silence."

The kora's thin lips twisted into an ugly line. "Can your silence be bought so cheaply? I think not. I think you would prefer to see me swimming in my own blood, Sarah Jane Rothko." Shifting, he pinned her against the desk and with one hand, ripped her sweatshirt down the middle. With one finger, he traced the rise of her breasts, laughing cruelly when she tried to squirm away. "I will enjoy you before I decide whether or not to kill you, Lieutenant."

"I'm not alone here," said Jane through clenched teeth.

"Of course you are. There is one hovercar parked outside. I have taken care of the ranger, so I doubt there is anyone here who could hear your protests."

Jane realized it must have been Morgan's car he saw; hers was in the tucked inside the little shed on the side of the house. She decided he had to have lasered the side door, judging from where he was when she came back in from the deck. On one hand, this provided the advantage of surprise when the captain returned, but on the other, she was trapped if Morgan wandered too far in search of Pete. Letting herself sag just a little, Jane sighed aloud as she looked down. "Your graciousness humbles me," she murmured submissively.

"That's better," said the Kora, loosening his iron grip slightly. "Look at me, daughter of Rothko, and think of what it will be like when we arrive triumphant on Jeylos."

He's crazier than I thought raced through Jane's mind. She let him raise her chin until her eyes met his. "I will be as you will make me, Kora Kaila."

"I will be more than Kora Kaila when we return to Jeylos, I will be Kaila Pana-Di. And you, little lieutenant, will be my first concubine. Produce an heir, and you will be Sarah-Di."

"I am humbled by your graciousness," repeated Jane, looking away.

This angered him. "Is that all you can say? I offer you honor beyond your wildest imagination and you talk like a parrot! There is no woman alive on Jeylos who would refuse me in this!" The crack of his hand against her cheek resounded through the silent room. Had he not held her arm, Jane would have fallen; instead, her head hit the shelf behind her. Pictures tumbled; shattered glass flew in all directions. Jane cried out but quickly stifled the sound; she would not allow him the pleasure of her pain. His hand came up again, but this time, she was ready for him. Wrenching her arm, she ducked as his fist made contact with the shelf. The kora only laughed as he jerked her up, a puppet on a tight string. "You will learn quickly, woman, or you will learn the excesses of pain!" He hit her again, leaving seven fingers imprinted on her face.

Stars danced before Jane's eyes. She tried to shake them off, but the pain was intense. She grit her teeth as she righted herself; his vise-like grip was cutting off the circulation in her arm and it throbbed as much as her head. Grasping the edge of the desk with her one available hand, Jane steadied herself in preparation for the next, inevitable attack. The words *the desk!* flashed in her brain; surreptitiously she moved her fingers to test the drawer. It was unlocked and she knew what lay inside.

The kora yanked at the strap of Jane's bathing suit. A deep, rumbling laugh shamed his victim, turning her beet red as he glared at the breasts now exposed to his glassy stare. He pinched an upturned nipple gently at first, then with increasing pressure. Jane clenched her jaw shut as bile rose in her throat. "I am more than ready to plow your field," he growled into her ear. Jane did not answer and the kora pulled back. "What? No appropriate response? Say it, woman," he shouted. "Say it now!"

She knew the ways of Jeylos well enough to know that if she answered, she will have agreed to bear his child. Through the fog of pain, her mind screamed *No!* while her lips remained tightly sealed. Jane saw the enormous hand draw back; she winced in anticipation of the next blow.

CHAPTER 30

A wrought iron chair sailed through the plate glass of the sliding door air, followed by Spike, his fangs bared. "Release her!" shouted Morgan as he charged through what was left of the door. The dog went right for the kora as he tossed Jane aside like a rag doll and she landed with the thud behind the desk. Spike's teeth ripped into Pana-Di's arm, but the kora managed to hurl Spike across the room. Morgan fired his laser missing Pana-Di as he dove behind the desk. He came up with Jane plastered hard against his chest, his laser pressed to her temple. "To kill me is to kill her, Captain."

From the corner of her eye, Jane saw Spike crawling along the floor. She waited until he was in springing range, then lifted her foot and brought it hard down on the kora's instep. He shrieked in pain, releasing her, and Jane spun around, at the same time jerking up her knee right into his groin. As Spike launched his attack, she ducked. The dog's jaws clamped around the kora's arm, but once again, he pulled the snarling animal off and tossed him aside. In the confusion, Morgan charged the kora and knocked him down.

Jane watched the struggle from the floor. The Jeylosian's strength was no match for Morgan no matter how powerful a man he was. Her head throbbed, her arms ached, but she could not just stand there. Crawling toward the desk, she grasped the drawer handle and slid it open. Even without looking she knew exactly where to find the gun. Her fingers closed over the pearl handle. Jane pulled herself up to sitting, checked the chamber, and unlatched the safety.

Morgan wrestled with the kora using every ounce of strength he could to keep the outworlder at bay. The seven fingered hands clawed at his face, neck and chest until blood ran. The Jeylosian, using the slippery blood to his advantage, twisted his body and flipped Morgan. His fist came toward the captain, but with a jerk of his head, Morgan avoided the blow. Pana-Di rose up on his knees with a shout, one hand around Morgan's throat, the other drawn back.

"Stop!" ordered Jane, the ancient revolver aimed directly at Pana-Di's head.

The kora's lips spread into a thin, ugly smile and he laughed. "I will kill you both," he growled and his fist moved toward Morgan's face.

There was a pop and the kora looked up at Jane before he pitched forward, greyish blue brain matter oozing from the hole in the middle of his forehead.

Jane clutched the desk, the gun smoking in her hand. She saw Morgan stand, his face and clothing red with his own blood, his eyes wide. "Are you okay?" she croaked at him.

"Are you?"

"Where's Spike?"

"He's over there." Morgan pointed to the corner where the dog was shakily coming to his feet.

Jane felt her head starting to swim. "Is he dead?" she managed to whisper. Morgan nodded. "Good."

"Are you sure you're all right?" asked Morgan again.

"I think so; but you're bleeding."

"I know."

There was a furious pounding at the front door. Spike started barking as he limped toward the offending noise. There was a resounding crash as the doorframe gave way. The door alarm shrieked. Into the room ran Blackjack and Tapper, lasers drawn.

"Holy shit!" shouted Blackjack as he skidded to a halt. His arm shot out, catching Tapper as the burly man charged in.

"Oh, my God," muttered Jane, "you broke Grandpa's door!"

The three men watched the lieutenant crumple.

While Tapper cleaned up, Morgan carried Jane, passed out cold, into the bedroom and deposited her gently on the large bed. He covered her with an afghan then leaned over and kissed her softly on the forehead before he checked her eyes; the pupils were neither fixed nor dilated.

She grumbled when he put a cool cloth on her head. "I should get up."

"Stay here and just breathe," said Morgan as he checked her pulse. In the bathroom, the captain found a med kit and took it back to Jane, along with a glass of water. Propping her up, he gave her a couple of aspirin before he let her lay against the pillows. "Tapper and Blackjack are sweeping up the mess. I'll let you know when whoever is coming gets here."

"Whoever?"

"We don't know yet. Mass Fleet is taking over."

"The kora?"

"Still dead."

"Will they arrest me?"

Morgan shook his head. "No, on a bunch of levels."

"I feel awful."

"I know it sounds lame, but try to sleep. I really don't want you in the living room right now."

"My folks."

"I'll call them. You can talk to them later. Okay?"

Jane sighed. "Yeah. I think I'll just lie here for a while."

"We found the ranger," Cardozo told Morgan when he came out of the bedroom. "He's pretty badly burned; they took him to Southwest Regional Hospital."

"They?"

"Yeah, they. When we got here, the ranger at the gate told us there was a single outlander in the park. We asked for and got back up from their station. We found the horse first, then Cabot. Pana-Di lasered the guy, but the ranger was wearing a deflector. He took it hard; enough to knock him off his horse, but not kill him. Said his shoulder hurt."

Tapper took the med kit form Morgan's hands and dragged the captain into the kitchen. As gently as he could, Tapper pulled the glass encrusted shirt off his friend and began tending to the wounds on his chest and face. "It's amazing you didn't cut S.J. to shreds with that shirt, Boston," he said drily.

Morgan winced as Tapper cleaned a deep gash on his shoulder. "That guy has nails like a hooker."

"Had, Boston, had. S.J. did a nice job putting him out of commission. Is she okay in there?"

"Yeah. She knows what's going on. Someone better call Rothkos." Cardozo shrugged and went over to the com to place the call.

The kora was pronounced dead by the attending EMT, and the body was carried out by the coroner's deputies. The EMT woke Jane long enough for a check of vital signs and a quick triage exam, and pronounced her well enough to let sleep, but elicited a promise from the Captain that he would bring her to the hospital in the morning. Two confused members of the Bennington Police Department wanted to arrest someone on the spot despite orders from Mass Fleet to arrest no one. Only when the admiral appeared on the com did they finally agree to go back to headquarters where they would meet up with Mass Fleet. Ambassador Xinthi-Ang was already en route to Vermont and it took all of Morgan's persuasive powers to convince the general that her presence was not needed at the cabin. "She'll be fine, General," repeated Morgan for the fifth time. "Let me do my job so she doesn't feel like you're hovering."

The admiral concurred and the mother was finally convinced. "Blackjack and Tapper are doing what they can with the door now; as soon as they're done, they'll be headed out."

"What about you, Morgan?" asked Admiral Rothko.

"I don't know, boss," he grimaced, "why don't you tell me?"

Rothko laughed for the first time in days. "I think a couple days off are in order, Captain. Jane can stay at the cabin if she wants, or she can go to the beach house on Cape Cod. Jackson can take her; he's been there often enough. Report back to the *Washington* with the lieutenant on Sunday night. You can ship out first thing Monday morning and head back to Kotuchar. You still have a schedule to maintain. Besides this'll give Tapper a chance to play with the changes to the reactor."

"Thanks, Ted!" shouted Tapper from across the room. "And don't worry about Grandpa Hersh's door. Me and Blackjack have it under control."

Liz's face appeared beside her husband's on the screen. "Why don't I trust those two, Ted?"

"It's not us you have to worry about," Cardozo tossed in, "it's the Bostoner Rebbe."

The Rothkos looked at each other, then at Morgan as he raised his right hand solemnly. "An officer and a gentleman," he intoned.

"That's it; I'm going up there, Liz."

The general patted the admiral's cheek. "Leave them alone, Edward; I trust him."

"One single hint of impropriety, Morgan, and I'll have your head on a pike," said Admiral Rothko although the twinkle in his eyes belied the seriousness of his words.

"Not me, sir. I'm very honorable."

"Uh-huh. I'll bet. I'll just send Jonathan after you."

"That's enough, Father Rothko," Liz teased. She looked directly into the screen at Morgan. "He's much better as an admiral, you know."

"I'm beginning to find out," countered Morgan with a grin of his own.

In the shed, Cardozo found a plank of plywood big enough to temporarily cover the door on the deck. He and Tapper hammered it into place and while it was ugly, it would serve until a glazier could be summoned to repair the damage. They cannibalized an old doorframe they found in the shed to fix Hersch Krieg's prized oak door well enough to be back in service, squeaky but lockable.

Morgan found a broom and swept up the last of the broken glass. As best he could, he replaced the fallen frames on the shelf over the desk. Those, too, would require some repair before they were right again.

"You'll make some lucky woman a great wife, Boston," drawled Cardozo when he came in from the deck. Morgan growled, but kept on cleaning. Blackjack went on. "Ah am just mighty sorry little ol' S.J. isn't awake to see this. Ah think she'd be duly impressed."

"Knock it off, Blackjack," yelled Tapper from outside. "Boston's had enough for one day."

Tossing the last collection of glass shards into the trash, Morgan stowed the dustpan and broom in the closet. "Don't you guys have someplace to go?"

"Y'all don't want us around, do ya, Boston?" laughed the southerner.

"Not in the least."

"And Ah'm guessin' you don't want me drivin' S.J. to the beach house."

"I am going to ask her to come to my folks for Shabbat. If she declines, I'll take her to Cape Cod."

Tapper raised an eyebrow. "Come on, Blackjack, let's go find ourselves some fun." Tapper slapped Morgan on the back. "See ya 'round, Boston."

"Just be back on board ship Sunday night by dinner. Staff meeting at eighteen hundred hours," replied the captain. "Now, shove off."

Blackjack and Tapper strolled out the door.

Morgan checked on Jane several times, convinced she was sleeping and not in any danger. Spike was curled up beside her, and Morgan was not about to move him. Between checks, he made calls to his parents and to Senator Collins. The senator had already been briefed on the events in Vermont, and she filled him in on her discussion with Admiral P'nucha. "How do you feel about hosting a small dinner party on the ship Sunday night?"

Morgan admitted he wasn't thrilled, but understood the need. "Contact Commander Lucas and have her set it up. You can tell her what you're thinking and just say I'm okay with whatever it is." They went over some of the details and Morgan promised he would extend an invitation to Ambassador and Lady Xinthi-Ang as well as the Rothkos when he spoke with them later in the day.

Ambassador Xinthi-Ang called as soon as he arrived in Bennington; Morgan reviewed the events of the afternoon with the ambassador, a representative from Interpol, and the local police via the com. It was mutually decided that other than a brief announcement to the press that the Kora Pana-Di died in an unfortunate boating accident while fishing on Branch Pond, no further investigation would take place.

"I would speak with Lieutenant Krieg when she is able," said the ambassador. "His Imperial Majesty would have me deliver a message of a most personal nature, Captain."

"I understand, Your Excellency, but I'm afraid the lieutenant is out of commission for the moment. Would you and Lady Xinthi-Ang be able to join us for dinner Sunday evening aboard the *Washington*?"

Ambassador Xinthi-Ang nodded gravely. "I accept on behalf of my lady and myself."

Their business concluded for the moment, Morgan called down to the Rothkos. Told they were at the hospital with Jonathan, he left a message asking them to join the dinner party Sunday night.

Left to his own devices, Morgan found something to eat in the kitchen. He wandered about the cabin for a while, pulled a biography of Maimonides from the shelf, and tried to read. He kept thinking he heard noises, so finally, in an attempt to quiet his own still jangled nerves, he went into the bedroom. Jane was curled up on the bed beneath the afghan, her breathing steady. Spike had already moved to his own bed in the corner. Switching on the nightstand reading lamp, the captain stretched out beside her. Morgan wanted very much to hold her in his arms, but sharp pang of guilt sliced into him; when she needed him, he was not there, just as on the ship. Then, too, he arrived too late to prevent the kora from violating her person. If, when she awoke, she was angry with him, if she asked for a transfer to another vessel, he would understand. Silently, he berated himself for running off into the woods in search of the ranger when he should have stayed at the house. Jane stirred and Morgan was almost afraid her eyes would open and she find him staring at her. But stare he did at her pale skin, the way her lashes rested dark against her cheek. He knew well the color of those stormy eyes behind the closed lids and he feared in the deepest part of his soul the way she would look at him now. Ugly purple splotches marked where the kora had repeatedly hit her. It would not be with respect, but with loathing at his inability to save her.

Save her? Ridiculous! Morgan shook the words out of his head. This was no shrinking violet lying beside him! She was an officer who survived the most rigorous training. She proved herself on the ship and again this afternoon. He would not be awash with guilt if she were a man. A small smile crept along his lips. *Good God, what a piece of work she is!* Morgan leaned back against pillow and closed is own eyes. Whatever she thought when she awoke, he would deal with it then.

The kora's face loomed large in Jane's dreams. The blue cast skin, the narrow, ice cold eyes, the huge seven fingered hands that reached out to close around her throat all grew larger and larger until she thought they would consume her completely. His thin lips in a twisted smile mocked her with harsh laughter; when she cried out, no sound could be heard. Jane saw herself reach for the gun; when she pulled the trigger, there was nothing but the acrid smell of burnt powder. She saw the bullet enter the kora's skull, but it seemed not to stop him. Jane's mouth opened to scream...

Something was pinning her down. She forced her eyes to focus and she saw the familiar shadow of her mother's dressing table cast against the wall. Her head throbbed mercilessly; any motion only made it worse. Someone or something was breathing steadily beside her. Fear raced through her brain and she held her breath. Turning as slowly as possible, she shifted beneath the afghan someone had tossed over her.

The movement caused Morgan to awaken immediately. "Well, well," he smiled, "look who's come back to the land of the living."

Jane almost bolted at the sound of a male voice, but when she realized it was Morgan, she let herself breathe once more. "What's happened to Grandpa's door?" she whispered through parched lips.

"Not to worry, it's back on its hinges, none the worse for the experience." He thought it funny yet typical that the first thing she would ask about would be the massive oak door.

"Where is everyone?"

"Gone."

"The kora?"

"Still dead. Mass Fleet took him to the local morgue. The ambassador is making additional arrangements. The official word is that he died in a boating accident."

"I shot him with the Derringer, didn't I?"

"Yes."

There was a long silence before she said "Good," and curled toward him. Morgan slid his arm under her shoulders and drew her close; she felt very cold despite the afghan. "My head hurts."

"It should; you were slapped around pretty good."

She reached up and touched her face. "Ouch," she murmured, "what color is my face?"

"A veritable rainbow." He wanted to kiss her. "It will fade in a few days." He wondered if the inner scars would heal as quickly.

Jane sighed and snuggled a little closer to Morgan. "Did anyone call my dad?" she asked before she drifted off again.

The next morning, they stayed at the cabin long enough to greet Ben Cabot when he came by with a glazier, then left him to close up the house. Ben, always ahead of the game, already made arrangements to ship the speeder and the dog down to Washington if Jane didn't feel up to driving. With a last hug for Spike, who seemed more than happy to stay with Ben, Morgan and Jane took off in Morgan's hovercar. Their first stop was the hospital in Bennington where a doctor checked Jane over, pronounced her concussion free, and in reasonable shape all things considered. Afterward, they found Pete Cabot sitting up in bed, swathed in bandages, telling his story once again, this time to Sewell and Jefferies. Morgan introduced the lieutenant to the two men and sat back while Jane told them her side of the tale.

"Ambassador Xinthi-Ang was here earlier to claim the body," said Jefferies obviously impressed by the Jeylosian. "I take it you've already talked to him, Ash."

Morgan nodded. "We're meeting with him on Sunday night. What happened to the other outworlders, the ones in Boston?"

"We picked up Katam-Enog and Hapa-Lin. Rega-Dop is still out, but we'll find him. Xinthi-Ang is requesting extradition with incarceration; whether or not he gets it, they will be on their way back to Jeylos before too long, one way or another. By the way, Lieutenant, the ambassador is sorry that you were the one who had to fire the shot, but is relieved the kora was, and this is a quote, "executed by his victim."

Jane looked Jeffries dead square in the eye. "I have never killed before, but as an officer, I was prepared for the possibility of such an event. This is something I can live with."

Morgan was relieved by her answer. "If you are finished with us, gentlemen, we would like to get on the road."

"Where are you off to now, Ash?" asked Sewell, a little envious of the captain's life.

"Boston, then back to the ship. We take off for Kotuchar on Monday morning; we were in the middle of a mission when we were called home." He glanced at Jane and caught the question in her eye.

Once out of the hospital, Jane caught Morgan's arm. "Aren't we headed back to *Washington* now?"

"We won't make it before sundown, S.J., so I thought perhaps we could spend *Shabbos* in Boston. Your parents said you could use the house on the Cape if you'd like, but I was hoping you'd come with me. My parents are expecting us. Is that all right with you"

She was more than a little surprised. "I guess so."

"Besides, there is someone I'd like you to meet."

Jane's hands flew to her face. "Like this?" she cried in horror.

Morgan put his arm around her shoulder and drew her close. "To tell the truth, he'll think you're a great hero."

CHAPTER 31

Belle sat at the comm station on the bridge filing night logs. Newhouse sat in the captain's chair, a star chart glowing on the main screen ahead of him, working out the new flight plan to be filed upon Morgan's return to the *Washington*. Near him, Lucas was skimming incoming Protocol Data-12 sets when news of the kora's death in a boating accident came in as a news flash on the public channel. "And if you believe that," commented Newhouse drily, "I've got a bridge across the Chesapeake Bay I'd like to sell you."

"What do you think really happened?" Belle asked, looking up from the panel.

"I'm sure we'll find out eventually," replied Lucas with a shrug. "Whatever it was, it's not going to make the evening news."

"That's for damn sure." said Newhouse, "but I'll bet the captain was there when it happened."

They were just finishing when Mass Fleet hailed the ship. Morgan's face appeared on the screen. "Good afternoon, ladies and gentlemen," he said with a smile. "Everybody working hard?"

"Hard enough to keep outta trouble, Captain. What's the good word?" Newhouse did not bother move from Morgan's chair.

"The good word is, take it easy until Sunday morning. I'll be back on board by 10 hundred hours. We've got guests coming in for dinner, but let's call a quickie staff meeting for seventeen hundred. Belle?"

The crewmate stepped forward. "Yes, sir!"

Jane took Morgan's place on the screen. "Let's meet as soon as I get back. I'd like to go over to the Pentagon library before the staff meeting. Is that okay with you?"

Belle nodded; she was too shocked by the condition of the lieutenant's face to say anything more than "Yes, ma'am."

"Great. I'll see you when I get back."

As soon as the screen went dark, Newhouse let out a long whistle. "Did you get a load of that?" he asked aloud.

"What happened to her?" asked Lucas.

"She looks awful!" Belle sputtered.

There was a brief moment of silence, before Newhouse ordered everyone back to work. "We'll find out when she gets here, gang. Now let's get cracking so we're ready for them."

❧

"Do you think they'll notice?" Jane asked Morgan as they pulled up in front of the Morgenstern house late in the afternoon

The captain squeezed her hand and grinned, "How could they miss it, S.J.? You're in livid color."

"Thanks. What's your mother going to think?"

"Would you stop worrying about my mother? She'll probably make you sleep with an icepack on your face tonight." Jane let him draw her close. "Frankly, Lieutenant, I think you look just fine. You're alive and that's all that matters right now."

Reuben was first out the door, whooping as he ran at break neck speed toward his father. Morgan jumped from the car, arms open, ready to scoop up the boy. "Glad to see me again so soon, champ?" he asked as he hugged Reuben tight against him.

"What do you think, Dad? Bubbe is in a lather trying to get a room ready for your friend. And she's made the biggest pot roast you ever saw!" He was about to say something else when Reuben saw Jane step out of the front seat. Quickly wiping his hand on his jeans, he stuck it out. "How do you do, ma'am? I'm Reuben."

Jane shook the proffered hand as she looked from son to father. "I'm so glad to meet you, Reuben, but please, don't call me ma'am; that's my mother. I'm..." she paused for a minute, "Jane, but my friends call me S.J."

Morgan beamed; he hadn't asked her what name she wanted to use. He was relieved she chose *S.J.* "Hey, Reuben, give your old man a hand with the bags."

The Morgensterns welcomed Jane into their home warmly and without reservations. As promised, Morgan's mother immediately insisted she apply an ice pack to her face, planting her firmly at the kitchen table where she could keep an eye on the swelling. The Morgenstern men were out in the yard playing catch. Feigie Morgenstern was happy to have company as she worked and this particular company was special. Since Tovah's death, her son had kept whatever romantic life he had away from his family and the minute Feigie saw Asher with the woman, she knew her boy was in love. Without being invasive, Feigie asked Jane about her family and the answers she got more than pleased her. "How is that you go by Krieg and not your father's name?" she asked casually, when Jane identified her parents.

"It's tough being the boss's daughter, Mrs. Morgenstern," she answered honestly. "My brother was the one who gave me the idea. Jonathan once said if he could change anything about himself at all, it would be his name. When I decided to apply to super-school, I decided I needed to do this without my parents. In fact, they didn't know until after I did it. It took a bit of doing to change the academic records, but since the name on my birth certificate was Sarah Jane Krieg-Rothko, it wasn't impossible. Simply a matter of switching a few initials."

"And this has worked for you?"

"Better than I ever expected, except when I met the captain." She grinned devilishly. "When he found out who I was, he didn't want me on his ship. He wasn't a very nice welcoming committee."

Feigie laughed imagining the black looks her son must have liberally passed out. "But now, you match each other; it's *b'shert!*" She looked at Jane. "You understand a little Yiddish?" she asked.

Answering in the old tongue, she said "Would you prefer to speak it now?"

"*Mein Gott* ! You speak Yiddish! Wonderful!" The woman was delighted. "Do they speak it in your home?"

Jane nodded. "It used to be they spoke it when they didn't want us to understand something, but we caught on. I'm the linguist on the *Washington* and it wouldn't be right if I couldn't speak both Yiddish and Hebrew."

Mrs. Morgenstern wiped her hands on her apron and studied the girl at the table with icepack on her face. "And what do they really call you at home? Lieutenant?"

She could not help but smile. "Sorke...at least my grandmother called me Sorke. My parents call me Sarah or Sarah Jane. Jonathan calls me Squirt, and my little sister and brother call me something I wouldn't repeat," smiled Jane.

"Just like any other family. Do you know what his brothers call Asher?"

"I hope it's something wicked."

Feigie nodded. "They call him Toby."

"Toby?" repeated Jane. "Why Toby?"

"Because when he was little, he always wanted to run away and join the circus...like that Toby Tyler in the story books."

"Oh, that's funny. I'm going to have to remember that!" Jane giggled until her face hurt.

"What are you going to remember?" asked Morgan as he came through the screen door with his father and son.

"Nothing, Asher," answered his mother with a wave of her hand, "so mind your own business.

Morgan frowned and looked at his father. "Dad, are they plotting against us?"

"Probably. But I wouldn't worry about it. Women have been plotting since the beginning of time."

Jane grinned, his mother beamed, and Morgan realized the conversation had just taken place in Yiddish. Shaking his head, he grabbed a bottle of juice from the refrigerator and motioned to his son. "Come on, Reuben, let's go back outside. It's safer there."

Reuben fell asleep on the couch curled up against his father. Jane, seated next to Mrs. Morgenstern on the other sofa, loved the way Asher continued to stroke his son's hair as he talked to his parents about the *Washington*. Occasionally, Jane would add something, but this was his show and she was more than happy to let him have center stage. At last, Mr. Morgenstern stood and announced it was long past a proper hour for sleep.

"There's tea on the warmer if you want some more," offered Mrs. Morgenstern as she prepared to go upstairs with her husband.

As gently as he could, Morgan managed to lift the sleeping boy in his powerful arms. "I'll be back in a moment, Sarah."

When he came back, Jane was not in the living room. Wandering out to the kitchen, he saw her through the door, standing in the yard, looking up at the sky. "What are you thinking about?" he asked softly as he came up behind her.

Jane snuggled against him. "Oh, I was just wondering how I ended up here, with your family, feeling so safe after..." her words trailed off.

Morgan led her over to the double swing out in the middle of the yard. "Come, sit with me and I'll tell you anything you want to know."

"Tell me about Tovah."

There was a long sigh. "Tovah and I were of the same world. I can't remember when I didn't know Tovah. We played in the same sandbox. I think I knew I loved her when I went to kindergarten, when I had to leave her in the sandbox. Everyone just assumed we would get married and we did."

"Were you happy?"

"Yes and no," answered Morgan honestly. "Tovah wanted me to be happy and if that meant watching me take off with the Fleet, she wanted that, too. I don't think it made her particularly happy. She thought she was marrying a rabbi, not a space cadet." He chuckled at some far off memory. "When Reuben was born, I think she thought I would leave the Fleet and settle down. It wasn't until she got sick that I did."

"And by then it was too late?"

Morgan nodded. "There was nothing anyone could do to save her and God knows we tried. But Tovah was funny about it. Funny odd, I mean. When she knew she was dying, when she knew there was no way to stop it, she told me that we weren't *b'shert*, that she knew it all along. She told me there was some other heart for my heart and that she was only a way station. I didn't believe her. I yelled at her, I told her that was stupid and she only smiled at me. God, that made me angry!"

"And now?" whispered Jane.

Morgan's deep chuckle was soft against her ear. "Upstairs, my mother said we are *b'shert*, and that's something she had never said about Tovah, not in all the years we were together."

Jane, in the deepest part of her soul, hoped Feigie Morgenstern was right.

⁂

While most everyone else was enjoying shore leave, the linguistics team worked late into the night, only to be up again early the next morning. During the week, they made significant progress on the new encoding scheme and now that time was growing short, they were not willing to sacrifice time in the various libraries for a few minutes in the bright autumn sunshine. They met briefly at breakfast to review the last minute assignments and once that was done, Belle grabbed her notes and left the ship. If her boss was going to be happy, there were still documents to be gathered before she arrived. She signed out a hovercar from the motor pool and, rather than drive all the way to the Pentagon, she headed for the National Center for Interplanetary Studies where the library contained a substantial linguistics section. She had been there twice already and Belle knew they would copy discs for her with just her Fleet ID. Glancing at her watch, she also knew she had only a couple of hours to get the work done before she had to be back at the comm-panel on the bridge.

Traffic was heavy as she crossed into the capital. Moving into the upper level of the hover lane, she quickened her pace, taking advantage of the fact she was driving an official military vehicle. Belle followed the signs to Capitol Hill, keeping her eye peeled for the A Street cutoff. She took no notice of the green hovercar following close behind her.

Parking around the center was tight, but not impossible. Most offices were closed for the day, so after a couple of passes on side streets, Belle found an empty space, thankful for the sticker the guy at the motor pool had insisted she put on the windshield. That little piece of paper would keep the D.C. cops from giving her a ticket for parking in an *official business only* zone. Bag in hand, she hurried toward the great bronze doors.

Hum Rega-Dop could not believe the ease with which he followed the red-haired officer from Andrews Air Force Base. The kora had told him about the red-haired woman called Winter and now that the kora was dead, his only hope of avenging his master was to reach the woman Krieg through her assistant. From the car, he watched her go into the Center, and then went in search of a parking place. He knew the lieutenant would not be meeting the woman Winter, but he was certain following her every movement would eventually lead him to his prey.

The death of Kora Pana-Di meant the death of Rega-Dop's dreams of a triumphant return to Jeylos. Not that he ever spent much time on his home planet, but it was the only place where he could ever be truly home. His family continued to live in exile; for the moment his father remained within Wa'atsi territory. It was not a good life, but it was life, when to set foot on Jeylos meant certain death. His father, once a powerful member of the Jeylosian ruling class, had gambled on a coup and lost. Since then, Nata Rega-Dop and his family had wandered from colony to colony, eking out a bare subsistence as a poli*tical* advisor to whoever had the cash to pay him. Hum, the youngest of four, remembered life before exile, when there were lavish parties in the beautiful stone house on the banks of the Rega River. He remembered the beautiful woman he called *mother*, and her screams on the night the coup failed. He had watched her fade from the loveliest flower in the garden to a sad eyed old woman who sat for hours singing dirges to the three sons she lost on that night so long ago. The father's hatred of the Emperor was transferred to his remaining son and in him, Nata Rega-Dop instilled a burning desire to see the government on Jeylos topple. Pana-Di, with all his bravado, had been his best chance at fulfilling the wishes of his father. Now he was dead and again, Hum was without hope.

At the library, Belle went directly to the front desk, flashed her ID card, and disappeared into the stacks, then returned a moment later with a container of discs. As she deposited them on the desk in front of the librarian, Rega-Dop came through the doors. He picked up a site map from the rack on the counter, then positioned himself close enough to Belle to hear what was being said.

"Mike, I'll need these three made into C-5s, no security code necessary," she told the librarian. "And then I'll need these five transferred to the Pentagon by Sunday noon. Address it to S.J.R.Krieg@DOD/wash/sec11582_311.mil. Bill the linguistics sector, U.S.S. *Washington D.C.* Okay?"

"Sure, but why not just come here? We're open on Sundays."

"I know. But we need the stuff at the Pentagon and we can't wire that here."

"Sure you can. If you come here instead of the Pentagon, you can have your data sent up on a secure channel to a Fleet terminal without having to bother with text check." He pointed at a closed door. "All you need is a valid password and you can get that from your C.O."

Belle considered the offer carefully, chewing her lip as she did. "I don't know. My boss may want to go to the Pentagon anyway."

"Look, I'll get this stuff ready. It only takes a couple of minutes to transfer, so call me when you decide. If you come here, I'll make sure you can get into the doc center without someone breathing down your neck."

"Can you do that, Mike? I mean, without getting into any trouble?"

"Sure. If you've got enough ID to wander around the Pentagon, this shouldn't be a problem. Call me when you're ready to come over and I'll clear a conference room for you."

"Deal," agreed Belle with a quick flash of grin. "I like this place better than the Pentagon any day, especially on Sundays. Thanks."

"Hey, Belle?" he called after her.

"Yeah, Mike?"

"Wanna have dinner with me tonight?"

The crewmate blushed prettily, but shook her head. "Thanks for the offer, but my boss is due back tomorrow and I'm swamped. Maybe next time I'm in town." She waved as she hurried up the stairs to the linguistics labs on the second floor.

Rega-Dop did not need to follow her. The Jeylosian was jubilant. If they came to the Center, he would most certainly be able to complete his final mission for the kora. And if he perished in the process, so be it.

The Rothkos were waiting for them at Dulles Airfield when the early sub-orbiter arrived from Boston. Morgan almost didn't recognize them in their civvies. General Rothko clucked over her daughter's face while the admiral stood silently by, his hands stuffed into his pockets. Like any father, he eyed Morgan suspiciously. "Your folks are well?" he asked the captain.

"My mother was very happy to have me home for Shabbos. She and Sorke got on rather well."

Ted Rothko did not miss the smug smile on Morgan's face, nor did the captain's use of *Sorke* escape him, either. No one other than his own mother had ever called her *Sorke* and gotten away with it. Something significant happened in Boston and he was just going to have to wait until someone bothered to tell him exactly what it was. Clearing his throat, the admiral interrupted his wife. "Jonathan's car arrived last night, along with Spike. You should call Ben before you shove off and thank him for driving down to Mass Fleet for you."

"Is Spike all right?"

"The vet checked him over before they left Vermont," said her mother, "and pronounced him reasonably fit. He had to take a little more glass out of his coat, but no stitches were necessary. He's got a little limp, but seems to be none the worse for the experience."

"That's some dog, General," whistled Morgan, recalling how the retriever sailed through the broken glass to attack Pana-Di. "He's relentless."

"Never fight with Sarah in front of him, Captain," smiled the general; "he'll go for your throat."

"So I was told," replied Morgan with great gravity. He reached out and caught Jane's hand in his. "Will you be joining us for dinner this evening?"

"Wouldn't miss it for the world," said the admiral. "Can I presume you will go back to being Lieutenant Krieg by seventeen hundred hours?"

Jane nodded. "I'm sure by now most people know, but I don't see any reason to officially go public."

The admiral started to protest, but his wife stilled him with a single glance. "I hope you'll have the chance to see your brother before you leave, Sarah. He's anxious to talk to you."

"More likely he wants to know if I dinged up his car."

"Did you?" asked her father.

"Nah. It was in the shed the whole time."

The Rothkos drove the two officers over to Andrew's. Morgan sat in the front with the admiral while Jane chattered away with her mother in the back seat. At the base, the guard waved them through and soon Admiral Rothko was pulling up beside the temporary gangway attached to the *Washington*. There was a flurry of quick hugs before Jane hoisted her duffle onto her shoulder and ran up the gangway, leaving Morgan alone with her parents.

"Before you go, Morgan, I would like to ask you something," said the admiral, leaning against the hovercar. He looked at his wife who smiled and slipped into the front seat. When the door was closed, he spoke again. "You and Sarah seem, well, somewhat closer now than when I last saw you together at our house the night she left for the cabin." He paused to compose the next sentence. "What are your intentions?"

Morgan resisted the urge to throw back his head and laugh; it would have been most inappropriate to laugh at Sarah Jane's father. Instead, Morgan stood up very straight. "Sir, my intentions toward your daughter are honorable. There is, of course, the problem of her being under my command, but I believe we will be able to...uh....deport ourselves with propriety."

The admiral looked him dead in the eye. "See that you do. I'm not going to interfere in any way, but if I get one word about any on board dalliances, I won't be able to protect either of you. Do I make myself clear?"

He felt like a raw recruit being taken to task, but Rothko's response was understandable. "Yes, sir," he answered smartly.

"Don't *yessir* me, fella. Just don't do anything stupid where my daughter is concerned."

"Permission to speak freely, sir."

"Granted."

This time, Morgan didn't have to suppress a laugh; his voice was deadly serious. "I took Sarah Jane home to meet my son and my parents. I wouldn't have done that if I didn't think..."

"Forget it, sailor," said Rothko feeling suddenly foolish. He looked more than a little sheepish when he added, "You're both adults. I'll keep my opinions to myself."

Morgan extended his hand, an uncharacteristic gesture between the two men. "Thank you, sir."

Rothko got into the car and leaned back. "There is a fine line between father and commander, Liz, and I think I just crossed it in the worst possible way."

The general laughed and patted him sympathetically on the hand. "There, there, Teddy; it was bound to happen sooner or later. Had Sarah not been such a late bloomer, I'm afraid it would have been much sooner. Just think of this as merely a test of your ability to changes hats in a new and unusual way."

"Are you suggesting I'm an inflexible stick?" asked the admiral, one eyebrow raised.

"Hardly that, dear; I'm simply reminding you that you are a father and it's perfectly normal to act like one. Let's go home; we have laundry to fold before we have to come back here for dinner."

"Hrrumph," snorted Rothko as he started the car.

Jane had barely changed into a clean pair of khakis when Belle arrived at her cabin. "Welcome back! How was your vacation?"

"Lovely, Crewmate Winter. Peaceful and relaxing." Jane turned around. Belle gasped when she saw the livid purple bruises. "Okay, so it wasn't so peaceful."

"Holy cow! We saw them on the screen, but they're much worse in person. Do you want some make-up or something?"

Jane shook her head. "I can't touch 'em; it hurts too much. Thanks anyway." She pried the docupad out of Belle's hand and scanned the contents. "Hey, this is pretty impressive, Belle. You guys did all this while I was gone?"

"Yep, and there's more. I made friends with the guy who runs the disc catalogue at the Interplanetary Center and he's can get us a private carrel with two linked terminals. I found a whole bunch of stuff over there I think you should see."

Jane glanced at her watch. "Let me look at my mail and the logs, then we can go."

"Meet you on the bridge, Lieutenant." Belle waved over her shoulder as she took off.

"I'll send someone with you," announced Morgan when she told him they were going to the center.

Jane bristled, but maintained her composure. "Thanks, but no thanks, Captain; we'll be fine."

"Are you arguing with me?" asked Morgan.

"No, I am declining your kind offer."

"Haven't you caused enough trouble for one week, Sarah Jane?"

"Please don't call me that here, Captain," she said sweetly.

Morgan scowled, "If you won't take an escort, take a side arm, Lieutenant. I would like to keep you alive at least through dinner tonight. After we take off, I can dump your carcass in deep space and conveniently forget to tell anyone for a month or two." He liked the way she frowned at him. Morgan reached out for her hand, then held it for a moment, thankful his office door was shut. "Come on, S.J., don't make me make it an order."

Jane pulled her hand from his; the frown deepened. "Do you really think I'm in any danger, Asher?" She saw him shrug. "Okay, fine. Maybe Blackjack will want to tag along. Is he aboard ship yet?"

Morgan hit the comm-panel and barked "Hey, Southern Boy, wake up!"

"What can Ah do for y'all, Boston?"

Belle was tickled pink when Jane said Captain Cardozo had business at the Center and would be accompanying them. Jane sat in back, letting Belle share the front seat with the dashing Blackjack. Zooming along the empty Beltway, they made the Center in record time. Blackjack parked the car right in front of the building. They raced up the broad white steps, laughing like school children on a field trip. Inside, Belle's friend Mike was waiting, discs in hand, to show them to the room he secured. 'We won't be more than an hour, hour and a half," promised Belle after the introductions, "we have a staff meeting at five."

Rega-Dop stood not ten yards away reading notices flashing on the bulletin board. The addition of a male to the little party added a new wrinkle to the delicate fabric of his plan, but it was nothing for which he could not adjust. He watched them as they walked up the staircase together. The Jeylosian waited until the one called Mike was gone, then left the building. If his plan was to succeed, he needed to come in from the outside when he first addressed the one called Mike.

He walked along the sidewalk thinking about the male. His face seemed most familiar to Rega-Dop yet he could not immediately place him; he had seen him somewhere before. He tried to picture the tall, curly-haired man in another setting, but no image fit. He was about to give up when suddenly, he remembered the face, but with a dark blue Amitidean pilot's cap. Rega-Dop had seen Captain Jackson Cardozo in action during the annual racing meet on Milabar, Amitides' outer moon. There had been an altercation in a local bar and the American had been in the center of it, swinging his powerful arms, all the while laughing. Rega-Dop thought the man a pompous fool up until the moment he picked up a pilot from Kotuchar and tossed him no less than ten feet in the air before catching him again. At the time it had been funny, but thinking about it now, Rega-Dop knew if he was to take the lieutenant, it would have to be without the man's knowledge.

In the room reserved for them, Jane and Belle set to work on the documents. Cardozo produced a tattered copy of **The Great Gatsby** from within a jacket pocket and stretched out in a beat up old easy chair someone must have donated years before, judging by its condition. It was tough to ignore two beautiful women, but he had no choice. Jane made it perfectly clear he was to keep his mouth shut and his hands off Belle. He was acutely aware of Belle's light, yet provocative scent. Besides, Jane hadn't been the only one to warn him about toying with the carrot-topped crewmate; Morgan threatened him with physical violence if he did anything untoward. Cardozo buried his nose in his book and pretended to ignore the women.

Close to the end of the hour, Mike rapped on the carrel door and poked his head inside. "Lieutenant, there's a call for you at the desk."

"Can you pipe it up here?" Belle asked.

"Sure. Hang on."

Jane stood up and stretched. "It's probably Jonathan. I left a message for him at the hospital. I'll be right back." As soon as it flashed, Jane hit the button and said "Hello?"

"I am most sorry to disturb you from your work, Lieutenant, but this is Hafcha Tor-Ba, Ambassador Xinthi-Ang's attaché. We have a messenger on his way to you at the Center with a new encoding packet His Excellency thought you might find helpful."

"Oh, that's very kind of the ambassador. When will your messenger be here?"

"Momentarily, Lieutenant Krieg. If you would wait at the desk, he should be along presently."

"Okay."

"I'll go downstairs," said Blackjack.

Jane shook her head. "I need the ladies' room. I'll be right back."

Rega-Dop waited a few minutes before he ran up the stairs and through the bronze doors. "Lieutenant Krieg!" he called as she came out of the restroom.

Jane turned around to see who called her name. The man was definitely Jeylosian, but his jacket was not traditional; it looked more Wa'atsi in design. His hands were empty. "I'm Lieutenant Krieg. Are you the courier?"

"Yes."

"Where is the packet from His Excellency?" she asked in Jeylosian.

Her accent took Rega-Dop by surprise. He grasped the laser pistol in his pocket. "If you would come with me, I would be honored," he said formally.

"The honor would be mine," replied Jane according to Jeylosian custom, "but I must decline. Please give me the packet."

Rega-Dop looked around the deserted lobby. The male behind the desk was gone. Sliding the pistol out, he pressed it against Jane's side. "You will come with me, Lieutenant." His free hand closed around her arm and squeezed. "You have no choice in this matter."

Jane refused to budge. "You must be kidding. Let go of my arm *now*."

He used his strength to twist her bicep, and smiled coldly when Jane winced. Half-dragging her, he moved toward the door.

"Where are you taking me?" hissed Jane through clenched teeth.

"Somewhere where you shall not be readily found."

"Who the hell are you?"

"My master's servant. Now shut up and walk." He kept her close to his side as he pulled her down the front steps of the Center.

"Maybe she went to the ladies' room, Captain," Mike suggested when he and Cardozo realized the lobby was empty. The librarian went over to his com panel and punch a couple of buttons. "Nope, she's not in there; the lights are out."

"Where the bloody hell did she wander off to now?" Cardozo stemmed the rising tide of panic. If anything happened to Jane, Morgan would have his head on a platter. He went out the main door and looked both ways down the quiet street. The only movement he saw was a green hovercar turning the corner onto Third Street. Running back inside, Cardozo took the steps two at a time as he tore toward the carrel where they had been sitting. "Get back to the ship now, Belle," he ordered, "and pray you don't run into the captain once you're there."

"Forget it, I'm going with you." They both tore out of the carrel.

"Belle, you can't. Go back to the ship. That's an order."

"The hell it is, Captain. I'm a black belt in Tai Kwando and I'm a crack shot. I've got combat experience," she yelled as they ran down the stairs.

"Yeah?"

"Yeah."

"Then keep up with me." Cardozo started out the door, then stopped, causing Belle to crash into him. He grabbed her by the arms. "You wearin' a pager?"

"Yes, and so is Jane."

"Buzz her."

Belle removed her pager from her belt and fed in the codes. At first, nothing happened, but then, right before the connection was broken, there was a flash of numbers. Belle looked up and smiled. "She's wearing a tag. We can find her, no problem."

CHAPTER 32

Before he pushed her into passenger seat of the hovercar, Rega-Dop tased Jane just hard enough to stun, then used a cable tie to bind her wrists. They were on the highway heading west when she started coming around and her pager beeped; Rega-Dop pulled off onto the emergency lane, stopped the car, and clawed at Jane's clothing until he found the offending device and, along with it, her little laser pistol. Through it all, Jane kept her mouth clamped shut. She knew it had to be Belle calling her and she prayed that her locator, fastened to her shirt pocket behind her nametag, would kick in.

Rega-Dop tossed the pager out the window and slipped the pistol into his pocket. "Let them look for that," he sneered, maneuvering back into the stream of traffic.

Jane swallowed the bile rising in her throat. She had no idea who this Jeylosian was, nor what he wanted with her. Obviously, he was one of Pana-Di's cohorts, but beyond that, there wasn't a clue.

They drove past Alexandria, and into Prince William County. This was her home turf; Jane saw one familiar place after another whiz by as they sped along in silence. Finally, the Jeylosian exited the highway and headed toward a place Jane knew well.

Long abandoned by the military, Quantico was in use as a private base for interplanetary ambassadorial personnel. Many of the outworld embassies had small, secure compounds on the base, and stored their smaller shuttlecraft, along with limos, hovercars, and anything else not currently in use in the old hangar area. Jane had been there with her parents on a number of occasions, usually family-friendly, informal affairs hosted by outworlders to demonstrate their particular form of home hospitality.

Jane doubted she was being taken to a compound. When Rega-Dop turned off onto an old paved road and used a flash key for an automated sentry, she guessed he was headed to what everyone called *the parking lot.* In the distance, Jane saw a hangar with two mini-orbiters parked on the tarmac. He pulled up to the second building. "Do not move, he growled as he got out of the car. He walked around to the passenger side of the car, and yanked Jane out. The taser was pointed at her throat.

Inside, the hangar was well lit. The walls glowed yellowish white with continuous light panels. The ceiling was a complicated series of baffles, the kind once used to deaden sound in a machine shop. Rows of spare parts lined the back wall, all neatly stacked and ready for use. A couple of older hovercars sat near the back, with a flashy new two seater between them. Their footsteps were sharp against the stainless steel floor as they walked across the hangar to where another Jeylosian sat at a table littered with documents. "Welcome, Lieutenant Krieg," he said. When he rose, he towered over Jane by at least a foot.

"I thought you were loyal to the Emperor, Lalo-Fa," spat Jane contemptuously.

Lalo-Fa's laughter echoed through the hangar. "A pity you persist in believing in fairy tales, Lieutenant Krieg. You have been deceived by the puppet Xinthi-Ang. He tells your people all is well on Jeylos yet this is not so. You have taken our one hope for a new order and we, in turn, shall take you."

"Where will you take me?" Jane demanded.

"For a short walk, Lieutenant." Lalo-Fa touched her cheek and laughed when she recoiled. "Our kora should have killed you when he had the chance; he would have enjoyed that immensely."

"He never had the chance to kill me, Lalo-Fa," Jane retorted, "I'm the one who put a bullet through his brain." Lalo-Fa's hand shot out; the sound of flesh against flesh rang out. "You are no more a man than Pana-Di; he got his jollies beating on women, too."

"Silence!" shouted Lalo-Fa. "Do not underestimate my power over your fate, Lieutenant. Anger me and you will die slowly, painfully, screaming for an end to your suffering."

"And the other choice? To be permitted to die with dignity?" Jane laughed harshly. "You are a fool, Lalo-Fa. Kill me and your own fate is sealed."

"My fate is unimportant; there are others who will succeed where we have failed...this time. The laws of Jeylos demand blood for blood. Your blood is red, but it will do." He walked to the table and removed an object from beneath the papers. "Have you ever seen one of these, Lieutenant?" He slid the stiletto-like object from its sheath.

Jane barely glanced at the finely honed blade, instead, she fixed her eyes on him. "A di-darood. So what?"

"Do you know its use?"

She knew he would tell her. Keeping her voice even, she answered "It is an executioner's device."

"And you are not afraid?" His eyes narrowed; he was obviously enjoying himself.

"No." She was not about to let him know she was terrified. Lifting her chin, she added, "There is nothing to fear. Since I have served the Emperor honorably and with truth, it cannot touch me."

"Take her outside, Rega-Dop." Lalo-Fa walked away, handing Rega-Dop the sword as he passed him.

It was the first time Jane heard her kidnapper called by name. He was the one Interpol was certain they would pick up after the ugly business at the cabin, yet here he was, free as a bird. Based on what Morgan had told her about Rega-Dop, he was a cool character, devoted to the kora, but definitely concerned about his own welfare. He was a notorious black-marketeer for the illegal Wa'atsi trade in the United States and considered *persona non grata* by the Jeylosian government.

Glancing casually about the hangar, Jane estimated her chances for an escape. With her hands so tightly tied, she was limited as to what she could accomplish on the run. She would have to create some confusion to give her time to free her hands; how she would do that, she wasn't quite sure. The door through which they entered the hangar was closed. A second door, behind the old hovercars, seemed to be ajar; a thin stream of sunlight spilled through the crack. Nearer to the table where Lalo-Fa was now sitting with his back to her, there were two more doors, but the nearby windows indicated these led to a secondary interior. Jane decided her best chance was through the far door.

Rega-Dop prodded Jane with the tip of the di-darood. His hooded eyes bore into her, hatred so clear it made her shiver. She started to walk in the direction of the first door, keeping her eyes on the one in the other wall. Waiting until they had reached a spot with a clear shot at the exit, Jane spun around, her leg extended. She caught Rega-Dop in the groin with terrible force. The Jeylosian howled as he doubled over in pain; the di-darood clattered to the floor. Jane kicked it as hard as she could, and ran. The smooth steel of the floor performed exactly as she needed; the di-darood slid beneath one of the cars. Not stopping to look behind her, Jane heard Lalo-Fa shouting at Rega-Dop. She dove behind the car in a forward roll, scooped up the stiletto with both hands, and threw her weight against the door.

Her shoulder ached but Jane clutched the di-darood as ran into a thicket behind the hangar. She stumbled when she caught her foot on a tree root and pitched forward. The di-darood flew from her grasp; she rolled away from it, afraid she would land on the blade. Catching her breath, Jane crawled to the weapon. She could hear Lalo-Fa still shouting, Rega-Dop answering as he thrashed through the undergrowth. Jane used the blade to cut through the plastic tie binding her hands, slicing her wrist in the process, but not enough to do any major damage. She crouched low, letting the shrubs conceal her while she tried to determine what direction Rega-Dop had gone. There was no point in running through the woods, the perimeter fence would prevent her from making an escape and if it was not live when they entered the compound, most likely it was now. Her only chance was to get back to the hangar and take the hovercar.

Rega-Dop was in the woods, slowly scouting for any sign of the woman. She could hear his clumsy footsteps and estimated he was about fifty yards to her left. Still crouching low to the ground, Jane began moving back toward the hangar, the di-darood in her hands, its blade turned outward, ready to inflict death on contact.

A laser beam shot past her ear, burning a hole in the nearest tree. Jane broke into a run, keeping herself on a course close to the trees. She wove in and out of the sheltering trunks, bobbing up and down as she went. Shot after shot was fired, but she kept going, even when one beam sliced through the fabric of her shirt. She felt the warmth of her own blood oozing down her arm. Gritting her teeth against the pain, she kept running.

The side door of the hangar was wide open. Lalo-Fa filled the frame; his hand locked around a laser pistol. At the first sound of crashing from within the woods, he fired. The shot went wide, the noise ceased. He listened closely for a moment. A sudden movement caught his eye, and he fired again. A squirrel dashed into the clearing, the disappeared beneath the dense brush. Again, there was silence.

Jane saw the furry gray flash and waited long enough to catch her breath.

All those years of sneaking about the woods with her siblings taught her to move without noise, and she used that skill to creep closer to the building. She wished she had her sidearm; Lalo-Fa was a clean shot away and she was powerless to take him down from this distance. Closer and closer she moved, listening between each step for the sound of Rega-Dop.

"East!" shouted Belle, "she's going east." She was watching the blip on the map screen moving eastward.

"Is she on foot or driving?" yelled Cardozo back at her.

"It's slow; she must be on foot."

"Whose land is she on? Have you figured that out yet?"

Belle entered the coordinates into the car's map screen. "Still no designation. It's not Quantico, but it's close. It's got to be in one of the embassy compounds." Her pager began beeping; it was the third time since they left the Center it had done so. Belle looked at the flashing numbers and frowned. "It's the captain again, Blackjack. I'm going to have to answer him sooner or later."

Cardozo growled; he didn't want Morgan racing down here, guns drawn, like the bloody cavalry. "Give me the damn thing." Belle handed it over and for a moment, Cardozo was tempted to throw it out the window like Rega-Dop had done. They found the pager lying in the grass, but when her tag wasn't with it, they knew Jane was locatable. "Whaddya want, Morgan?" he drawled as casually as possible.

"I hope I'm not interrupting anything, Southern Boy, but what the hell are you doing? And why are you on Winter's pager?"

"We're having an outing, Boston. Do y'all have a problem with that?"

"Where the hell is Krieg? She's not answering either and she's not at the library."

Cardozo weighed the benefits of lying against telling Morgan the truth. It was split down the middle. "If Ah had the answer to that, Boston, Ah wouldn't be tearin' down the highway at a hundred miles an hour."

"You're about ten miles from Quantico. I'm in a mini and will meet you there."

"Stay where you are, Boston. Let me handle this!" shouted Cardozo into the pager.

"Bullshit, Blackjack. I'm already on my way."

Cardozo hit the accelerator and the hovercar took off. He knew the way to Quantico, but he wasn't about to desert Jane either. "Don't go to Quantico, Boston, meet us at whatever it is that's directly east of the base."

"Prince William Forest?" asked Morgan

"No, near there. Pull a listing of the adjacent compounds. S.J.'s tag is pulsing at 77.625.38.439."

"Got it. Hang on." There was a brief silence. "That's a private site, owned by Limna-Kor Trading Company."

"We're hot!" said Belle suddenly. Cardozo glanced at the screen and saw the little light flashing red. "Captain, we're within three miles of Jane."

"I'm about five minutes behind you. Go for it."

Cardozo tossed the pager in Belle's lap and turned the hovercar sharply right down a dirt track.

The road ended abruptly at a fence. "Stay here," roared Cardozo as he leapt from the car. He ran as close as he dared to the mesh, then bent to pick up a small stone. Tossing it, he jumped backward when the area lit up.

Belle was beside him. "There's no time, Blackjack; I'll blow the fence. Get back," she barked, "this thing is hot." Belle leveled the pistol and fired. The fence ignited with a curtain of shimmering lights.

"Again!" yelled Cardozo when the flashing stopped and they could see the fence was intact.

Belle fired, holding the beam longer this time, until the mesh grew white hot. The ultimate explosion echoed through the silence and they ducked. Pieces of fence flew through the air, landing with hot crackles on the ground around them.

"You okay?" asked Cardozo, rapidly brushing burning bits from his clothing.

"Yeah. Come on."

They climbed back into the car and drove through the gaping hole.

Sirens went off all over the hangar. Lalo-Fa tore into the building. The control panel was ablaze with blinking lights, telling him security around the southeast corner of the perimeter had been penetrated.

Jane heard the alarm and saw Lalo-Fa's flight. Using it to her advantage, she moved close enough to the hangar to see the Jeylosian attempting to pound codes into the panel. She did not see Rega-Dop coming out of the woods until it was too late. He fired at her as he charged; the beam caught Jane as she turned, burning deep into her shoulder. Summoning every last bit of her strength, she stood with the di-darood extended. Before he could fire again, Jane shouted, "The day is mine!" and released the weapon. The stiletto flew into his body. Rega-Dop pitched forward into Jane, his eyes wide. He was dead before they touched the ground.

Fighting the waves of pain threating to overtake her, Jane pulled herself out from under the dead Jeylosian's and grabbed his laser. Leaves and grass clung to her bloodied shirt. She righted herself, keeping the useless right arm against her side to minimize the blood flow. Struggling to her knees, she aimed the laser at the open door.

Lalo-Fa fortified the rest of the perimeter system, hoping to impede any outside progress. He knew Rega-Dop was out there somewhere, but hoped he had enough sense not to cross the secondary defense line. The intruders were coming; this he could see on the panel screen, and he could see there were two in the hovercar. Crossing back to the open door, he looked out into the woods for any sign from Rega-Dop.

The silvery tunic Lalo-Fa wore caught the sun's rays and flashed against the alloy walls of the hangar. She knew he could not see her in the brush and she called to him. ""Rega-Dop is dead!" she shouted at the top of her lungs, using the formal Jeylosian pronouncement of an execution; "his blood wets the ground where the di-darood stands tall. Let those who dare claim his deed for their own!"

Lalo-Fa fired blindly in the direction of the voice. Harsh laughter was the only return.

"Do you fear me, Lalo-Fa?" shouted Jane. "Or do you fear the Emperor's justice more?" There was another volley of shots, one of which passed close to Jane's hiding place. "Face the sun, Lalo-Fa! Face the sun and face your mortality."

Her use of his own language made Lalo-Fa's blood run cold in his veins. He had sorely underestimated his opponent; she knew the law of his land and was using it against him. But this was not Jeylos and he was not bound by its code of honor. Shielding his eyes against the sun, he scanned the landscape looking for her. The hum of a hovercar was coming closer. If he was to avenge the kora, he had to do it now. Suddenly, he spied the di-darood standing straight upward. Leveling his pistol at it, he scanned to the right and saw nothing. Changing directions, he moved his eyes to the left. There, low to the ground, he saw her. Lalo-Fa aimed carefully; there would be only one shot at the woman Krieg.

"The day is mine!" shouted Jane; she was ready for him. When her eyes met his, she fired at the same moment he did. His beam went wide, but hers caught him right between his eyes. Lalo-Fa crumpled to the ground on his knees, before he fell face forward into the dirt.

Overhead, a tremendous whine made Jane look upward. A dun colored mini was descending from the sky, blocking out the sun with the dust it raised. A second vehicle came crashing through the tall grass, staying clear of the road. Sparks from the secondary perimeter line flashed as the hovercar crossed the line. For a moment, the car itself seemed to light up, then it glided to a dead stop. From above, the mini hovered. Four men jumped from the door before it touched the ground.

Jane knew the cavalry had arrived, late as usual. Willing herself to stand, she walked unsteadily toward them. Belle was running toward her from one direction, the men from the other. Jane stood still, letting them come to her.

Belle reached her first. "Oh, my God!" she cried when she saw the hole in Jane's shoulder. Immediately, she put her arm around the lieutenant's waist and felt Jane slump against her. "Can you walk?"

"Of course I can walk!" snapped Jane with considerably more bravado than she felt.

Morgan skidded to a halt in front of them. Wordlessly, he relieved Belle of her burden, scooping Jane up into his arms.

"Put me down, Captain!" she demanded.

"Shut up, Lieutenant." He carried her into the hangar. Cardozo ran ahead and swept the table clean. Morgan deposited Jane on the table; gently, he pulled the fabric away from her wound. "Get me a medkit!" he shouted to Cardozo. More softly, he said "Helluva job you did out there, S.J. How many more bodies did you leave in the woods?"

Jane winced as Belle pressed her handkerchief against the hole. "Just one. Rega-Dop."

"Who shot you?"

"Does it matter?" she replied from between clenched teeth.

Cardozo came back with the kit. "Y'all okay, Cousin Krieg?" He grinned at her smudged face. "That's one tough bird you've got there, Boston."

"Don't I know it. Why don't you go and collect the bodies, southern boy?" Morgan turned his attention back to Jane. "Can you move your arm, S.J?"

Jane laughed in spite of the pain. It seemed terribly funny to hear him call her that. Slowly, she raised her arm, but dropped it down again. "That hurts a lot."

"Of course it hurts!" said Belle." You've been shot." She went back to cleaning the shreds of material from the hole.

"I noticed." Jane gritted her teeth and closed her eyes. She was not about to cry out now.

Morgan pulled a small can from the medkit and popped the top with his teeth. "Hold still, S.J., I'm gonna spray you with sealgel."

She closed her eyes tightly and waited for the inevitable sting. "Ouch!" She opened one eye to see Morgan's face wrinkle with concern.

He gingerly pressed the skin together to make certain the spray had done its job. "There, that should hold it until we get you to Bethesda."

"No way!" snapped Jane, a little louder than she wished. The word echoed against the metal of the hangar.

"You have to go to a hospital; you don't have a choice."

"Dr. Vecchio can do this aboard the ship. These are not life-threatening wounds. We can keep this quiet." She looked at his raised eyebrows. "Okay, kinda quiet."

He suspected that was supposed to be code for *don't tell my parents.* "Quiet, my ass, Lieutenant; your parents have to know." Morgan glanced at his watch; it was only a matter of hours before the Rothkos would board the *Washington* for dinner.

⁂

"Boston, the MP's have landed and the Jeylosian attaché is with them," announced Cardozo "Y'all gonna be okay, Cousin Krieg?"

"Oh, yeah," replied Jane with a serious nod. "It hurts, but it looks worse than it is."

"And unless we get you to Dr. Vecchio, it's gonna be even worse than that. Belle, would you please escort the lieutenant back to the *Washington*? I'll catch a ride with this clown as soon as I finish with the MPs." Morgan took a last look at his handiwork before applying a sterile pad taken from the medkit. "Lieutenant, are you okay enough to give Winter directions?"

"Yes, sir, I am."

Cardozo escorted the Jeylosian to where Jane was now sitting up on the table. "Before you take off, this here's Matna Tchoca-Min and he would like a word with you…If you're able."

"I'm able." Jane managed a lopsided smile. "With profound sadness, Matna Tchoca-Min," said Jane in his language, inclining her head as prescribed by Jeylosian custom.

"No need for that, Lieutenant," replied the official in English. "I'd shake your hand, but….."

Jane's laughter was softly ironic. "But I truly am sorry, sir. I was unaware assistance was en route; I would not have killed Lalo-Fa had I known."

"Please don't feel compelled to apologize. He would have been executed in any event. It is well accomplished since the sentence was carried out by the victim, as is proper."

Jane grimaced; killing was not something she enjoyed, and there had been more than enough death. "I accept your kind words, but know that I am not joyous."

"None of us are, Lieutenant. Jeylos is a peaceful planet, but not without its problems His Excellency, Lord Xinthi-Ang wishes me to express his personal regrets that you were caught up, once again, in unsavory politics from our home world." He saluted her out of respect for her strength.

Morgan helped her off the table, steadying her until she seemed to be standing on her own. "Okay, Crewmate Winter, take her away."

"Aye, aye, sir." Belle took his place at Jane's side and helped her from the hangar to the waiting mini.

As soon as they were out of earshot, Morgan turned to Tchoca-Min. "Is everyone accounted for now?" he asked in a less than patient voice.

"Yes, Captain. Pana-Di's cell of petty revolutionaries is now properly disbanded. It is unfortunate that Lieutenant Krieg has suffered injuries twice in the hands of our own. She is to be greatly respected for her courage."

Morgan bristled at the way the Jeylosian looked at Jane's back nearing the door. "She performed well in the line of duty, sir, the way an officer of the Fleet should."

"And you do not think she is heroic?"

"Lieutenant Krieg is a competent officer; she did what she had to do."

"I see." Tchoca-Min had been on Earth long enough to read the signals in the captain's eyes. "Let us go and inspect the damage." Without waiting for a reply, he strode toward the door.

CHAPTER 33

The soft music wafting through sickbay gave Jane something on which to focus while Dr. Vecchio worked on her shoulder. "Lasers have a distinct advantage over bullets," mused the doctor as she peeled away the bandage and the layer of sealgel the captain used at the scene. "I don't have to go hunting around for shrapnel and usually the wounds tend to be cleaner. In fact, a well-placed blast can cauterize part of the wound, in effect, protecting the victim." She grinned at Jane. "Shall I go on, or have you heard enough?"

"It's okay; you can stop now."

The doctor continued her probe, her long fingers gently manipulating the injured area. "You're pretty lucky, kiddo; Lalo-Fa was a lousy shot. He missed the rotator cuff completely and there's minimal muscle damage. Mostly, you're burned."

"I don't have to stay here, do I?" asked Jane hopefully.

"Nah, you're ambulatory. Bethesda would've slapped you into the trauma unit and we would've gone without you, so it's just as well you came here. I'm much less hysterical than they are." Behind the joke, Dr. Vecchio was deadly serious. She had been in combat often enough and while most of her time was spent tending to various forms of space sickness, she was a crack surgeon and trauma doctor. "Okay, Jane, this is gonna hurt, so bear with me. I'm going to insert a nerve block into the wound." She waited until Jane grasped the side of the examination table. "Ready?" She leveled the hypo and released the spray.

"Yeow!" yelped Jane. In a moment, the pain subsided. "Hey, that's not too bad."

"Don't let it fool you, Jane. It's gonna hurt like hell when it wears off.

This is only so I can deep clean and close it up." She went to work, her face furrowed as she bent over the still gaping hole.

The nerve block allowed Jane to lie back and drift off to sleep. It was a black sleep, one without dreams. When at last she opened her eyes again, Dr. Vecchio was sitting at her desk. "Am I done?" asked Jane, testing her arm.

"Yep, for the moment."

"Can I take a shower and get dressed for dinner?"

"Absolutely...after the staff meeting. While you were sleeping, I took the liberty of sponging off your face."

With her good hand, Jane touched her own cheek; it felt clean, not gritty as it had when she came in. "Thanks, Doc." She sat upright, checked her balance, and gingerly slipped off the table.

"Here, put this on." She handed Jane a gray PRINCETON sweatshirt. "You can't walk around the ship without a shirt."

"No," giggled Jane, feeling a little light headed, "I suppose not."

"And do me a favor," said the doctor as she helped Jane into the sleeves. The injured arm went into a sling. "When you go back to your cabin to shower and change, take Winter with you. Let her give you a hand, and ask her to stay while you shower. That way, if you pass out, you won't drown. Remember, you've been hit. You're still running on adrenalin, so keep yourself quiet and stress free. If you don't, I'll haul you back here so fast you won't know what hit you...this time."

Jane laughed and promised she would enlist Belle's assistance. Feeling almost human, she headed up to the bridge.

The bridge was alive with activity. Every station was manned, all screens were lit and flashing. Tapper stood in the middle of it all, a docupad in his hand, shouting out orders. Belle looked frazzled as she punched code after code into the terminal, swearing softly to herself when her screen was slow to respond. Newhouse sat in the captain's chair, his eyes intent on the big screen as each exterior camera provided external shots in prescribed sequence. At ten second intervals, Lucas called out another designation and a flurry of flashes raced through the system.

Jane loved the preflight systems check. It gave her a rush of adrenaline, just knowing that soon the engines will begin building energy reserves only to release them at the moment of lift-off. Sliding behind Belle, she watched as her first assistant deftly manipulated the keypad with each command. It was good to see everything unchanged.

"Hi, I'm pitching in," murmured Belle between changes. "You okay?"

"Fine. Keep going."

"Wanna do this?"

"Can't. Only got one hand."

"Winter! Whaddya have now?" yelled Tapper without turning around.

"Two point one and rising. Three point four...five point six...eight point eight."

"Great! Keep it moving up in point two increments. Peters?"

"Pressure at eighty K and steady."

"Newhouse?"

"Peaking now at sixteen hundred RPS."

"Krieg?"

Jane was ready for him. "Thirty-two channels open; receiving on three. Forty-eight on standby."

"Open four and five."

"Opening," she called back.

"Status?"

"Open now, transmitting on five."

There was a pause while everyone waited for the screens to flash the next series. Jane kept one eye on the comm-panel, the other on the screen to the left of the main one, where her numbers would appear. All screens blinked yellow, then turned bright green, indicating all systems were congruent. There was an audible sigh of relief.

"Okay, people shut it down. Staff meeting in the wardroom in ten minutes." Tapper walked over to Jane. "Nice to have you back, Lieutenant."

"Thanks, Commander. Nice to be back."

Leaning close, he whispered "He's in his office. Go stick your head in the door."

Jane did as she was told. Pressing the intercom button, she said, "Permission to enter, Captain."

"Come." The door slid open. Morgan's face lit up when she came into the office. He waited for the door to close behind her before he jumped out of his chair.

Jane did not know what to expect, but it wasn't the lingering kiss he planted on her half-opened mouth.

"How do you feel?" he asked. Gingerly he touched arm in the sling.

"Stunned," Jane laughed. "I'm okay. I keep saying that to people, but it's true. I'm all right."

"No pain?"

"I wouldn't go that far." She looked down at her dirty trousers and the oversized sweatshirt Dr. Vecchio had lent her. "Permission to attend the staff meeting in my present state of disrepair, sir," she grinned.

"Frankly, you look beautiful. Alive and beautiful." His lips touched hers again.

Jane was unsettled by his kisses. Casting her eyes downward, she took a step away from him. "What happens next?"

"It's up to you." His voice was very soft.

"Maybe I should just sign myself into Bethesda and let you go without me."

"If that's what you want."

His answer brought Jane up short. "What about you, captain?" she snapped, angered by his passivity. "What do *you* want."

He refused to take the bait. "When I took you to my parents' house, I thought you knew."

"You work awfully fast for a guy who stays away from women."

Morgan sighed and leaned against his desk, his arms folded against his chest. "I'm too old for courtship rituals, Sarah Jane. I'm in love with you. I told you so last week, and I can say it easily, truthfully, again now. I know all the problems, all the pitfalls. There's an age difference between us...."

"It's only ten years," she said defensively.

"Eleven...closer to twelve. I've got a son."

"That's an excuse?"

"No, it's a consideration." He reached for her good hand. "And I'm your CO. There will be a certain amount of flack we'll both take, on a number of levels. One will be that you are under my command. The second will be the issue of cavorting with the boss's daughter. Third..."

"I can't think of a third, Asher."

"Third will be the resistance you will get from Speed, Tapper and Blackjack. While they will think this is all very cute, and I do mean cute, there will be a chorus of bloody murder if I announce I'm going to marry you."

"Whoa! Who said anything about marriage?" Jane protested, more than a little surprised.

"What did you think I was talking about?"

Her mouth opened and closed several times before anything came out of it. "I'm not ready to get married, Asher!"

"Not this minute, not tomorrow…Next week."

She knew he was teasing her. "Okay. I get it. We barely know each other. Just because you're Jonathan's friend, it doesn't mean I'm an extension of him…and anyway, he makes you crazy. Don't you think we should know each other a little better before we sign up for a lifetime hitch?" She pulled back from his embrace.

"Probably not a bad idea," he admitted

"And you can't pressure me."

"Agreed. Nor can this be public knowledge for a while. It has to be done slowly. If we agree to begin a relationship, it cannot be viewed by my crew as a political maneuver on either side."

"Agreed."

"Now, get out of here. I'll see you in the wardroom in five minutes."

As Jane went out, Tapper came in. "She looks pretty good all things considered, Boston," he said gruffly.

"Yeah, she does. You finished out there?"

"Yep. She's humming like a sewing machine. New reactor plate is working better with the mods the ground crew installed."

"Maybe it's just as well we came back. I'd hate to be stuck on some outpost with a sluggish propulsion system. Where's Blackjack?"

"In his cabin. Why?"

"Just wondering. He's planning on attending tonight's festivities?"

"As far as I know." Tapper eyed the captain suspiciously. "What's on your mind, Boston?" The only reply he got was an enigmatic smile.

The full complement of officers gathered in the wardroom to await Captain Morgan's final stateside briefing. Most were still dressed in non-regulation clothes and they made a colorful collection around the table. They were all curious about what exactly had happened to Jane since she disappeared five days earlier. Those who knew the truth weren't talking, choosing instead to listen to the speculation bantered about the room. The minute Jane entered the chatter ceased.

"I know you're all too polite to ask," began Jane with an impish grin, "I might as well tell you I was lasered this afternoon in the line of duty.

Dr. Vecchio will confirm that I am space worthy and will stay aboard ship. Until the matter is settled to the satisfaction of Fleet HQ, I'm…ah…" Jane pulled a wry face, "I'm not at liberty to answer any questions." She took the seat beside Lucas.

Morgan breezed in with Tapper. "Relax, people. This is nothing of any major import." Quickly, he reviewed the flight plan, filling in details as he went along. They were to resume the course from which they were diverted, with an additional stop added to the end for opening negotiations with the Wa'atsi. "We have the great good fortune to have been asked by the League of Planets to begin conversations with the Wa'atsi on a new treaty which will be the first step in admitting them to the League." Morgan beamed when his staff soundly applauded the achievement. "Thank you all; I appreciate your enthusiasm, but there's a hitch." He paused for the requisite groans. "Because we have had no *official* contact with this august race in the past, this first contact will require strict adherence to their protocol. During the next few months, all crewmates on all levels will be required to attend seminars on Wa'atsi culture. Those officers slated to attend the negotiations will be expected to learn the rudiments of the language. Ms. Krieg and Ms. Lucas will be in charge of aforementioned seminars."

There were several questions, easily fielded by the two women despite the fact this was the first they heard about it. "Anyone with exposure to Hatma languages should file with us as soon as possible," announced Jane.

"And I want to know if *anyone* on board this ship has visited any Wa'atsi outpost," added Lucas, "legally or not."

Morgan liked the way they automatically worked in tandem. Any doubts he harbored about Jane when she first arrived had long since disappeared. Hiding his grin, he waited for the last question to be answered before he continued. "There is to be a small dinner party this evening. This will basically be a debriefing. The guest list is distinguished and while I wish you all might be included, due to the sensitive nature of the visit, only the following will be in attendance: Bear, Cardozo; yes, people, Blackjack still walks amongst us; Krieg, Newhouse, Vecchio, and Lucas. The guest list includes Admiral Rothko, General Rothko, Ambassador and Lady Xin-thi-Ang, Senator Collins, and Admiral P'nucha." An impressed rustle went around the table. "I am asking, however, that we greet our guests in full dress uniforms all 'round. Since we will not be using the customary shuttle bay entrance, there will be a brief officer's review on the ground at eighteen hundred hours. There will be no general call for the crew. After that, those who are not on duty may have a last evening in town. Be back aboard by midnight, preflight begins at six hundred hours sharp. Any questions?" There were none. "See you on the tarmac at seventeen forty-five."

Jane didn't stick around for the usual post meeting banter. Belle was waiting for her at her quarters. "I wanted to get over to Bethesda to see my brother before we shove off," sighed Jane as Belle helped her out of the borrowed sweatshirt, "but I don't think I'll make it."

"Maybe after the dinner?"

"Maybe, if it doesn't go too late." When she got tangled in her pants, Jane started laughing

"I never imagined myself as a tiring-woman," giggled the yeomate, pulling the offending pant leg off.

"Where did you ever hear that word?" laughed Jane. "I thought I was the only one on the planet who still knew what it was!"

"That's how much you know, Lieutenant S.J.R. Krieg. You are not the only one who reads classic English lit! Just be thankful your yeomate is a woman!"

"You're right, you're right! This could be so much worse." Jane let Belle unhook the sling; she held her arm close, wincing at the sudden throb when the support was removed. "Make yourself comfortable; I'll manage from here." She left the door of the bathroom ajar, just in case she got into trouble. It was conceivable, thought Jane, that she might.

Instead of using the normal settings, Jane opted for a wide, steamy spray, figuring it would hurt less on her tender arm. Standing beneath the soft cascade, Jane closed her eyes and let the heat work its way into her bones. She used her good hand as best she could, but in the end, she was sure she hadn't gotten all the shampoo out of her long hair.

"Are you alive in there?" called Belle.

"Just getting out!" she called back. Painfully, she managed to wrap a towel around her torso. "I need help with my hair."

"You are leaving a wake, Lieutenant. Sit down." Jane did as she was told. Grabbing another towel, Belle went to work on her boss.

Dressed in sharp dress blues, Tapper rapped on Jane's door. "Are you decent?" he asked into the intercom.

The door slid open. Jane was at her desk, her nose buried in a pile of docupads. "Come on in. Are you here to escort me to the festivities?"

He doffed his hat and swept a large, gallant bow. "At your service, madam officer. How're you feeling?" He winced when he saw her arm in the sling.

"As well as can be expected. My face is still kinda purple."

"I'll say; you could almost pass for a Jeylosian farmer. Does it hurt?"

Jane shrugged. "What's a little pain when you've saved the universe as we know it?"

He grinned awkwardly, his hands playing with his hat. "S.J., there's been something I've been meaning to talk to you about," mumbled Tapper.

There was a strange, vaguely uncomfortable edginess in the way he shifted from one foot to the other, causing Jane to put down her papers. "What is it, Tapper? What's wrong?"

"Nothing's wrong, Sarah Jane. It's just... well, I was thinking....I mean...." He kept turning the hat in his hand, his face growing redder with every passing second. Suddenly, he stopped stuttering, took a deep breath, and blurted out "Will you marry me?"

Jane's mouth fell open. "Oh, Tapper!"

"When I heard what happened, Sarah, I got scared. I couldn't think about life without you! This isn't a mercy proposal, and I don't expect you to say yes without thinking about it, but jeez, don't you think we'd be good together? I've known you since you were a kid, and your folks like me. We've got all the right...the right...components."

Somehow, Jane managed to get to her feet without tipping over. She went to Tapper and put her one good hand on his very red cheek. "Joshua Isaiah Bear, you are the sweetest man I have ever known." She kissed his cheek lightly, "but as much as I would like to say yes, and you are right, we do have all the right... components, we are missing one very important one. It's true, I do love you very much, but it's more like the way I love Jonathan. Like a brother. But just so you know.....had you asked me ten years ago, I would have thrown myself in your arms." Her grin was infectious; he grinned back.

Tapper raised her hand to his lips. "I think someone has beaten me to the punch." He watched her nod solemnly. "I guess I've known for a while. Even before we barged in at the cabin. You did all the hard work, but

Boston was as pale as a ghost. Yeah, we made a lot of jokes, but Blackjack said he was a goner. You went to his parents', right?" She nodded again. "This is serious, isn't it?" There was a third nod. "Be careful, Sarah Jane; his ship comes first."

"I know. But I'm attached to his ship right now." She fluttered her big, grey eyes at him. "Besides, how can he possibly resist a veritable, real-life galactic heroine?"

"Speed's sister, real-life galactic pain-in-the-ass is more like it" snorted the burly commander, understanding that she knew exactly what she was getting herself into. He loved how she wiggled her eyebrows at him. Had she said *yes*, he would've married her in a heartbeat. Offering his arm, Tapper said, "May I escort you to the festivities, Mademoiselle Galactica?"

"Why, I'd be delighted!" Just a little shaky, she was glad to have someone to lean on.

Still on Tapper's arm, Jane stood at the bottom on the gangway talking to Lucas when Morgan came strolling down the carpet. Quietly, he slipped behind Jane and managed to give her good shoulder a quick, reassuring squeeze. If Lucas noticed the gesture, she made no comment. A ground crewmate piped the shrill boatswain's call from the terminal door. Instantly, the officers formed two lines and stood to attention. The wide glass doors slid open to reveal Admiral Rothko and a tall, veiled woman on his arm. Behind him walked Ambassador Xinthi-Ang, General Rothko on his arm. Lady Xinthi-Ang followed with the much shorter Admiral P'nucha along with Senator Collins on Blackjack's arm. Security swarmed around them, giving Jane the distinct impression that the newcomer to the group was of extreme importance.

The line of officers snapped a salute as Captain Morgan stepped forward to greet their guests. Much to everyone's amazement, he bowed slightly toward the veiled woman before taking her offering his arm. One by one, he introduced her to his officers.

"Allow me to present Lieutenant S.J.R.Krieg, Your Imperial Majesty," he said when he reached Jane.

The empress's green eyes peered through her veil, "I would convey my husband's apologies to you, Lieutenant Krieg," she said in Jeylosian. "His heart is most heavy with the sadness he has caused you."

Jane swallowed hard. The last person she ever expected to meet was the mother of Pana-Di and her faced flushed deep red. "My heart grieves with you at this moment of personal sadness," she managed to say.

The empress nodded and started to move off, then returned to Jane. "You must understand, Lieutenant, the pain outweighs the grief, and in words of truth, I tell you I bear no malice toward you for your actions, only the greatest of admiration. Had I been there, I would have been the one to end my son's life." Sliding her arm into Morgan's she glided majestically toward the gangway.

Lady Xinthi-Ang caught Jane's hand in hers. "Choma Ampat-Di is a strong woman, Jane," she murmured, "she would have ordered his execution long before this had her husband permitted it. Pana-Di was source of great embarrassment and there were many days his actions shamed her. My sister has only the greatest admiration for you and your courage, Jane."

"Your sister?" Jane's mouth fell open; she knew the ambassador and his wife were related to the royal family, but she had no idea the empress was her sister. "I am so sorry, Lady Xinthi-Ang," she whispered.

The lady shrugged. "It is not common knowledge here, as it is at home. Choma Ampat-Di is not well known off our planet. She has come to take Pana-Di back to Jeylos, but she would not leave until she met you." Lady Xinthi-Ang noticed the others waiting for her. "We will talk more later," she said, giving Jane's hand a squeeze.

The atmosphere in the observatory was subdued as the guests spoke quietly with the officers of the *Washington*. General Rothko cornered her daughter as discreetly as possible and began firing questions in a rapid whisper.

"Honestly, I'm okay, Mom," she whispered back. "There's no major damage and I'll heal up in a week or so." She tried to feel as confident as she sounded but it was hard.

"Your father is furious with your captain, Sarah Jane, as well as with Interpol. He thinks they were derelict in not telling you Rega-Dop was missing...."

"But I already knew. Look, there was one chance in a million he would find me the way he did..."

"Nonsense, Sarah. He was stalking you"

Jane smiled through clenched teeth. "Mother," she hissed, "this is neither the time nor the place to hash this out. If you want to argue with me about it, save it for the dinner table when I get home…in about a year."

"Lay off, Liz," murmured the admiral coming up beside them. "We can deal with this privately."

The general set her mouth in a firm line.. "I can't help it, Ted, I'm still her mother."

"We know that," father and daughter whispered in unison.

"I didn't think the empress ever travelled off planet," said Jane, turning to her father, happy to change the subject.

"Usually not, but the Emperor felt this was an important exception. Besides, Tasma Xinthi-Ang thought it best her sister handle this personally and the Emperor agreed." Rothko glanced at the empress sitting in the corner of the observatory deep in conversation with Morgan, Cardozo and Lady Xinthi-Ang. The ambassador stood nearby, his hands folded before him, listening to their discussion. "I suppose I should go over there," said the admiral. "Would you care to join me, lieutenant?"

"Do I hafta?"

Admiral Rothko laughed softly. "Yes, you hafta." He took her good arm and escorted her over to the little group.

As soon as the Rothkos joined them, Morgan rose and cleared his throat. "Ladies and gentlemen, Her Imperial Majesty."

The empress rose, lifted her veil over her head, and faced the assembly. "Gracious hosts," she began in heavily accented English, "as representative of His Imperial Majesty, Ampat-Di, Kaila of Jeylos and her surrounding moons, I have been given a task which is both pleasurable and solemn." She looked to the ambassador who stepped forward with a small box in his hand. "In return for your gracious hospitality, our son Pana-Di..." her voice faltered, but recovered, "repaid you with grievous crimes against your government and our own." She turned to Jane and took a step toward her. "You have sustained bodily harm at the hand of Pana-Di and his cadre and for this we are most pained. We cannot offer words of comfort enough, nor is any apology to you and your family sufficient to repair the harm done. Lieutenant Krieg, it is the wish of our husband that you be awarded the highest honor on Jeylos, Defender of Peace and Good Harmony." Ambassador Xinthi-Ang opened the box and the empress removed its contents. "Please accept this honor, Lieutenant, along with our hopes that you will visit our planet once more to be received and properly thanked by His Imperial Majesty." With elegant fingers, she pinned the star-shaped medal to Jane's uniform.

Jane was flustered and she looked to her father for help. The admiral merely nodded. "Your graciousness humbles me," began Jane in a quavering voice, "and I accept your thanks with my deepest heart. I am greatly honored by this kindness and wish Your Imperial Majesties quick healing of your own pain."

In an uncharacteristic gesture for a Jeylosian, the empress touched Jane's bruised face. "Your physical pain will heal, lieutenant; we can only hope your spiritual pain will fade with it. You do honor to your family." The empress smiled sadly; she wished her own son had done the same for her.

A steward entered with a tray. He moved around the room quickly, handing a slim flute of Jeylosian spring wine to each guest, then left. When he was gone, Ambassador Xinthi-Ang cleared his throat. "I would offer a toast in honor of the officers and crew of the *Washington, D.C.* Under the command of Captain Morgan, they have performed great service to the people of Jeylos."

There were murmurs of "Hear, hear!" and everyone raised a glass.

"His Imperial Majesty, Ampat-Di," continued the ambassador, "together with the Supreme High Chancellor of the Wa'atsi, Natchnat K'ladnam T'cha, has issued a battle ribbon to be worn by all members of this ship, in accordance with the custom of the League of Planets. We are all grateful for your aide in preventing an interplanetary war between our peoples."

Admiral P'nucha stepped forward to join the ambassador and raised his glass. "On behalf of the Supreme High Command, I salute you."

On Barb Lucas's advice, Morgan requested the table be set up as round, in keeping with Jeylosian custom. Seating was carefully arranged to maximize communication. Beginning with the Captain, the guests were seated in what Barb felt was conversational order. To the Captain's right sat Lady Xinthi-Ang, Commander Bear beside her, and Commander Lucas to his right. On Barb's other side sat Ambassador Xinthi-Ang, and beside him, Lieutenant Krieg. The admiral sat beside his daughter, with the empress on his right and, at her request, Blackjack on her right. Dr. Vecchio sat between Blackjack and Commander Newhouse, with Senator Collins to his right, and Admiral P'nucha on her other side. General Rothko sat between P'nucha and Morgan. The deliberation of the seating plan paid off; those who needed most to talk to each other did, while those who needed to observe, could.

Jane was relieved to have her father as a buffer between her and the empress. Despite the woman's kind words, Jane did not relish sitting near the late kora's mother. The woman seemed to be in complete control of her grief, something which simply amazed Jane. She listened to the empress converse easily with her father. She could hear the melodious sound of court Jeylosian and realized her father must have a translator tucked in his ear. The empress obviously understood some English, but Jane suspected she, too, wore a discreet device. Blackjack also listened to the empress as she related what appeared to be an amusing tale, judging by the smiles those nearby had plastered on their faces. Jane turned slightly in her seat, toward Ambassador Xinthi-Ang, who was deep in conversation with Tapper and Barb Lucas. Newhouse was talking quietly to Vecchio about something serious. Jane glanced at her mother, only to find the general involved in discussion with Admiral P'nucha. Feeling most isolated, Jane toyed with her salad, not really feeling much at all like eating.

From his vantage point, Morgan watched Jane while he talked to Lady Xinthi-Ang. His heart went out to her; she looked lonely, forlorn, and in pain. He regretted agreeing to this dinner party, wishing instead he could be sitting in his cabin with her, sharing a bottle of wine and a couple of steaks from his private stock.

"You are not completely with us, are you, Captain?" chided Lady Xinthi-Ang gently when she followed his gaze to Jane's downcast face.

"I'm sorry, Lady Xinthi-Ang; I'm concerned about the lieutenant."

"As well you should be, captain. If I were General Rothko, I would order her to bed immediately. I cannot imagine why you permitted her to attend this evening."

Morgan chuckled at the thought of sending Jane to bed. "I doubt if she would have listened to her mother, much less me, madam. Most likely, she would have told me to mind my own business."

"Pulling a different kind of rank, as it were?" laughed the lady.

"You might say that. In this case, I think she would have used her parents against me." He grinned, letting her know the remark was in jest.

Lady Xinthi-Ang did not let the remark pass. "And you can ill afford to have the parents displeased with you right now, can you, Captain?"

He noted the amusement in her eyes, and he could feel himself redden beneath his dark beard. "I'm not sure what you mean, Lady Xinthi-Ang."

She leaned closer to him. "Oh, come now, Captain Morgan; I would be a fool not to know you have feelings for the lieutenant."

"Is it so obvious?"

"Very." She leaned close to Morgan. "Do not feel awkward, captain; I am equally certain most people do not observe these things the way Jeylosians do."

Lady Xinthi-Ang was not the only one to notice Jane's discomfort. From across the table, General Rothko watched her daughter go from pale to paler and she began to wonder why she had not put her foot down and ordered Sarah Jane to remain in her cabin. But this was not her command and she could only hope her headstrong daughter would have enough sense to excuse herself from the party. Catching her husband's eye, she motioned to him to look to his left. The admiral did so, and his brows knit with concern. "Are you sure you're all right?" he whispered to his daughter.

"Yes, sir, I'm fine," replied Jane woodenly.

"I don't think so; you look awful. Why don't you go back to your cabin?"

Jane shook her head empathically *no.* "I'll be fine. I just need to eat something." She took a bit of salad on her fork and forced a smile as she pushed it into her mouth.

The taste was noxious. Jane could feel herself turning green as beads of sweat began to form on her forehead. Forcing herself to swallow, she felt ready to retch. The room began to swim and it took all her concentration to hang on to the edge of the table. "Sir," she rasped, "I don't think I feel so good. May I please be excused?"

All conversation ceased. Admiral Rothko caught Jane as she tried unsuccessfully to stand. Dr. Vecchio leapt from her place and tore around the table. Morgan followed in close pursuit, but it was Admiral Rothko who lifted Jane in his arms. "Your Imperial Majesty, if you would forgive us. I believe the lieutenant has had enough excitement for one day. Doctor?"

"The nerve block just wore off. Let's take her home, Admiral." Leading the way, Dr. Vecchio took the admiral to the cage and ordered the machine to E-2.

"If you wish to join them, Madame General," said the empress after a few moments, "please do."

Liz Rothko was torn. She wanted to go, yet she knew her husband and daughter needed to have a few minutes alone. "Thank you, but I think I will stay. I'm sure the lieutenant is in most capable hands." There was an appreciative ripple of laughter from everyone but Morgan who sat scowling at beside her. The general silently slid her hand under the table and rapped the captain on the leg. "Stow it, sailor," she whispered with a tight smile; "stay where you are and that's an order."

CHAPTER 34

The admiral gently deposited Jane on the bed and turned away to let the doctor do her work.

"I brought a kit with me to the dinner just in case," said Dr. Vecchio as she prepared a hypo. "I should've kept her in sick bay, but..."

"Don't apologize, doctor. I know my daughter and you couldn't have kept her there unless she was heavily sedated."

Angela Vecchio stopped midway to Jane's arm. "I did not know she was your daughter until today. That was a surprise."

The admiral shrugged, "I think...no, I *know* she prefers people not knowing. We're not exactly run-of-the-mill parents, I suppose."

"There's an understatement." Vecchio applied the hypo, then wiped away the excess with a swab. "That should take care of it for the moment. I tried to warn her she was running on adrenalin and nerve block, but I don't think she believed me. Jane's been through a lot these past few days."

"More than you might suspect."

"No disrespect, Admiral, but I saw the hospital report from Vermont. I have a pretty good idea of what's going on."

"Should she be off ship?"

"No; that would do more harm than good. She needs to be at her post, resuming her duties to ward off more serious, psychological trauma. I think once we take off, she'll settle down and give herself time to heal. I'll recommend she be given limited overnight duty for the next month. She needs rest, too."

"I hope you're right, doctor. We've already got one in the hospital; I'd prefer not to have two."

Dr. Vecchio smiled in sympathy. "I hear the major's going to be fine."

"If the nurses don't kill him; he's not an easy patient," chuckled the admiral.

A female voice called from the outer room. "May I come in?"

"Come on in, Belle," called Dr. Vecchio. "Did the captain send you?"

"No, Tapper beeped me," she answered as she joined them. "I'll stay with Jane so you both can go back to the wardroom. You should really be there."

The admiral looked at Dr. Vecchio and then at Winter. "If you're finished, I'll be along in a minute."

"Yes, sir," replied the doctor as she snapped her kit shut. "When Jane comes around, buzz me. It doesn't matter what time."

"Yes, ma'am. Anything you want me to do?"

"Just keep an eye on her. I've given her a light sedative, but not enough to keep her out. She'll awaken at will. Just let me know when."

Rothko waited for the outer door to slide shut before he motioned to Belle to join him in the sitting room. "What happened this afternoon was not your fault, Winter," he said softly.

"I beg to differ, sir. Had I been more alert, I would have recognized Rega-Dop at the Center." Belle was already doing a fine job beating herself up for the fiasco.

He shook his head. "I've read the initial report. There was nothing you could or should have done differently."

Belle frowned; there was plenty she and Cardozo should have done differently. "It would be unfair to assign responsibility to Captain Cardozo, sir. He reacted swiftly and appropriately."

Jingling his keys in his pocket, the admiral paced the cabin. Morgan had already been the recipient of his wrath, before the other guests arrived at the terminal. Morgan staunchly defended Cardozo, shifting any blame onto himself for even allowing Jane to leave the ship. The general had sided with Morgan in an effort to keep her furious husband from punching the captain in the nose. In the last analysis, Rothko knew they were right and he was wrong, but it was Winter's own decision to accept responsibility which made him stop to think about what he felt. Suddenly, Edward Rothko felt very old. "You know, Winter, that as Fleet Admiral, I am the one who should have ordered the lieutenant confined to quarters until Rega-Dop was apprehended."

"And in the end, *Mr.* Rothko," she said gently, "you are really just Sarah Jane's father."

Mr. Rothko. Admiral Rothko hadn't heard himself referred to as *mister* since parents' weekend during his daughter's freshman year at college. Oddly, it had a nice ring to it. "Yeah; I guess I am."

Admiral Rothko was stepping from the cage as Cardozo exited the wardroom. "I was just goin' to check on Jane. How's she doin'?" he asked, his voice filled with honest concern.

"Sarah's asleep." His expression was less than friendly as he brushed past the other officer.

Blackjack's hand shot out and grabbed Rothko. "Look, Ted, I know you're angry and I'd be too, if she were my daughter. But if you're going to hold anyone responsible, it should be me; not Morgan, not Winter. I was the one sent along as the bodyguard and I let her wander out of my sight." He dropped his hand from Rothko's arm.

"I ought to bust you down to mate, Jackson," snapped Rothko, his eyes cold as ice. "I ought to bust you right out of the Fleet. You're damn right you're responsible for what happened this afternoon. You, of all people, to under estimate Rega-Dop! Interpol was damn specific about the danger, yet you let her leave the room unattended. You're lucky she's alive, Jackson, or you'd be facing a court martial right about now."

"I'm not arguing with you, Ted," countered Blackjack. "But you have to ask yourself how much of this is because she is Sarah Jane. Would you be so all fired up over a mere officer?"

"What the hell are you implying, Jackson?"

"I'm saying straight out that you cannot apply two standards to your officers."

"You accusing me of nepotism?" demanded the admiral.

"Not nepotism, Ted, parentalism. Yeah, this was a bad situation, but Sarah Jane handled herself like the pro she is; any other green kid might've panicked, but she didn't. Y'know, she doesn't use your name for good reason, but this on her record will speak volumes for her ability. Why don't you quit kidding yourself and just admit you're damn proud of her as an officer, not as your offspring?"

Rothko's hands were balled into two tight fists. "Who the hell are you to tell me what to think, Jackson?"

"Just another product of your own indoctrination, Admiral, sir." He gave the admiral a cynical smile. "Aren't you the guy who taught me to tell the truth 'til it hurts?" When Rothko did nothing but glower, Cardozo shrugged. "I thought so." He turned on his heel and went back into the wardroom.

⊖⊖⊖

The main course was being served when Admiral Rothko rejoined the party. "The lieutenant is resting comfortably," he announced, "but I am afraid she will miss the rest of the dinner. Please accept her apologies." There was a murmur of understanding. He took his place beside the empress just as Cardozo strolled back into the wardroom. Ignoring him, Rothko leaned closed to the empress. "I know when she awakens, the lieutenant will be most embarrassed by her physical weakness, Your Imperial Majesty. I hope you will think kindly of her in spite of this."

"Your apology is unnecessary, Admiral. Your daughter has exhibited great strength, far more than we would have under these conditions. She has been injured, yet she insisted on attending. Give her credit, not criticism," she told him in his ear. "Perhaps, had we been more understanding of our own beloved child, we would not be returning him to his home in a shroud."

The parent in Admiral Rothko winced at her obvious pain. "May it be, Your Imperial Majesty, that we never grow too old as parents to learn."

"So be it, Admiral Rothko."

⊖⊖⊖

After dinner, when brandy was served in the observatory, the real business began. The captain slipped into the role of impartial moderator as Senator Collins laid out the proposals suggested in her meetings with P'nucha, Xinthi-Ang and the Rothkos during the last week. Morgan was greatly impressed by the empress as she asked probing questions of her ambassador. Her concerns, voiced on behalf of her husband, centered on the rights of safe passage for Jeylosian ships through Wa'atsi territory.

"If you are willing to prosecute pirate captains," the empress told Admiral P'nucha, "we will be more willing to turn them over to you. In the past, you have not responded to our requests for justice. Our people are prepared to send an ambassador to the Supreme High Command in order to open formal negotiations, but we must have guarantees."

"Those guarantees will be spelled out in the formal treaty, Your Imperial Majesty" said Collins. "In turn, the Wa'atsi want open trading routes for their goods."

"Provided those goods are not stolen, we can see no difficulty," countered the empress.

P'nucha snorted indelicately. "Not all Wa'atsi are thieves, Imperial Majesty."

"We did not mean to infer this was so, Gacham P'nucha. We are merely stating that our past experience has not been of the most positive nature. Our son became embroiled in a scheme in which your people played a major role and while we are ready to begin anew, we are not so naïve as to believe your history has not condoned such endeavors in the past." The empress had tossed down the gauntlet and sat back to watch the fireworks, all the while slowly sipping a glass of cognac.

The level of the conversation rose and fell as points were scored. Vecchio and Newhouse, while not directly involved in the process were there because Captain Morgan respected their opinions. Tapper and Blackjack lounged together against the wide windows, periodically calling out a point of clarification. It was only when Admiral P'nucha questioned Jeylosian motives that Cardozo finally took an active role.

"Ah am of the mind, ladies and gentlemen, that little will be accomplished here as long as backhanded name callin' is permitted. May Ah be so bold as to suggest we dispense with the jockeyin' for position and get on with layin' a groundwork?"

There was dead silence in the room. General Rothko was shocked, her husband appalled, the ambassador stunned and P'nucha.... laughed. The harder he laughed, the wider the mouths fell when the empress joined him.

"We believe, Gacham P'nucha" said the empress, catching her breath, "our esteemed colleague, Captain Cardozo, would like us to cut to the chase?"

"Exactly, ma'am," agreed Blackjack, a self-satisfied grin splitting his face.

"Then here is our proposal. Gacham P'nucha, we would be honored if you would consent to visit Jeylos as soon as possible, in order to present this concept to our august husband, His Imperial Majesty, Ampat-Di. I firmly believe an agreement can be more easily reached when the principals are face to face. After all, Gacham P'nucha, you are the one who will be hailed as hero when this is done."

The admiral's chest puffed out. "I would be pleased to come, Your Imperial Majesty."

The empress rose and everyone followed suit. "We thank you, Captain Morgan, for your gracious hospitality, but the hour grows late and we are fatigued. We are pleased with this evening's progress and will leave the details to be arranged by our ambassador, Repat Xinthi-Ang." She started toward the door then turned around. "Please give our kindest wishes for speedy healing to the lieutenant."

Morgan and the Rothkos escorted the guests down the gangway to the waiting hovercars. Pleasantries were exchanged, but it was Pat Collins' parting thumbs up that convinced Morgan everything would be worked out. Walking back up to the ship, the three met Tapper and Blackjack tearing down the gangway.

"And where are you two off to in such a hurry?" asked General Rothko with a frown.

"Over to Bethesda, Cousin Liz," answered Blackjack, pausing long enough to kiss her cheek. "We wanna see Speed before we go."

Morgan only shook his head. "There's always trouble when they're together," he muttered.

"And you're not part of that circus, Captain?" asked the general with a raised eyebrow. "If you didn't have us to contend with, you'd be running off with them."

"Frankly, I think it's me they're avoiding," the admiral shrugged, "not you, Captain."

"And for good reason, Ted," countered the general; "You told me you were pretty hard on Jackson tonight."

"Me? What did I do that was so out of line?"

"Oh, don't look so innocent, Ted," sighed his wife. "You hold Jackson, Tapper and Ash, here, responsible for what happened to Sarah Jane." She glanced at Morgan and saw guilt written all over his face. "You know it and I know it. They aren't and you're wrong."

"Yeah, well..." Rothko leaned against the handrail, his hands stuffed in his pockets. "I should've put Jane under house arrest. I didn't; what happened this afternoon is my fault. I can only thank God she's all right."

"We all have a piece of this," said Morgan.

"Don't contradict me, captain. You're not my son-in-law yet!" Rothko snapped, a little sharper than he would have wished.

Morgan's mouth flapped open, then closed. Only the look of amusement on Liz Rothko's face kept him from saying anything else.

Jane was sitting up on the bed, Dr. Vecchio in attendance, when her parents and Morgan arrived. "I'm really sorry, guys," cried Jane when they walked through the door. "I blew it. I really blew it."

"Don't be ridiculous, Sarah," answered her mother, sitting on the edge of the bed. "How are you feeling?"

"I have a headache."

"And your arm?"

"It hurts." Jane slid down the bed. "But worst of all, I feel like an idiot."

"Not nearly as idiotic as your father, sweetheart." The general looked up at the admiral, then smiled. "Dr. Vecchio, Crewmate Winter, would you be offended if we asked for a private moment with the patient?"

"Not at all, ma'am," replied Vecchio. "Jane, I'll be in sickbay for the next hour or so if you need me."

"And I'll be in my cabin changing out of this monkey suit," grinned Belle. "Just call when you're ready for me to come back."

"Thanks, Belle." Jane let her mother adjust the pillow behind her back. "Are you just going to stand around and make me feel even stupider?" she asked the men.

"I'll take off if you don't need me," offered Morgan stiffly.

"Sit down, Asher," commanded the admiral. The captain did as he was told. "I have something to say to the both of you." He paced the cabin a few times, then stood in the center of the room. "As Fleet Admiral, I am well aware that relationships often take root while a ship is cruising in deep space. As officers aboard the *Washington*, I need not remind you both of your positions." He paused, as though he expected some interruption. "Sarah Jane, your mother and I know you are an adult and we have every faith in your performance in the line of duty; you have never given us any cause to doubt your ability as an officer in this fleet. We have every confidence you will continue to make us proud."

"What your father is trying to say, Sarah, is that he trusts your judgment," said the general.

"Thanks, Mom," Jane said seriously, "I wasn't sure."

The Admiral turned to Morgan. "As for you, Asher, we are of the joint belief that your commission means more to you than just about anything else. As commanding officers, we know you do not routinely run about jeopardizing your officers or your ship. As parents, we can only stand back and keep our collective mouths shut." He glanced at his wife who nodded.

Morgan thought he discerned a certain amount of skepticism in Rothko's voice, but he would not risk even the smallest smile at this point. After all, he reasoned, this was, if all went well, his future father-in-law and he had no desire to alienate the man. Still, he felt he had a stronger ally in the general, judging by the way she held her daughter's hand. "I appreciate your confidence, Admiral," intoned Morgan with great gravity. "I hope that, given a little down time, Sarah Jane will be back at her station on the bridge."

"Should you and the lieutenant find yourselves....er....enmeshed in an interpersonal relationship, I am insisting you have the sense to keep it off the bridge. Do I make myself clear?" He watched two heads bob up and down. "Morgan, I'd like a word with you in private." He marched into the sitting room, the captain right behind him.

The door slid shut. "Sit down, Ash." Rothko pointed to the little table in the corner of the cabin. Again, the captain did as he was told. Rothko took the opposite seat and folded his hands on the table. "Usually, these kinds of interviews are done in my office after routine debriefing, but we don't have time for the amenities right now."

"I understand, sir," replied Morgan, wondering what was on the admiral's mind.

"I took the opportunity to review your file this morning. You've had, as we both know, a rather meteoric career, beginning with your chaplaincy. You've been assigned more than the usual number of hot spots." He raised an eyebrow. "You didn't get the *Washington* because you were a mediocre captain."

"I believe, sir, I got the *Washington* because of my skills in diplomacy and my ability to negotiate."

"Your training as a clergyman has served you well; but beyond that, other than the year you remained planetside during your wife's illness, you've spent your time in space. Have you given any consideration to what you'd like to do after the *Washington*?"

The question brought Morgan up short. *After the Washington?* Was the admiral hinting there would be a change in command? "I'm not sure; I've been so focused on getting this ship up and functional, I hadn't given it much thought."

"Your review comes up soon, Ash. You're due for a promotion...to commodore. What are you going to do, let it pass?"

"I didn't know that was an option."

"It's always an option; not a particularly intelligent one, but an option all the same."

Morgan scratched his beard. Rothko obviously had something up his sleeve and he felt obliged to take the bait. "Got anything in mind?"

"In or out of space?"

"Either. What are you thinking?"

"Tremna likes you. Would you consider heading the operation on Lomos for a couple of years?"

"What about Kip Lucas? I thought that was his thing."

"It is. We were thinking that a team could be put in place to oversee the construction of the new space port. It requires, at minimum, a five mate team: the chief architect, a ship engineer, a communications specialist, and the C.O."

"That's four; who's the fifth?"

"An ambassador...Barb Lucas." Rothko allowed himself a sly smile. "Kip wants to retain the chief architect post. You could take your son; it's about time you spent some real time with him."

Morgan winced at the rebuke. "I see you've already thought this out pretty carefully."

"And why not? It's the biggest outland base we've ever contracted and it's important. Would you be interested?"

"Possibly; it depends on the rest of the team. Who'd you have in mind?"

"That would be for the C.O. to decide. He'd pretty much have a free hand in picking his people. "Or her people," added Morgan.

"What's the timetable?"

"The engineer and the attaché have to be in place by next summer; communications and the C.O. by the end of the calendar year. Can you live with that?"

"Possibly. I'd have to talk it over with a couple of my people.

"I know one engineer who is interested…depending on the C.O."

"You talked to him?"

"Last May, when you were in port. He came over for dinner and the topic came up."

"He never said anything."

"I told him not to. I wasn't ready to pull him off this ship quite yet. And there were some details to be finalized before I asked you. Now, we're ready to move ahead.

"Who would take the *Washington*?"

"Coleridge, perhaps. Maybe even Jackson, on a trial basis of course. It would require him coming back into the Fleet on an official transfer...if I don't kill him first."

"Maybe he won't want her."

"Maybe he will."

Morgan eyed him suspiciously. "Have you already asked him? Or has he asked you?"

"Neither," shrugged Rothko, "it's merely a thought. One I will rethink, however, after today's debacle. I'm pretty pissed at him right now."

"He'd make a helluva captain for this palace. You might not have much control over him."

"That's what you think, Boston."

Morgan chuckled softly. "That's one I'd like to see. You'd be spending half your time shuttling all over the galaxy chasing him down." Morgan paused and studied the admiral carefully. "What about you? Why don't you and the general take her for a year? The general is getting ready to step down; she's said so herself."

It was Rothko's turn to laugh. "Don't think we haven't talked about it! The truth of the matter is we're thinking more of the *Merrimack* when she ships out for the first interplanetary Cadet Review next year. We thought we'd have Rebecca and Isaac join us for their summer vacation. If Liz is going to teach at super school next September, she'd have to be back by then. The timing is right."

"Are you going to retire, sir?"

The Admiral shook his head. "Nah, I was thinking more of a short sabba*tical* before I take my last rotation as Chairman of the Joint Chiefs. I haven't been on a grand tour in years and the *Merrimack* would be a nice change. The *Merrimack* has always been one of my favorites...." his voice trailed wistfully off.

Morgan knew the *Merrimack* had been under his command when she first sailed two decades years earlier. And he was right; the change would do both Rothkos good. "May I think it over? It's a lot to digest."

A soft chime from Jane's comm-panel caught their attention. "Newhouse here, Captain Morgan. You've got a call coming over from Bethesda. You want to take it there or on the bridge?"

"Here, Joe. Thanks." Morgan walked over to the screen and flicked it on visual. A pale, bruised but smiling face filled the screen. "Hey, Speed, what's up?"

"I should ask you why you're in my sister's cabin, more like it," laughed the pilot. He grimaced; laughing irritated the tube still running though his nose.

The admiral joined Morgan at the panel. "He's chaperoned. What are you doing making calls, Jonathan?" asked his father sternly. "You're not supposed to be out of bed, yet."

"I've been hijacked, Dad, forced to make this call by a couple of space-crazed sailors." His grin was as broad as his battered face allowed.

"Hrrumph. I imagine you called to talk to Sarah Jane. Let me see if she's up to it." Rothko rapped on the bedroom door, then went in, letting it slide closed behind him.

"Okay, Boston," said Jonathan suddenly serious, "cut the crap. How's S.J.?"

"Better than you think. I won't lie to you, Speed, she took a hit, but she didn't go down. She's a powerhouse and she impressed the hell outta me this afternoon."

"She's a fine woman, too, Boston, but she's my sister. Don't forget that."

"I took her to my folks for Shabbat."

Jonathan snorted. "Are you kidding?"

"Nope." replied Morgan, wondering if he was going to be interviewed by every member of the clan individually.

"You gonna marry my little sister, Boston?"

"I'd like to, if she'd let me ask her." There was a whoop of laughter, only it didn't come from Jonathan. "Are those bozos eavesdropping?" demanded Morgan.

"Damn straight, we are!" Cardozo howled, sticking his head beside Jonathan's. "She turned you down?"

"Hell, no!" growled Morgan.

"But she didn't say yes, did she?" prodded Cardozo with a wicked grin.

"Do you have anything to add to this, Tap?" asked Morgan, hoping for help.

Tapper's face joined the other two. He wasn't going to let anyone, not even Morgan, know Jane had already told him. "Don't look at me, Boston. I'm keeping my opinions to myself."

"Smart man. I would suggest your buddies follow your example and keep their collective mouths shut." He was about to add something else when the door slid open and General Rothko emerged from the bedroom. "Hang on, Speed, here's your mother."

"Sarah will talk to you, but she'll use the handset. She's a little too shaky to get out of bed." She waited until she saw the audio light blink on, then flicked off the screen. "Well, captain, I hope you know what you're getting into," she said gently. "She is not the easiest human being on the planet."

"Neither am I, or so I've been told… more than once," he shrugged. "It's far from a done deal, ma'am, but I'm hoping with some time it might work out."

⁂

The hour was late when Morgan escorted the Rothkos to the waiting car. The night sky was black; despite the lights of the base, stars were visible, twinkling sharply in the dark canopy. Morgan shook the admiral's hand one last time, but hugged the general, and thanked them for their wishes for a safe and easy journey. "If it's not," laughed Morgan, "you'll be the first to know." He stood beside the gangway, watching them drive off, a little reluctant to go back aboard. At last, when he saw the gate close behind them, he ambled back up the gangway and headed to Jane's cabin.

⁂

Belle was sitting on the sofa wrapped in a robe. "She's asleep, but I'm going to spend the night out here, just in case. Dr. Vecchio thinks it's a good idea."

"Thanks, but call me when she wakes up."

"No," said Belle firmly. "You need a good night's sleep, captain. Unless there's an emergency, I won't buzz you."

Morgan was about to protest, but the words faded before they reached his lips. "Yeah, you're right. I'll see you in the morning." Bone weary, he went to his quarters.

CHAPTER 35

Tapper was running the pre-flight check when Morgan strolled off the cage at 0605 hours looking refreshed and ready to go. His hair, still damp from a quick shower, curled around his ears, glinting in the bright light of the bridge. On the view screen, he saw the ground crew unlocking the pylon supports from beneath his ship while the last supply truck roll away from the loading portal. It was a sight he loved every time he saw it and this time, he was especially glad to watch the tethers which kept him planetside slide off into the distance.

Looking about the bridge, he silently counted heads. No station was left unmanned, but at the comm-panel, Ho Ngyuen, instead of Jane, was bent over the screen. A brief wave of disappointment washed over him, but he quickly shook it off. "Where are we, commander?" he asked Tapper.

"Lift off minus fifty-five minutes....right on schedule."

"How are the new mods working?"

"They're cold, but holding their own. I won't know until we've been up for a couple of days. They're pretty, captain," grinned Tapper, "but I'm not making any promises about efficiency."

"Good enough, commander." He headed toward his ready room. "I'll join you in time for countdown."

"Yes, sir." Tapper watched his friend disappear through the door then turned his attention back to the check procedure.

∾ ⊖ ∾

Morgan stared at the comm-panel on his desk for almost five minutes before he hit the button that gave him an outside line. Punching a series of numbers, he sat back and waited until his father's face appeared on the screen.

Before he could say anything, Aaron grumbled, "Who is this so early?"

"Dad, put your glasses on. It's me." He stifled a guffaw.

"Asher? Is that you at this hour of the morning? You'll wake everyone!"

"I thought I'd catch you before you go to *shul*, Dad. There's something I want to tell you."

Aaron Morgenstern pushed his glasses up his nose, sat down and stared at the screen. "This must be important, Asher. Are you all right?"

"I think so. You tell me."

"*Nu*?"

Morgan swallowed hard. "I've asked Sarah Jane to marry me."

"She said yes?" he asked solemnly.

"Not yet. But I think she will."

The old man mulled it over. "She's a nice girl, this Sarah Jane. Your mother likes her."

"Reuben likes her, too, I think."

"This is important. She will be his mother." A world of implication in his voice spoke volumes in its simplicity.

"Dad," began Morgan slowly, "if Sarah Jane does say yes, we will probably take a posting off planet when I come up for promotion next year."

"And Reuben will go with you?"

Morgan thought he heard his father choke as he spoke the words, but he could not be certain. "It depends…it depends on what Reuben wants to do. I won't force him to come, but if he wants to, I won't say no either."

"Your mother will miss him."

"I know."

"Will you tell your mother?"

"If and when it needs to be told." Morgan stopped for a moment. "Dad, it won't be forever and we'll be home on a regular basis."

Aaron Morgenstern gave his son a wry grin. "The Talmud tells us a parent must do two things: teach the child a way to earn a living, and to swim. I would not have chosen the profession you have chosen for yourself, Asher, but I will not deny that you have done well with it. As for swimming....you're not too bad at that either."

A surge of love for the old man swept thought Morgan and he wished he could have been in the room with his father to embrace him. "Thanks, Dad," he managed to say, feeling on the verge of tears.

"I won't say anything to your mother, Asher; you will talk to her when the time is right. You have a good head on your shoulders and I trust you. You won't do anything to make her unhappy."

"No, I think she'll be very happy......she'll eat in my house."

"You're sure?"

"Absolutely."

"Go with God, *mein kind,*" said Aaron. He held his hands up so his son could see them. "May God make you like Ephraim and like Manasseh. May the Lord bless you and protect you; may the Lord countenance you and be gracious to you; may the Lord favor you and grant you peace." He wiped his eyes with a finger. "I'm proud of you, Asher. *Gei gezheunt und kum gezheunt.*"

When the screen went dark, Morgan continued to stare at it for a moment. He breathed deeply, then prepared himself for the coming departure.

Bruised but undaunted, Jane relieved Ngyuen at the station and immediately fell into the patter of the pre-flight check. Unlike the last one done the day before, this was no dry-run. When Tapper ordered the engines on line, Jane felt a keen thrill as the vibrations increased in intensity. She could sense the power of the ship through the carpeted deck and the stronger the vibration, the more excited she became. In spite of everything that happened, this is where she wanted to be most: sitting at her post, listening to the chatter coming across the airwaves. When on her screen she saw the captain's commline flash, she didn't have to guess to whom he was speaking. And when the little indicator light went out, she calmed the racing sensation in her brain at knowing he would be joining them on the bridge.

Morgan saw her before she saw him. He was more than relieved to see the dark, auburn chignon bent over the panel. Her arm was in a sling, but it didn't seem to hinder her performance. He suppressed his desire to run across the bridge and sweep her into his arms. Instead, he leaned against the bulkhead, his arms folded across his chest, and watched his crew prepare for departure.

"T minus three," called Newhouse from the captain's chair at the center of the bridge. "Engines?"

"On line and holding," replied Tapper without looking up from his own screen in the corner. "Pressure steady, revs up to thirty K."

"Communications?" he called.

"We are priority one," Jane shot back almost before he finished asking. She glanced up and caught Morgan's smile. Although it still hurt, she managed to shoot one back at him before she resumed her watch.

"Okay, Tapper, let's do it," Newhouse announced as he vacated the chair in favor of his commanding officer. "She's all yours, sir."

Morgan dropped into his place and focused on the screen. "Tower, this is the *Washington*. Are we clear for departure?"

"What's yer rush?" came the voice over the speaker; "ya got more'n two minutes."

There were muffled guffaws from the crew. "Engage engines," ordered Morgan with a grin. There was a slight lurch as the thrusters began their downward push. In the background, a female voice from the control tower began counting the last sixty seconds before liftoff. Morgan knew everyone was counting with her.

At last the voice reached zero and the *Washington, D.C.* slowly started to rise straight up into the perfect blue sky above her city.

Made in the USA
Las Vegas, NV
25 July 2022